FLOWERS THAT GROW ON GRAVES

K.F. BLACK

Black Hollow Publishing

Flowers That Grow on Graves

This is a work of fiction. Names, characters, places, and incidents either are products of the author's imagination or are used fictitiously. Any resemblance to actual persons, living or dead, events, or locales is entirely coincidental.

Cover design: Cover Kitchen (Xavier Comas)

Edited by: Imbue Editing (Jason Letts)

ISBNs:

Hardcover: 979-8-9997772-0-1

Paperback: 979-8-9997772-1-8

Ebook: 979-8-9997772-3-2

Printed and bound in the United States of America.

First printing 2026

Library of Congress Control Number: 2025924967

CONTENTS

ACT I

TO BE FREE

CHAPTER ONE

THE BEGINNING OF THE END

> I knew I should've never had a daughter—let alone two! This is why I wanted a boy!
> ~Ravenna Ashryn

MISTAKES WERE NEVER FORGIVEN.

Lyra had just made one.

As the bucket of water slipped from her grasp, Lyra desperately reached for the handle to regain control, but her fingers brushed only air.

The bucket sounded a metallic ding when it collided with the ground, denting the bottom and ejecting water in a wave across the sidewalk. She froze, chest tightening, knowing what was coming next. She only hoped by closing her eyes that she wouldn't have to fully embrace it.

"Lyra Ashryn! The day I don't have to discipline you and your pathetic mistakes will be the day I die. Come here. Now!"

Ravenna's voice cut through the air, assaulting Lyra's ears and leaving no room for disobedience. Without hesitation, almost practiced in nature, Lyra sulked toward her mother, head tilted down to the cracked pavement. The city of Tenebral loomed over her, gray and oppressive, buildings of darkened stone surrounding the narrow streets.

Lyra followed her shadow, matching the neat and orderly line she was expected to follow. Her slow descent was merely a few paces but stretched into what felt like an eternity. Once she reached the polished toes of the pitch-black boots, she stopped, her heart pounding.

As Lyra lifted her head, the blow landed.

The frigid weather only amplified the sharp stinging sensation blooming on her cheek. It was a familiar feeling, but no matter how many times it happened, the pain never ceased.

She reflexively raised a hand to cover the sore spot, but reminded of her training and the threat of worse punishment, she resisted and kept her arms at her side, much like a soldier under scrutiny.

"Did your useless father teach you to fail, or did you manage that all on your own?"

Lyra had more than a few choice words for her mother but insisted on playing along. Staring up at her, she took in every unsettling detail of her mother. The unhealed gashes carved within Ravenna's cheeks, wounds buried under pale skin, and brittle strands of brown hair that clung to her high-collared coat. Her sharp teeth and talon-like nails were now stained, unusually long, and yellowed.

"No, ma'am, it was my fault. I'm sorry. I will let Father know."

Lyra's voice came out flat. She had to bite her tongue more than once with her mother, and as everyone in Tenebral knew, there was no winning with Ravenna Ashryn.

But it wasn't the slap or the insults that stung the most—it was the shame. The heavy, suffocating weight of failure that Ravenna foisted upon her, drowning in her own shadow. Lyra was trained to assume the blame from her mistakes, and that feeling would be nearly impossible to shake.

Her fingernails pierced painfully into the palms of her hands as she tried to withhold her emotions from boiling over. An eleven-year-old could only handle so much, but Lyra knew what rebellion would bring, something far worse than a mere slap.

Ravenna scanned the cobblestone streets, daring anyone to intervene. Everyone she made eye contact with turned their gaze and hurried past with swift indifference, minding their business.

Most would be outraged by such a sight, but in Lyra's case, this was treated as trivially as a typical day of snowfall. Most Necromites, those who are touched by death's forbidden powers and exiled to Tenebral, had seen Ravenna's wrath firsthand and were only glad it was Lyra on the receiving end and not themselves. Her powers were far too great for them; no one dared to intervene.

Lyra could see the wicked expression on her mother's face and felt the aura around her simmering like heat radiating off a furnace. She felt this all too frequently, often thinking to herself that the heat was so strong the snow would surely evaporate from under her feet.

"Quickly, let's return home to cover you up. Not a word more about this mess. Understood?"

Lyra stiffly nodded, wanting nothing more than to escape from the public lens. She carefully retreated to the empty bucket, staring down into it. The water had taken hours to collect, sourced drop-by-drop from far below the city, strictly measured for her father's experiments.

He would notice it was gone. He always noticed these things.

Reaching down and tightening her grip on the bucket, she hurried back to her mother and followed close behind in silence. Snow crunched under her boots as they walked, leaving a faint echo of her mother's scorn lingering in the air.

As Lyra continued to trudge through the intensifying weather, head down in shame, she caught a glimpse of a man out of the corner of her eye. He was no one remarkable, another passerby, but unlike the others, he was the only one to stop.

For a fleeting moment, she thought he may say something to her, shouting through the crowd to get her attention and free her from Ravenna. But the moment passed as quickly as it came. He disappeared back into the crowd, another shadow among the rest.

She peeked up to the sky as the sun began beaming onto her skin. The warm embrace of the light burned her cheeks, and though the sun was out for the first time in weeks, she felt today would be far darker than usual.

Finnian Valcrest watched helplessly from the backdrop as the sound of Ravenna's forceful palm made contact with Lyra's face. He wanted to step in, to say something, but with a baby on the way his feet stayed anchored where he was.

Lyra's bruised features and defeated stare remained etched into the recesses of his brain, as he eagerly excavated his mind in search of something to say.

After leaving his trance-like state, he made eye contact with Lyra for a moment. Was it worth the risk to speak out? Could he defend himself, or his pregnant wife, from Ravenna's wrath? Or even worse, what would happen to Lyra? Could he defend her?

Undoubtedly, he knew the answers to his deep-seated questions and hated all of them. Ravenna was too powerful, not just for him, but for anyone. Any kind of resistance wasn't just futile—it was a death sentence.

Not now, he thought. *Maybe later, when it's safer.*

Without a second glance, he picked up his belongings and hurried home.

Through the worsening storm, polar wind whipped at him, the snow under his shoes rising steadily, consuming each step forward. His mind continued to replay the scene he had witnessed; Lyra's image paired with Ravenna's prideful glare. He'd already let her down too many times, allowing Ravenna's violence to go unchallenged out of fear. Now, with his own child's future at stake, the burden of guilt pressed heavier on his chest. He couldn't bear the thought of watching helplessly again, especially if it involved his wife, Violet, or their unborn child. He clenched his fists, hoping the memories would soon wane once he reached home.

Upon entering, the smell of something vaguely edible caught him off guard. He could see Violet hunched over the stove, stirring a strange concoction in a large pot that messily dripped from the sides. Her baby bump was clearly visible now, stretching the fabric of her bright blue blouse. Her short hair was neatly styled, and a delicate chain of jewelry dangled from one ear.

"Another five-star meal for the baby, I take it?"

She turned to Finnian, rolling her eyes at the sarcastic remark. "I'll have you know, I happen to love boiled green slop with a side of mashed-potato disaster."

Their cramped apartment smelled of burnt starch, the walls stained, the tiles cracked through wear and tear over the years. The kitchen was barely large enough for the two of them to move comfortably, cluttered with cookware and cookbooks shoved into the corners, piled as high as the ceiling would allow.

Before he could respond, the shrill sound of the fire alarm pierced the air and blared through the hallway. Violet reached for a rag, but Finnian beat her to it, taking the cloth and waving it briskly over the sensor until silence returned. The chaos diffused, they embraced, Finnian pulling away with a sense of haste. Violet furrowed her eyebrows and studied him.

"Something wrong?"

He hesitated, his memory of the scene returning. Then the words spilled out urgently. "We need to leave this place, Violet. We need to pack immediately."

Finnian's stark proclamation hung in the air for what felt like minutes. Violet remained still, wooden spoon in hand, mouth partially agape.

"Leave? Right now? We haven't even packed or prepared—what brought this on?"

She looked to his face for answers but only saw a shadow of a man, burdened by something unsaid.

"Did something happen? What did you see?"

Finnian gazed past Violet, through the frost-covered window above the stovetop. The memories flooded him all in one instant, images of Ravenna and Lyra seared into his mind. Then came the images of what could be—of his soon-to-be child breathing in the same toxic air, growing up behind stone walls, in a city that devoured innocence and spat out violence. The longer he stood thinking, the more he could recall. Memories buried deep, hidden from sight all until now.

He stood eerily still, as Violet stepped closer to him to break his daze.

"Finnian?" The smell of jasmine pulled him back in. He looked down at her.

"We have to leave. There are dangers here that our child cannot be exposed to. For our family, I don't want to take any more chances."

She prodded again. "Did something happen? I need more to go off of, honey."

"It was Ravenna," Finnian finally said. "Out in the square again, tormenting that poor girl. And everyone just passed by, like it was just another day."

Violet's mouth tightened.

"And it's not just that," he went on. "Today I overheard the guards talking. They're planning to conscript another wave of children for the war. They plan to take them out to Valspire and try to pass through the barrier. There's even talk of sending more people to the Rift, to harness those forsaken powers and to do away with the others."

He stepped closer and grabbed her shoulders.

"I have a terrible feeling, Violet. Something dark is on its way, I can feel it. We can't afford to sit and wait around for it. We've talked about this before. For the sake of the child and for you and me both, we need to leave. This place is not suited for people like us, and if we want what's best for Aria, we must go."

Violet rubbed her belly, looking down at the increasingly large bump. She was never the type to believe in gut feelings or intuition, but the drawn look on her husband's face was all the proof she needed.

"All right..." she sighed, a hint of reluctance lingering. "Let's at least eat this mess of a meal I made, and I will pack up as quickly as I can. But there's a storm coming. If we're going to do this, we need to prepare for the worst."

CHAPTER TWO

A WORLD APART

> “You remind me of someone. Lyra, I think her name was. There’s something about you, and I can’t help but like it.
> ~Maeve Holloway

TAVIAN STROLLED DOWN THE NEWLY PAVED STREET.

His head was held high, radiating the confidence of a newly anointed king. He had just been awarded the title *Best in Class* for fervently defending Mariella during a heated classroom debate. When several classmates dared to question her teachings, Tavian stood firm, countering every argument with conviction. The praise that followed made him feel invincible.

He paraded through town, followed closely by his mother, Leora Fenwyn.

Lost in his triumph, he failed to notice an elderly man out in front. He continued moving, colliding head-first into him, the older man falling to the ground.

The pail of water Tavian was tasked with holding onto dropped to the pavement, its contents heaping over the edges and splashing onto the man’s robes.

The elderly man sat still, torn between anger and deference, as he glared at Tavian.

“Sorry, I couldn’t see you in my way,” Tavian muttered, flashing a smug grin. Paying no real mind to the accident, he brushed past and continued forward.

“Tavian! Please come back here and properly apologize to this poor man,” Leora said, shaking her head. “No son of mine will treat people like that.”

She knelt to aid the man who was attempting to wring out his robe, her calming demeanor masking the frustration and shame. She struggled to kneel all the way down, her legs buckling with each small movement. With a rueful smile, she handed her handkerchief over. Her son didn't budge an inch.

"But... wasn't he the one that ran into me?"

Leora's sharp stare silenced him. Unnerved by the intense expression in his mother's narrowed look and tightened jaw, Tavian turned back to the man.

"I'm sorry, sir." He mumbled, avoiding the man's glare.

With a slight nod of approval, Leora finished picking up the bucket and handed it over to Tavian.

"Good. Please be more careful."

Continuing home, Leora looked back to Tavian, who was sulking along, steps slow and heavy.

"Don't be upset. It was just a mistake," she said gently.

His head remained downward, as if gravity was working harder than the muscles in his neck. He mumbled, "I didn't mean it. He was in my way."

Leora knelt and lifted Tavian's head with a few fingers until she could see met eyes. "It's all right, sweetheart. I'm not upset, but I want you to understand that even if it's not your fault, it's kind to acknowledge when someone else is upset. Do you understand?"

Maybe she's right, he thought. *I probably shouldn't have been so mean to the old man.*

Tavian nodded slowly. "Yeah, I guess so."

Leora patted the top of his head. "Just try to imagine yourself in his place. Wouldn't you want someone to apologize and help you?"

Tavian agreed. He glanced back over his shoulder at the old man, who was now being looked at by some others that had passed by. One gave him a towel to dry off, another dusted off his clothes, and one young girl even took his arm to keep him balanced as he stood upright.

Then, a small bout understanding, a light flashed in Tavian's hazel eyes. He thought about the old man's hand, trembling as he tried to wring out his wet clothes that Tavian had ruined. Maybe it was about trying to do better, even when you didn't have to.

Suddenly, a smile overcame him.

"I get it now, I think. Thank you, Mom."

Almost like a car that jumped back to life, Tavian, with renewed confidence, ran as fast as his legs could take him back home. Leora tried to keep up, stumbling slowly, weakness and fatigue spreading over her body.

As they neared the house, Tavian was drawn to a group of three men dressed in strange gowns, whispering to one another. Their words carried enough to hear the faint murmurs.

"Eldric is here to stay. There's no need to worry. The Necromites will persist, as shall we."

One of the others, shorter in stature with an anxious tone, added, "But what if we can't control them? There's word of a girl, quite a powerful one. If we neglect them any further, we won't have much chance to reverse it."

They continued with their hushed conversation, and without realizing it, Tavian had stopped directly in front of them.

The trio noticed him at once, warily looking at one another. One of them tilted his head, trying to gauge Tavian's reaction. The others fell silent. Without another word, one of them walked up to Tavian. Leora, not noticing her son had stopped, kept walking ahead.

The man leaned in close, breath uncomfortably warm against his ear. He whispered, "Do not involve yourself in matters that don't concern you. Stick to your script, and none of this shall affect you." He flashed a wicked grin, exposing crooked rows of teeth.

Tavian audibly gulped, as if he was trying to swallow something that wouldn't move easily down his throat, sweat trickling down his brow.

The man returned to the group, and they carefully proceeded off, leaving Tavian still and in shock. All he was left to think about were the questions circling around his mind. Necromites? Eldric? Script?

There were far more questions than answers, and he was determined to find them.

Although Leora had walked far ahead, he caught up to her rather easily. His eyebrows were deeply furrowed, in intense thought as he fixated on the conversation.

The front gates to their home, the Royal Palace of Valspire, turned open slowly. When the gate gave enough room, Tavian rushed inside, working his way through the endless corridors and staircases toward his bedroom.

Minutes later, Tavian heard a familiar voice shouting to him from downstairs.

"Tavian! Tavian, get down here please!"

He groaned, sliding himself out of bed, heading back down the large, spiral staircase, wondering what he had done this time.

"Hold it right there!" the same voice croaked.

Blushing, he turned in time to witness liver-spotted hands reaching for him. With surprising speed, his grandmother pinched his cheeks firmly, slight pain rushing through his face, turning into embarrassment.

"Grandma! Not in front of everyone!" he protested, squirming from her steel grip.

He was able to wriggle loose, but not in time to evade the incoming spit-soaked kiss planted on his forehead.

"An old woman like me only has so much time left, so let me have my moment," Elyra said with a grin.

Tavian turned away, trying to ignore the comment. He hated the constant reminders of his loved one's mortality; he wished it never had to end. Except the kisses... he could go without those.

"Your Mom here told me about the mishap in town today. I trust you apologized to the poor fellow." Elyra said, turning him back around.

"I did. Mom told me to," he said.

"Good. She learned from the best after all!" Elyra winked toward her daughter.

Leora smiled faintly in return, then turned away, a sharp cough escaping her as she raised a hand to cover her mouth. As she glanced down to the palm that covered the cough, specks of blood dotted her skin. She quickly wiped it away before anyone would notice.

Tavian turned for a second, catching her movements, but she smiled too quickly for him to question it. She spoke with haste, diverting attention away.

"It should be time for the daily ritual. Grab the water and let's head over."

They made their way to the prayer room, past the courtyard at the heart of the sprawling 200,000-square-foot palace they called home. The palace was situated at the top of the hill, overlooking all of Valspire, but Tavian had become accustomed to it. The eccentric designs and masterful expanse had become commonplace, he now only ruminated over the words of the robed man that whispered to him earlier that day.

Script? He wondered. *Is someone watching me? Do they know something that I don't?*

Leora stepped through the chamber, now entering the center hallway of prayer room. The familiar marble underneath her feet provided little comfort. The ritual waited, just another daily task, but for her, each day felt heavier than the last.

Elyra recited the instructions, as she did each day. "Remember to say your grace, take the water, and rub it on both sides of—"

Tavian interrupted, mocking her tone, "Take the water and rub it on both sides of your feet. But don't forget the carpet! Heaven forbid you track in dirt or dust onto grandma's floors!"

Elyra grinned in a mildly facetious manner. "At least I know you've been listening. You go on first then Tavian, since you're the expert!"

With a face burning from embarrassment, he reluctantly took the water and began the first step of the ritual. Once completed, he approached the imposing statue of Mariella at the end of the room. The statue depicted a large, serene-looking woman, hands over heart, with a gaze both soft and eternal. He bent over, reaching out to place both palms on the stone pedestal in front. His hands began to emit a bright white light.

The statue responded with eyes glowing a vibrant orange; the color was so bright Tavian had to squint. Slowly, its stony arms groaned into motion, extending toward him like a divine offering. He stood up straight and poised, eager to continue, leaning his body toward the statue.

The stone hands touched him, and as always, it sent a jolt of energy surging through his body, down his legs, and back up to his head, electrifying every part of him before dissipating. The statue returned to its fixed position, hands held over its heart, eyes of orange dimming once more.

The ritual was complete; a rite performed only by those under Mariella's graces. The Fenwyn family were the few that were still able to contact their goddess directly and be granted a fraction of her power. The power to heal and protect.

And unlike the Rifts, these blessings required no sacrifice.

At least, not of their own.

The following morning, as the sun crept over the horizon, Tavian lay still in a mess of sheets, caught in the midst of a vivid nightmare.

In his dream, he sat near his mother, grasping onto her weakening grip. Her breathing was labored. She whispered something barely comprehensible in his ear. Though he could not pick up on the exact details, he knew it was about his father.

As her strength waned, she let go. Tavian firmly held onto her limp hand, refusing to let her die, but it was too late. Her chest stalled as the last breath exited her fragile body.

In desperation, he brought his palms up to her chest, willing the same white light from the ritual to manifest, in a feeble attempt to resurrect her lifeless corpse. Her glassy eyes stared directly upward, as if transfixed on something of acute interest only she could see.

He stared blankly down at his hands, realizing his limitations and inability to undo death, as his vision doubled then blurred from tears. They dropped from his eyelids, pooling at the tops of his hands like the droplets from an overflowing pail.

His mind refused to process the stillness in her chest. He just watched, silent and stuck, unwilling to accept.

As he stared at her, arms came down from above, reaching toward him without his notice. They forcefully pressed into his spine, carving away at his flesh, digging inside his body as if to pull something out of him. As its fingers neared his heart, a visceral pain erupted, and he violently bolted upright from the dream, drenched in sweat as if he had resurfaced from drowning.

The screams exited his body without restraint, reverberating through the stillness of the early morning. The door to Tavian's room swung open with a resounding crash. Vid, his best friend, stood in the doorway, expression brimming with panic.

"What the hells was that, dude?" he said, pinched with concern. "I was stopping by to get you for the performance, then I heard your horrible screams."

Trying to catch his escaping breath, Tavian fumbled for his glass of water on the bedside table.

"Just a bad dream," he said. "I just need some water."

He grasped the glass with both hands, his strength barely enough to hold it steady, tilting the glass and drinking it all in one large gulp.

Vid raised an eyebrow. "You must've been dying of thirst. Can't say I've ever screamed that loud for a glass of water."

"I guess you've never had a really good glass of water." Tavian placed it down, refraining from eye contact.

"Since you're obviously fine," Vid said with suspicion, "come down for my performance. It'll be a good one today!"

Saluting awkwardly, Vid merrily skipped along, heading for the central theater downstairs. Tavian sat still, vacantly peering at the empty doorway, putting together the pieces of his dream.

As he mustered the strength to stand, a sudden pain shot into his back.

Stumbling over to the mirror at a frantic pace, he removed his shirt and began investigating thoroughly, unable to notice anything of immediate concern.

Still worried, he began to scrub away at his back in the hopes that the pain would disappear through effort alone. But it persisted, and worsened, only disturbing him more as he wiped and washed vigorously. He had been labeled a hypochondriac by some. Whatever that meant, he was unsure, but was certain this was no mere delusion. The pain was real —maybe even deadly in nature.

He hurriedly put back on his shirt and fumbled out of the room, not wanting to cause any more concern. But in his alarm, he was unable to locate the scar that began to form at the base of his back.

Though, it wouldn't stay hidden forever.

He quietly descended the stairs, deliberately trying to avoid the groan of the ancient, wooded floors beneath. The faint echoes of what seemed to be a crowd of people gathered below caught his ear.

As he approached, a young girl with dirty-blonde hair, fidgeting with her polka-dotted dress and wearing bright-pink shoes, stood at the doorway. She wore a headband to match the dress, and was diligently scanning the room end-to-end, on the lookout for someone.

Tavian assumed it was him she was looking for, but was too nervous to initiate the interaction. He kept his gaze low to the floor, feigning obliviousness.

Her stare lit up as she spotted him, rushing over and playfully smacking him on the forehead with the base of her palm.

"Ow! What was that for, Aria?" Tavian protested.

"I dunno. I'm mad, I guess."

Despite her light tone, there were clear signs of distress in her features; a continuous fidgeting motion paired along with it. Looking closer, he realized she resembled a doll more than herself. Her dress was unusually formal, a stark contrast to her usual casual style.

Smirking, he said, "When did you start dressing like that? You look *different.*"

"Shut it," she shot back. "Orin made me wear this and it's so ugly. I wanted to take it off, but he didn't let me." Her face went red as a tomato as she shifted her feet back and forth nervously. "Do you think it's ugly?"

Caught off guard, he stammered, "Uhhh no, it's not ugly. I think it's nice—just... different than normal. There's nothing wrong with that."

Tavian's lack of social cues weren't a secret to anyone, except to himself. Aria had grown used to making things more obvious for him, though there were limits, of course.

"Thanks, I guess. Better than ugly," she grumbled with a shrug.

Before he could find better words, she grabbed his hand and led him through the crowd to their seats for Vid's show, her grip tight but not forceful.

Vid's performance was a wild success among the crowd per usual. He strummed vibrant melodies, delivered sharp but hilarious jokes, and executed phenomenal acts of gravity-defying stunts. And best of all, he told the most compelling, memorable stories. For a thirteen-year-old, he could outperform all the others in Valspire, earning the Fenwyn family's recognition and role as their prized performer.

Once it had ended and the audience dispersed from the halls, Aria, Vid, and Tavian gathered near the stage.

"Well? How did I do?" Vid asked, his chin up, already knowing the answer.

"It was awesome," Aria said. "I really liked the story about the vile non-believers and their run-in with Mariella."

Her tone was surprisingly lighthearted, considering the seriousness of the subject matter. But as she turned to look at Tavian, something seemed to be brewing.

Before she could ask, Vid's father appeared behind them, beaming with pride. He gave his son a firm pat on the back and pulled him in for a bear hug. "Another incredible performance, son. You never cease to amaze me."

Vid rolled his eyes but returned the embrace with a subtle smile, resting his head on his father's arm.

Beside them, Tavian lowered his head.

"You okay?" Aria asked, placing a gentle hand on him.

"Yeah." He exhaled slowly. "It's just... Dad stuff again. I hate remembering how he left us."

Vid's father caught the last few words and stepped over.

"You know," he said, with a sympathetic tone, "Vid's a real lucky guy to have a friend like you. You're family to us. Always have been."

Tavian flashed a brief smile and wiped the corner of his eye, removing a clinging tear.

"Thanks," he said earnestly.

When Aria looked at Tavian, she felt it again—that odd fluttering sensation, a warmth rising, both confusing and comforting. Her palms grew damp and a nervous smile played across her lips. Embarrassed, she wiped her hands against her dress, hoping that if they were to be held, he wouldn't notice.

That night, Tavian was restless, awake until the first light of dawn, ruminating over the same obsessive thoughts, replaying them again and again in his head.

Stick to the script. The words ricocheted through him, bouncing off the walls inside his skull.

As he tossed and turned, the pain in his back seemed ever so present. Knowing his tendency to over-inflate every ache and pain, he did his best to ignore the sensation, but this was growing far too great.

Anxious for relief, he turned onto his stomach. As the pain dissipated ever so slightly, his eyelids grew heavy and began to slowly close shut. But as he entered sleep, a figure appeared face-to-face with him, only speaking in fragments of sentences.

"You need to go..." The voice cut out. "And come to me. Only then can we help."

The figure had no recognizable features, obscured by a long, dark robe. It reached out to Tavian with the same hands that entered his flesh in the nightmare the previous day. These images continued to haunt his dreams, a homogeneous mixture of confusion and worry spiraled him deeper into agony.

Swiftly jolting up to eradicate the thoughts, Tavian instinctively felt along his back where the pain sat. And now feeling beneath his skin—raised, rigid, and real—was the unmistakable edges of a scar.

A mark he never remembered getting, and yet, it had been waiting for him all along.

CHAPTER THREE
CHAINS OF CONTROL

Were you the one that put these flowers in my hair while I slept? They're beautiful.
~Lyra Ashryn

RAVENNA STORMED THROUGH THE DOORWAY.

Lyra trailed behind, as the sharp stench of burning flesh and spoiled eggs hit their nostrils.

Ravenna's lip curled in disdain. "Corvin," she growled. "How many times do I have to tell that nuisance of a husband to keep his experiments confined to the basement?"

Lyra winced at the tone of her voice, yet even she could not deny the intrusive nature of her father's work. The house reeked of death, unknown substances smeared across the walls and floors; a section of wall partially scorched from one of his "accidents". What made it worse was how Anastasia, the newborn, was left unattended while the chaos unfolded.

"Corvin!" Ravenna howled.

Soon after her call, a withered man sidled into view around the bend of the doorway, his pale complexion highlighted by the dim light. He carried the look of a man long defeated, his expression distant.

Despite his timidity, he braced himself, knowing what was coming. Ravenna grabbed her "discipline device", as she called it, akin to an elongated pole arm with retractable blades at each end. In one swift motion, she vaulted over the couch that separated them, closing the distance. His fingers moved in a rehearsed motion, similar to that of a ventriloquist, freezing her midair. Invisible strings of power tethered her, controlling all parts of her body like a human puppet.

Lyra's stomach knotted. She had seen her father's power be used to snare animals, strangers, even herself—but never her mother. Ravenna's glare was still sharp, as if already calculating her next move.

"You ought to know better than to make a scene in front of the children. It's in poor taste," Corvin said in a jittery voice.

He lowered her to the ground, though not giving an inch to escape. The pole arm clattered against the floor, the clang loud enough to wake Anastasia. Her cries split the air, shrill and panicked, but only Lyra seemed to care. She shuddered as instinct took over and rushed toward the crib, with blankets tangled and askew.

As she leaned over her sister's crib, she reached over, but her wrists set in place. Corvin's free hand motioned toward her, ensnaring her outstretched arm just before touching Anastasia.

"You mustn't coddle that child any longer. Anastasia must learn her own way."

His once shy demeanor flipped in an instant, transitioned to a face stripped of all feeling. She was forced to remain still, watching helplessly as her sister continued to struggle and cry for attention. Seconds turned to minutes in this state, as Anastasia's sobs turned to hoarse whispers, her exhaustion evident.

Corvin loosened his grip on Lyra ones the cries died out, but firmly kept command over Ravenna. Puppeteering others became second nature, but Ravenna remained his greatest challenge. The threads binding her began to shimmer, a reminder of their fragile truce.

"Honey, let me go. You know I didn't intend to hurt you. I can *always* make it up to you," she said sweetly.

The fury she once held softened into a sultry glimmer. Corvin stiffened, recognizing the familiar trap she'd webbed before. Her allure was no mere charm; it was a power in itself, a force that could bend even the strongest-willed desires. Corvin had not been her only victim, yet no matter how much he fought, he could never quite break free.

His threads began to loosen unwillingly, fading away before he could manage to stop them. He was yet another fly caught in Ravenna's web, unable to squirm free. She stepped forward with a predatory grin.

She bent over and grabbed her discipline device, and before he could react, the blade whistled, striking his forehead with absolute precision.

Crimson ran down his temple and pooled over his vision, blurring all sight.

With a brisk kick to the chest, she sent him tumbling down and over the steps behind him, crashing down each stair, sending vibrations through the floorboards.

Lyra stood paralyzed as the events unfolded in front of her, the sound of her father's body colliding down each stair left their own individual imprint on her mind. She had known of the powers that both her parents possessed, but witnessing them left her breathless.

She wanted to help, but with no powers of her own, she stood little chance. She wanted to move, to do something to help her father, but she knew better than to interfere with Ravenna Ashryn.

All she could do was observe... and learn.

Violet pressed her back to the stone wall, cradling Aria close. The newborn cried as Violet gently rocked her, trying to mask the sound the best she could. Somewhere down the alley, the sharp click of boots striking stone echoed between buildings, approaching at a hurried pace.

"They know," Finnian whispered, ducking beside her. "One of the patrols saw me near the gate. We're out of time."

Violet's heart wanted to break free from her chest. For some time they'd been planning this, but there was no such thing as true secrecy in Tenebral. Not when every wall seemed to have ears, with eyes Ravenna had in places no one could reach.

"No one's made it out," Violet whispered back. "We're not going to make it."

That was the truth of it. To the outside world, Necromites were taboo. If word of Tenebral's secrets leaked—if someone escaped and was caught—it could lead to the demise of the city. That's why anyone who tried to leave, disappeared.

And worse yet, Tenebral was preparing again for another conscription cycle. More children to be taken to the Rift. Finnian had overheard the whispers himself: Aria's name was next on that list.

Violet would not let that happen.

"We have to take that risk. We'll go through the tunnels," he said. "Like we planned. We reach the pass by midnight. Then we head to the port of Valspire... on foot if we must."

She nodded, adjusting the satchel on her back. "Don't stop. Don't look back."

As they crept through the narrow alley, the old bones of forgotten burials watched silently. Violet kept her pace even, but her mind spiraled.

Ravenna had always spoken of Tenebral as a family bound in undeath, unbroken by time. "Families stay together," she used to say. "No one leaves, because no one needs to."

But that lie had vanished the day Violet saw what was done to the last mother who tried to flee this place. She'd begged and pleaded for her child's salvation, but they never gave in, her child sacrificed along with the rest.

They wouldn't let that happen to Aria.

Behind them, a horn blared. A hollow, warping sound followed by the hurried steps of boots on cobblestone. She could almost feel the city turning to look at them.

"The city knows," Finnian said, grabbing Violet's hand to quicken their pace.

A shout carried through the maze of walls, their voices distant yet near.

Violet tightened her hold on Aria.

"Then we run."

As Lyra grew, so did her resentment toward Tenebral, her family, and the life forced upon her.

Her training was grueling, more like a soldier preparing for deployment rather than the nurturing guidance of a parent. Day after day, week after week, she was beaten, bruised, and broken until she was pushed to the point of no return. Ravenna's vision of Lyra was clear:

her daughter would be the perfect soldier, a reflection of her own image.

But Ravenna's plans far outstretched the confines of Tenebral. The town was a stepping stone, a mere piece of the overall puzzle. Her mind was set on Valspire, and after that, all of the world.

Derewin was as harsh as they came. As Lyra's trainer, he was instructed to break her spirit and rebuild her in Ravenna's image. He learned from the best and followed her commands to a tee, delivering punishment with precision. Yet Lyra could not help but notice the small flicker of hesitation in him, the brief glimmer of remorse under his hardened exterior.

The relationship between Derewin and Ravenna had always perplexed Lyra, leaving her with an unsettling feeling. They seemed close, uncomfortably so. Ravenna's lingering stares and seductive tone did not go unnoticed. Lyra did not like to interfere in the affairs of others, but these thoughts left her stomach seething, thinking back to her father and his seemingly oblivious nature.

In time, those thoughts dulled but never fully disappeared, only resurfacing in the quiet parts of the night. And on what would have been her twenty-second birthday, though the Ashryn's never paid mind to such things, the same unease greeted her again. The house, usually humming with the noise of daily activity, was so quiet she wondered if she'd gone deaf.

She rose out of bed, shaking that same queasy feeling, and walked down the hallway. Whispers drifted from inside her parents' room, and as she approached, the voices were clear. Placing her ear on the door, attempting to listen in on them, she heard her mom, muffled but coherent.

"It's time to take her to the Rift. But you must ensure she's in top condition."

"I don't disagree," said another, the accent familiar but not her father's. "But keep her in line. We can't afford to be in bad graces with the Watcher *again*."

She didn't fully understand what they were talking about, but their concern told her all she needed to know. This would not end well for her.

Pressing her ear harder against the door, she strained to catch every word. But she lost her footing, and before she could catch herself, she stumbled—crashing through the door and landing at the feet of Derewin and Ravenna.

When she looked up from the floor, to her horror, she caught Derewin in her mother's bedroom with no sight of her father. His towering frame blocked the ceiling light, casting him in a silhouette. Broad shoulders, with strands of shaggy hair hanging low over his face, letting only the sharp gleam of his hazel eyes cut through the shadows.

"What in the hells do you think you're doing?" Ravenna wailed. "Have I not punished you enough lately? Do you need another reminder?"

Derewin stepped in, his tone as weak as his resolve.

"Let me handle it. In our next session, she'll learn to behave."

Ravenna stood unconvinced, seeing through his facade like a pane of glass. She honed in on him, glaring as a predator views its prey.

"Sometimes I think you forget who you are. Stop protecting her; you're doing more harm than good. Tenebral is nothing like where you came from."

Ravenna grabbed Lyra by the ponytail, pulling hard enough for a flash of searing pain to radiate over her scalp. "What do you say when you've done wrong?"

Lyra, internalizing the pain but showing a flat affect, recited, "I have done wrong, and nothing I do will change that. I shall carry this burden and repay my debt."

Ravenna snatched her pole arm and struck her daughter hard across the face. The metal cracked against her skin with a sickening snap, sending her to the floor, the taste of iron soaking into her tongue.

Her head hit the hardwood with a dull thud. She blinked once, then twice, her vision swimming. The continued clash of steel against bone resonated out the room and through the halls, but Lyra made no sound. She absorbed every blow in silence, as Derewin could be seen half-turned away, shielding his eyes. Tears slipped down Lyra's cheeks, but no cries were permitted to escape. Even when her instincts begged her to protect herself, she kept her arms at her sides, exposing her body, awaiting the next strike.

After the final blow landed, with blood trickling from each end of her pole arm, Ravenna tossed her weapon into a corner. She wiped her hands on her pants, not to taint herself with Lyra's blood.

"Maybe now you've learned your lesson... though I doubt it," she said dismissively.

As both Derewin and Ravenna exited, Lyra lay on the floor, crimson pooling at her sides. She felt no fear, little pain, no anger, only the familiar numbness.

A short knock at the door broke her trance, and as she turned her head sluggishly, a small figure peeked its head around the frame. It was Anastasia, her long black hair hanging in soft waves about her face. A single tear hung at the corner of her eye, threatening to fall down at any moment.

"Are you okay... Do you need help?" Anastasia asked in a hushed voice. Her focus was thoughtful; her innocence remained even in the face of tragedy. She was too young, she wouldn't yet understand.

Something released in Lyra's chest, a feeling she hadn't known in so long that it hurt to recognize it. The dam within her broke, sobs stormed free, uncontrolled and racking her body.

Anastasia lay down beside her, letting the blood soak into her tattered clothing. The sisters clung to each other on the hardwood, letting time slip quietly past them.

Later that same day, after an especially grueling training session, Corvin, Derewin and Ravenna summoned Lyra.

She'd been ordered to follow them to the Rift, their long preparations all leading to this moment. Lyra had only heard rumors about that place: a realm where vile creatures dwelled, offering power in exchange for a costly price. They were called Watchers, those who protected the Rifts and made use of their grand powers. The thought alone made her nauseous.

As she followed them, she could see the main gate of Tenebral appearing overhead, the steel frame casting long shadows over the entrance to the city. She watched the guards signal for the others, the gate now opening before them, exposing the outside world that she had yet to experience.

Her first step outside the city walls felt surreal, her legs shuddering as they moved over the compacted snow. She looked around at the bleak environment that now surrounded her, realizing they'd been trapped all along. Not just within the walls, but even beyond that, the world was nothing but distant nowhere.

There were no signs of life: no animals, no plants, not even birdsong traveled through the air, only endless miles of rock and jagged mountainsides.

For hours, the group marched in silence as if it were an unspoken rule. Lyra dared not to break the tension, worried it would lead to further punishment or, worse, abandonment in this desolate terrain.

At last, they arrived at their destination, a large crater leading endlessly into a dark void. The air around it changed as they approached, a strange energy spiraling around the hole.

"We're here. Follow me closely and don't step out of line," Ravenna instructed.

No one argued. The group descended a steep, cracked staircase leading further into the dark abyss, the light above fading away with each step.

At the bottom sat a massive door, its height immeasurable, the top of it disappearing into the darkness above. A line of people stretched endlessly in either direction, all leading to a single booth placed out front of the doorway. Behind a small window in the tightly packed booth, someone was chewing a mouthful of gum, flipping through the pages of a ledger. Ravenna led the group directly to the front of the line, bringing unwanted attention to themselves.

"Name?" the apathetic, elderly woman in the booth asked in a monotonous tone, not looking up from writing scribbles in her ledger.

"Ravenna Ashryn," she snapped. "I am here for Lyra Ashryn."

The attendant's pen paused. She looked up at Ravenna then shifted her attention to Lyra, eyes widening for a brief moment.

"Do you have a reservation? Can't enter without one, hon."

Ravenna took a step back, pride visibly wounded.

"Don't you know who I am? I'm not some commoner like those waiting in line. Ask your Watcher at once. He will surely know who I am!"

The crowd behind them began to grow impatient, soft mumbling growing into louder murmurs.

"Sorry hon, no reservation means no entry. Get to the back of the line, or better yet, make plans to reserve next time." The attendant scoffed and looked back at her ledger, shooing away the group with a simple wave of her hand.

Lyra could see Derewin's shadow shifting uneasily, and as she glanced over, his complexion had gone entirely pale. By contrast, Corvin appeared calm and collected, unbothered by the whole exchange, with his arms crossed in amusement. "This will end well, I'm sure."

By now, the crowd had lost its remaining patience as Ravenna refused to move, forming a restless mob behind them. Their frustrations spilled over, as they began to shout, "Lady, get outta line! We've been here for hours!"

Another shouted, "What's your problem? You think you're special?"

Ravenna donned a sinister smile, relishing the prospect of chaos.

"I would like to think so, yes," she said in a malicious manner, "I've been itching for some excitement. It's been awfully boring within the walls lately."

Lyra shivered at the sight of her mother's grin, knowing that was not the smile of genuine happiness.

Ravenna gave a subtle signal to Corvin. His hands lifted, fingers extending toward the attendant. Her body locked into place, eyes rolling back into their sockets until only the whites showed. Like a puppet with unseen strings, the old woman turned and marched to the door, pulling the lever that released the lock. The mechanism clicked open, and Corvin dropped his hands. The woman crumpled to the floor as the control ceased. He then turned to the crowd.

The mob, once riled and aroused with anger, stood motionlessly, unaware that they were in the presence of someone with such power. Their eyes darted to one another, and a heavy silence blanketed the chamber as people began to orderly line back up in front of the booth.

Ravenna was not content there. She reached for the holster along her back where her discipline device was stowed. She drew out the weapon, expanding the pole arm to its full form, emitting a current of energy that only she could perceive.

Corvin, Derewin, and Lyra stepped back without guidance, knowing what came next.

"What is she doing?" someone whispered from the line.

Ravenna tilted her head back, as if savoring the stillness, taking in deep breaths of cavern air.

Then she vanished.

In the blink of an eye, the once-packed line became a gruesome scene of bloodshed, a grotesque heap of bodies stacked on top of one another. Only flashes of Ravenna appeared among the screams, her form vanishing and reappearing in the span of milliseconds. She carved and slashed through the crowd, bodies falling quicker than Lyra could count. Cries of the many traveled through those hollowed caverns, while only a handful of survivors struggled to hang onto their last moments of fading life.

Ravenna retracted her device and brushed away a loose strand of hair blocking her view, wanting the full picture of her work.

"Well," she said with a renewed sense of calm, "shall we?"

The attendant was still lying on the ground in complete terror, her face as pallor as the moon hanging over the chasm mouth.

"What *are* you?" she croaked, voice barely able to escape her constricted throat. "Why are you here?"

Ravenna looked down at her. She formed a finger-gun, pointing it at the attendant's head, whispering, "Bang."

In an instant, the attendant's head snapped backward, severed cleanly from her body. It hit the ground with a soft thud and rolled over to Lyra's feet; the woman's eyes staring up at her.

Ravenna let out a modest chuckle. "I'm here for Lyra, didn't you hear me the first time?"

The group stepped through the doors and into the Watcher's chamber. Suffocating darkness swallowed them whole. There were awful smells drifting that Lyra could not place, and as she pinched her nose, she fought the urge not to vomit.

A deep, booming voice projected from all sides.

"Who has come to see me?"

Ravenna grabbed Lyra and nudged her forward, her nails digging deep into her sides. Lyra began to tremble but continued as rehearsed, speaking out into the darkness.

"Lyra Ashryn, daughter of Ravenna Ashryn. I seek the power rightfully bestowed to me."

The room exploded in a flash of blinding white light. She shielded her face until it began to dim into a subtle burnt-orange hue, revealing the layout of the room they were held in. The walls were metallic, and at each corner stood towering lamps. The one who spoke to them appeared right in front, raised high above a staircase.

It was something Lyra had never seen before, a kind of amorphous blob with greasy, gray skin pulsating to an odd rhythm. Three large eyes stared from its face, with a misshapen mouth hosting a sideways grin, revealing uneven rows of stained, jagged teeth. From its body extended countless appendages, arms and hands moving in a nauseating motion.

The creature emitted a guttural laugh, as though Lyra had told a joke.

"Rightfully bestowed to you?" He seemed slightly offended. "Do you know where you are?"

Ravenna stepped in before she could respond.

"Enough with the questions, Slug. Give her what she came for. We don't have time for idle chatter."

A fire burned within Slug's soul, his grin stretching his skin so thin it began to rip at the seams and emit a wretched smell, like burnt flesh left out to rot. Its body swelled, doubling then tripling in size, casting a shadow over the entirety of the chamber.

"You will not dictate how I use my time! And you should choose your words carefully. Do you not recall who endowed you with such powers? We Watchers, born of Mariella and the First Rift, don't take lightly to ungrateful humans."

For the first time, Lyra saw her mother falter, her confidence evaporating as she stepped back, head bowed.

"Lyra, step forward. Let me see you," Slug bellowed.

She shuddered, every voice in her head telling her to refuse. She wanted nothing more than to get as much distance between herself and this ugly blob as possible. But noticing her hesitation, Corvin pushed her forward.

She hesitantly walked up the stairs, the stench of his oily skin settling deeper within her nose. She looked down at her heavy feet, moving as if cement blocks were holding them down.

What's wrong with me? I'm not scared of this thing, am I?

"You seem to be," Slug said, somehow gaining access to her mind.

Stunned, she stopped moving, looking back up to its unsightly face. She could now see it in full view from the glow of the soft orange light, its body throbbing to the beat of her own heart. She could make out its legs hidden deep beneath the slug-like body, with hands crawling out from its gooey flesh.

"Come closer," he said, breathing heavier, struggling for air.

She inched closer, just enough to taste the rotten smell pouring out of its many crevices. Hundreds of appendages shot out like a flash of lightning, grabbing her from all sides, thousands of fingers moving, feeling, searching, and probing for something. They dug deep, reaching beyond skin, moving down her throat, and sliding between her eyes.

Suddenly they stopped, compressing their grip as if they found their prize, sending lancing pain through her body, simultaneous agony in each limb.

She shrieked. Often, she had embraced significant torment from her mother, father, and Derewin, but nothing like this. Her body convulsed under the creature's touch.

The limbs receded into Slug's bloated form, leaving her on the ground, writhing in pain.

Slug's many eyes flickered with severe interest, in awe of what they had discovered.

"You are far greater than I had anticipated, but the power I have chosen for you will come at a hefty price."

She pushed herself upright, with the strength to only mutter, "What... power? And what price?"

He snapped back to Corvin and Ravenna. "Your parents have a gift for manipulation, but you are different. You hold the potential for much more, for absolute control."

Corvin and Ravenna locked gaze, eyes glinting with hunger and ambitious ideas. Derewin stood further behind, covering his face with both hands, unable to watch what was coming next.

"You will be given the power to seize people's minds, to command them from their very roots. No thought, no memory, no one's will can remain outside your control. You can kill with just your eyes alone, but I shall also give you another memento," Slug turned back and grabbed a weapon from the wall; a polished, curved blade shone brightly in the soft light. "This scythe will be yours too. It's quite dear to me, so treat it well."

Lyra, for the first time, felt the thrill of ambition soak her mind. The power of total control, something far greater than that of her own parents, sounded appealing.

"But the price," he said, leaning in closer, "is your sanity."

Before Lyra could continue, Ravenna chimed in, "That's all? Her sanity? She'll take it!"

Lyra turned back to her mother.

"But I—"

Before she had time to object, a dull ache pressed on her neck, then her vision went black.

Faint images of bizarre figures coalesced below her. Her mind twisted as the images became clearer. They were people, all of whom she had known, writhing in torment at her feet, crawling up her legs. They were grabbing at her, pulling her clothes in a desperate attempt to get her attention.

As she looked down, they moaned. "Lyra! You did this. Why?"

She tried shaking them off, but they continued to claw onto her in an attempt to be freed.

"Lyra. Why? Why do you torture us? Let us go. Free us!"

She yelled and swatted away their hands, yet she was unable to free herself from these nightmarish images.

The noises stopped. All the faces looked up at her in unison, and in a perfect chorus, whispered her name. Her mother's face appeared from the swarm of heads, mouth lengthening far too wide to be human, screaming for Lyra.

She threw her fist at Ravenna's screaming head, her punch gliding right through her mothers form. The floor suddenly opened up like a trap door, sending her plummeting down into a sea of outstretched arms, all awaiting her arrival.

Right as she landed, the faces, arms, and bodies all vanished, leaving her back in the chamber with Slug, her body shivering vehemently.

Slug hovered over her, its words ringing with satisfaction.

"Welcome back, Lyra. Those will be your repercussions. You now have what you requested. With every kill, your powers will grow. But each time you use it, the visions will grow stronger. Your mind will distort further and further until nothing of who you once were, remains."

She could hear the muffled applause of her parents. The scythe was placed at her feet, her head throbbing in excruciating pain.

She wanted to stand—but couldn't.

She wanted to run—but was trapped.

A new victim of the Rift was born today—and a new life for Lyra, whether she wanted it or not.

CHAPTER FOUR
DYING LIGHT

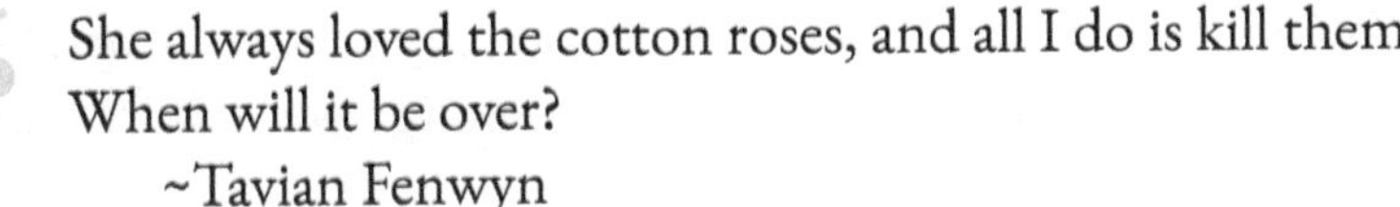

> She always loved the cotton roses, and all I do is kill them. When will it be over?
> ~Tavian Fenwyn

"GET MOVIN', TAVIAN!"

He ran as fast as he legs would allow.

"If you run any slower, your old grammy Elyra might catch up to ya!"

Orin's booming voice could be heard from streets over, rumbling across the training grounds. Struggling for breath, gasping for air, Tavian wheezed, "I'm going as fast as I can! Please—"

Dizziness struck as black spots clouded his vision. His overworked lungs failed to draw in enough air. His legs failed, as he crashed face-first into the dirt below. The world faded to black.

Water shot into his nostrils, yanking Tavian from his semiconscious state. He sputtered and gasped for breath, wiping his eyes to see clearly. Hovering over him stood Orin—the towering, bearded, barrel-chested man who looked more Viking than trainer. His leather-bound boots shone with golden buckles, though he could never actually see them; his stomach blocked the view.

"You all right there, my boy? Was worried for a second I worked ya to death! Boy, imagine explaining that to yer mother!"

Orin let out a hearty laugh, although Tavian didn't share his humor.

"Can I get a break now?" he grumbled.

"Maybe for a second, but don't go tellin' Elyra I went easy on you. I don't need another verbal lashing from her."

From the balcony above, Leora watched over her son closely,

pretending to water her cotton rose blooms. She gripped the railing, trying to avoid falling over, her strength diminishing by the day.

She turned back to the flowers, their blossoms were pale white this early in the morning—by afternoon they'd turn pink and by evening, a deep red. The daily cycle of change was what she loved about them: how they would alter as the day passed, always shifting, always growing.

She was the one who had insisted on starting Tavian's training early, but was a mother at heart, and her instincts refused to let her idly stand by. She peeked over the edge again, exposing the top of her head.

"You know you don't have to watch our every move, Leora!" Orin bellowed. "I know the boy well enough by now. I won't hurt him too badly!"

Orin caught the way Leora held onto the railing. He recalled why she had convinced him to start this so soon.

Leora flushed, quickly retreating from view. "Please keep him safe. He's still young, I don't want you pushing him too hard."

"I'm fine, Mom. You don't have to hover!" Tavian said, but immediately regretted it.

A brisk slap struck the back of his head, loud enough to reverberate the courtyard walls.

"Don't go talkin' to yer mother like that. She cares for you!"

Leora, still hidden, blushed and formed a tiny smile; unsure if from embarrassment or something else.

Tavian rubbed the back of his head where the blow had landed. He'd never admit it, but there was comfort somewhere beneath Orin's gruffness. Though right now, all he felt was a headache coming on strong.

"Okay, I'm sorry." Tavian dragged himself back inside, limping from sheer exhaustion. Leora met them at the bottom of the stairs, investigating the spot where the slap had landed, making sure he didn't strike her son too hard. Orin followed close behind, his stare lingering on Leora's reassuring smile.

"Are you all right?" Leora waved in front of Orin's face, pulling him out from his daze.

"Yeah, I'm fine, just thinkin' 'bout Tavian's progress is all," Orin said, burying the truth deeper into his chest.

He had loved her for as long as he could remember. He dreamed of a life where she chose him instead of her husband, Gareth, but it was a thought he dared not speak aloud. At least not yet.

"He's gettin' stronger," Orin added, crossing his arms, "but has a ways to go. He can fight all right, but his healing prowess is not where it needs to be."

Tavian shifted uncomfortably, not meeting their eyes. Leora surveyed him with her hands on her hips. "It's all right, sweetheart. Some things take longer to blossom, but the longer you wait, the more beautiful the transformation."

Tavian smiled under the dirt that rimmed his lips. He went up to his mother and hugged her, then hurried upstairs to his room.

Leora looked down into her palms, her fingers reeling slightly as she rubbed them together.

"Our family has always been blessed by Mariella's graces," she murmured, "but Tavian... He's just a late bloomer." She looked over to the array of flowers lined in the window. It was the start of the fall season, yet they had not bloomed. She thought that to be peculiar.

Orin nodded. "Give him time. I'm sure he'll—"

Midway through his statement, Leora's knees gave out under her, and she collapsed. Maroon-red blood splattered across the floor as violent fits of coughing tore from her lungs.

"Leora!"

Orin rushed to her side, clutching her frail figure. She weakly pushed him away. "Don't let Tavian see me like this. He'll start to worry."

Orin's stomach coiled. Seeing her so fragile, so breakable, left him helpless. He wanted to stay beside her through it all, but she wouldn't allow it.

"I just need some rest. Don't worry... I'm already feeling better, I think." The quaver in her words betrayed the strength she tried to show. He couldn't convince her otherwise. All he could do was nod and put on a forced smile.

She lifted herself with brittle arms and shuffled cautiously toward her room, stopping to look back at Orin for a brief second. He pictured this as an invitation to join her, but before he could make up his mind, the moment had passed, and she continued down the hallway, locking the door behind her.

In his own room, Tavian gawked at the mirror.

His sweat-stained shirt clung to his back and outlined his body. He ripped it off, revealing the dark, twisted mark etched into his skin. It looked larger than before.

"Three point seven inches," he quietly remarked, jotting the number into his notebook before settling at his desk. He looked to past measurements, the last one recorded at 2.4 inches. The mark had grown over an inch since last he checked. He felt like the boy who cried wolf, trapped between disbelief and reality. Who could he tell? Who would believe him? Would they dismiss it like the rest of his concerns?

He traced his finger over the mark, wincing as the pain shot through his spine.

"Help us."

The sound was faint but unmistakable. He spun around, but the room was empty, no one there to claim the voice.

"You must come to me. Find us, outside Valspire," the words faded in a dying echo.

He could hear his pulse thrumming in his ears. The silence that followed felt more ominous than the message itself. The voices he'd heard: from the robed men in the group on his way home, to the whispers in his head, still clung to his mind like smoke that refused to clear.

He couldn't decide if this time had been a warning... or a plea. What he did know was that the same voice haunting his nightmares always returned during the mark's flare-ups. But he told no one: not Orin, not Aria, not Vid, not even his mother. If they dismissed it, he'd be alone with something he didn't understand—and if they believed it, he wasn't sure what that would mean for him.

Days bled into seasons. The mark was no longer a lingering curiosity; it was a consistent presence. Sometimes it burned hot enough to take his breath away, while other times it lay dormant, whispering familiar sounds into the back of his mind. Tavian learned to fight through it in time, and lived with this shadow as a new part of his own self.

Leora's laughter had become less frequent in those upcoming years, her steps shorter, her visits to her garden fewer. Although she tried to hide it from her son, he could see the change in Orin most of all; always watching over Leora as if he were witnessing a soul slowly finding its way home to a grave.

Small cracks started to form in the translucent barrier that surrounded and protected Valspire as well, although Tavian could not quite understand what it meant at the time. It had always kept their city safe from the Necromites, but over the years it seemed to weaken.

When Tavian had turned twenty-five, his posture was firm, his strikes were heavier, his healing powers steadier... but not to Orin's satisfaction. As his mother's health continued to decline, his training continued to intensify. This was Orin's feverish attempt to grow a bud that was not yet ready to bloom.

"I'm trying... I really am! But it's never enough, is it?"

"You mustn't give up now, son. You need to be ready."

"Ready for what?" Tavian snapped. "I've done everything you've trained me to do. Why push harder? What are you afraid of?"

Orin didn't reply. He was focused on the shimmering barrier surrounding the city. Cracks grew larger, now easily visible to the naked eye, snaking through the protective shield.

"Your mother is sick, Tavian. She won't always be here to keep us safe. You need to be the one to take over once she can no longer..."

Tavian glanced at the barrier then back at Orin. "She'll fight through it. She always does." But his voice hesitated; even he didn't believe it this time.

Leora lay in bed, her skin drained of color, each breath shallower than the last. Elyra sat by her side, tending to a bouquet of flowers.

"They're blooming beautifully," Elyra hummed. "But they could use your hand. I'm not as good at this as you are." Elyra's fingers moved carefully over each petal, but her attention was reserved on her daughter.

Leora managed a small smile.

"Thank you, Mom. But please focus on Tavian now. I worry about him, and he needs you more than I do."

"Don't say things like that. He's stronger than you think! He's no longer the little boy you remember."

The door to Leora's room creaked open. Orin entered, his expression grim from one glance at Leora's condition.

"How's she holdin' up?" he asked, putting a hand atop Leora's forehead as if trying to gauge her sickness through the intense heat radiating into his palm.

Elyra shook out a fragment of her thoughts. "She's a fighter, you know that. But..."

Leora struggled to twist her head over to Orin. "He's not ready yet," she whispered. "Tavian can't maintain the barrier like I can. The Necromites will break through... I can't let go yet."

"Tavian's a tough one. He'll step up," he said as his teeth clenched. He placed his hand into hers, grasping onto the boney fingers that remained. Elyra watched over them both, tears filling her eyes to the brim. Soft droplets rolled onto her lap.

"My time has come, Orin. I can't delay the inevitable much longer," Leora rattled a cough into her hand, with no more blood, only thick balls of saliva and mucus. "Promise Valspire will be safe without me."

The light in Orin was beginning to dim. He was not ready for her to leave, not before he told her his truth.

"I promise, Leora, but let me say—"

She cut him off, wanting to make the most of her limited time. "Go get Tavian for me, quickly. I need his face to be the last I see."

He looked over to Elyra, who nodded and promptly left for Tavian.

Elyra walked back into the room with Tavian, his eyes scanning the scene. By this time, a small group had gathered around her bed, watching Leora's final, fading, few minutes of life. They all brought beautiful bouquets of various flowers, each with a single cotton rose at the center.

"What's wrong? What's happening?" He pushed through the bodies of onlookers and fell to his knees beside his mother. "Mom? You're okay, right? Why is Grandma saying all these things? You said you were getting better..."

Tears had already taken over, his throat too tight to speak. Leora's fingers brushed against his face, wiping away some of the stray drops rolling down his cheeks.

"Don't cry, dear," she said, forming a taxing smile. "There was so much more I needed to tell you, needed to teach you, needed to protect you from... but time is working against me, and now I can't do any of that. I'm so sorry, Tavian." Her smile faded to despair, her lips pressing together, trying to hold back a sob.

The sight of his dying mother apologizing to him brought about an emotion he had never experienced before. A miserably confused wave of anger and distress overcame him.

"Why are you apologizing? This isn't the end. Can't someone heal you? Haven't they been trying?"

She shook her head. "It's progressed too far now, honey. I'm lucky to have even made it this long."

He grabbed her hands, his palms started to emit the same white glow, but just as quickly as it came, it faded away. His powers had no effect, even Mariella's grace couldn't manage to break through.

"Let me see you, Tavian."

He looked to her thinned face, a shadow of what it had been.

"I love you. But unfortunately, everything that blooms must wither. That's what makes the blossom so beautiful." She brushed her fingers through his hair. "I just wish this wasn't the first death you had to witness... though maybe I should be content, since you'll know you were loved to the last second."

Every word felt like the cold, sharpened blade of a knife burying deeper inside of Orin's chest, knowing he would never hear those words spoken to him. He looked over at her soft hair spread across the pillow. He wished he could lay next to her, to comfort her just once, even if for a mere second.

Tavian's mother's shattered voice tore at him; he squeezed her hand snug. He wondered if he should say it, even though he knew it was wrong, but someone had to.

"We can still bring you back, right? Like those Necromites do?"

A collective gasp swept through the room, a taboo never to be mentioned within the walls of Valspire. Several of the onlookers stepped back, one even covered their ears, mumbling prayers to Mariella. Just the mention of necromancy was enough to garner suspicion within the confines of the city, the Necromites—an exiled evil, forbidden from ever returning to the holy city.

Leora's eyes shot to a glare, a side of her Tavian had never witnessed. "Promise me, Tavian. No necromancy. Never fall into their wretched ways."

Her glare faltered as if she were trying to hold onto something for just a little longer. Her breathing slowed to a halt, her fingers began to slack, the warmth draining from her skin.

Before he could answer her promise, the glow in her eyes had gone out. A single cotton rose petal drifted from the vase beside her bed, spinning slowly until it came to rest on the floorboards.

It was white.

The room seemed to tilt, every sound muffled under a blanket of silence. Tavian waited expectantly for her chest to rise again, but it never came.

He seized her shoulders and shook her body in an attempt to wake her up.

"Mom. Mom—stay awake. Don't go to sleep. Please don't let go!"

Regardless of his pleas, her body remained lifeless, now an emptied shell where life once took root. The air felt heavier, making each labored breath thick and difficult to swallow. His legs threatened to give way beneath him, yet he continued his efforts, refusing to let her enter a permanent slumber.

Her body grew colder as he scrambled to save her.

"Someone grab her a blanket! What are you all doing? Stop staring and help her!" he cried, voice cracking at the seams.

But no one moved, their attention fixated to the floor, helpless and heavy with grief.

"No, no, no—Mom, *please*!"

He clung to her body, but could hear no pulse. He looked into her vacant, glassy eyes, their light faded away. He folded himself over her, face planted into her pillow, his sobs muffled by the fabric. He could still smell the faint perfume of rose in her hair, and it broke him all over again.

Orin approached, hand resting lightly on Tavian's back. Without saying a word, he reached over and gently shut Leora's eyelids.

Orin's light had died inside him that day; a part of his soul was taken with Leora, never to be returned. He loved her in silence and now would never have the chance to tell her. He wished to have said something sooner, then maybe it would have never ended this way.

Tavian's vision turned cloudy from the excess tears forming in his eyes. He collapsed back over her brittle frame, his body continuing to heave with sobs. He had yet to face death before, and losing his mother, his anchor to life, was more than he could bear.

Orin pulled Tavian back and hugged him, holding on tight. Tavian glanced outside the window past Orin, watching the faint outline of the barrier surrounding their town shimmer weakly. It was fading, lowering inch by inch, exposing the world beyond. The truth began to settle within him, that the one who maintained the barrier, keeping them safe from the Necromites, was gone.

The world outside looked far darker than he remembered. Much harsher and colder than when he was a child.

The ground shook; a sudden dread loomed over the inhabitants of Valspire. A world that had remained hidden for years revealed itself—a darkness watching over them in a sheet of black.

Whatever they were now exposed to, they were not ready.

CHAPTER FIVE
DESCENT TO DARKNESS

> Have you ever asked yourself what *you* want?
> ~Rowan Lysander

"Please let me go. Why keep me here?"

The utterance carried in Lyra's ears as a legless torso crawled up her body, tearing at the fabric of her clothes.

The weight of the mangled torso knocked her off balance, forcing her backward with a crash. Before she could get up, another half-dead corpse came up from underground, and grabbed onto her shoulders, holding her firmly in place. Around her, a sea of hollowed faces emerged from beneath—they were ghastly, fragmented, and pleading. Their calls merged into a painful symphony, echoing, "Don't leave us... Please, let us go."

Each of their hands pulled her apart in every direction, and even through her struggles, they were unfazed. Her limbs began to split at the seams, a wet tear of flesh from bone.

Her eyes flew open from the nightmare, her mouth preparing to scream, but no sound came.

For a moment, she couldn't tell if she was truly awake. The ceiling above her rippled like water, shapes moving in disorienting waves, like being adrift at sea. A pounding rhythm, her heartbeat perhaps, sounded in her ears. Then came another noise just behind her; the scrape of nails grinding against the floor. But when she turned her head, the sound vanished.

She sat up slowly, but a rotten stench greeted her. She looked down to discover the vomit-covered sheets sticking to her skin.

Sleepless nights led to restless days, a cycle that persisted ever since she was *blessed* by the Watcher. The victims clawed at her sanity, continuing to haunt her mind day and night, bleeding over in her waking hours like oil spreading through water. She started to wonder where the nightmares ended, and where reality began.

And with these newfound powers meant the need for testing, or so Corvin claimed.

Each day, new captives taken from beyond Tenebral's walls were dragged into the chamber beneath their house, where Corvin had conducted most of his experiments. He forced their ragged bodies into the iron chair sat at the center, while Lyra watched in the corner, silent and detached.

Corvin treated it all as careful science, pushing the limits of her newfound abilities. His journals overflowed with notes and crossed-out names, large red X's marking the failed experiments. Yet even the so-called successes ended the same way... lifeless, discarded bodies joining the rest before a new batch were brought in.

One man stood out to her, the merchant with a family of four, frost still clinging to his beard. He was pulled into the chamber, cursing them in every language he knew, thrashing against his restraints and spitting at their feet. Up until his sight met Lyra's.

His words died mid-insult. Heat flared behind her sockets, a red haze flooding her vision as blood seared down her cheeks in hot streams. The man's pupils dilated in terror before he collapsed, whispering for his wife, for his daughters, for anyone to pull him back.

Then the illusions took hold. His body convulsed, nails raking his own skin in a futile attempt to rip the visions from his skull. When the screams turned to hoarse cries, she finally let him die... only to bring him back moments later, just to watch the horror bloom again.

All it took was eye contact. Every soul that met her gaze came face-to-face with their greatest fears, with grotesque monstrosities, with creatures that seemed to defy reality, gnawing at their minds and stripping away any sanity they once possessed. They clawed away at their own flesh to escape the nightmare Lyra had created. And when they broke, death being their only escape from these visions, Lyra would bring them back again, repeating the cycle endlessly until nothing of who they once were remained.

Over the next few months, Lyra was able to hone her craft with frightening precision. She could bend wills, kill with ease, and shatter minds into insanity. The scythe gifted to her by Slug had also become the weapon of choice, a powerful red glow emitting from the curved blade, allowing her to cut down anything that stood in her path.

Each time she crossed a new threshold, with a body count now tallying in the hundreds, the line between her and the Watcher she once feared grew fainter.

Derewin, appointed to oversee these experiments along with Corvin, was conspicuously absent. On the rare occasion when Lyra was allowed outside of the chamber, she would catch Derewin in passing. His look was always averted; shoulders slumped with the weight of tremendous guilt. Lyra studied his expression, noticing his shame-riddled face, leaving him haunted as though he held a secret far too heavy to disclose. She had also noticed around that same time, a drastic shift in his relationship with Ravenna, often overhearing glimpses of their heated arguments.

Lyra continued to hear the word "Valspire" during these debates, though all she knew of that place was its location far to the south, near the sea, but she had little idea of its significance. Derewin's unease was evident whenever this topic was brought up, his discomfort magnified by Ravenna's pressure.

On one occasion, she'd passed the chamber doors where their voices rose sharp enough to overhear the conversation, even through the thick stone walls.

"We're not ready for Valspire. Give it some time." Derewin's voice strained.

Ravenna's reply was a hiss, too low for Lyra to make out, but the tone made her neck prickle. Something crashed against the wall from within, dust sifting from the beams above Lyra's head—then the room fell silent.

Over the coming years, the Lyra who once existed was gone. Her reflection became unrecognizable. As she stood in front of the mirror, she now only saw a hollow, expressionless, indifferent woman staring back at her. Her eyelids were ringed with perpetual shadows; knuckles scarred from fights she didn't remember starting, bruises unhealed from frequent beatings. Bloodstains became the norm, death itself a daily ritual. The transformation was nearly complete, and much to Ravenna's joy, Lyra had become her perfect soldier.

One day, after another grueling training session, as Lyra was headed home, there were whispers of death from across the street.

"They say she's finally dead," a woman muttered to her husband.

"It's time," he responded in a low voice, brimming with hope. "The one who exiled us is finally gone, the horrid woman that ruled Valspire. We can be freed of this place at last."

The wife cradled her baby, wrapped in many layers of blankets, swaying it side to side to distract from the bitter cold.

Dead? Do we have plans to take Valspire? Lyra pondered the thought as she continued through town.

It appeared news spread like a cold front sweeping through Tenebral; word traveled fast and relentlessly. The streets buzzed with muted celebration; a rare sight for a town defined by silence and death. Some people were even dancing and singing, their boots stomping upon the icy cobblestones as children screamed with joy, chasing one another down the streets. Lyra watched it all unfold, feeling nothing other than confusion.

Is death really worth celebrating?

Joy felt like a foreign language to her; one she could hear but no longer speak. Watching them made her feel heavier, as though other people's happiness had pressed her down further into her own misery, rather than lifting her out of it.

A young boy ran past her with a steaming sweet bun cupped in his hands, laughing as if the cold couldn't touch him. A pair of old women trailed behind him, whispering and giggling as they tried to keep up. Someone pressed a steaming cup of cider into Lyra's grasp.

"Don't look so down, celebrate! Our time is near!" The old man smiled, continuing to push his cider cart down the street, handing out free samples to everyone he passed.

Don't look so down? How do I look?

Lyra held the cup, savoring the warmth seeping into her gloves. She looked down into it, watching snowflakes land on the surface of the cider and vanish one by one, swallowed by the amber swirls. When the surface finally stilled, her reflection emerged; a bleak face framed by tangled hair, eyes dulled to opaque circles. The cider trembled in her grip as she realized what she saw.

A face that resembled her mother's.

Less than a week later, talks of a grand festival were in the works, the first one ever to be held in Tenebral.

"She's dead." Ravenna's voice slid through the air, catching Lyra off guard. There was an air of lightheartedness to it, but with severe implications.

Lyra turned to her mother, who hoisted an evil smile, setting down the local papers.

"She's finally dead. The matriarch of the Fenwyn family that exiled us so many years ago, is finally gone. The chains are breaking, Lyra, don't you see? The time of our resurgence is upon us."

Lyra blinked. "Does that mean anything to me?"

"It means everything. This is what we trained you for. You will be the one to lead the Necromites to salvation. The next coming of a true god, one to restore our former glory. Forget Mariella. Think, Lyra."

Lyra was never fond of religious ideals, especially the ones held by the Necromites. Mariella, the originator of the Rifts...

How can Necromites idolize such a figure? What good has come from those Rifts?

Lyra snapped back to reality and replied, "Yes, ma'am."

Ravenna's face lit up with evil excitement. A new beginning for the Necromites was upon them, and soon the world would know.

Far from Tenebral, within the bowels of the Rift, the Watcher known only as Slug leaned back with a wide grin. Through unseen connections, he watched Lyra's unraveling; her suffering a source of his twisted delight.

"Slug, you've given her far too much." A resolute voice sliced through his connection.

He turned to look for the one responsible, but no one was there.

"Balance is overrated," he mockingly replied. "But even so, the repercussions of its use are far too great. She won't last long."

The mysterious voice roared. "Slug! You exist to provide balance, not chaos! This girl could ruin everything we have built. Mariella will be displeased."

Slug's grin faltered. As he looked back over to Lyra through his distant connection, something stirred within him for the first time in centuries.

A flicker of uncertainty.

CHAPTER SIX

BLINDING EMOTIONS

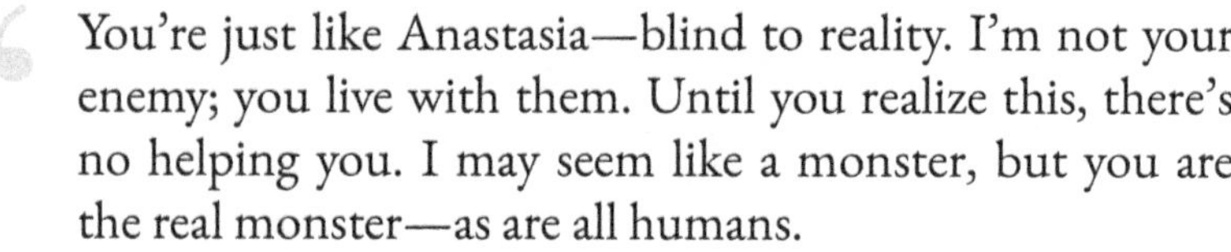

> You're just like Anastasia—blind to reality. I'm not your enemy; you live with them. Until you realize this, there's no helping you. I may seem like a monster, but you are the real monster—as are all humans.
>
> ~Slug

CONFUSION RIPPLED THROUGH VALSPIRE.

The barrier continued to fall. Mobs gathered in the streets, demanding answers.

"What's happening?" someone yelled.

"Where's Leora? Why has she stopped protecting us?" another had protested.

Their panicked voices continued to rise in pitch as more joined the evergrowing crowd. A great choir of troubled voices sang out. All eyes turned toward the Fenwyn palace, where Tavian stood behind the balcony's heavy velvet curtains, peering out at the relentless mob below.

"This is getting out of hand," Tavian muttered, rubbing his temples. "Orin, what do I do? Mom never taught me how to retain the barrier. What am I missing?"

The grief over his mother's passing lingered like a persistent wound that refused to heal, but the burden of leadership pressed even heavier now.

Orin stood beside him with arms crossed, staring down at the unruly mass of people. His typical calm demeanor cracked ever so slightly.

"She wanted to prepare you, lad," he said. "But time wasn't on her side. This is on me. I should've pushed you harder when I had the chance."

"No, none of this should've happened. She shouldn't have died." Tavian clenched his fists, his voice steadying as resolve took hold. "I need to bring Mom back. That's the only way."

Orin jerked his head, his piercing stare making Tavian flinch; the same look his mother gave him when mentioning the Necromites and their taboo ritual. "Don't even think of it. That's heresy, not to mention suicide. You've no idea the price of such foolishness."

Tavian responded with anger. "But why mourn the dead when there are those with the means to fix it? Necromites do it all the time. Why can't someone tell me *exactly* what makes it so wrong?"

Orin's massive hand came slamming down on the table between them, rattling a vase of fresh flowers Elyra had arranged.

"Enough!" he barked, inflection brimming with authority. "You want to protect our people? Forget your damned ideas of necromancy. We need to focus on what's happening *here* before it's too late. The Necromites will be marching over as soon as word gets out."

"What makes you so sure they're coming?"

Orin grimly glanced back out the balcony window. "They've waited for this moment for years. They'll come... with an army that we cannot face alone."

Tavian rushed through the halls of the expansive palace in search of Elyra. Orin had instructed him to go after her, to provide insight into the barrier.

He found her in the East Gate Garden, bent over Leora's beloved flowers, hands shaking uncontrollably as she tended to their petals.

"Grandma," Tavian called out to her, but she didn't respond.

"Grandma? Grandma, are you—" He reached out to touch her, with a slight graze causing her to recoil. She turned around, exposing her tear-streaked face.

"How could Mariella take my daughter away from me?" she whispered. "What did I do to deserve this?" Her watering can began to tilt, spilling over the flowers until they began to droop from oversaturation.

Tavian's own tears began to well up at the sight of his grandmother's grief. Elyra broke out of her trance and quickly wiped away any evidence of remorse.

"I'm sorry. You shouldn't have to see me like this. What do you need?"

He took a deep breath, managing to catch his runaway exasperation. "I need to know how to restore the barrier. Mom didn't tell me anything, and Orin said you may know more about it."

Elyra looked up at the barrier-ridden sky. "There is a way," she admitted. "Your mother wrote everything down, every detail on the barrier and its formation. But the book... It's encoded. She created it in a language only she could read."

Tavian's heart sank. "So there's no way to decipher it?"

"There may be, but unlikely that it could be done quick enough before the Necromites arrive. For now, the best you can do is keep the townspeople calm and figure out how to protect Valspire without help from the barrier."

Tavian shook his head, his frustration resurfacing. "That's not good enough. I can't wait around. Someone must act."

Elyra studied him, and for an instant she saw Leora's defiance in his clenched jawline, and Gareth's recklessness in his furrowed brow. She wasn't sure what his true motivation was. Did he really care to protect the people from the Necromites, or just to get his mother back?

"I can't believe the time has already come. I wonder what she'll get!" Ravenna's tone was brimming with elation. "Imagine what awaits Anastasia. After what Lyra got, it's bound to be extraordinary!" She turned to Lyra with an unusual display of affection, wrapping her up in an enthusiastic embrace. "You must be so proud to watch your sister grow up *just* like you."

"I'm not going," Lyra said flatly.

Ravenna pulled back, her joyous expression faltering for the first time that day. She scrutinized Lyra's face, inspecting for the source of her defiance.

"Not going? This is an important moment for us and all of Tenebral! You need to be there for your sister."

"This isn't for Anastasia, for me, or even for Tenebral. It's for you. I won't be there to experience that again."

Her icy words didn't waver, cracking Ravenna's composure. "How could you speak to your mother like that? Like I'm some self-centered, careless woman. I do everything for this family, *and* for Tenebral!"

Lyra remained motionless, her bitter watch meeting her mother's with unsettling stillness. The silence between them was deafening, the tension in their relationship growing by the day. An unfamiliar sensation washed over Ravenna—a tinge of fear.

"Fine," she said, recovering quickly. "If you must stay, at least make yourself useful. Go see Derewin. He's being as useless as you are about this. Lord knows he'll never join us."

Lyra turned on her heel and headed for the front door, catching a glimpse of her sister in the corner of her eye. Anastasia had grown, but even still, her small frame was only a tiny shadow beside Lyra's. She wanted to warn her of what was to come, but some things were better left unsaid.

Be careful, Anastasia, she thought. *But Slug should be the one worried, not you. If I find out he touched her...*

She trudged through the snow to Derewin's home, her boots falling through the frozen surface into unknown depths. The small, crooked house stood near the edge of town, its windows dimly lit with candlelight.

She knocked, the door creaking open under the weight of her touch.

"Derewin?" she called, peering into the shadows past the doorway.

A sudden slam came from deep within the home. Her muscles tensed as the sounds of clattering books and hurried footsteps grew louder. She stepped back, her fists at the ready.

The door swung wide, revealing Derewin, disheveled and morose. His complexion was gray, his eyes red and swollen, and his hair looked as though it hadn't been washed in days.

The sour stench exuding from his pores confirmed that suspicion.

"Lyra," he said, a bit unsteady. "Sorry, I didn't hear you. Something came up, and I... needed a moment."

"It's fine. I just needed to get away from Ravenna. They're taking Anastasia to the Rift, and I couldn't watch," Lyra admitted.

She expected him to dismiss her, but instead his features softened.

"I don't blame you," he said under his breath, as if wary of an onlooker. "I couldn't bear to watch you in there either. Come in. I can find something to keep you occupied."

Inside, the warm air was a haven from the city's freezing winter. They spoke little, Derewin keeping busy with odd tasks and preparations that he kept hidden from Lyra. She decided to spend most of her time around the fire, trying not to think about what was happening beyond the walls, within the bellows of the Rift.

After several hours had passed, Lyra figured it was all over. "It's about time for me to go back home. Thank you for having me."

"No thanks are needed. Consider it repayment for all the punishment I've been putting you through." He hesitated, the next words catching on his tongue. "On an unrelated note... do you know much about Valspire? About the people who live there?"

Stiffly, almost rehearsed, she nodded. "Yes. They're abominations to this world, the wicked ones who cast us out here to die." She grimaced as she pictured the people of Valspire—Spirians—their faces altered into something inhuman. In her mind, they were beyond redemption.

Derewin somberly looked down at the cracked wood floors, nervously shifting his weight from foot to foot.

"As you set out, consider keeping an open mind. Not everyone from Valspire agreed with what they did to us."

Lyra frowned. "What makes you say that?"

"Nothing," he said too quickly. "It's late. Go—before Ravenna gets angry at me for keeping you too long."

Lyra nodded, but a lingering unease stuck with her. *Why would he tell me this? How could someone from Valspire not be evil?*

When Lyra returned home, a visceral smell of metallic tang met her at the front door. A crimson-stained trail cut through the snow to her doorstep that she had traced all the way home. The blood led inside, snaking through the halls and up to the door of the room she and Anastasia shared. She followed the trail, gripping her scythe, careful not to make a sound.

She stopped at her bedroom door, where the trail had ended, her hands deliberately floating over the doorknob. Human groans leaked through the thin wood, growing louder until they became anguished screams. Her vision tinged with red, boiling anger accumulating in her throat. She grabbed the doorknob and pushed the door open suddenly as if bracing herself for what was beyond.

Ravenna stood at the foot of Anastasia's bed, exasperated and drained. Corvin was at her bedside, fumbling with bandages that did little to stop the blood pouring out from Anastasia's face. The sight of her sister—her tiny form writhing in pain, bandages soaked through—made Lyra's stomach seethe.

"Finally decided to show up? Your sister won't stop crying," Ravenna impatiently snapped. "Can you do something about this? It's disrupting your father's work—"

Lyra grabbed Ravenna by the collar and threw her hard against the wall. Corvin barely had time to flinch before Lyra's hand shot out, gripping his throat with enough force to lift him fully off the ground.

"Don't touch her," Lyra growled. "Leave. Now."

Ravenna and Corvin scrambled out of the room, slamming the door behind them. Lyra knelt beside her sister, whose frequent screams diluted to raspy cries. Blood continued to gush down onto the sheets, puddling around her small, trembling body. Lyra began to unwrap the crude bandages covering Anastasia's eyes, revealing the raw, cratered, pink flesh now taking their place.

Slug had taken his price, her sight for whatever powers he'd promised in return.

Lyra's anger surged tenfold, but she forced it down momentarily, hastily attempting to reapply fresh bandages.

"It's okay," Lyra whispered. "I'm here."

Anastasia clung to her, quaking.

Damned Slug, she thought. *The next time I see him will be the last time he sets foot in this world.*

"Lyra... it hurts. Please... make it stop."

Her broken pitch stabbed at Lyra's heart, and for a fleeting moment, she considered ending her sister's suffering. But no, she couldn't. There had to be another way.

She desperately did what she could, using the supplies they had on hand—disinfecting, bandaging, and providing Anastasia what medication she could find scattered around the house.

Lyra cradled her sister through the night, doing everything in her power to help ease Anastasia's pain. When her sister finally went silent, her body limp from exhaustion and need for rest, Lyra stayed awake by her side. Her mind was a storm of rage, sorrow, and guilt. All she thought about was Slug, and how she could get him back. How she *would* get him back.

When Anastasia awoke late into the next morning, her sockets were covered by fresh bandages, with a blindfold covering the crude work that was done. Lyra's hand rested gently on her sister's forehead.

"Anastasia," Lyra began, dense with emotion, "I must leave soon... to Valspire, as Ravenna instructed. I hate leaving you like this, but I promise I'll fix whatever was done to you. I'll kill those people that forced us here. I'll find a way to set us free."

Anastasia kept silent for a long while, tracing her fingers over the blindfold. Finally, she said, "I don't want to see anything again. Not like this."

Lyra stared curiously at her sister, not understanding what she meant. Before she could ask, her vision went hazy, and her body began to move without her control. She impulsively brushed Anastasia's arm with a hand, and moved her head and neck as if it were her first time discovering her own body and the world that surrounded her.

She was being controlled by an unknown force so powerful that she could not fight to regain control.

Then her vision cut to black. Lyra lurched back into herself, lungs struggling for air, her vision now returning. She stared down at her sister in shock.

"It's one of my many *gifts,*" Anastasia said bitterly. "But it's no gift. It's a curse."

Tavian strode toward the entrance of Valspire, his footsteps burdened with determination. Behind him, Elyra and Orin hurried in pursuit, their voices resounding in a panicked unison.

"Tavian! Have you lost your mind?" Elyra's yell carried over the murmuring townsfolk.

Heads turned as the scene began to unfold, the gathering crowd growing denser. Among them, Aria and Vid stood silent.

"You can't leave," Orin implored. "We need you here to help protect Valspire! Without you—"

"Without me, what?" Tavian shot back. "We can't do anything about the barrier by just sitting around and waiting. Only Mom could manage it. I'm doing what I should've done from the start, I'm bringing her back."

Gasps rippled through the packed crowd. A woman covered her child's ears from Tavian's blasphemous words. Orin's face darkened, his tone increasing into a thunderous roar.

"Bringing her back? Are you mad, boy? You've no idea what you're saying! You're too naive to understand."

"Tavian, please," Elyra called. "Your mother would've never wanted this. She warned you about these things. Come back home and we can figure this out. If you leave, you'll die out there."

Tavian turned back to face them with an unwavering resolve.

"It's not about what Mom wants anymore, it's about what Valspire needs. I'm not going out there to die," he said firmly. "I'm going out there to restore what was lost."

He spun back, his pace quickening as he approached the edge of the city.

"Tavian!" Aria shouted from the crowd. She darted toward him, grabbing his arm and spinning him back around. His breath tensed at the strength of her grip.

Has she always been this strong?

"What in the hells do you think you're doing? You'll get yourself killed. Don't be an idiot, make the right choice."

Vid's head popped into view over Aria's shoulder. "She's probably right. That said, it's making for some great drama. I admire your crowd work." He grinned.

Aria shot Vid a withering glare. "Not the time."

"Right, sorry." He threw up his hands in mock surrender. "But to be fair… I've been itching to get out of these confines for some time now. I don't know where you're planning on heading, but if it means seeing what's beyond these walls, I may be convinced to join you."

Tavian seized the opportunity. "Yes, come with me! I'm sure you can meet all sorts of people out there and gather more stories for your acts. Who knows? You might even meet some foreign princess and fall in love."

Vid's grin intensified. He nodded so enthusiastically his head seemed ready to detach from his neck.

"This is ridiculous," Aria interjected. "Don't drag Vid into your suicide mission. I get that you're in pain, but don't you see what you're doing to everyone here?"

Tavian looked at her. "Didn't you plan to leave this place too? To finally find your *real* parents?"

For years, Aria had dreamed of finding them, their identities a shrouded mystery hidden behind the lofty walls that kept her constrained within the city. She'd been raised in Valspire but had always felt an unshakable distance from the people who lived there. The thought of finally uncovering the truth filled her with equal parts hope and dread.

"I…" Aria paused as her thoughts raced, the cogs of her mind turning vigorously. "I don't even know where to start. I don't know what they look like, their names, where they came from… nothing."

"You'll never find out by just sitting here," Tavian pressed. "Come with us. We'll figure it out together. What's there to lose?" He extended his hand in front of her, palm up. Aria studied him, her heart aching at the sight of his ignorant decisiveness. She'd always admired him, flaws and all, and she couldn't let him face the unknown alone, or at least not only with Vid to protect him.

Is this stupid? Am I being stupid? She took a second to think, admittedly not that long, considering the severity of the situation.

She placed her hand on top of his, her palms greased with perspiration. Her face turned several shades of red.

Has it been this hot all day? she thought. *Why am I so sweaty…*

"Fine," she said, "I'll go—partly for my parents, mostly so you both don't do something stupid without me. But Tavian, don't get caught up in this mess. You're no Necromite. You're a part of the royal Fenwyn lineage, an heir to Mariella's gifts. Promise me you won't forget that."

Tavian offered a small nod. "I promise. I'll do this for Valspire and for Mom."

Orin and Elyra stood silent as Tavian, Aria, and Vid faced them.

Tavian spoke to them again, his words heavy with emotion. "I'm sorry to you both and to everyone in Valspire, but this must be done. With Mom back, we can all be saved. I'll come back with the knowledge to restore her and the barrier."

To everyone's surprise, Orin let out a hearty laugh. "You're just like your father," he then looked away. The words tasted wrong.

"Orin!" Elyra shouted. "Don't you dare bring up that man."

"It's true," he said sternly. "It's obvious we can't stop this stubborn boy." He glanced back at Tavian. "But I happen to have my own business outside these walls. If you're so adamant on killin' yerself, I'll be comin' with you."

Elyra smacked his arm. "Have you gone mad too? Why am I the only one with sense around here?"

"What changed your mind?" Tavian asked suspiciously.

"I won't ruin your fun, my boy, but you'll need someone who knows what they're doing out there. Besides..." He reached deep into his pants pocket, pulling out a set of keys. "You weren't plannin' to walk, were you?"

Tavian and the others exchanged uncertain glances before tilting their heads in agreement.

"This is ridiculous! I've just lost my daughter, and now my grandson is next. What have I done to deserve such punishment?" Elyra dropped to her knees with hands covering her face. Orin stood beside her, placing a hand on her back.

He whispered in her ear. "I'll take good care of the lot, I always have. They need me more than you do—Mariella will guide you all. We'll be back in no time, just hold off for us. Stay strong, Elyra."

She pushed away his hand that was resting on her. "When you reach him, that awful man you plan to go and see, tell him my daughter's blood is on his hands."

Tavian, Aria, Orin, and Vid piled into the car, the crowd behind them growing restless. Tavian felt a pang of guilt as their angered faces appeared in the rearview mirror.

"What about us?" a man yelled. "You're just leaving us here to die?"

Stones clacked against the wheel's rim, the townsfolk gathering loose stones and hurling them at the vehicle.

"We'll be back!" Tavian tried shouting over the commotion, but the sea of maddened snarls washed away his efforts. "But until Mom returns, there's nothing I can do."

"Tavian, get the car started. You're speakin' to deaf ears," Orin stated plainly. "I don't have your blood, the engine is linked to you, not me."

As the car rumbled to a start, Tavian felt the presence of countless eyes on his back. Nearing the front gate to the city, someone caught both Tavian and Aria's attention—a little girl no older than four or five. She was petite, with golden curls tumbling over one shoulder and a curious look on her face, watching their departure.

In her hands was a toy; small, vibrant flowers that seemed worn down through frequent use. Even so, she held onto them tightly, her most precious possession. Tavian tried to wave at her, but she only looked down, admiring her flowers and picking at the fake petals. One of them fell.

It was pink.

The car reached the gate, then passed through, and for the first time in his life, Tavian had crossed the threshold of Valspire. The world outside appeared marvelous, with rolling green hills, crystalline rivers, and vibrant forests stretched as far as the eye could see. Aria glanced at Tavian, her heart lightening at the sight of his wonderstruck face.

But Orin's gaze lingered on him, Tavian's reflection in the rearview mirror unnervingly familiar. His mask had slipped, and who sat behind Orin was no longer the young, innocent boy from Valspire, but a boy who trusted their enemies.

He could see it clear as day, the face of Tavian's father staring back at him.

CHAPTER SEVEN

DEATH'S DEPARTURE, LINGERING SHADOW

> Don't think of it as heaven or hell. It's a waiting room; you stay until their arrival. Once they're ready, you'll know. We make it easy for them.
>
> ~Luna Gray

"You look so good, Lyra!"

Ravenna commented in an unusually chipper tone, straightening her daughter's long black hair. "I can't believe you're ready to set off. This has been a long time coming, you know. Corvin, Derewin and I have put so much work into this."

Lyra abruptly stood up from the chair and readjusted her hair, undoing Ravenna's efforts. "I need to talk with my sister first."

Ravenna put down the comb with a sigh and waved Lyra away, rolling her eyes.

Lyra walked over to her sister who was staring at the closed front door to the house. She gently tapped on her shoulder. Anastasia flinched and turned around.

"Lyra?"

"I'm heading out soon. I wanted to say goodbye before I left... Are you feeling any better?"

Anastasia shrugged. "As good as someone who lost both her eyes can be. But thank you. No one would've helped me if you didn't. I'm better now because of you."

Lyra smiled, but it quickly faded. Anastasia couldn't hold onto her emotions any longer, now pleading to her sister.

"Please don't go," Anastasia said, tears accumulating beneath the blindfold. "I can't be alone with Mom and Dad."

For a fleeting second, she imagined herself staying. She imagined leaving the front door closed and daring their family to try and say anything. But Slug still had to pay for what he'd done, and her duties at Valspire called for her.

Lyra grabbed her sister's small hands and held them close. "I'm sorry, but I have to. You know that." Anastasia shook her head, unwilling to accept it as truth.

"You're a strong girl, Anastasia. I have no doubt you'll be okay." Lyra cupped her sister's cheek. "And were you the one that put these flowers in my hair while I slept? They're beautiful." She showed Anastasia the flowers adorned in her hair, although her sister couldn't see.

"Yes." Anastasia looked down, tears leaking out of the blindfold, dripping onto the tops of her untied shoes.

Lyra knelt and tied them, whispering, "I also left you some medicine, food, and extra bandages in your bedside cupboard. Don't let them find it. And I used the rest of my money to buy some Amberlucks. They're in your sock drawer."

Her sister's excitement showed briefly. Candy was a rare treasure in Tenebral, and Amberlucks were her favorite.

They embraced, holding on as if their lives depended on it. Corvin, watching from the side, mumbled, "Please get going. Who knows how long we can keep that barrier down."

Anastasia turned to Corvin. A stabbing pain shot through his forehead, his mind consumed by a sharp, relentless ache. Anastasia's vision returned momentarily as she took hold of his senses, the way she'd been practicing, honing her control.

"He's scared, Lyra," she noted. "He's worried that once you're gone, they won't be able to control me."

Corvin strained against her influence, his body locked into a statue-like state. Anastasia motioned him to the couch and sat him down. Lyra stepped closer, his fear oozing from every pore, almost tangible.

Good, Lyra thought. *Fear is a language even Corvin understands.*

"I'll leave when I choose," Lyra said menacingly. "And take special care of Anastasia. I'll know if something happens."

He nodded as fast as his neck would allow. The color had already drained from his face, with his weight bearing down onto the couch cushions until they completely folded inwards.

Lyra turned back to leave, planting a small kiss on her sister's forehead as she made way to the front door. She could hear mumblings from Corvin behind her as she opened the door, the freezing cold air rushing into the living room.

"Let go, Anastasia. I wouldn't want to have to tell your mother about this..."

Approaching Tenebral's front gate, Lyra stared at the imposing stone walls, an uneasy feeling brewing within. As she neared, her vision flicked. She witnessed flashes of her victim's faces, their bodies mutilated and lifeless. A front of suffocating darkness covered her, as the victim's hands sprouted out from the ground like flowers, trying to drag her down into the earth to join them. She wrestled with the appendages, but a spotlight suddenly illuminated a lone figure—a small girl standing in the distance.

Everything went still, save for the girl's vague and struggling weeps. A man, with eerily similar features to her father, emerged from the dark and grabbed the girl by the hair, yanking her off the ground. Lyra's heart plummeted as the girl turned to the light. Her face exposed from the shadows, revealing her sister dangling from the man's grasp.

He presented a sword, the metallic scrape of blade on sheath drew painfully in Lyra's ears. He placed the blade against Anastasia's throat, as she began to scream out for her sister.

"Lyra, help me! He's gonna kill me!"

Lyra tried to speak, but her throat collapsed shut. The cold air invaded her lungs, stabbing her insides like she was swallowing the sharpened edge of a knife. Her legs felt frozen in place, her feet secured by the stout hands that kept her planted, powerless to intervene.

The sword flashed, slicing clean through Anastasia's neck.

Lyra's scream finally broke free, tearing through the lining of her throat. The dizziness set in, just in time for her to draw one last shuddering breath, before collapsing into the snow, surrendering to the dark.

She woke to a boot nudging her side. Men with confused looks filtered through the haze. Two Tenebral guards hovered nearby.

"Ma'am? Ma'am, are you all right?" one of them asked.

Lyra sat upright, brushing snow from her coat.

"I'm fine," she said, but the words stung her sore throat.

She rose unsteadily, scanning the area for the man or Anastasia's body, but neither was anywhere to be found. Even as she stood, a phantom sting burned along her throat lining, and her boots felt heavy as if she'd truly fought off the clawing hands that dragged her down.

She moved briskly toward the front gate, her mind reeling.

Was it a dream? A vision?

She couldn't be sure, but there were bigger concerns to address. She shook her head, forcing the afterimage of Anastasia's execution out of her mind.

Stepping foot outside Tenebral's walls was much the same as the inside. The world stretched out in bleak white and gray, snow-covered plains sat under a lifeless sky. Lyra adjusted her tattered scarf, her breath visible in the chilled air, and set off toward the Rift.

Valspire could wait. Before she could face what lay ahead, there was unfinished business, someone she couldn't ignore.

Slug.

She would make him answer for what he'd done to her and her sister. He needed to pay, and she intended to collect.

The only guidance she carried was a crude, hand-drawn map from Ravenna. It was enough to lead her toward Valspire, but she didn't need it to find Slug. The Rift's pull guided her like an internal compass; its presence called to her with every step.

She had barely taken a few paces beyond Tenebral's gates when something weakly tugged on the corner of her coat. She immediately drew her scythe, swinging it behind at whatever had grabbed her. But before the blade could fully cut its way around, her eyesight halted, as she dropped to her knees, body slacking.

She lost her sight for only a second, but when it returned, it was Anastasia who knelt beside her.

"What are you doing here?" Lyra demanded. "Go back home!"

Anastasia shook her head. "I heard Mom and Dad talking as soon as you left. They wanted to kill me. I had to run away."

Lyra wondered if her mind was playing tricks on her again—was this another illusion? She looked carefully at the blindfold, waiting for the seams to split apart and reveal something monstrous underneath. But the fear in her sister's tone seemed too real to fake.

Lyra's brow furrowed. "That's not possible, I already warned them. Why would they even consider it?"

"I don't know, but I swear it's true! They were gonna wait until tonight, once you were far enough away."

Lyra was torn. She couldn't put such treachery past them, but found it hard to fathom that they would be so bold as to kill her sister right as she left. Looking at Anastasia, her helpless, blind sister, she couldn't help but feel remorse. That in some way, it was her fault, and it was her duty to protect her.

"You can come," she said reluctantly.

Lyra hesitated longer than she cared to admit, her mind replaying all the possible scenarios in which bringing her sister could be more dangerous than leaving her behind in Tenebral. But she could only see the faces of Ravenna and Corvin, bearing down on her sister, ending her life.

"But only if you follow my every word. This isn't a game, especially once we reach Valspire."

Snow clung to the tops of Anastasia's laces, once again untied, and without thinking she went to one knee to retie them; just like she had before she left.

Anastasia happily agreed and pulled out two wrapped Amberlucks from her pocket. "I even saved these for us," she said with a gleaming smile, handing one over.

The crinkle of the candy wrapper pulled Lyra back to her childhood. She remembered the two of them huddled together in their room, with a single treat to split between themselves. Even if the memory was simple, nothing out of the ordinary, she had felt safe then... maybe even happy.

"He's so handsome... Why can't all the boys be like him?" one girl whispered, peeking around the corner.

"Don't get so caught up, he's gonna be mine," another girl replied, yanking her friend's ponytail to get a better look.

A small group of young women gathered to ogle Rowan as he browsed a munitions stall. His expression stayed focused; lips pressed in a faint line as he lifted a weapon to test its weight. He looked as though he belonged on a recruitment poster: tall, tailored clothes, neatly trimmed hair, broad-shouldered, with golden eyes that radiated confidence and self-assurance.

Noticing the girls' presence, he glanced over and offered a polite smile. The girls erupted in giggles and scattered, realizing it wasn't an invitation, more of a courtesy.

"Must've been the wind," Rodrick, Rowan's father, said dryly. "Let's head back. You've got packing to do... and you're still sure about this?"

Rowan's ambition was unshaken. "Mom would've wanted this. She set out to make the world a better place, and I plan to do the same."

Rodrick exhaled through his nose. "You're so much like her. I wish you weren't sometimes." He fidgeted with his necklace. Inside the center lock was a picture of Aidra, his wife.

Nearly a decade had passed since Aidra walked out of Westwick for the last time. Everyone said she'd joined the Riftbound Order, working to balance the powers granted by the Rifts, but Rodrick wasn't convinced. No letters came, no word from her, no signs. Rowan had just turned thirteen when she left.

What Rowan didn't know when she disappeared, what Rodrick had never found the strength to tell him until much later in life, was that his mother's path led her straight to Maeve—a sinister Necromite hailing from Tenebral. Aidra had been sucked into his orbit, like so many others who believed they could fix the broken world. And as Aidra found out first hand, no one came back from Maeve.

Still, Rowan's mind was set. He'd trained relentlessly, poring over old field logs, practicing survival drills, and sharpening his marksmanship. To the people of Westwick, he was a golden boy with a bright future. But to Rowan, this was something deeper, something unfinished he had to see through. He didn't just want answers, but to prove he was worthy of what lay beyond Westwick. And if Aidra wasn't out there anymore, then he'd finish what she'd started.

But sometimes, into the late of night, the doubt crept in. *What if she hadn't vanished, what if she chose to stay away? What if she found someone, or something, that made her forget about us entirely?*

He hated himself for thinking it, but the questions gnawed at him all the same.

That night after returning from the munitions stall, he sat at the edge of his bed, staring at the weathered photo of himself and his mother. He habitually traced his fingers along the thinned edges of the photo, adding more to the wear. It had been taken just days before she left Westwick, the last time he'd seen her. Her arms wrapped around him, her smile full of strength and hope. He tucked the photo into his satchel, finishing the rest of his packing before the morning.

That morning had arrived, and Rodrick stood by the van, his shoulders slouched.

"Be careful out there, son," Rodrick said as Rowan finished his preparations. "Your mother is out there somewhere, but she won't be the same. And Maeve... well, he'll find you if you're not cautious."

Rowan dipped his chin in agreement. "I'll be fine," though doubt creeped in.

Cloud, his old mutt, barked and circled the van excitedly, leaping in beside him before Rowan could protest. The dog nudged his head into Rowan's arm, demanding affection. Rowan gave in and scratched behind his ears.

"Guess you're coming with me, then." Cloud wagged his tail, leaning into Rowan as if he understood.

As he drove out of Westwick, he waved goodbye to the townsfolk who had gathered around to watch his departure. A local hero set free to the outside world, following in his mother's footsteps.

Cloud's ears perked, before breaking into a fit of barking at something unseen beyond Westwick's border. Less than a mile outside of town, Rowan spotted a still and bloodied man lying by the road, next to an overturned vehicle. He slammed on the breaks and jumped out from the van, running to the man's side.

"Sir, are you okay?" he called, dropping to his knees.

The man's chest lifted weakly, his breathing shallow and forced.

"The dead are..." he rasped. "Among us... His name..." A rattling exhale followed, breathing his last breath.

Rowan stayed there for a long moment, hands braced against the man's chest as if sheer willpower could bring him back. But the body stiffened, the cold already seeping in, sealing his fate.

Rowan closed the man's eyes as Cloud growled low beside him.

"This is why we're out here, Cloud," Rowan said grimly. "But for this one... we're too late."

Leora awoke to warmth blanketing her body.

She couldn't remember falling asleep, yet here she was, feeling a cool breeze brush against the back of her neck.

The gray sky above shifted, wisp-like clouds drifting aimlessly. There were silhouettes of others far away, but too distant to make out. Around her, familiar structures began to form: halls of the palace at Valspire, stores she would often visit each morning, the central square where festivals were celebrated, and her garden with cotton roses growing plentiful.

Some blossoms were white, others pink, and a few already deep red. Even here, wherever "here" was, the petals changed color within the day. Leora admired them for a moment, the way they bloomed pure in the morning, softened in the sunlight, then darkened at night. A reminder that nothing stayed the same forever.

Someone was pacing in her garden, their outline familiar but too blurry to see clearly.

"Tavian? Orin?" she called out into the void.

No answer.

A soft touch grazed the back of her neck, causing the hairs of her neck to stand straight. She turned around, revealing a slender woman that stood before her, veiled in gold, the designs of her clothing intricate and otherworldly.

"It seems you've made it," the woman said. "Come with me. I've much to do today."

Leora didn't move. "Who are you?"

The woman pointed toward the garden, where the mysterious outline paced around the flowers.

"It seems someone has taken interest in your work."

It moved among the cotton roses, wilting each flower with a simple touch. The stranger's cold presence sent chills down Leora's spine; her limbs began to tingle and numb.

"What's it doing? Why is it killing my flowers?" Leora sounded as if she were going to break.

The woman's face remained composed, with only a thin smile forming, like one who'd already seen how it would end.

"Some choose life. Others prefer death," she said, watching the roses wilt into the dirt.

"Which do you think Tavian will choose?"

ACT II

YOU MUST FIRST BE LOST

CHAPTER EIGHT
THROW CAUTION TO THE WIND

> Be careful out there, son. Your mother is out there somewhere, but she won't be the same. And Maeve... well, he'll find you if you're not cautious.
> ~Rodrick Lysander

THE AGE OF THE CAR SHOWED WITH EVERY BUMP.

The vehicle sputtered as rusted machinery whirred and groaned in protest. Through each twist and turn, it felt as if the whole thing could fall apart at any moment.

"This is why we need to go back to the days of cars runnin' on oil. This magic-powered who-what's-it machinery doesn't work the same." Orin scoffed, pounding on the dashboard with his fist. "Damn thing's barely holdin' together."

The rolling hills and wide-open fields stretched endlessly beyond them, a stark contrast to the enclosed, towering structures of Valspire. Tavian sat in awe, staring at the beauty of the outside world.

This was what he had left for.

Aria remained unbothered, her attention fixated on the pages of her book.

"Do you see that?" Tavian interrupted Orin's rant.

He pointed at a great expanse of waterfalls cascading down jagged cliffs into a shimmering lake. His face glowed with wonder, and even Aria, who was usually indifferent to most things, sounded impressed.

"Wow, that's—"

A car suddenly veered in front of theirs. A violent crash put a swift end to their sightseeing.

Tires screeched as the windshield shattered, its glass breaking into sharpened shards. Metal twisted and crunched. The car lurched forward, sending them all flying inside the cabin. Their screams filled each crevice of the inside. Tavian's head collided with the front headrest of the passenger seat, Aria narrowly avoided a sheet of metal heading toward her, and Vid's forehead split open from the impact with the dashboard. The world spun around them as the car flipped end-over-end, tumbling across the road like a toy discarded by a child.

Everything came to a sudden halt. The sounds of car alarms rang in the background, rising smoke filling the cabin.

When Tavian's vision sluggishly returned, he was upside down, his seat belt the only thing keeping him from collapsing onto the ceiling. Aria's hair, soaked with blood, stuck to the floor beside him; she looked dead.

He unbuckled himself, falling and hitting his head into the roof before scrambling over to her.

"Aria! Aria, wake up!"

He pressed his hands over her deep gashes, trying to stop the profuse bleeding. A white glow emitted from his palms, warmth spreading throughout her body.

Aria mumbled awake, her eyes fluttering open.

"You okay?" she whispered hoarsely.

Tavian nodded. "Yeah, stay still. I've got you."

He carefully unbuckled her from the seat, pulled her through the broken glass, and rested her against the car's side.

"You still doing okay?" he asked, continuing to work on her major wounds.

She nodded, placing her hand on his forearm. "Yeah. I'll be all right."

Vid and Orin soon emerged from the wreck, beaten and bruised. Vid groaned dramatically.

"I'm okay too, if anyone was wondering," he said, brushing the remnants of splintered metal off his collar.

Orin observed the scene, pondering the circumstance.

Why did they drive head-first into us on this wide-open road? He thought. *There was plenty of room for them to move... unless they—*

Smoke erupted in the distance, and a screeching wail echoed from where the smoke originated.

Tavian stiffened. "We should check that out."

Orin immediately reached for his weapon. "No, we wait."

"But someone could be hurt, we have to help them."

Orin grabbed Tavian's arm, a vice grip, almost painfully so.

"You don't get it, boy. This isn't Valspire. The outside world doesn't work the way you think it does. We need to be cautious."

Vid, uncharacteristically serious, agreed with Orin's concerns. He stepped closer behind Orin, letting his large body hide him.

Tavian pulled free of Orin's grasp. "I don't care, I'm going. Look after Aria and Vid, I'll be back."

He limped toward the rising smoke, no weapon in hand, guided only by compassion and reckless hope. Aria, still unsteady on her feet, followed him without question.

Two bodies sprawled on the ground, stuck beneath the overturned vehicle that was responsible for the crash. Tavian hobbled to the nearest body and tried to pull it out from under the car. The sound of wet flesh tore, as the body separated in half. Tavian recoiled in horror and let go, now seeing the woman's face. It was unrecognizable, her skull caved in, her mouth frozen in a perpetual scream. Her torso was now split in two, separated from its legs, intestines plopping to the ground.

The color from Tavian's face evaporated. He barely managed to crawl backward before he vomited onto the pavement, his stomach retching and twisting in pain. His breathing hastened to a sprinter's pace, unable to control the hyperventilation. He grabbed at his chest, his heart beating at an exponential rate. A sharp pain flared on his left side —he gripped at the area where his heart was held, praying it wouldn't give out.

Aria crouched beside him, rubbing his back. "Don't look, just breathe," she forced his head away from the corpse, guiding his gaze toward her. She could see the genuine fear in his eyes, those of a boy who rarely witnessed death.

Vid and Orin followed, rushing over to examine the second body. Unlike the first, this one was still intact, but something wasn't right. Their skin was still warm to the touch, with a shallow pulse thumping in uneven bursts. At first glance, it looked like another corpse, but this body seemed far from dead.

The corpse's eyelids snapped open.

A shrill voice left its lips. "Wrong choice."

Vid took a step back, following the corpse's gaze into the adjacent forest. A low, rhythmic pounding came from beyond the trees, a sound like drums beating to a strange pattern.

Orin recognized the drumming at once, now realizing what was coming, but it was too late.

"Stay behind me," he instructed.

Tavian wiped his mouth and stumbled to his feet, Aria slowly supporting his efforts.

"Why?"

Orin reached into his side pockets and pulled out a set of cleavers.

"You'll see."

Vid, who had no weapon nor training in combat, jumped onto Orin's back like a child clinging to a parent. Aria sprinted back to the trunk of their car, rummaging through its remains, and pulled out a sword longer than her torso, its steel as thick as a tree trunk. As she dragged the blade against the ground, the road rumbled in its wake.

Tavian stared at her lugging the weapon. "How the hell are you lifting that?"

She merely turned to him, her face wrought. "I've been training for times like this. Just hide... please don't come out until this is over."

"I can fight. Let me help," he said, but the tremor in his voice undercut the confidence in his words.

Quickly scanning the surrounding area for a weapon, he noticed a staff lying near the half-torn corpse. He reached down to grab it, but its separated half lunged at him.

"That's not yours to use, kid," the half-dead woman sneered, gripping the staff with both hands.

She lifted it overhead. Her body began to reassemble, bones snapping into place, blood surging back into her skin, flesh knitting together like a hideous puzzle. She let out a hysterical, strangled laugh as her body finished mending.

Then, without hesitation, she bolted into the woods.

"What the hell?" Tavian stumbled backward, tripping over his feet.

"Let her go." Orin put an arm in front of Aria before she could strike.

"What? Why?"

Orin sighed. "Because... *you* can't kill them."

The drumming stopped, the trees grew still, all the wind was sucked out of the forest. Birds circling overhead dropped dead to the ground, falling like rain in a storm. There was death dragging in the air, and no living thing near the tree line could survive any longer.

Beings emerged from the trees, unnervingly alert, gore smeared across their faces. Their ages varied—some much younger than Tavian, barely old enough to wield a weapon, while others were so old and brittle it seemed impossible they were still alive. Yet they all moved in unison, as if bound by something, or someone, unseen.

From the center of the group, Maeve stepped forward, his arms crossed with a smirk forming at his cracked lips. He swept over the group before settling on Orin, his focus narrowing.

"Orin?" Maeve's voice was smooth, laced with amusement.. "Didn't expect to see you again."

Tavian glanced over to Orin, noticing his body was far more tense than usual, gripping tighter onto the cleavers.

"I'm helping the boy look for his mother. None of your concern, friend." Orin seemed calm, but his posture was anything but relaxed. "Let us leave. We don't want any trouble."

Maeve crooked his head, then his dark pupils landed on Tavian.

"You know better than to get caught up in one of our ruses." He let out a quiet chuckle, now focused fully on Tavian. "Don't let this kid make you look so stupid."

The crowd behind him erupted in laughter, a mixture of growls and cackles, their looks loaded with something feral... hunger, perhaps.

Maeve took another step forward. "Our allegiance only lasts for so long, Orin. Once our boss says it's through..." his lips curled into a wicked grin. "We're coming for you."

Another wave of laughter rippled through the group. Vid could be heard swallowing audibly.

An uneasy silence followed. Aria and Vid exchanged glances, unsure of their next moves, waiting for Orin's direction.

After a moment, Orin exhaled sharply. "Where's your boss, nowadays?"

Maeve's smirk subsided, several members of the mob behind him stiffened, their expressions bent with discomfort. "He's where he's always been... but I wouldn't go poking around places you aren't wanted."

He stole another look at Tavian, then back to Orin.

"It seems our little car accident ploy took a toll on you and those kids. I'd say it's time for you to go, before I consider forgetting about our deal."

Orin scanned through the crowd behind Maeve, realizing the sheer number was far too much for them. He took a step back, shoving Tavian, Aria, and Vid toward the direction of the car.

"Move. He won't repeat himself."

Vid hardly needed convincing, already scrambling toward the passenger seat. Tavian hesitated for a split second, catching once last look at Maeve, before running back to the car and opening up the hood to kickstart the engine. The car sputtered back to life, its engine groaning as if reanimated back from the dead.

"Let your boss know I'll be seeing him soon. He's been expecting me, I'm sure." Orin turned around and followed the group back to the car, leaving Maeve and his army behind.

As Tavian climbed in, he looked to Orin. "Who were those people? And that woman who put herself back together. Was that... a Necromite?"

Orin's jaw tightened, continuing to look forward as the car rolled ahead. "The power Necromites possess is more than you can imagine. I understand you want this for your mom, but sacrifices will have to be made."

Vid, ever the mood-breaker, cleared his throat. "I think I'll pass on being sacrificed. Nose goes!" He tapped his finger to his nose; an idiot's grin plastered to his face.

Tavian smirked and slapped Vid on the back of the neck, his shrill yelp could even be heard from outside. Aria promptly slapped Tavian twice as hard.

Orin paid no mind, his hands gripping the wheel, lost in his thoughts.

Tavian had seen Orin worried before, but not like this. He grew nervous. Orin knew something and wasn't telling them.

And for the first time, Tavian began to understand what everyone had been warning him about. Maybe this wasn't going to be as simple as he'd thought.

Rowan parked at the train station, gravel crunching beneath all four tires. The air was warm and carried the scents of oil and wet concrete. Inside, a regional news broadcast played on the half-static, mounted TV. Two men sat and watched intently, holding their cups of train station coffee steaming in their hands, fixated on the newscaster. Rowan walked by the television, overhearing the broadcast.

"This just in. Our on-field reporter has informed us that the barrier surrounding Valspire has fallen. More to come shortly."

"Serves them right," one of the men said. "Been hidin' for too long. Those suckers don't know what's comin' to 'em."

The other one scoffed, taking a sip from his cup. "Now hold on a second. Tenebral deserves worse, don't you know? Think about what Ravenna did all those years ago."

Rowan's grip fastened on Cloud's leash. Then the screen flickered once more. Another news report flashed onto the screen.

"BREAKING: Hundreds of armed and dangerous undead spotted outside Ashford."

The image cut to another on-field reporter outside the small town of Ashford, the silhouettes of a massive horde creeping over the horizon. Cloud growled deeply, his tail tucked between his legs.

"As you can see, I'm standing outside Ashford, where there appears to be a large mob of undead beings, possibly in the hundreds, heading toward Ashford from the north. The name Maeve has been brought up, although we can't confirm their Necromite origins as of yet. We are unsure of their intentions, but we know that—"

As the reporter continued to broadcast, an undead woman rose up beside him, a long pair of kitchen shears held in one hand. The reporter turned in time to watch the shears nearly reach their face—

The TV was cut off.

An error message appeared on the screen, reading:

"We apologize for this inconvenience, we are having technical difficulties. Please stay tuned for your daily broadcast on WDN - Westwick Daily News."

Maeve, Rowan thought, his vision pulsating.

"Damn undead freaks," one of the men grunted. "I say kill 'em all. Ain't that what they always do in the movies?"

The second man frowned. "You know they aren't all bad, right? Most of those poor souls were forced back to life; they don't wanna be there any more than we would."

"Well, if it were up to me, I'd—"

Rowan placed a hand on the ranting man's shoulder. The man withheld his words, coffee slipping from his hands and spilling across the floor. His gaze drifted to Rowan's face, then widened in recognition.

"You're... Rowan, ain't you? The Watcher killer?"

Rowan didn't answer.

"Reconsider your choice in words," he said calmly. "There are people out there that need help. Not judgment nor ignorance."

"I didn't mean nothin' by it," the man stammered, catching a glimpse of Rowan's holstered weapon.

Rowan said nothing more.

"I don't want no trouble," the man added, getting up out of his chair and slowly stepping back, arms raised up in surrender.

Rowan only gave a nod, then waved a hand toward the exit. Both men scurried out in silence, only the soft sounds of their hurried steps could be noticed.

He turned and scanned the waiting room. The others stood frozen, locked onto the blank television screen, clinging to the hope the broadcast would resume. They didn't yet realize the truth.

There wouldn't be another update. Soon, there wouldn't be an Ashford to report on.

Rowan approached the ticket booth.

"One way to Ashford, please," he said.

The clerk paused, eyeing him closely. "You sure? Didn't you just hear the news?"

Rowan's knuckles turned white against the handle on Cloud's leash. "Yes. I'm sure."

Elsewhere, far from the quiet tension of the train station, the Rift was in Lyra's reach, although smaller than she remembered. The abyss emitted the same powerful sensation as before, momentarily freezing both her and her sister.

"We're here," Lyra muttered. Anastasia's fingers dug into her sister's hand without meaning to. "I need you to wait here. It's too dangerous."

Anastasia shook her head. "No, I want to watch."

Lyra looked down at her sister. Her petite form seemed too innocent for the darkness festering within her.

"Fine. Then stay behind me and hold my hand tight."

They proceeded down the familiar steps, going hand-in-hand, snaking their way into the darkness below.

At the bottom, things appeared mostly the same as last time, although a new attendant stood at the booth in front of the massive door where Slug resided. There were people waiting their turn in front of the door, some huddled around a massive fireplace in the corner, and a line of prospects filing into the booth.

Lyra and Anastasia caught stray glances as they cut in front of the line, working their way to the booth. Someone stuck out a foot in front of Anastasia, tripping her over onto the floor.

"Get in the back and wait like the rest of us!"

His daughter snickered and his wife dimly smiled, mocking Anastasia and her blindness, covering their eyes and stumbling in place. Lyra picked Anastasia off the floor and carefully placed her to the side, just out of range.

"Ignore them, let me handle it. Just cover your ears, I don't want you to hear."

Not wanting to hear the screams of another victim, Anastasia cupped both ears.

Lyra stood tall and walked back over to the family who were still waiting in line, still laughing at Anastasia's misfortune. Lyra grabbed a hold of her scythe, a red glow erupting from the blade.

Their laughter died at the sight of the weapon.

They had only seconds to react, the mother cowered and put her hands out in front to shield herself. The father attempted to step in front of their daughter. Their pleas didn't reach Lyra, they were muted by her desire. She could feel their fear, but it was nothing new, she had grown accustomed to it.

The flavor of each victim's terror tasted sweet on her tongue—it was an acquired taste.

And Lyra had long since acquired it.

In one sweeping motion, the man, his wife, and his daughter were beheaded. Blood sprayed onto the bystanders in line, causing hysteria to ring out in the halls.

She could feel her power growing, each soul melding into her own.

People scattered in a panic, fleeing to escape Lyra's terrifying display of power. The door to Slug's chamber burst open, and a familiar, putrid voice called out.

"Who dares make such a mess of my chambers?"

A wet, slithering sound came from within the darkness that lay behind the cracked doors. Out came Slug, his body oozing with mucus, each movement leaving a trail of slime on the cement floor.

"Lyra?" he rasped, more amused than concerned. His milky-white eyes labeled her in an instant.

"What is it with you Ashryns, killing everyone before I can see them?"

Lyra stayed motionless, her scythe dripping with fresh blood, its red glow covering her hands. She leveled the blade toward him.

"You should've never touched my sister." Her voice was restrained with rage. "It's time to pay. For me... and for her."

She lunged forward, swinging the scythe in a wide arc, an attempt to sever him in half. A thick, glistening hand launched from his side, catching the blade mid-swing. The impact sent a jagged vibration up her arm; her muscles contracted from such a sudden blow.

She yanked back the weapon, but Slug's grip was like iron. His strength was overwhelming.

A second appendage burst from his torso, hurtling toward her head. She twisted mid-air, kicking off of the limb and propelling herself upward while dragging her scythe along with her.

A pulse of red haze emerged from her body, surging in violent waves. The energy coursed through her scythe and into Slug's hand that still gripped the weapon, sizzling his skin, burning through the outstretched hand. With a sickening hiss, the limb dissolved into a blackened puddle.

But Slug barely flinched.

"Stop this foolishness," he said condescendingly. "You're just like Anastasia—blind to reality. I'm not your enemy; you live with them. Until you realize this, there's no helping you. I may seem like a monster, but you are the real monster—as are all humans."

Lyra ignored his sermon, pushing forward, her scythe igniting in a brilliant red, brighter than before. The energy spiraled like a cyclone, engulfing the weapon from blade to snath.

She managed to strike part of his body. A deafening explosion of power rained down in a red hailstorm, piercing into Slug's oversized mass.

With inhuman speed, he had raised another hand. In a blink, his flesh morphed, forming a thick, protective shell that absorbed most of the attack.

As the red haze dissipated into his body, Slug condensed it and shot it back. She narrowly dodged it, only a few red drops managing to burn through her shirt. The ground shattered where she had landed, the force so great it sent fragments of flesh-laden debris into the air.

Her vision swam. Crimson poured from her eyes, running down her cheeks as tears. Static images of Slug pulsed in and out, the reality of the chamber distorting. She tried to force it back, withholding her eyes from taking control, but the power opposed her struggles.

No, not now, she thought. *I can't risk using it here.*

Slug smiled, noticing her internal battle. "I gave you these powers, Lyra. Nothing you can do will surprise me."

The ground quaked. A hundred hands came out from his body, rocketing toward her like a pit of writhing serpents. Lyra's scythe cut through them with ease, but limitless more followed the fallen. The chamber swarmed with them, an endless tide, each severed limb replaced with another, then another, and another.

She fought them off as long as she could, but they finally caught hold. Cold, vicious hands wrapped around her ankles, her wrists, then her throat. They slammed her to the ground, pinning her beneath their weight.

Slug then took another arm and reached down his own throat.

A sickening wet sound filled the space between them, as he pulled forth a sword from his insides, its edges coated in thick, dripping bile.

He turned to Anastasia, not to Lyra. A cruel smile split his features. "Once I kill Anastasia, you'll be easy to finish."

Lyra thrashed against the hands that bound her in place. "No! Anastasia, he's coming!"

"You two should have never come here," Slug said, steadily sliding toward Anastasia. "I wanted to test your limits and watch the power grow, but if this is how you repay me, I cannot stand idly by any longer."

His many arms continued to withhold Lyra, her efforts futile. He raised the viscera blade high above his head, nearly touching the ceiling above.

"Goodbye, Anastasia. I had so much hope for you."

He forced the blade down, but it stopped just before touching the top her head. His arms could move no further.

His entire form was seized. Expression, thought, and sight vanished all at once. His muscles locked up as if bound by a supernatural force.

Lyra tried to squirm free while Slug was vulnerable, but the same paralysis gripped her. Pain exploded behind her eyes, spreading through her skull like her mind was trying to rip itself apart. Lyra's entire body lurched, screaming in a bout of nausea.

Anastasia started to cry. Tears fell in rivers down her pale cheeks.

"I'm sorry, Lyra." Her voice shook, removing her hands from her ears. "I tried to control it, but I can't."

Slug's mouth opened in desperate petition. "Wait! Don't do this, Anastasia. There are things only I can tell you!" Fear had crept into his voice for the first time. "The other Watchers, Mariella, the Riftbound Order, they'll come after you! You don't—"

Anastasia lifted a shaky hand and pointed at the roaring fireplace in the far corner.

Slug's body began to move in accordance with her directions. His body slithered toward the fire, despite his jerky attempts to resist.

"No! You don't know what I did to give you those powers! You're making a mistake!"

The flames grew stronger as he neared, the fires growing hungry at his arrival.

"The others will find you... this isn't over. I gave you far too much Anastasia. I—"

His body rolled into the red and blue flames. The room picked up a smell of burning flesh and rot as his skin began to pop and crackle in the fire. His screams were laced with despair and torment. Sounds of cooked flesh over fire seasoned the chamber, his many hands dissolving away into the charcoal.

Lyra watched, Anastasia used her sister's eyes to spectate.

Neither spoke, neither mourned.

Anastasia clasped her hands together, now standing by the fire, a growing warmth covering her palms. In the ash grew a few strange flowers, somehow enduring the incredible heat of the flames.

The chamber was silent as they warmed themselves up by the fire. But soon after, a low rumble came from above.

Lyra's head snapped up, and from the shadows of the ceiling, pairs of glowing eyes blinked open in unison, watching them with intent.

A single voice drifted through the meeting hall.

"We must act now. The Eyes at Slug's Rift witnessed his death and the extent of Anastasia's powers."

The words were carried by the rhythmic tremors beneath the floor. Burning incense curled smoky wisps along the walls, mingling with the scent of decay.

The speaker stood near the edge of the semi-circle; a small figure in formal attire. His tone was sharp and anxious.

"With Slug now gone, and Westwick's Watcher killed, we're losing traction. These failures are a stain on us. If we hesitate any longer, the seams will unravel. Our balance is thinning."

Around him, figures sat in a semicircle, their faces hidden beneath heavy hoods as dark as midnight. A few nodded in grim agreement, while others sat quiet, unwilling to voice dissent.

A voice broke the silence from further down the circle. "What should we do, Eldric? People will soon realize our intentions. We can't afford to wait."

All focus turned to the man seated at the center: Eldric, the commanding officer of the faction tasked with stabilizing the powers of the Rifts, formally the Riftbound Order.

He said nothing at first, with a small shift in his seat cracking his spine. He adjusted the folds of his robe with care.

"We wait." His voice was eerily calm. "Patience is a virtue. I do not fear the unknown." His smile widened. "The brightest lights often herald the darkest shadows."

He again adjusted himself, moving uncomfortably this time. His fingers drummed against the wooden armrest. No one dared to interrupt him, even the most hardened among them felt a chill as Eldric's gaze swept over the room.

"Although… I do fear Anastasia," he added.

"So you *do* fear her?" one voice challenged.

Eldric turned to face the speaker.

"Fear is not the same as weakness, and weakness is not tolerated. We'll let our friends handle her."

CHAPTER NINE
WHAT COMES AFTER LIFE

> I'm not writing you this because we want you back. I'm writing you this because we need you back. Please, come home.
>
> ~Elyra Fenwyn

"Lyra, help!"

Anastasia's screams tore through the stillness of the night.

Lyra bolted upright from her makeshift bed, her heart racing. She grabbed her scythe, scanning the darkness.

"It's on me! Hurry!" Anastasia wailed.

Lyra sprinted through the dark toward where she remembered Anastasia had set up her bed, reaching her sister's side within seconds. Anastasia was rigid as stone, unwilling or unable to move.

"What is it? What's wrong?"

Anastasia pointed to her leg. Lyra followed where she'd pointed and found the culprit, a spider no larger than a coin, perched atop her skin.

"Please kill it," Anastasia squeaked. "It's so gross. I can't see it, but I know it's there."

Lyra exhaled sharply and mumbled under her breath.

"Oh my gods, kill the thing yourself," Lyra said, already turning away. "Go back to sleep."

Anastasia flinched at the coldness in Lyra's tone. "Don't leave. I… also don't wanna be alone."

Lyra paused. She looked back over her shoulder to her sister, who was now looking up at her and absentmindedly picking at her nails, no longer paying mind to the spider crawling up her leg.

"You could've asked me that from the start," Lyra bent down. "I figured you'd want your own space, now that we don't have to share a room."

Anastasia shook her head. "I don't like being alone. I liked how we used to sleep."

The corner of Lyra's mouth lifted. "Okay, bring your stuff over. You can sleep by me."

Anastasia threw herself upward, the spider flying off her body, rolling onto the dirt floor and scurrying away. She hopped in excitement and grabbed all her belongings in a messy pile, rushing over to where her sister's bed was.

They laid close; Lyra could feel a warmth untouched by the outside air, lulling her into the first truly restful sleep in days.

By the time morning broke, the burnt-orange hues of the rising sun set the sky ablaze. They packed their meager belongings and prepared for the road ahead. It had been ten days after Slug's demise. Ten days of exhaustion, hunger, and relentless cold. Their path toward Valspire was slow and uncertain, with only vague directions to guide them.

"Is Mom's map working?" Anastasia whined. "This is taking a long time."

"What we need is a boat," Lyra replied, shaking off excess snow from her coat. "Ravenna told of a port further past the hills. If we can find it and get on the ferry, we can make this quick."

Anastasia shivered nonstop, her body rattling like an old, dying furnace. Lyra sighed, wrapping an arm around her, trying to transfer some of her own warmth.

"We'll get there," Lyra murmured. "I promise."

"Are we there yet?" Vid asked for the hundredth time. He groaned dramatically, restlessly stretching his legs, his fingers picking a scab on his arm.

Orin gritted his teeth. "No."

Vid grinned. "Maybe you should turn—"

"Would you like to drive instead?" Orin snapped. "Hate to make ya bored, sittin' there doin' nothin'."

Vid huffed, slumping back into his seat. "Y'know, I could sing a new song to pass the time—"

"FOR THE LOVE OF MARIELLA, PLEASE NO MORE!" Aria shouted from the back seat, delivering a swift kick to the back of Vid's chair. His body flew forward, his already-injured head smacking the dashboard once more. A small dent now marked the spot where it had hit several times before.

Orin smirked at the scuffle, but glanced over in the rearview mirror to Tavian, who sat silent and distant. The boy hadn't spoken in nearly an hour, his swollen and bruised hands limp on his lap.

"You all right back there, Tavian? Could use a voice that ain't Vid's for a change."

No response.

Aria leaned over and placed her hand on Tavian. He flinched, startled out of whatever trance held him.

"Huh?"

"Orin was asking if you're all right. You seem... off."

Tavian looked from Aria to Orin then back to his hands, flexing his fingers.

"Yeah, I'm fine," he said unconvincingly. "I'm just hoping this hand doesn't get more infected. You think it's spreading? Should I go see a doctor? Will I die if I wait too long?"

Orin sighed. "No Tavian, you're fine. We'll be stoppin' soon anyway. We're all in bad shape... and by the looks of it, we're all sick of sittin' 'round each other."

A unanimous silence filled the car as they exchanged knowing looks.

Another few hours into the trip, the landscape ahead began to change. On the horizon, a colossal tree—larger than most cities—rose into view, its vast canopy blotting out the evening sun. The sky behind it blazed with pinks and purples, painting the sky like a coloring book. The tree climbed higher than a hundred stories, its branches sprawling outward, each supporting a community of homes, shops, and businesses built seamlessly into the living wood.

It was a city born from a single tree, alive and breathing.

"My gods," Aria whispered, putting down her book, tilting her head upward to get a full view.

The car slowed to a stop in standstill traffic before the massive tree. Out the window, Tavian noticed something lying by the roadside —a dead animal, he thought at first, though it was too far to make out.

He squinted. *What kind of animal has two arms and two legs...*

As his eyes adjusted, the truth settled in. It was no animal, but a human in its place... or had been. The body was more fungus than flesh, with growths and spores ejecting from every crevice.

Tavian sucked in a sharpened breath, the sound drawing Orin's attention. He looked over to the same corpse, his grip tensing on the steering wheel.

"Do you know what that is, Orin?" Tavian asked, noticing his sudden shift in demeanor.

Orin didn't answer.

As they inched forward, the line of cars wound toward a bridge at the tree's base, opening up into the heart of the city. At the checkpoint stood a guard, a man... or at least something resembling the shape of one.

His body, much like the corpse on the side of the road, was laced with growths; his skin oily, his features partially human but unmistakably akin to a mushroom.

When they pulled up to the checkpoint, the mushroom-man leaned through the window, staring at them unblinking. "Do you have an ID and proper registration to—"

His head switched to Orin. "Oh, well I won't be needing yours actually."

Then narrowing his gaze, he added to the rest, "And please stop staring."

Tavian, Aria, and Vid immediately snapped their heads down, faces burning.

Orin sighed. "Sorry about them. First-timers."

The mushroom man scoffed. "They don't mention us in Valspire? That checks out. Move along."

As they crossed the bridge, Tavian exhaled. “So you do know of this place.”

“Didn’t seem like somethin’ important to mention,” Orin quickly responded, keeping his sight planted on the road. “But there's plenty of world outside Valspire, Tavian. Welcome to it.”

A sour, briny smell drifted into their nostrils as Lyra and Anastasia neared the ocean. The ferry port was in sight.

“There’s a small shack over by the docks,” Lyra said, spotting the abandoned building. “You’ll wait there while I handle the ferry.”

“But—”

“Remember what I said, if you came with me, you’ll listen to what I say.”

Lyra left no room for argument. They walked over to the shack, Lyra opening the door for her sister. Anastasia grumbled but relented, stepping into the old building. The floors reeked of dead fish.

“First time I’m glad I can’t see anything,” Anastasia muttered, wrinkling her nose and pinching her nostrils shut. “Wish I couldn’t smell, too.”

Lyra left her sister and approached the dock workers. At the edge of the pier, a colony of arctic puffins wheeled near the cliffs, their calls trailing over the water. But as Lyra drew closer, the birds faltered mid-flight. One by one, sickening thuds of their bodies slammed into the docks; the sound calling the worker’s attention.

The mark of death that shadowed the Necromites had surfaced again, leeching life from anything nearby. Grass withered and blackened beneath her boots as the workers slowly backed away.

Then, the port went still. Only the slight creak of mooring ropes and the gentle slap of water against the ship's hulls broke the silence.

“Where does this ferry go?” Lyra asked, pointing to the boat nearest her.

One worker, shivering, bowed to her.

"P-p-please, ma'am," he stammered, "we ain't asking for trouble. We're just doing our jobs."

"Then answer me." Lyra's patience thinned.

"I... It goes to Ashford," he finally admitted.

Ashford, She looked back at her map. *Closer, at least.*

"Good. My sister and I need passage immediately."

The men exchanged frantic glances with unanimous nods. "Yes, of course. Right away, miss!"

But before they could move, a woman stormed forward from a nearby office.

"Hold up a damn second! Who the hell said you could pack up and leave?" The woman towered high, at least 6'2, built like a bear with thick shoulders and patches of fuzz for facial hair. "I don't know who you are, lady, but we ain't going to Ashford anymore. There are undead—"

She stopped, looking over to the dead birds then to the rotting grass... then to Lyra's face. Her next words clumsily wobbled out of her mouth.

"W-What is a Necromite doing all the way out here?"

Lyra remained silent, taking a step closer. Her scythe dipped lower below her waist, catching the light, now in full view.

The burly woman, assumed to be the harbormaster, slunk back a step, her bravado draining.

"Wait, please! I'm sorry, I didn't know. We'll be sure to get this boat set for you immediately, ma'am. It was silly of me to overreact like that. If I'd known, then I would've—"

A salty, metallic taste coated the inside of her mouth. Her body jolted for a second, and as she looked down...

Lyra's scythe was embedded in her torso. The blade twisted, releasing chunks of innards onto the ground. They sounded spongy as they slid over the tops of her shoes.

Lyra leaned into her ear, her voice deathly calm. "Were you saying something?"

The woman collapsed. Lyra withdrew the blade, next slicing through the neck. The harbormaster's head rolled off the dock and into the sea; a swarm of fish surfacing, beginning to feast on her scalp.

Lyra turned back toward the workers, their bodies petrified.

"Have we been given permission to proceed to Ashford now?"

They scrambled to prepare the ferry for departure to Ashford without another word.

They would finally be leaving Tenebral for good.

A step closer to Valspire.

A step closer to their freedom.

The inner workings of Mycordia were unlike anything Tavian had ever seen.

There were shops, vendors, food stalls, and homes nestled into the hollowed walls of the spacious tree's interior. Large bioluminescent fungi illuminated the walkways, their soft light creating an eerie yet comforting glow. Miniature fungi waddled along in clusters, bumping aimlessly into crates and benches with no real sense of purpose nor direction. The townsfolk seemed to move at an unhurried pace, taking their time with every exchange, as if time itself had slowed.

Yet as Tavian's group passed, fungal eyes seemed to linger on them longer than expected; far longer than appreciated.

"Not sure if I like it here," Aria said, giving back equally uncomfortable stares to each passerby.

"I think it's beautiful," Tavian corrected, though he wasn't sure if he believed it, sensing the presence of a small group forming around him.

Vid, however, was already distracted by something in the distance. He pointed at an open-air market, his eyes sparkling under the luminescent glow.

"Look, over there! Look at all the clothes, and the food!" His mouth began to salivate. "And over there... Are those baby mushrooms playing flutes?"

"Vid, focus." Orin slowly dragged his hand down his face. "We're headin' to the medics first."

Tavian flexed his sore hand, still tender from the car crash. He couldn't get it out of his mind, the hypochondria working overtime to negate the awe and expanse of the new world surrounding him.

The queue outside the Mycordian clinic was agonizingly slow. One would've thought for all their medical brilliance, the Mycordians would've mastered the art of efficiency.

Ahead of them in line, stood a stocky man covered from head to toe in burns. Some wounds leaked a strange-smelling black pus, and others had hardened into dark scabs.

"Ughh," the man rocked slightly back and forth, his knees beginning to give way under exhaustion.

Orin reached out, catching the burned man before his body finally gave way. "This man needs urgent help. We're gettin' you inside."

He shoved past the line, carrying the man as his body slumped over. The receptionist, a mushroom-hybrid woman with long fungal tendrils draped over her shoulders, didn't look impressed.

"Can I help you?" she droned, her expression blank.

"This man is on the brink of death. He needs immediate attention."

The receptionist barely reacted. "Like I told the others... You. Must. Wait. Your. Turn. In. Line."

"Look at him, dammit! Can't you see—"

"Orin?" A man dressed in tight-fitted formal attire strutted out from the back of the clinic. The gait of his walk would suggest he owned the place.

Turns out, he did. "What brings you all the way out here? And why do you look worse than usual?"

Orin tried looking away, hoping the distance would turn him invisible, but with a dying body in his arms, that seemed impossible. "Kaelen? Didn't think I'd run into you again."

Kaelen's facade faded. "Yeah, funny how things work out."

The burned man groaned in Orin's arms, reminding him of the urgency in the moment. Kaelen clapped a hand on the receptionist's shoulder, a small spark of energy crackling between them.

She stiffened as if momentarily stunned. Then she nodded haltingly. "The doctor will see your friend immediately. We apologize for the inconvenience."

Tavian shivered, that was beyond normal.

Kaelen summoned his false smile and turned to open the doors. "C'mon, let's get your friend to the back." But before opening them, he turned back to Orin. "Also, Orin, I would love to catch up when you have a second."

The twisting hallways of the medical center were dimly lit, the air damp with an herbal, earthy scent. The walls were made of splintered wood, mushrooms sprouting from every angle. People rushed by with urgency, but not a word was spoken. Only through small electric pulses in their touch, much like Kaelen with the receptionist, did they communicate.

Aria and Tavian looked to one another.

"What was all that back there? Sounds like Orin and this guy aren't too friendly." Aria whispered.

"No idea, but if it gets us in quicker..."

Vid was still openly gawking at the mushroom-covered people rushing by. Unfortunately, one of them caught his stare, narrowing its gaze. Without warning, thin, spore-veined tendrils erupted from his palm, lashing toward Vid. He was still grinning in awe, not even flinching at the oncoming tendrils.

Aria reacted in his place. She drew her mammoth sword and swung in a steep arc, slicing the vines in half before they could reach him.

Cutting the vines appeared to be the wrong move, a sudden stillness swept over the halls of the clinic. The old wooden floors quaked. From beneath their feet, thick wooden branches burst from the floor, wrapping around each of Aria's limbs. The mushrooms resting on the walls came to life, their caps glowing an ominous red; they vibrated in place, emitting clouds of powder that stung to breathe in.

"Why must humans always disobey the colony?" The speaker could not be seen, but the voice could be easily heard.

Aria bucked against the branches, but with every movement, they constricted tighter—soon turning her skin purple. Spores that littered the branches crept toward her, working their way up her skin and through her hair.

"Wait!" Orin shouted. "She's new! I'll handle it. Let her go."

There was a momentary pause. The spores ceased their crawl, the branches loosened their grip, and the Mycordians fell still. From the shifting fungi seated on the walls, hundreds of eyes blinked open, and from up above, the ceiling split wide, revealing a single, gaping mouth.

"Was she not made clear of the expectations?"

"No, but I'll be sure she understands."

Kaelen interjected. "This is Orin, The Harvester, he means no harm. It was an honest mistake."

"If I knew The Harvester were paying a visit, I would've requested more bodies." The mouth on the celling smiled, exposing rows of dagger-sharp spikes as teeth. "Even *you* only get one warning, Orin."

The spores vanished, the branches receded back into the floors, and the Mycordians returned to their normal routine as nothing had changed.

Orin turned to Aria, his fear palpable. "You can't go makin' such brash decisions. These people are *sensitive*."

Aria scoffed then turned her back to him. "I saved Vid from those freaks. Besides, what harm does cutting down a few tendrils do anyways?"

Orin grabbed her by the shoulder and twisted her back around, his expression far more serious than before. "Look 'round yerself. How do you think these people turned out like this?"

She caught movement through a cracked door, opened just enough to see the faint outline of an operating table. A patient laid strapped to it, a human... just like them. Before she could blink, his legs spasmed, as minuscule fungi worked their way under his skin through precise surgical incisions. He struggled mercilessly, his mouth sealed shut by roots pressed over his lips, his hands and feet locked into iron clasps.

Bit by bit, his body began to morph into something much like a Mycordian, parts of his flesh now giving way to fungus.

A nurse passing by noticed the door ajar and hurried to close it.

Aria swallowed, the truth crawling under her skin much like the fungus she'd just seen. These people weren't born as mushroom-hybrids. They had been forced.

The nurse opened a new door and motioned them all inside. Aria grabbed Tavian and Vid and pushed them in. The nurse then quickly shut the door behind them, locking away what they had just seen.

As the medics tended to their wounds, Aria looked back at the closed door, wondering how many others hid behind these walls, tortured and converted to these awful creatures.

And how long until it may become them, instead.

Several days had passed, and by now, Tavian, Orin, Vid, and Aria had mostly recovered from their encounter with Maeve and the undead.

On the morning of the third day, Orin led the group, except for Vid—who was more fascinated with thrift shopping than reunion—to check up on the burn-riddled man they'd rescued from the perils of medical clinic wait list.

When they entered his room, the man, now fully conscious and sat upright, turned his head toward them. "Welcome to my new digs," he said, smiling. "I don't think I ever had the chance to properly introduce myself. I'm Cassius."

He sat up further and adjusted himself. His charred hands still bore evidence of his wounds, but his face radiated warmth.

"And I have you to thank for getting me seen in such a hurry, I don't know if I could've lasted much longer in such condition."

"Don't ya worry," Orin said. "It got us in quicker too, so I should be thankin' you for the good excuse."

Cassius laughed, coughing between each note.

"What brought you all to Mycordia?" Cassius asked. "Spirians tend not to wander too far from home."

"How could you tell we're from Valspire?" Tavian chimed in.

Cassius looked him up and down, itching his stubble. "The way you dress and how you speak. It's quite obvious, for someone like me."

Tavian looked down at his clothes, the loose-fitting shirt and worn-in pants didn't seem too out of the ordinary, but he shrugged it off and continued regardless.

"We came here for rest," Tavian now answering Cassius's earlier question.

"And you? You look like a man who never rests."

A slight tinge reverberated in Orin's back. "I'm with the lot; we just needed to recover from our travels."

Cassius's head tilted. "You've got quite the reputation around here.

To me it seems like you had other plans for choosing a place so far out the way. But I'm not always right... although rarely."

Aria turned to Orin. "What does he mean by that?"

Cassius leaned back, watching with amused detachment.

"I've got nothin' to say."

Kaelen scoffed from the doorway, "'Nothin' is one way to put it."

They all turned to him; he had been silently observing from a distance. His arms were crossed, his polished shoes lightly tapping onto the floor.

Tavian's eyes narrowed. "Orin?"

Orin's arms slumped to his sides, and for the first time since Tavian had known him, he looked tired. Not the kind of tired you experience after a grueling battle or from miles of strenuous travel, but from something deeper. Something old that had worn him down over the years, slowly eating at his consciousness.

"You ever wonder how a place like this survives? How a community built inside a tree can get so massive?"

Aria frowned. "What are you saying?"

Orin rubbed his temples, as if saying it aloud was more draining than any fight he'd faced. "I created this place. I gave them life—I gave them bodies."

"You what?" Aria's hand reached for the hilt of her sword.

"Not Spirian bodies," Orin added. "The bodies of others."

"Who? And... why?" Strange veins under Aria's skin distended like emerging roots below a tree.

"Because I owed them," Orin said.

The room went silent, except for Cassius, who became more profoundly interested by the minute. "Owed them? Your debt came in the form of sacrificing human lives? *The Harvester*, yes, that name suits you well."

The silence pressed in thick. Cassius looked between each of them, waiting for someone to speak.

Suddenly, someone ran in behind Kaelen and pushed him to the side, stumbling into the center of the room.

"YOU ALL NEED TO SEE THIS SHIRT!" Vid announced, proudly pointing to the decal pasted on his sweater. It read: "I'm a real *fungi.*", complete with the cartoon image of a mushroom wearing sunglasses.

He paused, taking in the grim faces around him. "Did I... interrupt something? I know it's kinda corny, but..."

Orin dragged a hand down his face. "You got no idea, boy."

That night, per Cassius's request—and his generous offer (or rather, *bribe*) to pay for them to accompany him—the group went out for one last meal in Mycordia before departing. There was stiff tension between them after Orin's revelation, and no further explanation had been given.

Aria sat nearest to him, her hand never straying too far from her weapon. *What debt could he possibly owe?* she wondered. *Would he offer us next?*

Vid, as expected, ate like he'd never seen food before. Aria and Tavian, however, poked around their food nervously, uncertain of what to believe.

"This is phenomenal!" Vid shouted, scarfing down another serving of the unlabeled meat. "Seriously, do you guys even realize how good this is? Beats anything I've ever had in Valspire!"

Cassius chuckled. "Best restaurant in Mycordia. I couldn't let you all leave without trying it... and I know my way around food. How do you think I got so big?" He rubbed his distended stomach with a laugh.

Though his laughter faded quickly, replaced by a thoughtful look over to Tavian. He set down his fork, studying Tavian from across the table.

"I do have one question," he said, finally lifting the fork again and pointing it to Tavian.

Tavian raised a brow. "Yeah?"

"That mark on your back. I noticed it when you removed your shirt earlier today. It's unusual. How'd that end up there?"

Tavian shuddered. The scar, he'd almost forgotten about it.

"Uh, excuse me one second," he replied, rushing into the nearest bathroom.

He yanked off his shirt and twisted in front of a mirror.

The mark had grown again. Still no pain, but as he traced along the edges with his finger, a faint warmth bloomed. He scratched at it, rubbed at it harder, but it only seemed to throb as an answer. He quickly put back on his shirt so as to not arouse suspicion and returned to the table.

"Sorry, held it in for too long," Tavian said, managing something that slightly resembled a smile. "But I have no idea what the mark is. It's probably nothing, maybe an injury from training."

"Hmm..." Cassius studied him, scratching his chin. "Can't argue with that."

There was a long, awkward period of silence where only the sounds of forks and knives scraped against glass plates.

Cassius cleared his throat. "So... where are you all headed?"

Orin nearly choked on a piece of meat, pounding on his chest, dislodging it. "It's a long story... one you're probably not interested in."

"Oh, I wouldn't be so sure. Still, I can't say much, I've got my own secrets—ones best kept from strangers."

Tavian looked up. "Well then, where are *you* headed?"

Cassius flinched at the question, looking down to his burnt palms and picking away at the scabs absently. He readjusted himself in his chair, exhaling a single, deep breath.

"I'm in search of the afterlife."

Tavian's fork clanged against the plate. Leora's helpless, dying face flashed before him. He wondered if Cassius could help him... if he could help her.

Tavian leaned forward. "Have you found anything?"

Cassius placed down his utensils and pushed his plate away. "Haven't found much yet. I have my ideas, although when I tell people, they think I've gone mad."

Aria still hadn't let her guard down around Orin, but Cassius's words drew her attention. Even Vid had stopped eating—whether because his plate was empty or because of what he'd just heard, it was difficult to tell.

"How mad?" Tavian asked.

"Mad enough to visit Ashford. Word is, a Necromite and an army of undead have taken refuge there. If anyone could teach me about the afterlife, it would be those who command it."

"We'll join you." Tavian said.

Aria, Orin, and Vid exchanged uncertain looks, confused by

Tavian's brash decision to recruit Cassius so impulsively. Cassius leaned back, his eyes wandering off in distant thought. A long silence stretched thin between them.

"I'm not sure our interests are aligned, Tavian. I think—"

"Please," he interrupted. "We could use the help. And believe it or not, our goals are very much aligned."

Cassius sat on the proposition for a bit longer, mulling over his thoughts. He studied Tavian once more.

"You all can tag along," he said at last, "but this is for my family, I won't let you get in the way."

"Don't think of it as heaven or hell. It's a waiting room, and you stay until their arrival. Once they're ready, you'll know. We make it easy for them," Luna said, walking Leora through a field of cotton roses. Luna moved right beside her, but never left traces of footprints.

The sky was a swirling mix of gray and silver, formless yet vast, with the white-topped tips of mountain peaks far into the distance. The air smelled fresh and clean, far more so from the garden Leora once tended.

Leora reached out, brushing her hands along the flower's delicate petals, feeling their soft and familiar texture. It reminded her of home, of her own garden, and everything else she had to leave behind.

She couldn't help but to take notice of the same shadowy figure following close behind them, far enough away as to not cause concern, but close enough to feel its cold radiance. The figure left a wilted path of death behind them; her vibrant rose petals curling inward, shriveling into decayed roots.

"You still haven't told me *exactly* what this place is," Leora said.

Luna tilted her head, as if the answer was obvious. "It's what comes after."

Leora exhaled, her fingers curling around the flower she had picked off the stem. "After what?"

"After everything." She pointed a delicate finger back to the figure trailing behind them.

Leora turned back around to look at the shadow, now only a few feet away from her. It somehow managed to close the distance within seconds, without sound, but she was oddly not afraid.

"Who is that?" she whispered to Luna.

Luna clasped her hands together. "You could try asking it yourself."

The figure reached out a hand toward Leora. She extended her own, revealing the flower resting in her palm.

She felt something unnerving crawl over her skin as the hand approached. A cold, numbing sensation spread from her fingertips to her wrist. When the shadow's fingers brushed the flower, its petals withered and collapsed to dust.

Leora recoiled, pulling her hand back. The touch burned like frost.

The shadow looked up at her, tears rolling down its empty face.

CHAPTER TEN

FOUR'S COMPANY

What was his name again?
~Vid Merriweather

Tavian,

Things in Valspire have grown bleak since you left. The townsfolk worry you'll never return. I try to reassure them you're out finding answers about your mother, but even I'm no longer sure what it is you hope to find.

Mobs have begun to gather. Shops and homes are broken into nightly. Factions are rising, and anarchy spreads faster than we can contain. I no longer feel safe here, and it only grows worse by the day.

I feel the presence of Necromites drawing closer, no more than a year out. And there is a girl, one Mariella herself has sensed, who troubles even her. Through Mariella's vision, I've seen them: thousands of those horrid Necromites and wicked creatures waiting for their moment to strike.

As for Orin... I still don't know what possessed him to leave so rashly, but I hope he finds whatever peace he's looking for.

I'm not writing you this because we want you back. I'm writing you this because we need you back.

Please, come home.

Love, Grandma

Elyra set the pen down, her hand still struggling to maintain composure. Outside her bedroom window, she could see the local meat market littered with shattered glass and a small fire smoldering within. Spirians rushed out, arms full to the brim of stolen goods.

The town had devolved to chaos, and there was little Elyra could do.

Mariella stood behind her, silent and stilled, an omnipotent figure, yet with little control over the lives of the commoners. Her translucent hands rested on Elyra, radiating a warmth only a goddess could provide. Elyra handed her the folded letter, sealed with the intricate crest of the Fenwyn family.

"You said what needed to be said," Mariella spoke, sensing Elyra's indecision. "There's no need to dwell."

Mariella accepted the letter, folding it between her palms. A faint white light formed in her fingertips, and with a sudden pulse, the parchment vanished in a streak of energy through the ceiling, into the sky. It would find the one bound by the family name; Tavian would receive it soon enough.

Outside, a scream echoed, followed by the crash of broken glass—closer this time. Someone pounded on the doors down the street as rallying shouts began to gather in the square.

Elyra moved to the window and drew the curtains shut. "Please, Tavian, come back quickly... before there's nothing left to come back to."

Ravenna slammed her fist on the dining room table, the force rattling the half-lit candles and tarnished silverware. "That damned girl! What a good-for-nothing brat!"

Corvin continued to read the note left behind by Anastasia.

I'm going with Lyra on her mission. She wants me to keep her safe, but I will be okay. Please don't come for us. My eyes feel better too, in case you wondered.

Ravenna snatched the note from Corvin's hands and tore it to shreds. "Who told her to leave with Lyra? She had so much potential! What a waste."

Corvin leaned back in his worn felt chair, fingers drumming against the wide armrest. "She's a fool, but she's still ours to manage. We can't have Anastasia wandering on her own, with an untrained hand."

Derewin stood silently in the corner of the living room, fixed on an old, crooked framed photo. He adjusted it until it hung perfectly level—just as Ravenna spotted him.

"Derewin!" she screeched, pounding her fist against the dining room table once more. The frame rattled and tiled askew again. "Tell your lackeys to find them! I couldn't care less about Lyra, but we can't lose Anastasia. She's our strongest asset."

Derewin sighed, abandoning his futile pursuit of symmetry. "I'll be sure Maeve hears about this."

He left the house and moved straight through town, leaving no time for distractions. Ravenna's orders were law.

Deep beneath his home, within the confines of his hidden basement, sat a steel contraption shaped like a helmet, wired to a vat of swirling reddish-purple vapor. The device was fastened to a chair, its frame cluttered with dangling instruments and flickering gauges.

He settled into the seat, lowering the helmet over his head before flipping an array of switches at his side. Oblong tubes drew the smoke inside the helmet, one of his eyes lighting up to life, glowing with the same color as the vapor. Through it, he could locate and communicate with Maeve.

"Maeve, it's Derewin. Anastasia has gone missing, likely alongside Lyra. We need her back at once, and reports from the port confirm they're headed to you in Ashford."

Maeve stood up from his seat. The crunch of a skull beneath his boot barely registered over the rowdy crowd and cheers that surrounded him. Drunken men and women sang, clinked glasses, and stabbed the lifeless bodies littering the floor.

"Boss! You always call when you need something. Ever care to ask me how my day was?"

Derewin's patience thinned. "This isn't a joke. Anastasia is far more powerful than you or I could imagine. Do not take this lightly."

Maeve burst into hysterical laughter, falling over and rolling onto the blood-smeared floor. The crowd exchanged uneasy glances, but one by one, they forced out nervous chuckles, uncertain what he found so funny.

"Relax, Derewin!" Maeve gasped between laughs, hauling himself upright, his clothes clinging to the sticky crimson ground below. "I'll handle it, but you'd better make it worth my while."

Derewin grumbled. "You'll get the next round of bodies once we have Anastasia."

Maeve grinned. "Deal! And while you're at it—"

Derewin cut off the connection and threw the helmet onto the floor. "Damn beggars. This is why I can't stand dealing with them."

Behind him, the empty house creaked. Derewin looked around at the stale walls and empty chambers, then sank lower into his chair and closed his eyes.

But I asked for this life. For better or for worse, this is what I deserve.

Maeve stretched his arms above him, rolling his shoulders back. "You hear that, boys 'n girls? We have our next targets! Lyra and Anastasia Ashryn."

The crowd erupted in cheers, downing their drinks in hasty gulps.

Maeve's grin widened. "Let's kill 'em both."

The ferry took two days to reach Ashford. On the final morning, the ringing of the ship's bell signaled their arrival. Lyra woke Anastasia with a gentle shake.

Together they stepped off the ship and onto the dock, where the warm sea air greeted them with thick humidity sticking to their skin. The contrast to Tenebral was staggering: the sun burned high, and the sky stretched wide and impossibly blue.

Lyra swept over the vast size of the town that sprawled before her. Its scale dwarfed anything she'd ever pictured; an intimidating backdrop from her once humble beginnings.

"Look through my eyes," she whispered to Anastasia.

Anastasia guided Lyra's head, turning it slowly to take in each corner of the city. She stomped with Lyra's feet, no longer feeling the familiar crunch of snow under her shoes. Heat pressed against her, and for the first time that she could remember, she started to sweat—a strange but oddly comforting feeling.

She beamed. "This place is amazing! No snow!"

She severed the connection with her sister, tearing off her jacket and tossing it aside, only to hear it slide off the dock and splash into the ocean.

"Oops."

Lyra chuckled. "It's all right. We'll need lighter clothes for this heat anyways."

Anastasia giggled. "You just wanna go shopping, don't you?"

Lyra raised a brow. "No, we need to prepare—properly."

Anastasia looped her arm through Lyra's, still wearing that mischievous smirk. "Whatever you say."

They strolled along the street, sunlight spilling across open balconies and lines of clothing strung between buildings. Most of the shops appeared closed, their doors hanging ajar, the interiors ransacked and stripped bare.

For a while, the town felt peaceful, quiet in a way that allowed for silent retreat. But that same quiet lingered too long.

"Lyra..." Anastasia's tone shifted. "When I looked through your eyes, I didn't see anyone. Do you?"

Lyra's stomach dropped, a queasy unease pooled inside her. She turned to get a full view of the port behind her, scanning the markets, shops, streets, and vendors.

There were no footsteps, no chatter, no workers piling crates onto ships, nothing.

The city that had seemed so bright and alive moments ago was hollow; void of life. They were alone.

At least, for now.

Rowan stepped off the train at Ashford Station with Cloud at his side. He'd been the only passenger on the line, the conductor giving a nervous nod before pulling away the instant Rowan stepped foot off the ramp.

Cloud let out a low growl, faced toward the city just beyond the platform, his hackles rising.

Rowan rested a hand on his gun. "Let's make this quick."

They moved through the port district, past abandoned shops and hollowed-out homes. The silence ate at him, with each glance a reminder of the damage that the undead would leave behind. Although there were no bodies, he could pick up the familiar scent of death. Not of the dead, but of the undead.

He ducked through the collapsed entrance of an ammunition supply shop, rifling through whatever remained, pocketing any rounds that could still fire. As he continued to scour, behind him, Cloud's ears perked up to a murmur coming from outside.

The dog padded to the door, his nails clicking on the floor, slipping just beyond Rowan's view. Rowan sat up, listening as the sounds of Cloud's nails faded.

"Cloud? Cloud, here, boy!"

No response, just the sounds of sea wind blowing through the exposed, half-torn apart shelves.

He hurried outside, looking in either direction for a glimpse of white fur. He spotted Cloud standing rigid at the entrance of a nearby store and sprinted toward him.

"What is it? What did you hear, boy?"

The dog stood unmoving, looking straight ahead through the cracked window of a beauty supply store. That's when Rowan caught the trace of a girl's voice coming from within.

"Did you hear that?" Anastasia asked her sister, who was diligently applying winged eyeliner to either side of her eyes.

Lyra carefully drew the tip of the makeup from the outer corner of her eye to the marked wing point.

"No. Give me a sec."

Anastasia heard a whisper again, and this time, what seemed to be the sound of a dog whimpering.

Rowan's hand went to his holstered gun at the sight of the girls.

Other Necromites? I thought it was just Maeve and his undead army.

Cloud's growling deepened as a small girl waddled closer. Her complexion was ghostly pale, almost translucent, and long, dark, tangled hair cascaded messily past her shoulders to her hips. A frayed blindfold hid the space where her eyes should belong, drawing attention to the sharpness of her cheekbones and the softness of her features. Her ears were slightly too large for her narrow face, and the small grin she wore seemed at odds with the dark energy radiating from her.

Rowan then noticed the girl's clothing—a faded shirt several sizes too large, the sleeves reaching well past her wrists, paired with worn-out trousers. It was a messy patchwork of clothes scavenged from nearby shops, the outfit suggesting she was unprepared for their venture, yet something about her frightened him.

A small tremor ran through his grip, the sweat slipped up against the butt of his pistol. He drew the weapon and leveled it at the girl who was now fully in view.

“Come here, doggy...” Anastasia whispered under her increasingly large smile. She stretched an arm out in their direction.

Rowan took a steadying breath and pulled the hammer back. The barrel wavered with uncertainty.

Anastasia took another step closer, now within inches of them both. He closed his eyes and relaxed his breath, finger moving and clasping around the trigger.

But when he opened his eyes to take the shot, someone new was shadowing behind Anastasia. They made eye contact.

Scalding pain exploded in his head, he lost all control of his body as he floundered onto the ground, clutching the sides of his skull as the world fractured into ringing noise and lights.

Lyra stood behind her sister, her eyes bleeding red, streaks of it cutting through the smeared eyeliner at the corners. It flowed down her cheeks and dripped onto the top of Anastasia’s hair, mingling with the black makeup until it pooled in a darkened, maroon sheen.

“Stand behind me,” Lyra instructed.

“I just wanna pet the—”

“Now.” Lyra’s ferocity left no room for discussion. She promptly followed her sister’s orders, huddling behind her.

Lyra held firm control over Rowan, who writhed and clawed against the burning agony that ate away at his consciousness. Cloud barked frantically, positioning himself between his master and Lyra, ready to defend.

Anastasia slipped a thread of connection into Rowan's thoughts as Lyra pressed deeper. What she found startled her—there was no malice or hatred, but instead something warm and inviting. He'd felt different than the ones they'd faced before.

He didn't seem like an enemy, he seemed rather familiar. Similar to Lyra, someone driven not by hate, but by the need to protect.

She ran past Lyra's protecting arm that tried to hold her at bay, past Cloud that was too focused on Lyra to notice, and fell over to Rowan's side. "Please don't kill him, Lyra."

Lyra furrowed her brow. "What? This boy nearly killed you."

Anastasia sputtered. "But we don't have to kill everyone. I think he's safe."

Safe? He nearly shot her, and she thinks he's safe?

Lyra looked back to Rowan thrashing on the ground and spotted the gun beside him. She stepped over and reached for it, but the moment her fingers brushed the metal, her skin began to smolder.

She hissed in pain and dropped the weapon, shaking out her hand as the scorch marked her palm.

Releasing her hold over Rowan's mind, Lyra studied him as he lay gasping on the floor, recovering from the torment that nearly ate through chunks of his thoughts. He was lean but solidly built, his body showing signs of wear and tear from frequent travel and combat. Short, light hair hung halfway across his forehead, dampened with sweat. A rough stubble highlighted his jawline, accentuating his piercing hazel eyes.

Beneath his worn shirt were layers of leather and reinforced cloth protecting his torso, with scars that traced both his forearms, slightly hidden under the sleeves.

Cloud lay pressed close beside him as Rowan's breath steadied.

He looked up at Lyra, swallowing hard against his dried throat. "Why haven't you killed me yet?"

Lyra looked over to her sister and sighed. "She thinks you're worth sparing. I'm still deciding whether to listen or not."

She looked back to see Rowan quietly crawling toward his gun. She withdrew her scythe. "What's with the gun?"

Rowan lunged and grabbed it, but didn't raise it. Instead, he slid it back into his holster with slow and deliberate movements, careful not to provoke her.

"I carve a tally on the barrel for each of the undead I kill. It's to show—"

"No… I mean why does it burn to touch?"

"It's specially crafted to handle the undead. They can't touch it, the protective barrier burns their flesh."

I'm not undead. Lyra thought. *What's he hiding?*

Anastasia knelt near Cloud, her small hands outstretched in an attempt to pet the dog, though looking in the opposite direction.

"If I leave you here," Lyra said, watching over Rowan carefully, "how do I know you won't use that gun on us?"

"I'm no fan of Necromites," he admitted. "But your sister spared me. And besides, I'm not here for you." He skimmed over the abandoned city. "I'm here for Maeve."

He peeked back up at Lyra and got a good, long look. He let out an unexpected chuckle.

"What's funny about this?" Lyra demanded, grabbing hold of his collar. He could feel her cold hands digging into him, with sharp nails scraping the edges of his throat.

"Didn't think Necromites cared about things like makeup."

Lyra's face flushed with warmth, but this wasn't the sweltering Ashford heat. An odd, nauseating sensation swirled in her stomach, but she shoved it down.

"You'd better watch your mouth before—"

A glass beer bottle shattered at Lyra's foot. A whistle came from the left.

Lyra, Cloud, Rowan, and Anastasia all turned.

One man stood alone, picking his grey teeth with a sharpened bone. Gradually, murky figures began to appear from the shadowed alleyways, some stepping out from behind corners and gathering steadily along the street. Their numbers swelled quietly, soon becoming a mob of over one hundred.

Lyra released Rowan's collar, stepping in front of Anastasia with her oversized scythe resting at her side.

Rowan scurried back up, grabbing Cloud's collar and holding him at bay.

The lone man, a bold, scarred figure draped in ragged leather, stepped forward. His teeth were deadly sharp and plentiful, a mouth like a shark.

"We hate to interrupt the reunion," he said with amusement, "but I believe we have business with the two of you. Lyra and Anastasia, I assume?"

"What's it to you?" Lyra's accent was as sharp as the blade resting by her side.

The man shrugged, feigning innocence. "Name's Maeve, just takin' orders from the boss is all. The small one is a runaway, and runaways always get brought back home." His steel-tooth grin stretched further. "Her loving family misses her dearly."

The mob erupted in laughter. Some were so drunk they stumbled over one another, retching onto the cobblestone, while others dragged their tongues across bloodstained blades in anticipation.

The earth beneath Maeve's feet melted to oily tar that spread in ripples. In the nearby markets, food began to sour with his mere proximity; fruit turned into split, blackened rot and meat spoiled instantaneously in its carts. Out at sea, fish surfaced belly-up, their lifeless bodies bobbing in the waves.

The necromantic energy radiating off Maeve was strong, seemingly amplified by the swarm of undead surrounding him.

Rowan stepped ahead of Lyra and Anastasia, his chest noticeably rising and falling.

"They are mine to handle. You two step back." Rowan scanned the crowd, looking for someone in particular. "Where's Mom?"

"Mom?" Maeve repeated, raising an eyebrow. "Who's Mom? She gotta name besides Mom?"

Rowan's face twisted with fury. "Aidra Lysander. The woman you killed and turned into one of those undead freaks."

Maeve's smile shifted to a sneer. He turned to face the crowd behind. "Aidra? Oh, Aidra?" he called out lazily. "Sound familiar to anyone? Going once... going twice... three times...."

The crowd hushed. A frail, battered woman stepped forward. Her body was half-decomposed, her bones visible through flesh. In one hand, she held a pistol, and in the other a small, rusted dagger.

Rowan could recognize her instantly, even through the layers of decomposition. He caught a glimpse of her outline, of her eyes, of the gun that mirrored his. His heart stuttered. It was Mom, she really had been taken in by Maeve. She was his captive now, and he planned to set her free.

Maeve snorted. "Aidra, huh? That's your name? Weird, I've always called you *wretch*."

Maeve threw back his head and laughed loud enough for the next town over to hear.

Rowan staggered forward. "Mom, it's me, Rowan! Dad and I have been waiting for you."

Aidra's hollow and sunken eyes gave a flicker of recognition, stirring for the briefest moment before hollowing back out. Whatever light had sparked had died just as quick, leaving only an empty stare as if he were a stranger.

He broke into a run before his mind could stop himself, launching him forward in her direction with no regard for the others.

"Mom!"

But as he neared, she recoiled in terror, hurling the rusted dagger at him. The blade sliced through the air straight toward his head, but he was too entranced in the moment to react.

Lyra made it just in time to deflect the dagger with her scythe; just missing his face by a mere two inches.

Aidra disappeared back into the crowd at the sight of Lyra, vanishing into a pile of the undead.

Rowan screamed, "Mom, no! Come back!"

Maeve scoffed. "Enough of this pity party. This isn't family bonding time, I'm here for the girls."

He pulled open half of his jacket, revealing a long iron staff cradled at his side. When his hand gripped the base, the staff extended upwards of three times its original size. An orange glow surged from its tip as energy condensed into a crackling beam of light. He pointed it at Rowan, leveled with his head.

The beam fired fast, but Lyra was faster. Her scythe caught the shot midair, deflecting it into a nearby building and splitting the structure in two. The redirected blast crashed along the pavement, ripping deep holes into the ground as the energy sprayed wildly from its misdirection.

Maeve's smile remained, though if you listened closely, a tinge of hesitation wove through his words. "I almost f-feel bad having to kill you. You'd make a great addition, Lyra." He shifted the staff toward Anastasia. "But my eye is on her."

With a subtle wave of the hand, the mob charged forward.

Lyra shoved Anastasia in the direction of the docks. "Run! Go back to the ferry."

Anastasia obeyed, grabbing Cloud's collar as she sprinted, her legs pumping as fast as they could. The dog jerked and twisted, fighting against her pull. She seized control of its sight and movement, forcing their steps into sync as they tore down toward the boat.

Maeve chased after her, leaving Lyra and Rowan to his undead army.

Lyra scanned for an escape route and spotted a stack of crates piled outside a storefront. She pulled Rowan by the shirt and pointed to safety. Gathering her strength, she vaulted up, stepping onto each box and propelling herself onto the rooftop. Rowan followed suit, stumbling over the crates in far less graceful attempts.

She peeked over the ledge, the two of them huddled side by side against the brick. Below, hordes of undead looked up with ugly grins and weapons brandished with the blood of their previous victims.

Lyra turned to Rowan with a stare that shot to his core. "Stay. If you get close, you die with the rest."

Rowan drew his gun.

"I can help from here."

One deep breath was all she needed. On the exhale, she tightened her grip on the scythe with both hands, the energy between her and the weapon sharing the same red glow. She stood over the ledge and looked down into the crowd below.

"What do you plan to—"

She plunged into the swarm.

The mob engulfed her. She swung in a perfect arc and a dozen heads rolled. Another wave rushed from behind, and she drove the scythe into the ground. The blade bit deep, as spires of hardened dirt shot up like redwoods growing in seconds, skewering the undead as easily as insects on a sharp pin.

Even amid the chaos she unleashed, there were still too many to handle alone. Arms restrained her from behind, where a group of three men held firmly. From the front, an undead woman stepped forward, a bone saw glinting in the sunlight as she swung for Lyra's throat.

A single bloody tear dripped from Lyra's eye, but before she could even make eye contact, the sound of a gunshot struck in her ear. In an instant, the saw-wielding woman's head burst into mist, coating Lyra in a soft bloodied spray. Three more shots followed in rapid succession; the clasping hands that restrained her falling away like discarded cloth.

She spun back to the source of the shots, catching a brief glimpse of the one behind the smoking barrel. Rowan stood atop the ledge, hands trembling as the gun wavered in his grip.

By the docks, Maeve had caught up to Anastasia and Cloud. He took his staff and pointed at her; orange-tinted vines emerging from the ocean like the tentacles of some massive sea creature coming up for air, coiling around her limbs and pulling tight.

Maeve stepped in close, reaching out to pat her head.

"That's it? Should I have expected more from a blind, miniature girl as yourself? If I knew it would've been this easy—"

A sudden, invisible gut punch hit Maeve like a dozen boxers unloading all their might onto his abdomen at once. Blood burst from his mouth as he was hurled backward, slamming through the first floor of a nearby building. The three-story structure came crashing down on top of him, burying him deep beneath brick and concrete. The vines that constrained Anastasia had loosened, slipping back into the sea.

He emerged from the rubble, groaning, shaking the excess pebbles from his hair. "Damn," he said, licking the blood off his lips and lightly guarding his stomach. "That kinda hurt."

Maeve limply waved the staff overhead, emitting a screeching siren that wailed loud enough for all of Ashford to hear. The thunder of approaching footsteps echoed from deep within the city. Hundreds more undead reinforcements poured from the alleyways into the streets.

Lyra retreated back to Rowan on the rooftop. One final shell clinked against the ground before the hollow sound of empty clicks came from the chamber—the last bullet spent. The smell of burning flesh and blackened earth covered them in a thick layer. Lyra was bruised and battered from holding off the endless waves of undead, and Rowan's hands were raw, the gun's recoil having shredded the skin from his palms.

"We need to go," Lyra said. "There's too many, we can't keep this up forever."

"I still need to get Mom out of here." Rowan frantically searched to find more bullets, patting down his chest and feeling the sides of his pants.

"Leave her for now. If you stay any longer, you won't live to have a second chance."

A long silence filled the gap that separated them.

"But I've been—"

"But, nothing. Stay and die, or come with us and live. Choose—quickly."

Rowan closed his eyes. He thought back to his father's warnings of the reunion with his mother and Maeve. He wanted to stay, but he hated that Lyra was right. Better to live and fight another day than to die a stubborn fool.

"Okay," he said with a smidge of remorse. "I'll follow you."

He pressed both hands to his face, as if to hide from the guilt that shrouded him. His mother, Aidra, was somewhere in that horde, trapped out in the sea of undead. And he was leaving her behind, after finally finding her.

Lyra stood, gathering in as many of the undead as her eyes could find. The bleeding began, profusely pouring out of both sockets, as pain stabbed deep into her temples. Every unfortunate soul that fell into her gaze toppled over, squirming in agony so fierce they could barely see. They flailed and stumbled, bodies dropping one after another, as some invisible force pinned them down and consumed them from within.

Maeve stared in Lyra's direction. Dust and rubble tangled in his black hair, and his eyes—pitch black with red rims—locked on the soldiers falling like flies under Lyra's sight. Rage twisted his face from a contorted grin into a snarl.

"What the hells are you all doing? Get up and fight, damn it!"

Lyra took advantage of this distraction and ran off toward the ferry, motioning Rowan to follow. He forced himself to get up and trail behind, taking one last look back into the crowd, hoping his mother wasn't caught within Lyra's snare.

He didn't know why he trusted a Necromite like Lyra, but he was certain this was the better choice—it was either this, or Maeve.

"Run all you want, pretty boy!" Maeve shouted, firing one last blast from his staff. The shot missed by a wide margin, melting the ground beside Rowan. "Ain't nowhere in this world you can hide from what's coming! And Lyra..." He exposed his gnarled, spotted gums. "I'll be seeing you soon."

He turned back to his army. He was still reeling from the pain Anastasia inflicted, not able to remove his hand from his stomach.

"Stand up, you worthless piles of trash! What do I even pay you for?"

Lyra spotted her sister up ahead, still clenching Cloud's collar with both hands. The ferry remained docked, its engine rumbling, but the workers had long since vanished.

Rowan's lungs burned from his attempt to keep pace with Lyra. When he glanced back, he saw one of Maeve's men circling wide—moving fast to cut them off. Rowan shouted a warning just as the undead soldier launched into the air and came crashing down in front of Lyra. His freakish grin stretched wide, splitting his face in two. Dark saliva clung between broken teeth as he raised a rusted sword and shield.

"Maeve may be done with you, but I want more."

The creature drew back his sword to strike. Rowan lifted his gun but it only clicked. Lyra couldn't muster the strength to move, her body failing to react from copious fatigue that had hollowed out her strength.

Anastasia, though, stood firm. She lifted a single hand in quiet defiance.

Rowan could barely comprehend what happened next. One moment, the undead soldier stood before them, alive and ready to kill. The next, he was at Rowan's feet, carving away at his own flesh. His neck snapped to one side, the sound of bones cracking happened all too easy. His arms thrust the sword into his own torso before clawing through what remained of his flesh from body, separating himself into a messy jigsaw puzzle.

Then, at last he slumped over, like a puppet with its strings severed.

All Rowan could do was stand still, mouth agape, staring at the pile of whatever mess that lay before him.

Lyra grabbed Anastasia's wrist. "Don't do that again. It's not good for you to use those powers like that."

Anastasia bit her lip. "But I had to."

Lyra looked back to Rowan, still dumbfounded and petrified at the gore. She grabbed his hand and pulled him forward, as more of Maeve's men were gathering behind.

The dockhands had left in a hurry, but the engine still idled, coughing up salt and water from the exhaust. They hastily boarded the ferry and lifted the ramp behind them. The boat lurched forward as Rowan frantically searched for the controls.

The distant roars of Maeve and his army grew fainter as the waves carried them away, out far into the ocean.

Once he managed to steady the boat, as much as anyone could call it *steady*, Rowan made his way to the starboard side and leaned against the railing, watching Ashford fade into the distance as the soft sea air caressed his cheeks.

But his hands wouldn't stop twitching. His mother was out there, still trapped in that hellish nightmare. He had waited his whole life to find her. And when he finally had...

"I left her there," he said to himself. Cloud rested his large head on Rowan's foot. "And even if I took her with me, she wouldn't even know who I am."

"She's still in there." Out of the corner of his eyes, a small outline came round the corner.

Rowan turned. "What?"

Anastasia sat cross-legged on the deck beside him, tilting her head in his general direction. She ran her hand over Cloud's fur in small, uneven strokes. The dog tolerated it, for now, too exhausted from the day to protest.

"I took a peek through her eyes, just for a second. She was confused, but she remembered you."

"Then why did she try to attack me? Why did she run?"

She shrugged. "I dunno, maybe she was scared? Maeve probably wouldn't have liked it if she joined you."

Rowan looked back out into the ocean, the sunlight gone past the horizon, turning the once blue water into a black abyss. He didn't know if he could believe Anastasia, but he wanted to. He wanted that to be the truth more than anything.

Lyra leaned against the adjacent railing with her arms crossed. "Your obsession with this is going to get you killed."

Rowan bristled. "What's that matter to you?"

"It doesn't," Lyra followed his gaze into the dark water. "But I don't need dead weight hanging around."

"And what if it were your mother?"

Before any memory of Tenebral—of Corvin, of Ravenna and her cruel *discipline device*, of all the things she was desperate to bury in the depths of her mind—could resurface, she scoffed and shook her head.

Rowan rolled his eyes. "Yeah, that's what I thought."

An uncomfortable silence settled between them. Cloud was snoring by now, and Anastasia had finally curled up on one of the ship's benches, her breathing steady as she entered a peaceful rest.

Rowan ran a hand through his hair and pulled out several loose strands. The pressure on his eyelids battled against his will to keep them open, the exhaustion now setting in.

"You're heading for Valspire, right?" he whispered. "That's what your sister told me, at least."

Lyra nodded. "But don't think you have to join us, although Anastasia refuses to let me leave you and the dog alone."

She looked over to her sister, now deep into the pull of sleep, her hands resting under her head to prop it up above the hard wood. "I don't know what she saw in you; she won't tell me."

Rowan smirked. "I've got my charms. But I won't interfere, I'll just tag along until I can go my own way, back to find my mother again."

"I wouldn't say charms—I'd say you're more of a liability."

He snickered. "Don't count me out too quickly."

A breeze rolled across the deck, stirring Lyra's hair. Rowan looked over at her, and under the moonlight, the angle caught her face just right. Oddly enough, even in the mess they'd just escaped, she still looked... nice. Nothing about her seemed out of place.

Lyra suddenly turned to face him, and he looked away at once. She raised an eyebrow, brushing at some imaginary speck off her cheek—whatever it was she thought he'd been staring at.

Rowan sighed, rubbing the back of his neck. "I must need some sleep."

Lyra nodded. Her head had been throbbing mercilessly since the encounter with Maeve. Strange images continued to appear from the corners of her eyes. Each time she would look for them, they vanished.

She needed rest, yes, maybe that was the issue.

He looked over at Anastasia one last time, reminded of the undead man at the dock she brutally ripped apart. For such a small and unassuming girl, she had potential to do some horrendous things. His spine tingled, the hairs on the back of his neck stood upright.

He found a cramped cabin below decks to rest for the night, and slid the bolt across the door, checking the lock multiple times for insurance.

He planned to sleep with the doors locked tight tonight.

CHAPTER ELEVEN
STEEPED IN REALITY

> You wouldn't understand. My choices are not your problem. Don't tell me Leora meant that much to you.
> ~Gareth Fenwyn

THE BRACKISH AIR CARRIED THE SCENT OF DEATH.

Death to last night's catch, fish freshly harvested from the sea; as waves slapped against the docked ships. Finnian and Violet stood at the port of Valspire, bracing themselves against the night's cold gusts of wind. Their daughter Aria, bundled in Violet's arms, slept peacefully, unaware of the weight of the decision being made.

"Violet, we can't take her with us," Finnian said, pained from those seven words alone. "The danger across the sea is far too great."

Violet clutched Aria closer, her nails digging into the thick fabric of the baby's blanket. "Then why did we bring her in the first place?" Her voice cracked. "If we want to escape, then she needs to come too!"

Finnian exhaled, laying a hand near her collar. "They're after *us*, not her. She isn't a target... but if she comes along, she will be."

Violet's lips began to quiver. She looked down at Aria's soft, untouched face. Her world had always been small—her parent's arms, their warm embrace... safety. How could she rip that away from her?

"I can't let her go, Finnian. She's my baby. Our baby."

He swallowed hard, a lump lodged in his throat that refused to budge. He ran a delicate hand over Aria's head, his heart constricting at the thought of leaving her behind. "I know it's hard, but you want what's best for her, right? You want her to be safe?"

Violet shook her head fiercely. "Where would we even leave her?

Drop her off here at the port, like some abandoned orphan? What happens when they discover who she is?"

Finnian remained still. He hadn't figured that part out yet.

A short distance away, a tall, burly man finished unloading cargo on a ship. He wiped sweat off his brow and turned to the sound of the argument, studying the couple.

"You need to stop yelling before someone hears us," Finnian warned, lowering his pitch barely above a whisper.

Violet slapped his arm with surprising power. "Don't tell me to calm down! This is our child we're talking about, not some stray dog!"

Their argument continued, fear and desperation erupting in silent shouts. The burly man approached cautiously, his curiosity piqued. "Eveythin' all right over here?"

Finnian turned to the man, panic sharpening his features. "Please… I don't have time to explain, but we need help."

"Finnian Valcrest, don't you dare!" Violet snapped, turning her back on both men.

"I wouldn't unless we had no other choice!" he snapped back. "They've already found us. We can't outrun them and worry about Aria. It will only be temporary."

The burly man raised his hands warily. "I don't know what this is about—"

"You don't have to," Finnian cut in. "Just—please. Take our daughter somewhere safe. Anywhere safe. It won't be forever, just long enough for us to come back for her. I beg of you."

The man turned to Violet, who refused to look at him. She was focused on Aria, brushing strands of hair from her tiny forehead. "Please don't take my child," she whispered. "I don't know what I'd do without her."

"I know how this sounds," Finnian continued. "But we're not criminals, we're doing the only thing that gives her a chance."

The man continued to look between the parents and child. "I do know of a place where they could help her. People that could take her in for the time being."

Violet shook her head again, clutching Aria to the point that the blankets folded inward. "I carried her for nine months. I could feel her kick. I lay with her every night," she buried her face into the baby's blanket. "I'm her mother. I'm supposed to protect her."

Finnian placed another hand on her back. "And you are. You're protecting her right now, Violet. Even if it doesn't feel like it."

She stood unmoving for a long moment, letting her head bury deeper into the blanket. Then slowly, her grip loosened. Violet finally looked up at the man.

"Please... no harm should come to her."

The burly man knelt beside her. "I swear it won't... I don't know who you are or what you've done—but I know what this means to you."

Violet looked back to Aria. She swallowed thickly, her tears soaking Aria's blanket. The baby slowly woke, her eyes shimmering like polished stone. She giggled and reached out, grabbing her mother's nose.

The same sounds of horns that followed them from Tenebral blew in the distance. Violet turned and spotted several Necromites on the hills, racing down the steep slopes toward the port.

"They've already caught up. We must go now, Violet!"

"I can't believe I have to do this. Aria, please forgive me." She kissed her daughter on the forehead and wrapped both arms around her. "Please wait for us. We'll be back. I promise."

She hesitantly handed Aria over to the man. Finnian pressed a final kiss on Aria's cheek, then turned to the man.

"Sorry sir, but I never caught your name."

The man gave a small, almost reluctant smile.

"It's Orin Olmstead."

There were faint views of the ocean and a woman's face, narrow and pallid. The waves carried whispers of an argument soon forgotten, a decision being made that would alter the course of her future.

The woman's voice called out softly. "Aria..."

A slight warmth tickled her skin, a soothing motion rocked her back and forth between linen sheets. The scent of salt and jasmine filled her nose, almost nostalgic.

She giggled.

"Aria."

The voice was clearer now. Growing louder.

"ARIA!"

Aria jumped awake, flailing her hands around wildly, the imprint of one hand still remained on her cheek. Her vision swam as she tried readjusting from her dream-like trance, the world sharpened into view. She was in a car.

Tavian noticed her pallor complexion and reached out a hand to calm her nerves. "Sorry," he said. "Didn't realize you were asleep. I couldn't feel you breathing, I was worried."

Aria rubbed her eyes, frowning. "Worried about what?"

Tavian hesitated then looked away in embarrassment. "It's nothing, sorry."

Orin peered into the rearview mirror at her. "You okay? Havin' some bad dreams?"

Aria stared out the side window, watching the hills roll by in smooth lumps, trying to recollect whatever lost fragments of the dream she could gather.

"Yeah, weird dreams again."

Orin continued to prod. "Same ones?"

Aria nodded. "Yeah, the port by the ocean. That woman."

He tapped the steering wheel nervously to a nonexistent tune, trying to drown out the panic in his mind. "I wouldn't put too much thought into it. You'll give yerself a headache."

"I can't help thinking it's my mom. It sounds crazy, but it feels so real."

Cassius, twisted like a pretzel in the limited space of the far back seat, chimed in. "Do you have any plans on where to start looking for them?"

Aria reached into her pocket and pulled out a worn scrap of parchment. The name "Valcrest" was scribbled onto it.

"All I have is this," she passed it back to Cassius. "Those Mycordians said we were the first humans they'd seen freely enter Mycordia since the

Valcrests came through years ago. I asked them to write down the names of those people that came before us."

Cassius looked at the name for a long while, thinking intently to himself.

Orin went rigid.

"They think the woman's first name was something like Viola, Verona, Violaine, or Violet. Something like that..."

Orin turned his head completely away from the road, letting the steering wheel drift off on its own. "Let me see that paper." His inflection was unusually tight.

"You all right there, old man?" Cassius said. "How about you grab that steering wheel before we get into another one of your famous accidents?"

Tavian could see the beads of sweat accumulating on Orin's bushy brow.

Orin reached back to snatch the paper, leaving Vid to take hold of the drifting car. He grabbed the paper from Cassius with a forceful rip, then muttered something under his breath. All Aria could hear was a name.

"Violet..."

They traveled far along winding roads that cut through grassy plains and stretched past large expanses of dazzling water, their search for answers carrying them from dawn to dusk. By nightfall, the group decided it was time to pull over and rest.

They came upon a small town. To their left stood a playground, a new and polished swing set moved with lubricated hinges as two children swung effortlessly through the air—though in the darkness, their shapes seemed not entirely human. To the right, a liquor store sat dark with locked doors, closed for the night.

The car slowed to a stop before an enormous, oddly shaped building that looked as if it had been carved from petrified chitin. It appeared to have been built from the top down—its architects seemingly unsure of where it was going. The roof lay tilted to the right, sloping into a tunnel, with an entrance on the left, like an old accordion left to gather dust.

Windows were scarce; a few let thin streaks of candlelight slip through, while the rest were sealed by a gooey film that hung like a curtain. The word *Gheget* was etched across the front, and Cassius nodded, indicating it was an inn.

"We're stopping here?" Aria asked, wrinkling her nose.

Orin sighed, stretching out his arms over his head and emitting a yawn that rattled the car frame. "No better options around. All we need is sleep."

As they stepped out of the car, a pair of neon white beetle-like eyes blinked down at them from the crooked awning. An Erreeckan, perched on the rafters, observing them in silence.

Aria suppressed a shiver. "What is that thing? It's watching us."

Cassius adjusted his collar. "They always are. Just ignore them and don't stare."

He moved forward without hesitation, the rest of the group following close behind. Beneath the awning came a sharp, rattling chirp of the watchful Erreeckan above. Tavian slipped inside quickly, eager to put as much distance between himself and that *thing* as possible.

The inn's interior was lined with wooden plaques framing black-and-white photos, shelves of liquor bearing unfamiliar labels, and patches of spongy moss that cast a greenish glow along the walls. The air was heavy with humidity, carrying an earthy, organic scent—one that hinted at something alive and growing, like an oversized petri dish.

At the front desk, a short, stocky Erreeckan innkeeper stood waiting. His skin had the hard, armored texture of a beetle's shell, his many jointed fingers tapping on the counter. He wore a bright silver chain around his large, rounded neck, with a sizable opal stone placed in the center. The initials "RC" were carved into it.

"Rothanna rea iuo beneve?" the innkeeper asked.

Silence. None of them understood. Tavian shifted uncomfortably and looked down at his watch.

"Rothanna rea iuo beneve?" he asked again, this time with the sharp edge of impatience.

Cassius stepped forward and spoke in the same dialect. "IIuos menencan beneve ghitlia."

The innkeeper's antennae twitched. He stared at Cassius for a long, unblinking moment before letting out a low hiss. The bar adjacent to the front desk went quiet: glasses ceased clinking, drinks went unpoured, and the waiters froze in their tracks. One by one the patrons turned to watch, silently observing the tense exchange between the two.

The owner replied to Cassius. "Iluos no sekkarian iuo beneve. Polop, iuo gnabaratya yot, iuo vvexsias retrat."

The patrons broke into laughter, more of a heckling sort of laugh, the kind meant to sting. They weren't laughing with him, they were laughing at him.

Orin muttered to Cassius, "What's he saying?"

Cassius turned back to the others and sighed. "We can stay, but Spirians have to pay triple the rate. I told them we'd cover it, since arguing with an Erreeckan is a good way to end up missing a few organs."

Vid scoffed and lifted his chin into the air. "Sounds like a scam."

The innkeeper extended his hand with a palm open for payment, waving them in.

Cassius reached into his coat pocket and produced a thick bundle of cash, dropping over half of it into the Erreeckan's palm.

Orin's jaw clenched. "I'll be damned if I let some oversized bug rip me off! There's a reason we—"

Cassius snapped his fingers, and Orin's voice cut out. His lips kept moving, but no sound escaped.

Orin's face reddened in a fury as he pointed first to his throat, then at Cassius.

Cassius smirked. "Let's not piss off the flesh-eating beetle men, please. Promise?"

Orin seemed to settle, at least as close to calm as he ever got, and gave a solemn nod. With another snap of his fingers, he released the hold on Orin's voice.

"What the hells was that? And I'd be better off dead than letting this racist *bug* swindle me!" he shouted, storming out of the inn and slamming the thick wooden door behind him. The impact rattled the walls; a few pictures wobbled, and one slipped free of its hook, falling to the floor. It depicted the innkeeper smiling beside a woman and a small girl.

The innkeeper's amusement grew, fanning himself with the cash Cassius had generously provided him. "Iious vvexsian gnabaratyaas yot, xertarea iou."

The bar's patrons shook their heads and returned to their drinks. Though one did not. A lone patron remained seated at the far end of the counter, his attention locked onto them.

"Iou fliout, derate, millonth! Iour benieres awesterry lvoioa nebes lla!" the patron shouted.

The angry Erreeckan's breath reeked of hard liquor and juniper berries. The door Orin had stormed through creaked open again, and he slunk back inside. The drunken Erreeckan stumbled over to him, swinging as he stepped in—but the strike went wide, missing the mark by a long shot.

"Iou lla grechinoa hharatch!" he screeched, taking another messy swing at Orin.

Cassius stepped in between the two, intercepting the oncoming strike with a quick movement. "Orin, move out the way. I'll handle this."

"This drunken idiot's lucky you're here! I would've killed him by now." Orin grumbled his way over to Aria. "Sorry you had to see that. I shouldn't be actin' this way in front of ya." He ruffled her hair.

Meanwhile, Cassius worked to calm the patron. They exchanged words in the Erreeckan tongue for nearly half an hour. Eventually, after Cassius bought him another drink, the creature relented.

He walked back over to the group waiting at the front, thumbing through a few spare papers and old photographs. "Let's head to the room, I'll explain everything there."

They gathered their belongings and made their way up the precarious, crooked staircase that twisted sharp around the corner. Orin lagged behind, casting one last glare back at the drunken Erreeckan, before giving him a quick middle finger and heading up the stairs.

Their room was surprisingly spacious, and was separated into two conjoined spaces—one with a single bed, the other with two.

Orin threw his pack onto one of the larger beds. "I'll claim this one. No one's fitting with me anyway."

Cassius took the other, Vid squeezing himself into the small space beside him.

That left the single bed in the conjoined room for Aria and Tavian. They both looked at it, then at each other.

Tavian paused. "... I'll take the floor."

Aria rolled her eyes. "Don't be dumb, the bed's huge. It's only weird if you make it weird."

Tavian shrugged but agreed quicker than expected. He was clearly overthinking it... right? It didn't take much convincing besides that; he tossed his belongings onto one side of the bed.

Aria turned to unfold the sheets, half-hiding a smile obscured by a curtain of dangling hair. Her stomach fluttered, as if hundreds of frantic butterflies were fighting for space inside of her.

As they settled in for the night, Cassius cleared his throat. "All right. Before we sleep, I want to address some of the things that went on downstairs."

Vid perked up from his half-drowsy state. "Yeah... how were you able to talk to them? And why were we judged so hard?"

Orin, Aria, and Tavian joined in, gathering around Cassius. By now, everyone was dressed for the night—Orin in a plaid shirt and shorts to match, Tavian in whatever he'd manage to scrounge from the depths of his bag, and Aria in a flowing nightgown with flowered inlay. Tavian kept sneaking glances her way, only to snap his eyes elsewhere the moment her head so much as turned.

"I'm quite well-traveled," Cassius said. "I've found that the more languages you know, the better you understand people; whether it's their culture, their customs, or simply their way of life. It's fascinating, really." He crossed his arms. "That's why I speak Erreeckai. But they hold little fondness for Spirians. The looks you got? That's because their people were nearly wiped out years ago. Some called it an act for peace; the Erreeckans called it genocide."

"What did the Erreeckans do? They must've done some horrid things to have caused that," Tavian asked, leaning in closer.

Cassius paused for a long moment. "They simply existed. That's all I've ever heard, at least."

Orin shifted uneasily. Aria could feel the tension from where she stood, the same kind of unease he showed whenever Mycordia or his nickname, *The Harvester*, came up.

Cassius continued. "There was a woman, though her name eludes me. She saw the Erreeckans as an obstacle to her vision of peace, so she set out to eradicate them. Along with the other… unfortunate souls."

"That's blasphemy," Tavian fumed. "Who would justify killing innocents in the name of peace? Isn't that irony at its worst?" He shook his head in disgust.

Cassius nodded, straightening as if lifted by Tavian's passion. "Yes, quite disturbing, isn't it? But the good news is, she's gone now. Only recently, in fact. I must admit, I'm a bit surprised you haven't heard of this sooner. Then again, Valspire has always favored a somewhat closed-door policy…"

Orin flexed his fingers, beads of sweat gathering in his palm before slipping down and falling onto his shoes. He scratched at his thigh, chasing an invisible itch that wasn't really there.

There was a long silence. Aria and Vid slowly looked over to each other sharing the same dawning realization, both their eyes glazed over. Tavian appeared unbothered on the surface, though his chest felt empty, his heart hammering in an erratic rhythm. He didn't know why—only that he couldn't catch up with his escaping breath. There was something missing, but he couldn't reach the last piece of the puzzle and make it fit.

"Valspire… her death wasn't *that* recent, was it?" Tavian asked, though part of him didn't really want an answer.

"I believe she was still around when you were! She ruled over your land for quite some time." Cassius threw his head back in sudden realization. "Oh! I remember her name now. It was something like Leora Fennwick… or was it Fenwyn?"

Tavian could no longer feel the spit in his mouth—a sudden desertion of all moisture from tongue to cheek. His hands were unsteady, his face sucked of any color. Aria tried looking over to him, but the side of his face was hidden under strands of hair. She didn't need a full view to know what expression lay beneath.

Without a word, Tavian lumbered out onto the balcony, leaving the door ajar behind him. Aria followed close behind.

Far within the midst of the Riftbound Order, Eldric stared naked at his reflection. His wrinkles and liver spots were covered by scars, bruises, and torn-apart flesh. He grabbed, pinched, slapped, and pulled his decaying meat off bone, tossing it to the side like trash. A look of disgust and disappointment showed in his face, staring at an elderly withered man; a shadow of who he once was.

"Still not enough," he said. "Still not perfect."

He trudged into the cold and unwelcoming shower like a zombie, rinsing away the blood and pus that clung to his skin. Bits of his own flesh slid from him in sheets, clogging the drain as they gathered in a pulpy mass. The water at his feet turned red, rising around his ankles until it lapped at his shins. He tilted his head back, letting the water wash over his skeletal face.

I must hurry, he thought. *I can't continue to wither like this, the rot is spreading too fast, and fewer and fewer Watchers remain to help.*

He stepped out and patted himself dry, careful not to tear the fresh and delicate remaining skin. With a weary sigh, he donned his robes, pulling them over his fragile frame. He moved his way toward his throne at the far end of the chamber. It stunk of stale incense and the familiar metallic tang of blood. The ground below shook intermittently, to a slow but steady pace, like a march echoing from underfoot.

Seated upon the cold metal throne like a king awaiting judgment, he lowered a metal contraption—much like Derewin's helmet—over his head and extended his arm.

On the balcony outside the inn, where Tavian had just learned the news about his mother, Aria had found him hunched over the railing, retching in painfully harsh, dry heaves. Pain seared up his spine; the scar along his back was burning hot, a heat like molten lava flowing from his back, radiating all the way through to the tips of his fingers.

"Just breath, Tavian. It's going to be okay." Aria caught him by the shoulders and refused to let go as he pushed himself off the railing, collapsing onto the floor in bouts of convulsions. She had seen him injured and exhausted before, but never like this. Never this broken.

"My scar," he managed through locked teeth. "It's burning."

That voice, the familiar and dreaded voice, the voice of Eldric, slithered through his thoughts. "Tavian, you must come to me at once. There are rotten apples in our orchard."

Tavian's fingernails dug into his scalp, tearing at the thin skin. "Get out," he snarled, but the voice only laughed. Though half-lidded eyes, he caught a glimpse of a throne, and a face half bone, half rot. The pungent funk of incense and blood filled his nostrils. The sounds of a ticking clock replayed.

"You're so much closer. Come to me... Let me help you." The words were ever so clear now. "Don't forget me. Don't lose sight of your goal."

Eldric's presence faded with those final words, and with it, the burning in Tavian's scar began to cool.

"Tavian? What's going on?" Aria tried to steady him, but he fought against her, struggling hard to stand upright. He staggered backwards, gripping the railing for balance.

"He's calling me," he rasped. "I don't know who—but he wants to see me."

Back in his chamber, Eldric grinned as he removed the helmet and sank into his throne. Below, the council of men stood in quiet reverence.

Those two rotten apples—the sisters—must be dealt with immediately, not even Maeve could handle it. Eldric thought, wrapping his fingers tight around the arms of his seat. *The boy will do it for me, and when he breaks, I'll have even less to worry about.*

"Necromancy shall not die, and neither shall we," Eldric boasted to his council.

Then softer, almost gleeful:

"But Tavian might."

CHAPTER TWELVE
THE ECLIPSED BAZAAR

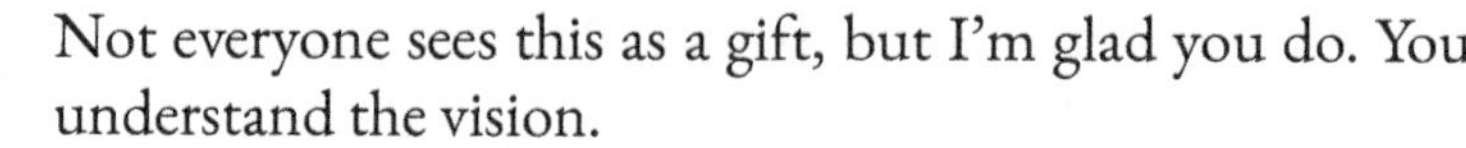

> Not everyone sees this as a gift, but I'm glad you do. You understand the vision.
> ~Eldric Wynthal

"HOW COULD YOU HIDE THIS FROM ME?"

Tavian struggled to get the words out. "And how could Mom..." he sat on the floor, dropping his head into his knees, wrapping his arms around them so tightly it looked like he feared they would fall off if he let go.

With a labored exhale, Orin replied. "Nothin' is so black-and-white. There's more to the story than—"

"There's no excuse for it!" Tavian propelled himself up, his shoulders rigid, fists tensed at his sides. The dark circles under his eyes spoke of a restless night, his exhaustion unable to tame the storm brewing inside. "But Mom wouldn't—couldn't—do something like this. That's not who she is."

"Tavian..." Orin's hand hovered near Tavian's shoulder but never quite reached. He knew better than to push any further.

Aria and Vid kept their distance, still trying to process everything themselves. Maybe Valspire really did keep its secrets close to the heart. Maybe they had been lied to all along. Maybe... *they* were the bad guys.

That morning was a tense one, as they slowly packed their belongings and climbed into the car. The silence from the night before, after revealing the news, seemed to follow them wherever they went, hanging overhead like a personal storm cloud.

Cassius fidgeted with a small spice pouch in his pocket, brushing it with his thumb like an old nervous habit. He'd carried it everywhere since the accident—a subtle reminder of his wife. Guilt ate at him; it felt like somehow this was his fault, for revealing the truth before they were ready. But how could he have known? How could they not have known themselves?

"I spoke with the innkeeper before we left," he said, attempting to brave the personal storms of silence they created for themselves. "I know we're not in the best mood, but there's a market I think you all should see. Particularly you two, Tavian and Aria."

Tavian's fingers hovered near his mouth as he bit down on the last of his nails, his cuticles already peeled raw at the edges. Aria, a quarter of the way through her book, looked up half-heartedly.

"What kind of market?" Tavian asked through clenched teeth, biting onto broken shards of nail and skin. "And why would we care?"

Cassius leaned forward between the two headrests. "You'll understand once we get there. It's not your average street stall."

Aria shrugged and went back to her book. Tavian kept gnawing at his nailless fingers, his thoughts circling back to his mother. "Just make it quick. Mom can't wait forever, and now I need answers."

Orin looked back and nodded toward Cassius, a mutual understanding between the two. He merged onto the road and followed the half-tattered signs pointing south to the Eclipsed Bazaar. If Tavian was searching for answers, he might find them here. Or maybe, instead, he'd discover something else. Someone else.

The road stretched for miles into the deepening night, until a faint glow appeared ahead, piercing through the black sky. Drawing closer, the stars began to dim as the radiance of artificial lights swallowed them whole, leaving behind a sky that shone as bright as day. The steady thump of music pulsed from somewhere far ahead, the melodic vibrations carried by the wind. If you squinted, you could just make out the tail end of distant fireworks, their bursts flaring in silence before the delayed rumble followed seconds later.

The closer they drove toward the market, the more the car's headlights would flicker in rapid, unsteady bursts. The only parking available was situated nearly a mile and a half away. Along the roadside stood obscured figures in a measured line, all guiding the endless stream of arrivals with dying, sputtering lanterns in hand, all pointing in the same direction. They didn't all look human. At least, not anymore.

Their trench coats, flowing and riddled with holes, brushed the ground as they moved. Beneath the lantern light, their faces were little more than bare skulls, the hollows swirling with a colorful, ethereal mist that cascaded out of the gaps where their eyes, ears, and nose once were.

As they parked and stepped out of the car, one of those bare-skulled figures turned toward them. Even without eyes to see, they could feel it glaring straight through them.

"What's with them?" Vid asked, narrowing his focus as he moved closer to one.

His foot caught on something solid and unmoving; his body lurched forward—tumbling into the mysterious figure. There was no resistance, no impact, only a sickening sensation of his own existence slipping through something that *should* have been solid. A rush of cold swept through, like plunging headfirst into an ice bath.

He hit the ground on the other side, leaving him with a mouth full of dirt. He scrambled to his feet, spitting out soil and gasping for a steady breath like a man breaking the surface after nearly drowning.

"The Bazaar is that way." The figure pointed toward the marked signs. "Please, watch your step."

"Ahhh!" Vid yelped, sprinting back toward the group, his heart slamming against his ribs. "I fell through him... like air! What is that thing?"

Cassius watched him brush off dirt, his feelings caught somewhere between amusement and mild disappointment. "They're Vespari, Vid. Spirit guides of the true dead... here for the semi-annual Eclipsed Bazaar. This is a rare chance to trade for things you can't find anywhere else in the world. Anyone and everyone comes to visit. It's one of the few places you might find something, or someone, you'd never otherwise encounter."

All Aria needed to hear was the word *spirit* before her hands clenched at the fabric of her sleeves. "They're... dead?"

Cassius gave a small shrug. "Technically, yes. I suppose it depends on how you define it."

Ghosts. As a child, and even now, she feared them—the unseen shapes lurking in the dark, the shadows waiting behind closed doors and under beds. But now they were everywhere: walking, trading, laughing, as if they still belonged to the world of the living.

"I-I don't do ghosts..."

A family passed by them, or rather, *through* them: a father, a mother, two teenage boys, and a little girl. Aria shivered as she felt their chilly presence drifting through her body.

The small girl trailed behind the family, entranced by the night sky. She giggled, reaching for the moon with tiny hands, trying to catch its shifting glow. Her mother turned back, light with laughter, and scooped her up, spinning her through the air. The child shrieked with delight, her arms flailing as if she could better catch the stars the higher up she went.

Their voices were soft, joyful, and alive.

But they weren't.

Watching the family of spirits poked at something deep within Aria, a hushed ache that she tried to repress. Her thoughts turned to her own parents, her own family. What if she saw them here, walking among the dead as another lost spirit? Would she even want that truth, if they were gone?

The Bazaar spread miles long in each direction; an entire city of pop-up tents and restless commerce. A melody of scents drifted through the air, weaving together in an intoxicating blend: spiced meats sizzling over open flames, the sharp tang of rare incense, the cloying sweetness of candied fruits, and stranger aromas still, ones so foreign they felt they were still undiscovered by the living world.

The stalls themselves were immense, some raised as high as buildings, their boarders glowing with a sickly greenish neon that clung to them like ghostly residue. Most tents seemed to appear by the second, but not constructed by workers, instead unfolding on their own, inflating rapidly like pulling the cord to an emergency life raft. These, more than anything, truly earned the name *pop-up tents*.

And most impressive of all was the sheer diversity of people. It was unlike anything they'd ever imagined, and even Aria, still shaken by the ghastly encounter, couldn't help but stare in awe. Humans and Vespari mingled freely with Mycordians, Erreeckans, and other beings beyond description. Some walked backwards on twisted legs, their bodies bound in ceremonial cloth, where only their eyes were exposed. Others appeared almost alien, their skin shifting like liquid silver, odd grey amorphous forms studded with octagonal eyes shoved into their rounded bodies. High above, winged creatures perched among the canopies of tents, served by floating lines that ferried goods between land and sky.

Vid's attention darted between the surreal sights with a childlike sense of wonder. Even Tavian and Aria—as burdened as they were—couldn't help but be drawn in.

Aria pulled Vid, Cassius, and Orin to the side while Tavian continued to gawk at each passerby, careful not to stare too long and draw suspicion. "We should get Tavian something," she whispered. "He's been going through a lot."

The others nodded in agreement.

"He likes rings," Aria continued. "Sweets, shoes, board games. Violet—his favorite color. His birthday's April twenty-fourth. Oh, he also used to love this one brand of food... it's a purple bag but I can't remember what it's called. He also sometimes does this thing where—"

She cut herself off, heat rushing to her cheeks as she caught their looks. Their smirks were instant.

"What?" she demanded.

Vid chuckled. "Nothing. It's just... you seem to know an awful lot about Tavian."

Aria's face flamed deeper scarlet. "Forget it! Just get him something nice!" she snapped, throwing her hands up before storming off into the market.

Tavian lingered for a moment, his eyes following Aria as she rushed off into the crowd, flustered in a way he wasn't used to seeing. His eyes trailed from her shoulders to her hips, then a little lower, from her hips to her...

"You okay, man?" Vid's voice cut through his daze.

"What!" Tavian feverishly flipped around. "Yeah, I'm fine! Just saw a cool store, gonna go check out their shoes—"

He hurriedly shuffled off toward a nearby tent with a sign that read *New Age Treasury*.

Maybe they sold shoes, he told himself, though it was just a last-second guess. He could use a new pair.

Yes—that's why he was in a hurry. New shoes. Definitely the shoes.

Wow, she was right, he really does love shoes. Vid thought.

He too slipped away into the crowd, drawn by sheer curiosity and the thrill of the unknown, while Cassius wandered off in search of ingredients. If he couldn't take back what he'd said, he could at least make it up to them with a meal worth remembering.

"Be sure to meet back here at sunrise!" Orin called out over the bustle, realizing the group was splitting apart by the second. "Guess I'll wander by myself..."

Vid wove through the sea of bodies, his head snapping in every which way, trying to take in everything all at once. Colors blurred together, voices overlapped, strange scents clashed. It was an overwhelming, intoxicating, and utterly thrilling experience. This is exactly what he'd left Valspire for: a change of scenery, and the rush of something *real*.

But amid the din of haggling merchants and buzzing conversation, something cut through the blur.

Screaming.

Not the lively calls of salesmen trying to allure new customers. Not the excited chatter and bartering of a deal being made. Something far more pronounced, distinct from happiness, the unmistakable sound of terror.

Vid scanned the expressions of others, expecting heads to turn, for anyone to react, but no one paid any mind. The market carried on as if the screaming didn't exist.

Why isn't anyone else hearing it?

He chose to follow the sound.

Meanwhile, Cassius stood in line at *Deep Fried Life*, a stall that proudly advertised its motto: *"If it can be eaten, we'll fry it!"*

The menu lived up to that promise—a glorious, grease-soaked parade of excess. Double-fried ice cream, triple-crunch pastries, fried meats, fried-and-lathered vegetables, ultra-fry butter, entire sandwiches dunked in batter and shoved onto a stick, and whatever questionable creation you could dream up after a night of drinking one too many.

Just a quick pit-stop before the shopping. His stomach rumbled in anticipation. *Can't shop while hungry, right?*

Patting his pockets for his wallet, he felt the lump beneath the fabric and reached in to grab it. He flipped it open and frowned. Empty.

He patted down his back pockets next, a tad more frantically this time, as if money might magically appear through desperation alone. A quick glance over his shoulder showed the line had doubled behind him. If he left now, there'd be no getting his spot back.

Amid his panic, a heavy hand clapped onto his shoulder.

"I'll cover ya' this time!"

Orin was already waiting for him, flashing a smug grin and waving a wad of cash.

"But you owe me next time. Us bigger men gotta keep our form." He merrily rubbed his bulging stomach.

Cassius snorted, shaking his head. "Are you calling me fat?"

Orin shrugged, eyeing Cassius's shoes. "When's the last time you saw yer feet? Bet ya' didn't know yer laces were untied!"

He bent down to look at his shoes, and sure enough, they were. He barked a laugh, but it soon faded, replaced by a pang of sadness that slipped in behind it.

"You all right?" Orin asked, noting the sudden shift in Cassius's demeanor.

"Just thinking of my wife, is all... the way she'd disapprove whenever I spent too much on food. She always let me though, I just think she pretended not to care."

He didn't stop there, the memories continued to resurface, uninvited.

"And the way she knew exactly how to season a roast duck. I used to help cook beside her every night, even though she was far better than I ever was."

"What happened? If you don't mind me askin'."

A dull ache struck behind his forehead. He forced a half-smile at Orin before turning back to the stall, moving a little farther up in line.

"Food first. Reminiscing later."

Aria ignored the stalls of perfumes and candies without a second look. Her focus was unwavering, Tavian deserved something meaningful, something beyond simple trinkets anyone could buy. She wanted to prove that she cared more than the others. That she knew him. *Really* knew him. That's when something caught her attention.

An assortment of rings lay spread across a display, but one stood out in particular; glowing colors shifting in a rare, prismatic brilliance. The sign above bore foreign lettering, nearly impossible to decipher, though she could make out two familiar words: *cotton rose*.

She elbowed through the crowd that stood in the way of her and the ring, disregarding the glares she received as she shoved passed. Human or not, no one was getting it before her.

She made it to the front, where an array of workers mingled with other customers, their hands flashing over other types of jewelry. She scanned diligently, shifting through and tossing aside the cheap bands that held no value to her.

Then, she finally spotted it... a ring with a prism at its center, housing delicate fragments of cotton rose petals. The silver band shone with ornate inlays, each carved with near-perfect precision. As her hand went for it, a frail, wrinkled hand smacked hers away.

"No touch. Only look."

Aria was taken aback as she looked up at the elderly woman standing behind the counter. Her skin had the hue of something long deprived of oxygen, a mottled blend of purple and blue. From her scalp sprouted a tangle of spiraling horns that twisted in their own directions. She had no hair, but instead an assortment of piercings studded along her head like her own personal jewelry display.

"Very rare. Very expensive."

"Why can't I touch it? What makes it so rare?"

The purple-skinned woman exhaled, as if debating whether it was even worth the effort to explain. Instead, she tapped a long, bony finger against the sign behind the ring, translated into Aria's own language.

Cotton Rose Ring — Crafted from the rare petals of the illustrious cotton rose flower, set into the finest silver. Just like the cotton rose, the ring changes throughout the day, transforming into beautiful new colors by nightfall.

Aria ignited in a passionate glow.

A ring: win one.

A ring containing the petals of his and his mother's favorite flower: win two.

A ring containing the petals of his and his mother's favorite flower that also changed color within the day: win three.

She whipped out her wallet without a second thought.

"How much?" She asked.

The woman hardly glanced at her. "One hundred and fifty."

Aria grabbed a handful of coins, one hundred and fifty, and slid them across the counter. The woman snickered and pushed them back. "One hundred and fifty... *thousand*."

Aria shot her a snide look, then yanked open her wallet again, rifling over the creases with frantic fingers. "One hundred and ten thousand... one hundred and twenty-five thousand... one hundred and forty-nine thousand."

She couldn't afford it, still a thousand short. All of her savings, and it wasn't even enough for this one thing.

Even so, she shoved the entire amount forward, silently praying the woman wouldn't count it.

"One thousand more," the vendor said, her patience thinning. "Or leave."

As she was about to give up, a young man's hand appeared beside hers, placing the final stack of coins on the counter. She looked over to him, and found a warm smile greeting her. He was tall, handsome, though she hated to admit it, and... armed. A pistol with tally marks engraved on the barrel was holstered to his hip.

"That one's on me," he said with an easy confidence. "I can tell that ring means a lot to you."

"Oh, no, you don't have to—"

"Nonsense." He flashed a grin. "No girl goes ringless if I have anything to say about it!" He nudged the coins closer, and the woman snatched them up without comment.

"That's very generous of you, thank you. May I ask your name?"

"Rowan Lysander. It's a pleasure to meet you." He dipped into a dramatic bow. "And you are?"

"Aria, the pleasure's all mine."

The woman behind the counter gave an exaggerated tilt of her head and said nothing, carefully packing the ring into a box. Aria stopped her, pointing to a violet-colored one tucked in the corner.

"Please. That box."

The woman grabbed the one Aria picked out instead, huffing and puffing while exchanging boxes, nonetheless.

"I'll have to be on my way," Rowan said, stepping back. "My group isn't the forgiving type when I'm late. But I hope to see you again sometime!"

"Bye, Rowan!" Aria called after him. "Hope to see you again..."

Aria clutched the violet box, a slow, satisfied smile creeping across her lips. It was perfect.

Tavian's going to love me, she thought. *I mean... it.*

Vid followed the screams, each step bringing them closer, louder. They lead him toward a colossal, coliseum-like structure, something that looked as if Mariella herself hand carved it from the bones of the earth. It rose like a cliff of marble and pearl, its pillars dusted in light orange from the fires lit above. Vast windows spread across its facade, mimicking the unblinking eyes of giants.

He pressed his hands against the glass, leaning forward to peer inside. Blurred figures moved within, engulfed by golden light. Fire ejected from cannons, illuminating the arena in waves of yellow and orange. The crowd roared, an overwhelming chorus that shook the glass beneath his palms and rattled him to the core.

It seemed to be some kind of performance. The screams he'd followed weren't that of terror, but terrified amusement. A sound Vid knew all too well from his own shows in Valspire. But this crowd was massive, the theatrics far more advanced than his simple tricks. He needed to see more.

He rushed through the front doors, barely skidding to a halt before two imposing guards blocked his path. They were formidable; clad in armor as thick as the coliseum walls, each hoisting a spear tipped with a curved blade. Their faces were expressionless, carved from stone, perhaps the very same that built the walls around them.

"May I enter?"

The guards exchanged a solemn look, then broke into laughter.

"No," one of them said bluntly. "The Hidden Moon Circus is an exclusive performance. Entry's for those with royal permissions only."

The other guard leaned in close, a punchable sneer lifting his cheeks. "Go find yourself a nice princess to vouch for you. Maybe then we'll consider it."

Vid clenched his jaw as their laughter grew all the louder, the two doubling over and wiping away their tears like it was the most fun they'd had all night. He forced himself to turn away, muttering curses under his breath as he stormed off.

He plopped down onto the front steps, dragging his hand down his face. Rejection stung, but the guards' laughter burned more than anything. He needed a distraction.

Noticing a few rounded stones scattered nearby, smoothed by years of wear, he scooped them up without thinking and began tossing them into the air like his old juggling routine.

Up. Down. Catch. Release.

The rhythm was second nature, muscle memory kicking in like a forgotten habit. At least this was something he could control.

A quiet gasp pulled his attention. A small boy stood a few feet away, wide-eyed, watching the stones dance between Vid's hands before arcing high into the sky.

With a flourish, Vid added more stones to the rotation, spinning them faster, switching hands, looping them behind his back. The boy clapped, giggling at every new trick.

Vid's confidence swelled.

He spotted shards of broken glass, a pair of rusty nails, and a few discarded curved blades from the guard's old spears. Vid snatched them up, adding each to the precarious rotation. People began to gather in hoards as the juggling routine turned perilous, captivating each onlooker as they walked by to witness the man defying gravity and death with every toss.

The small boy's smile faltered, now focused on the sharp edges. But Vid juggled even faster. His hands became a blur, the objects soaring higher, higher, higher, until with one final toss he sent everything skyward simultaneously.

As gravity took hold, sending the nails, stones, glass, and blades back down to earth, Vid flung open his satchel and caught every piece in one smooth motion. The now one hundred-person-deep crowd gasped as he ended with a graceful bow, the applause thundered louder than from inside. The guards that once discarded him were now among the crowd, clapping as spectators, their smugness erased.

The boy ran up, grabbing Vid's hand. "Show me how to do that!"

Vid ruffled the kid's hair. "That one was a little dangerous. Here, start with these."

He took the stones from his bag and placed them into the boy's cupped hands. "Practice with these first. Then one day, when you get really good, you'll get to do the cool stuff."

The kid beamed, squeezing Vid with all his might.

"Quite the trick, young man." A warm voice interrupted.

Vid looked up as the boy's parents approached, a well-dressed couple with an air of muted authority. The father, though short and plump, carried himself as if he towered over everyone around him. His barrel-chest pulled against a finely tailored suit, a thick gold chain hung across it. A dark, carefully groomed toupee sat neatly atop his head, though just slightly askew, completing the picture of self-assured confidence.

Beside him, his wife's hunched posture spoke of years spent caring for others more than herself. Though fatigue lined her eyes, her graceful gait hinted at a once-regal life. Her gown, elegant yet practical, lacked the flamboyance of her husband's attire.

"You should be an entertainer," the father continued. "Why aren't you inside performing in the circus?"

Vid turned back toward the coliseum. "I don't work there. They wouldn't even let me in to watch. Said I needed some kind of royal permission or whatever."

The husband and wife exchanged looks then turned back to Vid. "Lucky for you, we have a little influence around here." He dug into his front suit pocket and produced a set of five tickets, all assigned to the Trubbman family for access to the Hidden Moon Circus.

Vid's jaw nearly hit the marbled steps. He gawked at the tickets, handling one as if it were made of gold, careful not to crease the delicate edges.

"How did you get these?"

"Don't concern yourself with the details." The father winked, letting Vid hold onto the one ticket. "Why don't you join us inside? That ticket happens to be an extra."

Before Vid could reply, the man continued.

"And how rude of me to not introduce myself and the family. I'm Agusto Trubbman, and this is my wife, Arnette."

Arnette smiled warmly, shaking Vid's hand. "Pleasure to meet you."

"And this little one," he added, motioning to the boy attempting to juggle his new stones, "is Baron, our youngest."

Baron didn't even look up to acknowledge him, too busy tossing a stone into the air, trying to mimic Vid's routine. He wasn't nearly as successful, the stones clattering against the steps with every toss.

"And last but not least," Mr. Trubbman pointed to the young woman that was hidden behind him and his wife, "is our blessed daughter, Seraphina."

Seraphina stepped forward, her golden-blonde locks catching the firelight, her hair cascading over the delicate embroidery of her opal-colored gown. Her eyes, a penetrating silver-gray, studied Vid with intrigue.

She extended her hand, fingers poised with noble grace. Vid, half-dazed by her beauty, reached out and shook it. Seraphina recoiled, jerking her hand back and shaking it as though she'd touched something filthy.

Vid too retracted his hand, unsure what he'd done wrong. Was he really *this* bad with women?

Her father sighed. "Seraphina..."

"Apologies," she said coolly, "I assumed this boy is a performer, the servant class, yes? I expected the traditional kiss to hand."

Mr. Trubbman let out another heavy breath, shaking his head. "Here, we are all equals. Let's enjoy ourselves. No worrying about titles or any of that nonsense."

Seraphina pursed her lips before looking back at Vid. "Forgive me for that oversight. What do you call yourself?"

Vid found himself staring longer than he intended to. Her features seemed to be painted meticulously by hand, in careful detail. The faint smattering of freckles beneath her right eye, the way her gown curled at the edges and hugged around her curves, her sun-kissed skin against the vibrancy of her painted nails. For the first time in a long while, he was completely at a loss for words.

"Vod," he said without thought.

Seraphina giggled. "Vod, is it? How peculiar." She extended her hand again—this time, palm facing in anticipation of a handshake.

Vid took it gently, but instead of shaking, he turned her hand over and brushed a light kiss on top. Seraphina's tan skin flushed a softened red.

Tavian drifted from tent to tent, finding no luck with the shoes he wanted. His movements were aimless, his mind elsewhere. The vibrant market had allured him initially, but now barely registered. His thoughts churned, circling right back to his mother.

Was she really a bad person? What had her plan for peace been... did it truly justify what happened? Did she actually kill all those Erreeckans?

No. He shook the intrusive speculations from his mind. *Mom wouldn't do that.* She cared too much for others. She was the kindest person he knew.

He could still picture her fragile hands tending to the cotton roses, the sweet sounds of her humming while she worked. She would never put innocent lives in danger. This had to be a mistake, Cassius must've confused her with someone else.

Lost in the obtrusive rush of thoughts, Tavian bumped into someone.

He staggered back as a cold wave of dread slammed into him. It was an instinctual warning buried in his bones, screaming at him to run as far and as fast as he can.

The young woman before him exuded power beyond anything he'd encountered before... but more than that. Something sinful rested dormant inside her, itching to be awoken.

From behind, he noticed miniature flowers intertwined within her lengthy, dark hair. She turned around, and in one arm, she cradled a bouquet of flowers. In the other, a small girl held her.

The small girl by her side wore a blindfold, or something more intricate than that. Delicate, beautiful patterns wove across the fabric, shimmering in multicolored threads. Looking at it made Tavian's mind twist ever so slightly, as if a hand were shuffling through his thoughts the longer he stared at it.

"S-sorry... a-a-about that," Tavian stammered.

The young woman deliberated for a second, weighing whether his mistake warranted punishment. Instead, she only looked at him, eyes rimmed with dried blood; as though she were peeling back his skin, his thoughts, his very soul in the process. The little girl tugged at her arm, breaking her from the menacing fixation.

In a voice as smooth and unshaken as the night, the young woman said, "It's fine."

They turned away.

Tavian's limbs began to tingle, a sensation like brushing past death itself. "Wait," he blurted, unsure why he'd spoken at all. But the flowers... they were dahlias, he needed to know where they came from.

She glanced back over her shoulder.

Tavian pointed. "Where'd you get those flowers? I need ones just like that."

The little girl spoke before the older one could. "They're over there." She pointed out to a distant stall called *Odds and Ends*. The older girl redirected the hand of the younger one to the correct location this time.

The older one said, "They're running out, but there are other options."

Tavian barely registered what she'd said. His attention moved onto something else—a sharp edge of a scythe, peeking out from the woman's side. A cold sweat broke over his skin. He didn't want to prolong this conversation any longer.

"That's okay. Thank you." Tavian said swiftly.

Before he turned away, his gaze fell on the little girl once more. "I... also like the thing you're wearing," he said, directing toward the blindfold.

"He's talking about your eye cover, Anastasia." The older one mumbled to the youngest.

Anastasia smiled, her fingers tracing over the delicate silk inlays.

"Thank you," she said. "Most people think it's weird. Only one other guy ever said he liked it."

The oldest gave a slight nod then turned, melting back into the sea of people. Anastasia waved a small goodbye, and Tavian lifted his hand in return, unsure if the gesture was meant for him or for whomever she was waving to.

No one stood in their way; the mass of bodies parted around them.

Tavian released a chest full of breath that was trapped inside, not realizing how tightly wound he'd been. Forcing down the knot of apprehension, he made his way toward the flower stand.

He caught sight of the sun cresting around the bend of the stand, soft golden light bleeding into the edges of the sky. Orin's voice replayed in his memory: *Be sure to meet back here at sunrise!* Tavian hurried through the array of flowers, eyes darting between stems and petals as he searched for the familiar rounded tops and vivid colors. Then he finally found them, the last ones left. An elegantly wrapped bouquet of dahlias, with assorted colors of deep red, soft white, and pink.

Perfect.

Tavian grabbed them, handing over his last bit of change, and took off toward the meeting spot.

His heart was still pounding, but whether it was from the flowers, the woman, or the blindfolded girl, he wasn't sure.

Vid sat between Seraphina and her mother, the heat of the grand performance washing over him. It was unlike anything he'd ever seen.

Hundreds of performers moved in perfect synchrony, their costumes shimmering like gold beneath a canopy of light—each one brighter than the stars over the Bazaar's night sky. Cannons ignited fires in bursts of orange and blue, the heat palpable even from the furthest seats of the audience.

Beasts of all sizes prowled the stage, some draped in flowing silks as they paraded in formation around the stage, others balanced on impossible perches, performing feats that would challenge even the most skilled humans. Above them, acrobats soared, weightless as spirits, twisting and tumbling through the air as if the laws of nature held no dominion here.

The crowd erupted in collective gasps and cries with every death-defying stunt. Yet, to their astonishment—and relief—the performers always landed on their feet, defying both gravity and fate.

And then there was Seraphina. Vid wasn't sure which spectacle captivated him more, the dazzling show or the girl seated beside him. Every so often, she caught his wandering gaze, a subtle smile curving her lips.

"Is there something on my face?" she teased, tilting her head. "I know I don't wear much makeup, but I didn't think it looked *that* odd."

Vid nearly choked on air. His face burned hotter than the flames bursting from the cannons. "No! Of course not! I—"

Before he could finish, she placed her hand on top of his. Vid forgot how to breathe.

She leaned in close, her voice a whisper against his ear. "You must be careful, some things are dangerous if you look too long." Her smile turned mischievous. "But don't worry... I promise I won't bite."

Vid's mind short-circuited. His lungs forgot their purpose, his heart stopped—or maybe the world did. A singular pause in time, where everything narrowed to her. To Seraphina.

The crowd roared as the performance reached its climax, but Vid couldn't hear. The extraneous sounds dulled to a hum, replaced by a faint ringing in his left ear. His vision went in and out of focus, his mouth felt unbearably dry.

Then, she rested her head upon his shoulder. The warmth of her touch sent a signal through him, both grounding and unraveling all at once. The world could have truly stopped turning and he wouldn't have cared. He only wanted this moment to last forever.

The final act concluded in a cascade of dazzling lights and thunderous explosions, drawing a standing ovation from the crowd. Seraphina lifted her head off Vid, stretching as the audience began gathering their belongings and filtering out of the stands.

Vid panicked. He wasn't ready for this to be over. "We should walk around the market together," he blurted, reaching for her hand. "Will you join me?"

Seraphina looked over at her family, already making their way toward the exit.

"I'm sorry, Vod."

He blinked. *Vod?*

"I have to return home," she continued. "There's much to do." She glanced down to her open-toed shoes. "But... I invite you to visit. We'd love to see you again. Or rather..." her smile returned. "*I* would love to see you again."

"How far is it? Where's home?" he asked quickly, not wanting the chance to slip away.

"Aipiron," she said, "along the westward mountains. If you know of Tenebral, it's nearby."

Vid shook his head. "I have no idea where that is."

There was now a hint of sadness that softened the lines on her forehead.

"You'll find it... if you're meant to."

The first streaks of morning light spilled through the coliseum's stained-glass windows, painting the stage in a rainbow wash of colors.

Vid's heart lurched. Sunrise. He had to go back.

"Listen," he said in a hurry, "I know we just met, but I think there's something between us. You're beautiful, and I know—"

She lifted a finger to his lips, silencing him. "You flatter me, Vod. But if you truly mean that, come find me. I'll be waiting."

Before he could finish his desperate attempt at stalling her, she leaned in and pressed a soft kiss to his cheek. Her lips lingered for a split second longer, and as she pulled away, a strange white wisp drifted past her face like smoke caught in the overhead light. She then turned and rushed off toward the exit, her dress flowing behind her.

Vid's fingers feebly grazed the place on his cheek where her lips had touched. The spot felt too fragile to disturb.

As she disappeared, a single thought crossed his dazed mind: *Why did she call me Vod?*

Orin sat slouched on a bench near the meeting point, his stomach waging war against him. A pained groan escaped as he clutched his rumbling gut.

"Lesson learned. Never eat anythin' labeled *quadruple-fried mystery meat of the day.*" He let out a weak chuckle, cut short by another bout of nausea that enveloped him.

Cassius arrived to him first, arms overloaded with ingredients, bags teetering on the edge of collapse as he struggled to keep them all balanced.

Vid arrived next, but something about him was off. The usual chipper attitude was replaced by a sulking boy whose long-distance dreams had just come crashing down.

Cassius bent his head around the pile of ingredients stacked in his arms. "Vid, you all right? For such a spectacle of a night market, you seem awfully down!"

Vid gave him a halfhearted shrug, looking back in the direction he'd come.

Aria soon came after, holding the small violet box in her hands. She scanned the group then sighed.

She asked expectantly, "What did everyone get Tavian?"

Orin moaned, sinking deeper into the bench. "I forgot," he admitted. "My stomach's wagin' a full-blown rebellion against me!"

Cassius motioned toward his armful of supplies. "I'm planning a meal," he said with a fond smile. "One of my favorites."

At the mention of food, Orin's face turned a shade paler. He clapped his hands over his mouth, using pure willpower to keep everything down.

Vid kicked at the dirt, his voice low. "Sorry, I got nothing. Something came up."

Aria threw her hands up. "Guys! You had one job!"

Orin smiled weakly through his suffering. "But I'm sure you did good. What'd you get him?"

She lifted the box and cracked it open. Inside, the ring sat nestled in silk, gleaming in the early morning light. The polished silver band petaled with cotton rose cast soft reflections across their faces. Beneath a prism of clear resin, hard as glass, preserved petals began to change color as if they were still alive.

"It's a ring," she explained. "Made from the flower he and his mom loved most."

Tavian approached, his hands tucked behind his back. For the first time in days, he appeared lighter. Aria quickly shut the box and hid it behind her back.

"There's the man of the hour!" Orin grinned, despite the ongoing battle in his abdomen. "Hope since you were this late, you got somethin' for dear ol' Orin?"

Tavian shook his head, though there was no edge to it. "You look like you're having enough fun already," he joked, then turned to Cassius. "But this was great. I'm glad you brought us here."

Vid, Aria, and Orin, who was barely holding himself together at this point, nodded in agreement.

Cassius beamed. "My family and I used to love it here. It was nice coming back."

The group began the long trek back to the car, but before she could join, Tavian snagged Aria's sleeve, pulling her aside.

"I got something for—" they both said at once, cutting each other off.

"You go first," Tavian said.

Aria presented him with the violet colored box.

"I know things have been tough, and I thought this might help, even if just a little."

Tavian set down the flowers behind him, out of sight, and carefully took the miniature box. It was violet, his favorite color. A good start.

He lifted the lid and unwrapped the silk that shrouded the box's contents. His breathing slowed as the ring was unveiled. Gently, he picked it up, turning it toward the sun to study every intricate detail. The smooth silver band, the fine engravings, the way the light caught onto the prism's surface, the color-changing petals.

He slid it onto his right middle finger, beside the ring already resting on his index.

Tavian said nothing throughout the entire process. Aria fidgeted with her hands. "It's made from the petals of the cotton rose. I know you and your mom loved those. I hope you like it—I can return it if not. I know it's not, like, the *coolest* thing, but I thought it was pretty. And I figured—"

Tavian pulled her into a tight embrace before she could react, his arms locking around her, his face buried in her shoulder. Warm tears soaked through the thin fabric of her shirt.

Tavian's shoulders shook. Unrestrained sobs escaped him, raw and unfiltered. "Thank you."

Aria's arms tightened around him; a small, relieved smile forming.

When he finally pulled away, Tavian wiped at the stray tears, sheepishly scuffing the dirt with the toe of his shoe. "I got something for you too... but it's not nearly as nice."

"You did? Why?"

He bent around and grabbed the bouquet of flowers, presenting them to her.

"I hope you didn't think I forgot about your twenty-fourth birthday," he said, shifting around awkwardly. "You only get one of those. So... happy birthday, Aria."

She stared at the flowers. Tears welled before she could stop them.

"How did you remember I love dahlias?" she asked, taking them gingerly and holding them close.

Tavian shrugged. "I remember the things that matter, I suppose."

Aria wrapped her arms around him again, squeezing the life from his lungs and nearly all the oxygen from the flowers' stems.

A short distance away, Vid turned to watch them. He couldn't help but smile.

Then he looked back toward the Hidden Moon Circus... and farther still—perhaps toward Aipiron.

CHAPTER THIRTEEN
FUGITIVES

Valspire? I can help you with that, you know. But I need Tenebral. I need it gone.
~Seraphina Trubbman

"To be honest, I have no idea what I'm doing."

Before Lyra's group ever reached the Bazaar, they were still adrift at sea on the ferry, narrowly escaping Maeve's grasp.

Rowan wrestled with the boat's salt-crusted controls, twisting knobs and pulling levers in a futile attempt to stabilize the vessel. The sea rocked, rolling waves smacking against the hull. Each movement became more and more unpredictable under the blistering sun.

Lyra sighed, unfurling the crude, hastily sketched map Ravenna had given her. She rotated it in different orientations, trying to make sense of the mess of tangled lines and landmarks. The parchment was already damp from the ocean air, worsened by the swells of water crashing over the sides of the boat.

The humid weight of the sea breeze clung to her. Sweat streaked down her forehead, beading along her temple before falling onto the map, further disorienting the ink. She wiped at it absentmindedly before glancing toward the back of the boat.

Anastasia's laugh rang faint in the background, with Cloud close on her heels.

Peering out, Lyra saw her sister chasing Cloud in wild, delighted circles; the dog's tail wagging furiously as he effortlessly dodged her grasp. It was a game of Marco Polo, though Anastasia's sightless pursuit turned it into something more like a confused dance—one she seemed to be enjoying immensely.

Lyra's lips twitched, amused by their antics, until the pain struck.

A sudden dagger of agony drove into her head. She gasped, gripping her forehead as the world warped and spun in sickening disorientation. A low rumble came from across the sea, followed by a chilled gust of freezing wind that slammed against the ship.

Then came the thunder.

Seemingly out of the sea's blue depths, the once-calm waves erupted into a violent, churning chaotic spray of water rushing overboard. The water crashed up and onto the deck, as the tide surged higher.

Lyra forced herself to focus through the blinding pain, blinking rapidly as the sun felt like it was burning brighter than ever. She locked onto Anastasia, who was still playing with the dog, unaware of the monstrous tide swelling behind her.

She can't see it, Lyra thought. *But why can't she feel it?*

"Anastasia! Get off the deck!"

But she remained oblivious, giggling merrily as Cloud circled around her again.

Wet, rotting hands slapped against the back deck, fingers curling over the railing. A chorus of wails tore through her eardrums as half-decayed bodies dragged themselves aboard, smearing trails of blackened blood in their wake. Some were missing eyes, their sockets hollowed and leaking coagulated fluids; while others had grotesquely twisted mouths frozen into permanent, toothless sneers.

They crawled toward Anastasia, skeletal fingers reaching for the hem of her shirt, narrowly missing as she kept chasing the dog, blissfully unaware.

"Leave the dog! Run!"

Cloud kept wagging his tail.

Lyra turned to Rowan, but something was wrong with him too. He stood perfectly still, his hands plastered to the controls, posture rigid, knuckles white as bone. He didn't react to the creatures, to her screams, to the increasing tide, to anything at all.

"Rowan!" Lyra grabbed him. "Help her! We need to—"

Lyra's breath left her in a single rush, leaving no space for another inhale. Rowan's head turned, but his face was gone. Smooth. Featureless. No eyes, no nose, no mouth—only a blank expanse of skin.

She tumbled back, tripping over a loose life preserver and crashing hard onto the deck. Hands burst from below the floorboards, the fingers resembling snakes, slithering up her arms and legs, grasping for her pupils.

She struggled against the wet hands binding her, but their ironclad grip constricted her limbs until all sensation of feeling drained away. Her body began to sink into the ship as if the deck itself turned to quicksand, undead arms dragging her deeper and deeper.

Anastasia's voice broke through, now directly behind her, devoid of all emotion. "You should've never killed them, Lyra. We don't have to kill everyone."

Cloud, once playfully darting across the deck moments ago, appeared at Anastasia's side. Then, without warning, he lunged at Lyra, sinking his teeth into her ribs. Meat tore under his jaws, exposing the pallor cage of bones underneath her flesh cover.

The pain was excruciating, yet Lyra couldn't stop it. She wanted it to all end, for her suffering to finally cease, but her mind refused to let her drift away. She was forced to stay conscious, to live through the nightmare until its bitter end.

Rowan's faceless body jerked like a bolt of lightning had struck him. One arm lifted, his stiff pointed finger extending toward Lyra's left eye.

Her vision fractured as the fingertip neared, the space around her going dark. She tried to pull away, but one of Anastasia's hands clamped the top of her head and forced it still.

A horrid squelch—-the sounds of finger meeting eye. Lyra screams vanished beneath the raging storm, masked by thunder and wrecking waves. The finger dug deeper, sliding behind the eye and into the nerves that sat deep within the socket. Her own warm, thick, blinding blood ran down into her lap.

Her screams finally ripped through her chest, but no one seemed to notice. The torture dragged on for what felt like an eternity, until her mind at last gave way, granting her the only mercy left: silent release.

The next thing she knew, ice-cold water slammed over her, shocking her back into reality. She gasped, flailing as her senses returned all at once. Her lungs burned as if she'd been underwater for hours, her throat raw from past screams. Salt coated her lips in a film; she spat immediately.

"Breathe!"

Rowan's voice. Cold water dripped from his fingers—he'd doused her with a wash bucket of seawater. He was kneeling beside her, one hand steadying her side, the other hovering uncertainly near her hip. His face was taut with worry, as though he was scared to even look at her.

She swatted his hands away and tried to stand, but her legs gave out beneath her. Rowan caught her before she could fall again, easing her back down to the spot where he'd first laid her.

"Easy there," he said. "You were out for a while, give your body a chance to reacclimate."

She pressed her fingers into her temple, the pain still pulsating behind her left eye.

"What... happened?"

He frowned with uncertainty. "I should be asking you that."

She rubbed both hands over her sweaty forehead, trying to massage away the pain.

"One second, you were looking out toward the back of the boat," he continued, "then you started screaming at Anastasia. I couldn't understand what you were saying. Then you turned to me, calling for help... but there was nothing wrong. And then you just collapsed."

Nothing wrong? Had they not seen the storm, the undead, Rowan's faceless body?

A small weight pressed against her side. Lyra urgently grabbed for it, the same spot where Cloud had torn through her flesh. But it was no longer an open wound, now covered by layers of skin, bone, and meat. It was just Anastasia, hugging to her ribs, her small arms encasing tight.

Her sister's face was buried in her. "Remember what Slug said," she whispered. "Please stop using your powers. I don't want you to go away."

Lyra thought back to Slug and the warning he'd given her when she first entered the Rift.

With every kill, your powers will grow. But each time you use it, the visions will grow stronger. Your mind will distort further and further until nothing of who you once were, remains.

She shuddered at the fragmented memory of Slug's disturbingly grimy fingers digging into her skin. Drawing in a slow breath, Lyra ran her fingers through Anastasia's hair in a calming motion. "Don't worry. I've got it under control."

Lie, Anastasia thought. Control was slipping, and her visions were proof of it.

Yet another aimless day at sea had passed. The ocean became an unbroken expanse of dark water that refused to yield to their makeshift directions. Above, birds wheeled in the sky until, one by one, they plummeted lifelessly onto the deck. The trace of Lyra and Anastasia's necromantic energy clung to the ship like a layer of skin, snuffing out whatever life dared to come near.

Cloud had taken it upon himself to retrieve the fallen birds, his large frame weaving between their limp corpses. He nudged each one close to the edge of the deck, giving a final push overboard. He worked tirelessly, tail low, ears flicking back at every dull thud of another body hitting the wood.

Lyra woke before dawn, her body stiff and her head throbbing with phantom aches from a sleep that never reached deep enough. She was tired of the nightmares, tired of the thoughts that never stopped swarming her mind. It was growing harder and harder to differentiate the visions from reality, the sleep from waking, the nightmares from daydreams.

She drifted into the ship's cramped, lightless kitchen, rubbing the exhaustion from her eyes. A dying lantern flickered, casting shadows against the walls. The air smelled of something earthy and perfumed, like coffee mixed with disinfectant.

Rowan stood at the counter, pouring what appeared to be coffee into two mismatched mugs.

"Want one?" he asked, holding out a steaming cup of the potential coffee. "Figured you'd need something to keep alert. This one's extra strength."

Lyra peered at the drink with suspicion, watching the way the coffee clung unnaturally to the inside of the cup. She put her nose up to it, and the sharp sting of liquor entered uninvited.

"No," she said flatly, pushing it away.

Rowan raised an eyebrow. “Not a fan of the finer things in life?”

“I don’t drink.”

Noticing his disappointment at the declined gesture, she softened a bit. “It’s not you. I just don’t usually have something like that this early.”

Did I really just apologize? Why do I feel so bad?

Rowan gave a disheartened shrug. He took the rejected cup and dumped it into his own, doubling the drink until it nearly spilled over the rim. The moment he took a sip, his face contorted at the burn of whatever concoction he’d created.

“It’s a strong one,” he coughed, clearing his throat. “But maybe *this* you won’t reject.”

He pulled a small rectangular device from his pocket. The moment it powered on, it began to beep in a slow, steady rhythm like a heartbeat monitor. Its dim screen revealed a singular, pulsing dot beside a large, uneven brown mass. Other shapes appeared farther away, scattered across the empty grey expanse.

“This thing shows our way back to land,” he said. “We’re that dot, and that huge brown thing is our destination.”

Lyra straightened up. “Valspire?”

“Not quite...”

She scowled. “Then where?”

He tapped on the screen of the device. “Aipiron. It’s a city built into the mountains, along the coast, nearest Tenebral. Heard of it?”

Lyra’s already straight posture tightened further into perfect alignment, as if a string had been pulled taut along her spine. The back of her neck prickled. Miserable memories clawed to break free, but she forced them back into their cages and locked the doors shut.

“No,” she said, “we can’t go there.”

Rowan leaned over the counter. “We don’t have a choice.”

She stared at him, the fires within her scorched through her cornea.

“You don’t get it,” she said in a tone reminiscent of her mother’s. “That’s the opposite direction. We need to head toward Valspire. Not anywhere near Tenebral.”

He showed her the screen. “Look. This thing tracks the nearest landmass,” he continued. “Aipiron’s the closest port for hundreds of miles.

If we don't dock there, we'll be stranded out here for weeks, maybe even longer."

He gestured toward the barren shelves, where only a few cans of weeks-old fish and stale bread remained from the previous crew. "We don't have enough to last."

Her anger was slipping out of its confines. A deep, red heat built inside her, begging to be unleashed. Not even Rowan's gun could stop her.

The air warped around her as shadows coiled at her feet. Her hand slid to her back, feeling for the scythe's handle. The wood beneath her creaked and splintered, as if the ship itself were bracing against the force radiating from her. He felt the danger rising but didn't step back, instead placing a cool hand on the butt of his holstered gun.

A smaller, warm hand clasped Lyra's wrist. Anastasia had slipped into the room without a sound. She looked up at Lyra, whose rage abated. Her breathing slowed; the tension in her shoulders eased. The swirling energy around her dissipated then vanished into nothing.

Anastasia leaned against her. "It's okay. We'll go to Valspire after."

"Fine," Lyra relented. "But once we get what we need from Aipiron, we head straight there."

Rowan nodded and took another sip of his drink, visibly regretting it. He swallowed with a grimace, the bitter liquor burning the lining of his esophagus. Leaning back against the counter, he watched her carefully, his hand still hovering near the pistol.

"I haven't asked," he said, "but what's your deal with Valspire? Who are you looking for?"

"It's my duty," she shot back. "Nothing more, nothing less."

There was neither hesitation nor warmth in her voice. "That place is responsible for my people's exile. They owe a debt, and I intend to collect."

He clutched his mug with both hands now. A beat of silence.

"I gotcha," he said, finally taking another sip. "Glad I asked."

Several hours later, land finally appeared off the starboard side.

The familiar sting of the cold wind sent an unwelcoming reminder of Lyra's past inching down her spine. Her skin dried out on contact, and her ears went numb to the brisk seaside gusts. Anastasia clutched her coat, teeth chattering.

Rowan let out a breathless laugh, rubbing his hands together, trying to muster any warmth he could summon. "Gods, it's freezing," he muttered, shoving his rough, scaled hands into his pockets. "How'd you two ever live like this?"

Cloud let out a small, pitiful whine, anxiously pacing along the dock trying to warm himself up.

"There were things far worse than the cold to deal with back home." Lyra moved forward, seemingly untouched by the weather, her gaze drifting through the light snowfall as she walked. "Let's get moving." She pulled her sister alongside her.

Aipiron was built directly into the mountainside. The city resembled a mammoth beehive, sprawling along the rocky cliffs in an intricate network of bridges, tunnels, and stacked dwellings. Vehicles darted in and out of shadowed passageways, disappearing into the massive tunnels that carved deeper into the mountain's heart. Workers dangled from ropes hanging over the cliff's edges, chiseling new craters into the stone. Below the hive, the port jutted out over the ocean, boats coming and going in a constant stream, unloading crates onto the shore.

Rowan made a low whistle. "This place isn't half bad," he grinned. "I think we could stay here a while."

Lyra snapped him an unamused glare at yet another sarcastic remark, then turned her attention to the passageways and lofty structures ahead—her mind already mapping and calculating the fastest routes in and out. She needed to be ready. Something in her gut told her this city wasn't safe. How could it be, with Tenebral so close?

As they stepped into the nearest shop, Rowan paused by the door. Outside, a weathered poster flapped in the wind, half-torn from its tape, its corners curling in the cold mountain air. He caught the name *LYRA ASHRYN* listed at the top, along with the words *WANTED NOTICE* pasted right above.

"Lyra." He grabbed her arm and spun her around. "Look."

She followed his gaze to the poster.

WANTED NOTICE - KEEP POSTED

LYRA ASHRYN
ANASTASIA ASHRYN
ROWAN LYSANDER

If you see these individuals, report to your nearest authority at once. They are armed and dangerous, presenting a critical threat to public safety.

Alleged Crimes:
Treason, Murder of Rift Watchers

REWARD: DEAD OR ALIVE

Issued By: The Riftbound Order
Head Commissioner: Eldric Wynthal

Lyra read the fine print, studying the crudely drawn portraits. "What the hells is this?"

Rowan sank onto the nearest bench, anxiously running a hand through his hair. Lyra turned to Anastasia and read the details aloud.

"The Riftbound Order... who are they? Why do they care what happened to the Watcher?" Lyra asked, directing the question at Rowan.

He stared blankly out at the water. "They're the ones who maintain the so-called 'balance' in the Rifts. They oversee the Watchers, and they're made up of very powerful people." He exhaled. "This complicates things a bit. They don't take kindly to their Watchers being killed."

Lyra now fully turned toward him. "Why are you on that poster? You killed one yourself?"

He stayed silent. For a long moment he didn't meet her gaze, keeping his eyes fixed on the water instead.

"I did," he finally said, "as did you, it seems."

He placed a hand over his gun that was strapped at his side. Lyra investigated it, sensing a strange energy emanating from it, something unlike any weapon she'd encountered before. It reminded her of her scythe, yet felt fundamentally different. Crafted for another purpose.

"That would explain the gun," she said. "Seems obvious now, it's something only a Watcher could grant someone... for a price, of course."

She took a step closer, her voice dropping to a near whisper. "What did they take from you?"

He looked down, then glanced around nervously until locating a nearby sign. "We should focus on getting our supplies and leaving quickly, right? To Valspire?"

Lyra narrowed her eyes but didn't press further. She kept her distance, though her focus lingered on him longer than he liked.

"Let's head to the market," he said, gesturing toward the sign he'd been staring at. "It should have everything we need."

She nodded, taking Anastasia by the hand and pulling her close. Together, they followed the narrow path leading deeper into the bowels of the city.

Aipiron's market wound through a maze of tunnels and cliffside shops, nestled into the city's stone husk. Each storefront glowed with brilliant neon signs, emerald and violet letters flickering over the hustling crowd below. Massive sculpted statues hovered above the shops, marking their trade: meats, clothing, trinkets, tools—all delicately chiseled and painted in eccentric hues. The air was thick with the mingling scents of saltwater, fresh linen, and grilled fish.

The group drifted deeper into the neon-lit confusion of a market. A street performer, a young girl draped in silver and gold, twirled bright ribbons as she simultaneously played a beautiful melody, drawing in a wide crowd. But as Lyra stepped within earshot and the girl caught sight of her, her performance snapped to a halt. The ribbons fluttered to the floor, and her instrument let out a harsh, metallic screech.

The young performer ducked and ran offstage as a low murmur spread through the crowd. Lyra looked down, double-checking her scythe was concealed and her coat pulled tight—nothing exposed.

They kept walking.

Rowan pulled Cloud closer as a shopkeeper smiled a little too wide while they passed. Then, the moment they were gone, the door slammed shut. A hand-painted sign swung into view over the windowsill.

CLOSED.

Masses of people pressed tightly together in the restricted alleys of the market, the hum of voices layered over one another like a rising ocean tide. But it wasn't just noise, Lyra could hear the whispers; subtle shifts in tone, darting eyes, fingers pointing at them.

"Is that them?" a woman said to her husband, clutching her son's hand. "Do the Trubbmans know they're here?"

A group of tourists paused amidst their scheduled route, gawking openly in their direction. One even lifted a device and snapped a photo.

Cloud growled and flattened his ears as more eyes locked in on them.

"We're being watched," Lyra spoke in Rowan's ear. She leaned in close under the guise of showing him a piece of fruit from the adjacent stall.

Rowan gave a subtle nod, taking the fruit and turning it over in his hand. "What makes you say that?"

"Three men in uniform, right behind you. They've been tailing us since we passed the performer at the entrance."

Rowan cautiously glanced back, pretending to reach down and adjust Cloud's collar. Sure enough, three tall, slender men stood half a block away, each clad in matching purple and brown robes, leather braces, and weapons strapped across their backs. One of them lifted a hand, gesturing to Rowan as the others turned to follow.

Rowan turned back to Lyra. "Let's cut into the side alley. See if they follow."

Lyra gave her sister's hand a quick squeeze. "Stay close to me and don't let go. Okay?"

Anastasia gave a quick thumbs-up with her free hand, tightening the other that held onto Lyra.

They veered sharply into the alleyway, zigzagging around corners only lit by sky blue lanterns. The sound of the crowds faded behind them. Here the walls rose higher, canyon-like within the cliffs, damp and moss-covered, the stone beneath their feet slick with mildew.

Close behind, the three men pressed on, joined now by several more who had taken up the chase.

Rowan cursed under his breath. “They’re closing in.”

Lyra drew her coat tighter. “Take random turns. Try and lose them.”

They darted around corners, weaving through side paths and abandoned alcoves. They burst into a side street, startling a group of elderly women sitting around an outdoor stove. One shrieked and hurled a pot in their direction, the clay shattering at their feet.

But the footsteps of the men didn’t falter. A sharp whistle pierced the air. Another group appeared out in front of them—four more men, dressed the same, blocking their escape.

Rowan stopped short. “Damn it.”

They were now boxed in. The forward guards lifted their spears.

“We’re not looking for a fight,” Rowan called out. He lifted his pistol but didn’t aim it. “We’ll leave.”

Two of the guards hesitated, but the rest advanced, spears raised with stained tips.

Lyra drew her scythe, her eyes darkening to the same maroon shade as the blood seeping from the waterline. A surge of power flared beside her, but as she looked down to Anastasia, a sudden force struck her from behind. She slammed into the stone floor face-first. Her muscles locked as the weight of gravity seemed to multiply ten times that of the usual force, pressing into her spine.

She gritted her teeth, rage building inside her, but her limbs wouldn’t obey. The powers within were suppressed, trapped and rendered useless under the immense pressure.

A split second later, the same force struck the others. Rowan fell to his knees, choking and struggling for air. Cloud whimpered and sank to the ground. Anastasia was pinned face-down, neither resisting nor seeming to care.

The crushing force amplified, then eased for a moment, as if someone found the dial and adjusted its settings.

A girl knelt before Lyra, cheerful and elegant. Her golden locks were tied back in a loose braid, her smile sparkled radiant, like a gardener watching her flowers bloom for the first time.

"A pleasure to meet you, Lyra," she said sweetly, her voice bright and incongruous. "I'm Seraphina. We have sooo much to talk about."

CHAPTER FOURTEEN

TROUBLE, IN THE NAME OF TRUBBMAN

Davie. Not David. Just Davie.
~David

LYRA WOKE TO THE TAP OF METAL AGAINST STONE.

Her vision was hazy, clearing slowly as she caught a glimpse of Cloud barking furiously, snapping at a guard who awkwardly held him at bay.

"I told you I don't do dogs! Can someone else take him?" the guard pleaded, his voice strained.

Laughter echoed among his companions, indifferent to his canine plight.

Once she blinked away the fuzz, Lyra thrashed against the guards gripping her arms. "Let go of me, you—"

A heavy blow silenced her, and darkness enveloped her once again.

She woke a second time to a pounding headache and a tender lump where the blow had landed. Her hands reflexively flew to her temple as her vision adjusted to the darkened, damp surroundings. She was alone in a decrepit cell; no Rowan, no Cloud, no Anastasia.

Footsteps tip-tapped closer down the corridor from outside the cell. Instinctively, she reached for her scythe, but it was nowhere to be found. With no weapon to defend herself, she pressed into the shadows, holding her breath as the steps neared.

A silhouette stopped in front of the cell, sharp heels clicking purposefully. The sound brought memories of her mother flooding back; those proud, commanding, ruthless heels striking against the splintered floors of their home. Seraphina paused at the bars, cutting into the darkness with her piercing gray eyes. She looked no older than her mid-twenties, of average height, her skin sun-warmed and tan.

She pulled Lyra's scythe from behind her back and tossed it into the confined cell. Lyra lunged forward, snatching the weapon, her knuckles whitening as she braced herself for a fight.

"Please don't make me regret that," Seraphina said.

In an instant, an oppressive force bore down on Lyra, driving her to the ground, the same sensation as before. It felt as if a crowd of women in heels stood along her spine, each step sending sharp points of pain stabbing into her nerves.

"Please... stop." Lyra managed through clenched teeth.

"You feel that? Remember it. I'll free you, but know I can crush you whenever I wish." The pressure lifted, leaving Lyra gasping and rubbing her wounded spine.

"Where's my sister?" Lyra demanded, shakily standing upright and moving closer to the cell door.

"She's safe," Seraphina said, fumbling with a ring of thin, metallic keys. "Though something was... unsettling about her. We took extra precautions."

A key jammed into the rusted lock, and the old metal cell door swung open with an eerie creak.

Anastasia? Lyra's mind raced. *What's wrong with her?*

"Follow me," Seraphina instructed, pointing toward the bright light at the top of the stairs. "I'll bring you to the others."

After ascending the staircase, Lyra emerged into a hall utterly unlike the grim dungeon below. Her breath caught as she took in the magnificent space. It was vast and shimmering beneath the soft, golden glow cascading from crystal chandeliers. Each one, crafted from thousands of glittering diamonds, cast delicate rainbows that danced across polished marble floors and silk rugs woven in deep shades of royal purple and brown.

Along the towering walls hung portraits of stern, regal figures, with their watchful gazes casting silent judgment over the room. Lyra lingered on a particularly striking image of Seraphina, beautifully rendered yet wearing an expression of distant melancholy and dissatisfaction, her poise reflecting the heavy burden of her position.

Massive pillars, carved with elaborate floral patterns and spiraling ivy designs, rose endlessly toward a ceiling painted like the sky at dawn. A harmonious melody drifted from background musicians, a blend of classical symphonies and the soulful rhythm of jazz.

At the hall's far end, upon a raised dais, was an enormous throne adorned with diamonds and gold, sparkling yet intimidating in its grandeur. Seraphina lounged there and allowed Lyra to regroup with the rest.

At the room's center, Anastasia stood bound in weighted chains, flanked by visibly anxious guards. Nearby, Rowan knelt beside Cloud, soothing the agitated dog.

"Anastasia, are you okay?" Lyra asked, trying to get near her through the wall of armored men.

Anastasia nodded. "Yeah, I'm fine. But these chains are itchy."

Lyra looked over to Rowan, who was still crouched over, petting his dog. "I'm doing okay too," he added, dryly.

Lyra rolled her eyes. "I'm glad."

Seraphina looked to Lyra, her voice resonating clearly from the far end of the hall. "The Riftbound Order fears you all. That intrigues me." Her eyes glittered like the diamond chandeliers, with calculated interest. "I propose an alliance."

Lyra tensed. "Why do you need us?"

Seraphina leaned forward, the diamonds on her throne catching and reflecting fragments of light. "I know where you're from, and that means much to me."

Rowan looked over to Lyra and caught the shrewd look on her face. The same one she'd worn when he mentioned Tenebral on the boat. He could see her fury building beneath the surface, her composure beginning to crack.

"Tenebral, correct? You are Lyra, daughter of Ravenna? And that girl is Anastasia Ashryn, your sister?"

Lyra looked down at her feet, trying to steady the surge of emotions threatening to spill over. She thought of home. She thought of Ravenna, of Corvin, of Derewin. Of the training, the killing, the torture, the torment.

"That's irrelevant." Lyra said.

Seraphina glanced down at her nails, fanning her fingers to inspect their edges and polish. "I wonder what brought you to Aipiron. Why would Ravenna send her only two children into the world beyond Tenebral? It doesn't seem like her. I can't help but worry you're here to harm us. What if I sent you all back to the cells? What if I keep you here indefinitely? What if I let the Riftbound Order know you're here?"

"I have business at Valspire," Lyra quickly responded. "We didn't intend to be here long, just passing through."

Seraphina looked up. "Valspire?" She scoffed, looking back down and picking away at her well-maintained nails. "I can help you with that, you know. But I need Tenebral. I need it gone."

Lyra's rage flared. "Gone? My home?"

Seraphina's expression softened with mock sympathy. "You call that place your home? Do you even know what Tenebral has done? How many suffer in that treacherous wasteland, how many of my people they've stolen and killed?" She straightened in her throne, now ignoring her nails, tone hardening. "As the old adage goes... the only Necromite you can trust is a dead one."

The words struck Lyra and left a bruise; no one had ever spoken of Tenebral that way before. She reached for her scythe, only for Rowan's firm grip to halt her.

"Wait."

Reluctantly, Lyra loosened her hold on her weapon and looked back up at Seraphina. "Why would we help you with Tenebral?"

Seraphina sighed theatrically, reclining once more. "Do you really have a choice? I'm being generous by offering you something in return—assistance with whatever you need in Valspire. I'll help you, but only if you help me." She sank deeper into her throne. "Until you come to your senses, you'll stay here... as *guests*."

Lyra turned to Rowan. "What do we do?"

With Rowan unarmed, Anastasia bound, and Lyra in no position to face Seraphina alone, he made the only choice that made sense. Stepping forward, Rowan bowed respectfully.

"We would be honored to stay as your guests. We appreciate your kindness."

Seraphina smiled. “I like this one! Rowan, was it? Handsome, polite, charming—rare qualities in a man. You have good taste, Lyra.”

Lyra’s cheeks flushed. “It’s not like that.”

Seraphina raised an eyebrow at Rowan, who remained bowed, hiding a subtle grin beneath his composure. “Right. Of course, my mistake.” Her gaze shifted, sharpening as it settled on Anastasia. “She is the only one I worry about. Are you a cause for concern?”

The nearest guard glared at Anastasia, pulling at the chains that bound her. “Answer her already!” he barked, shoving her hard and forcing her to her knees. The others guards laughed cruelly, whispering their mockery under their breath.

“Did I instruct anyone to touch her?” Seraphina hollered, her voice suddenly razor-sharp. The guards froze, no one daring to be the first to speak.

“I hear only silence. Let me ask again, since clearly I wasn’t loud enough, *did I instruct anyone to touch her*?”

One of the guards stepped forward, trembling as he bowed low enough to nearly kiss the floor. “No, ma’am. You did not.”

“Then why was she touched?”

“He’s new,” another guard blurted, pointing toward the offender. “It won’t happen again, it was an honest mistake.”

“You’re right,” Seraphina replied, “it won’t happen again.”

With a casual wave of her hand, the offending guard imploded, reduced to a muddied smear of viscera and bone. His body was flattened into a human-sized pancake, the floor slick with gore. The blood splattered across the ornate rug, staining its intricate weave.

The other guards were sent into an internal panic, but stood stiff as boards, shaking as they loosely held onto the chains that confined Anastasia. Even the background musicians fell silent, their tunes cut off by the sounds of crunching bone.

Lyra and Rowan mimicked the guards, afraid to move, unsure if even breathing might earn them the same fate as the flattened one. Cloud spotted a loose bone from the guard, tugging at his leash, eager to fetch it.

A hunched woman entered the hall, out from behind where the throne sat, after hearing the commotion.

"Seraphina Trubbman!" Her voice shrieked authoritatively. "What did I tell you about staining the rugs?"

Seraphina slumped down in embarrassment. "Mother, please, not now."

Her mother stormed forward, seizing Seraphina by the hair and yanking her upright in the throne. "Don't you dare give me that attitude! Must you always make such a spectacle? Clean this up, now!"

Her mother's expression softened as she spotted Anastasia wrapped in chains, surrounded by the iron-clad troops. "Oh, dear girl, are you all right? Get those chains off her!"

"Mother," Seraphina protested, "Father said—"

"Hush! Your father hardly knows his head from his ass." She shook her head as the guards hesitated, then reluctantly began unfastening Anastasia's restraints.

Anastasia slipped a hand free with ease, waving off the guards. "I got it."

The chains melted off her body, liquifying into silver metal that seeped into the fibers of the rug. The guards stumbled back, shielding themselves. Seraphina laughed and shook her head, pressing her face into her hand.

"Anastasia! Are you okay?" Lyra rushed to her side, checking her forehead and patting down her arms and shoulders.

"I'm fine!" she said quickly. "I didn't wanna be rude. I waited until I was allowed to take them off."

The woman smiled, though a trace of fear lingered in. "I'm Arnette, it's a pleasure to meet you all. Please forgive my daughter; she's still learning."

"Ugh, Mom! Can you please just direct them to their quarters? I have *cordially* invited them to stay as guests for a while."

"How splendid! Right this way, you three... and the dog, of course!"

As the group followed Arnette toward their quarters, Anastasia felt an indistinct pressure brush against her shoulders as she passed Seraphina. It was barely there, like a thumb pressing a scale ever so softly. Anastasia ignored it and kept walking.

Seraphina watched her go, astonished. *She can withstand all that force? What a frightening girl.*

Tavian turned the ring Aria had given him at the Bazaar over between his fingers, admiring how the sunlight streamed through the car window and shined off its surface. He slipped it back on, fidgeting with it fondly. When he glanced at her, a small smile touched his lips. Aria's face warmed, and she quickly buried her eyes back into her book.

Vid, staring out the passenger window, caught a sign as they drove past.

Welcome to Ashford—home of the world-famous Pepper Loaf!

"Pepper loaf?" Vid asked, lighting up. "We should stop and check it out!"

Groans erupted from the crowded backseat. Tavian shook his head impatiently. "We need to keep moving. Valspire is waiting for us, so is Mom."

Orin chimed in cheerfully. "But pepper loaf, Tavian! Think of the possibilities! Besides, we're headin' that way anyways. What's the harm in a quick pit stop?"

Tavian slumped back in his seat with a heavy sigh. Aria rested a reassuring hand on his arm. "We'll find a way to get her back. I promise."

Their eyes met, remaining there for a long moment, until a thunderous boom came from outside, shaking the car and startling everyone inside.

Cassius peered out the window toward the explosion. "Sounded like that come from Ashford. Maybe we should listen to Tavian and keep moving."

But Tavian's attention was already fixed on Ashford. His face pressed against the warm glass, mesmerized by the strange, powerful streaks of orange and purple energy dancing across the sky above the city. The sensation was unmistakable, the same power he'd felt when he met Maeve after the accident. Could there be Necromites? Was this finally his chance to find more of them, to find what he'd been searching for?

"I've changed my mind. Let's go," he said.

Orin looked back. "Why in the world would you want to—" The

realization dawned on him. He'd read at the Bazaar, in some papers he'd found in a news stand, that Maeve and his men had overtaken Ashford.

"Tavian, you can't go in there. If they catch you, you'll be torn apart."

"What's the harm in a quick pit stop, Orin? You knew this was why I came. Drop me off alone if you have to, but I need to see it for myself."

The car fell into tense silence as they neared the exit for Ashford.

"Turn," Tavian urged, leaning in close to Orin's right ear.

Aria tugged at his arm, trying to pull him back. "Tavian, maybe we shouldn't—"

"Turn. Now." He was firm, his determination overruling any preoccupation that once held him back.

Orin didn't look back, instead reluctantly steering the car onto the exit ramp.

As they entered the city, the strange energy molded the air in such a way, bending it until heat waves shimmered in plain sight. Each moment became more oppressive, more grim than the last. Bodies lay contorted along the streets, mangled beyond recognition, old blood pooling beneath them. Blackened grass and the carcasses of dead birds added to the scene's horror. Collapsed buildings forced Orin to steer carefully through the wreckage, weaving around broken bricks and shards of glass scattered across the pavement.

Orin brought the car to a stop. "We can't go any farther. The road ahead's blocked. You chose this, Tavian. I'll be waitin' here."

Tavian's confidence wavered, fear rising in his throat. "Y-You're not coming?"

Orin shook his head. "I warned you, boy. If you want answers, you'll have to go find 'em yerself."

Tavian looked to Vid, who tried awkwardly avoiding his gaze. Cassius turned away as well, clearly curious, but too nervous to act. Finally, Tavian's looked to Aria, who was already climbing over Cassius to get out.

"Hurry up, Tavian," she urged. "Let's get this over with."

Swallowing his fear, he reached for the door handle.

"One more thing, Tavian," Orin warned, eyes meeting him through the rearview mirror. "If you hear the name Maeve, run."

Aria retrieved her hefty sword from the trunk, causing the vehicle to visibly lift from the reduced load. Tavian eyed the weapon skeptically.

"How do you manage to use that thing? It has to weigh a hundred pounds," he remarked, incredulous.

She shrugged, effortlessly spinning the blade. "Good training, I guess. Orin was never easy on me."

They walked down the desolate streets of Ashford, leaving Orin's car far behind until it vanished into the shrouded mist that blanketed the city. An eerie quiet settled over them. Only their own footsteps broke the silence, accompanied by a warm sea breeze that brushed against their skin like an uncomfortable whisper far too close to the ear.

Aria snapped the tension. "Do you really think they'll help you? These Necromites you're looking for?"

His stride faltered, uncertainty edging into his speech. "I'm not sure, but I have to try. Cassius says Mom did terrible things, but I need to know the truth... and Valspire needs her back."

Aria studied him, her thoughts drifting. "Whatever happens, I'll be here for you."

He paused, troubled. "Why do you always help me without question?"

Aria stared at the cracked pavement, noticing her worn shoes and frayed laces. "It's what... friends, do. And honestly... I care about you. When I see you hurting, it hurts me too, Tavian. And—"

"And I'm useless?" he cut in, turning to face her, eyes intense.

"What? No, of course not! Why would you say that?"

He looked upward, as though seeking comfort from the stars just beginning to peek from their nocturnal hiding places. "You and Orin are strong. Vid is witty, and Cassius is more well-traveled than anyone I've ever met. But I always feel like the weak link, the burden everyone has to carry."

Aria knew his feelings weren't unfounded, yet something about him defied easy explanation. To her, he was different—special in a way words could never quite capture. She wished he could see himself the way she did. If only he could see himself through her eyes—to understand how extraordinary he truly was.

"Tavian, it's not like that. You—" She couldn't articulate it.

He waited expectantly, but the silence only grew louder the longer he stood there. "That's what I figured," he said at last, distant and resigned.

They continued walking in strained unease, Aria fumbling for a way to tell him how she felt.

Why can't I just say it? Why am I so nervous?

The sun finally resigned behind the horizon, casting long shadows over the broken city. Night brought a chilling wind, and still, there were no signs of any Necromites.

"Maybe we should turn back," she suggested, eyes shooting around every blind corner and darkened alley. Only then did she realize how sprawling and unfamiliar the city had become. "Though I'm not sure we'd even find our way back."

"We should find somewhere to sleep for the night," he said, pointing toward an abandoned hospital erected in the distance. "There should be beds in there, right?"

She grimaced. "An abandoned hospital? That sounds like the perfect place for trouble... or something worse. Like ghosts."

He chuckled. "For someone so strong, I figured you'd be brave too! Come on, I'll protect you."

She scoffed. "Right, *you'll* protect *me*. Shouldn't we try to go back to Orin and the others? They're still waiting on us."

He waved her off. "Forget them. They said they'd help, then abandoned us when it mattered most. For all we know, they've already driven off without us."

The dark pressed closer, oppressive and heavily weighing against Aria's back. She felt eyes on them, an unshakable presence that intensified her fear. The distant lights from within the hospital appeared as a fragile beacon of safety in the consuming night.

"Fine," she conceded, quickening her step. "But hurry, I can't shake the feeling we're being watched."

Behind them, concealed in the deepening shadows, a small child watched closely. He had trailed them unnoticed, moving quietly through the alleys and hidden passageways he knew now by heart.

The automatic doors of the hospital slid open with a hesitant creak, revealing a vacant lobby. Somewhere, a backup generator coughed back to life, sputtering to keep the emergency systems running near empty. Flickering lights pulsed sporadically, presenting ghostly shadows that crawled across the peeling wallpaper. The stale air was thick with dust and mold, punctuated by the whir of ceiling fans stirring scattered paperwork across the grimy floor.

Tavian bent down and picked up one of the scattered documents. His eyes skimmed the page, stopping when he saw the name *David*. According to the file, David was a seven-year-old boy diagnosed with a condition Tavian couldn't pronounce. The photo, stained and distorted by old coffee spills, showed a child with strikingly green eyes framed by straight, jet-black hair. Beneath the diagnosis, a footnote caught his attention:

Don't call him David. He goes by Davie.

Tavian shuddered and dropped the paper, rising back to his feet.

They moved through the corridors, weaving around left-out stretchers, overturned chairs, and empty beds stained with unidentifiable fluids. Every creak and groan of the building made Aria flinch; she tightened the grip on her sword, muscles tense and at the ready.

"It's fine, Aria," Tavian laughed, amusement lighting his voice. "It's the building settling. Relax. No ghosts this time."

She nodded but didn't lower her sword. She could never be completely at ease, surveying each nook and cranny of the rooms they moved through.

Tavian sped up ahead of her, disappearing around a blind corner before she could catch up. When she looked around the bend, he was gone.

"Tavian?" she whispered.

No reply. Sweat trickled down her forehead, her pulse thrumming in her ears. Then came a sudden crash from one of the rooms around the corner, objects clattering to the floor, followed by the shuffle of frantic footsteps.

"Tavian?" she whispered again, rounding the corner toward the half-open door where the sounds had come from. Peering inside, she could just make out someone hunched over, rifling through a box of some sort.

Gathering all her courage, she took a deep breath, counted to three, and burst into the room with her sword raised high. She screamed with eyes sealed shut, swinging wildly in a frenzied assault.

"Aria, stop! It's me!" a familiar voice shouted.

Her eyes flew open as she halted mid-swing, realizing her mistake. Tavian was crouched low, shaking with his hands covering the top of his head. His hair was mussed and uneven where her blade had just missed.

"Watch it, you nearly took my head off!" he exclaimed, brushing through his chopped strands of hair.

"I'm so sorry!" she gasped, heart still pounding. "You disappeared. I thought the noise was—"

The same banging resumed, louder this time. They stopped, exchanging anxious looks.

"Don't move." She whispered firmly, edging back toward the door.

"Wait! Why are you going *toward* the noise?" he picked up a stray scalpel off the floor, clutching it awkwardly in both hands.

"I'm going to kill it before it kills us."

They stepped back into the hallway, following the noise to the next room over. As Aria stood before the locked door, the noise ceased, replaced by hurried scuffling sounds. Holding her breath, she reared back, preparing to kick the door down.

Before her foot could strike, the door swung open on its own. A small boy stood in the doorway, staring up at them.

"Hi," he rasped.

Startled, Aria stumbled back and fell hard onto the floor. An involuntary shriek escaped her.

"It's all right, Aria! It's just a kid!" Tavian reached down to help her up.

The boy repeated quietly, "Hi." He scratched furiously at his skin, eyes twitching.

Aria, regaining her composure, cautiously asked, "What are you doing here?"

The child glanced around with a look of confusion. "This is my room. Why are *you* here?"

Tavian studied the boy, feeling an unsettling familiarity in his piercing green eyes and straight black hair.

"We're looking for a place to stay tonight," Tavian explained, kneeling down to meet the boy's eyes. "Are you all right? Are you here all alone?"

The boy shrugged, eyes flickering back and forth toward blank spaces on the wall. "I have friends too. I live here. It's *my* room."

Tavian offered his hand with a warm smile, introducing himself and Aria. "What's your name?"

The boy reached out a shaky hand in response, his fingers twitching erratically. "Davie," he said. "Not David. Just Davie."

Tavian's gaze drifted to the chart clipped to the bed rail behind Davie. The name *David* had been crossed out in thick red marker. The name *Davie* replaced it.

Orin's roaring snoring reverberated through the parked car's metal frame, turning it into a deafening echo chamber. Cassius squirmed in his seat, shifting restlessly as he tried to drown out the noise. Vid, however, sat wide awake, gazing thoughtfully out the window. His mind wandered back to his encounter with Seraphina—her mesmerizing silver-gray eyes, her gentle touch—each memory vivid and nostalgic. Yet something was off. Fragments were missing, pieces he tried to put together but couldn't recall.

"Hey," Vid poked Orin's sizable belly. "Wake up."

Orin stirred, grumbling groggily as if emerging from deep hibernation. "What's it now, boy?"

"Have you ever been to Aipiron?" Vid asked, anticipation evident.

Orin sighed, rolling onto his other side. "Once—briefly. Too cold for my likin'."

"I want to visit. Do you think we could?" Vid persisted, hopeful.

"Sure, kid, whatever suits ya," he mumbled, already drifting back into sleep. "Still gotta see if Tavian survives till mornin'."

Vid smiled, content with the vague promise. He opened his mouth to thank Orin, but no words came. Orin's name slipped just out of reach. Then Orin spoke again, his tone clearer now, edged with warning.

"Though Aipiron isn't for the faint of heart. Those Trubbmans are trouble."

Vid's brow furrowed. "Trouble? What do you mean?"

Orin's voice began to fade again at the prospect of sleep. "Mind-Eaters. They'll consume your memories before you even know what hit ya'. Drive ya' mad if you're not careful."

Vid's heart skipped, his thoughts spiraling. *Mind-Eaters? Has Orin gone mad? Seraphina wouldn't do something like that to me... right?*

He clutched his head in distress. Memories felt hazy, had he forgotten something vital? Had their moments together even been real?

Orin rolled over, returning to his harsh, rattling snores. But Vid sat awake through the endless night, anxiety gnawing at him. He glanced toward Orin, realizing with sudden dread that something felt incomplete. He remembered the man sleeping beside him: their friendship, their journey... yet something vital was missing.

What was his name again?

Dawn broke, sending rays of sun piercing through the car windows, turning the interior into a suffocating greenhouse. Vid woke from what little sleep he'd managed, thrashing upright with sweat-soaked clothes clinging uncomfortably to his skin. His fragmented memories flashed to the surface once more. The Trubbmans... he couldn't let the others know he'd met them—or that he might have already lost parts of himself to their twisted powers.

Orin stirred shortly afterward, his large body stretching as he yawned. He noticed Vid's discomfort, patting his back with a heavy but gentle hand.

"How ya doin'? Sleep all right?"

Vid nodded meekly, forcing a convincing smile. "Yeah."

Orin eyed him skeptically. "Somethin' botherin' you? Tavian got you freaked out, or you upset about the pepper loaf?"

Vid nodded again, grateful for the excuse. "I'm worried about him, and the bread, of course. We should probably go look for them. They still haven't come back."

Orin stared out the window toward where Tavian and Aria had vanished the previous night. "Yeah, you're right. I just hope Maeve hasn't beaten us to it."

A sudden, terrified shout came from the backseat. Cassius bolted up, hands clutching at his chest as he gasped for additional breaths.

"What happened?" Vid asked, spinning around.

Cassius stared blankly forward before gradually relaxing into exhaustion. "Nothing, just a nightmare," he muttered.

He looked down at his hands, the burns still a reminder of his past. Although the wounds on his body were healing, his mind wasn't recovering the same. The screams of a woman and children were seared into his memory, burned there like a brand from the man who caused their deaths.

CHAPTER FIFTEEN
MEMORIES LOST

> But remember this: people aren't born evil. They're shaped into it, taught it, and can be changed for the better. The Rift doesn't have to be a permanent scar, a constant reminder of your plight.
> ~Thalia Moonbrook

"N-Nice to meet you... Davie."

"Have you seen the bad men in white clothes?" Davie asked fearfully, backing deeper into his room. His body quivered with miniature tremors, almost insect-like, radiating unsettling vibrations. "They tried to hurt my friends."

"Hey, it's okay," Aria reassured him, placing a hand near his head. Davie flinched, recoiling from her reaching arm.

"Don't touch me!" he shrieked, eyes wild. "You want to hurt me like they do!"

Aria looked to Tavian helplessly and leaned in close. "We need to go. He freaks me out. I don't want to abandon a kid, but there's something really off about him."

Tavian stared at the boy, his heart twisting at the sight of Davie's tears. Curled up on the floor, Davie murmured to himself, words barely audible. "Friends... David..."

"We should try to help." Tavian crept toward Davie in slow, deliberate steps. The boy's eyes snapped wide, and he swiftly retreated into the shadows, running behind a rounded corner deeper in the room.

"I'm waiting here; I'm not going any closer," Aria called after Tavian as he too disappeared around the corner. "Please... be careful."

Tavian rounded the corner into a hallway that shouldn't have existed. It ran on forever, doors lining both sides, smaller corridors branching like veins through the body of a colossus. He turned in confusion, already dizzy from the sheer number of choices.

"Davie?" he called out. Only sobbing answered.

Tavian opened door after door, each revealing nothing but haunting emptiness. By the seventh room, he spun around and realized he no longer recognized the hallway behind him. It stretched on in both directions, featureless and unfamiliar.

"Aria?" he shouted, his voice failing. "Can you hear me?"

Silence.

His breathing grew ragged as he started sprinting through the veins of the limitless halls, flipping open doors to identical, emptied rooms.

"Davie!" he called again. "Where are you?"

The sobbing stopped.

"You came for me?" Davie's voice whispered, impossibly close, echoing from everywhere at once as if spoken through a hidden loudspeaker. "Did you want to be my friend too? You can join them."

"Sure, Davie. We can be friends. Tell me where you are so we can get out of here."

"Open the door to your left."

Tavian pushed it open, instantly dry heaving at the pungent smell assaulting his senses. The room was lit only by the moonlight spilling through a single window. David stood in its pale glow, fixated on a closed closet. Tavian took one step forward, his shoe sinking into a thick, viscous liquid. Each step after came a wet, sucking sound, like walking across a floor made of honey.

"Davie?" Tavian swallowed but the saliva couldn't move past the closed-off epiglottis. "Are you okay? How do we get out of here?"

David ignored him, speaking into the horizontal slats of the closet door, his voice shifting between gentle pleading and harsh reprimands. Tavian crouched, fingers dipping into the liquid pooling beneath him, a minor sting as he held them under. He lifted his hand up to the dim moonlight.

Bloodied bile.

His stomach lurched.

"They said it's okay now." David announced, throwing both sides of the closet door open.

Tavian watched, horrified, as countless mutilated corpses cascaded into the bile—limbs twisted, chunks eaten out of their sides, bodies torn apart in grotesque displays of violence. Their remains began to dissolve, little-by-little, the bile eating away at the last scraps of flesh.

David looked at the bodies expectantly. "Introduce yourselves!"

Clearly, no response.

"C'mon, you all are never this shy." David poked the head of one of them. It detached from its neck with a wet pop and splashed onto the floor. He lifted it and pressed its mouth to his ear, listening and nodding as if to a secret meant only for him.

Tavian gagged, rolling back on his half-dissolved shoes. David turned sharply, eyes narrowed in a predatory fashion. "Geoffrey says you're lying to me. He says you don't really wanna be friends," David turned fully toward Tavian, dropping the dead into the acidic bile. "And he's never wrong."

"David, please—" Tavian stammered, his hands fumbling behind him for the doorknob. "I mean Davie—"

"David? You're like the rest of them, aren't you? You want to hurt us!" David yelled, his small figure contorting horrifically. His belly split open with a wet rip, unfurling into a cavernous mouth ringed in jagged teeth and hot, reeking breath.

Tavian screamed as loud as his lungs would allow, throwing himself against the stubbornly locked door. "HELP! PLEASE! ARIA!"

He heard David's footsteps pounding toward him, each one heavier than the last, until hot breath grazed the back of his neck.

Aria followed the shouts, the voices carrying true even as the halls deceived. The door flew open as Aria stormed in and drove her sword straight through David's monstrous form. It smiled around the blade. Flesh ripped and closed over the steel, forcing the weapon back out as its body swelled, knitting together around the shards that remained.

She reached down to retrieve the rejected sword, now soaked in blood and hot bile.

"Run!" Tavian shouted, grabbing Aria's hand as they sprinted down the endless corridor. Behind them, David's monstrous howls echoed.

Room after room revealed only more horrors—walls and floors of meaty flesh, heaps of corpses in white uniforms, the reek of death from unfriendly encounters. They could hear David approaching quickly, his shrill screams able to pierce their ears. His stomach split open, and from it shot an elongated tongue that lashed down the hall and coiled around Tavian's leg like a snake constricting its prey. He fell hard onto the floor.

Aria spun back and struck in one motion, her blade severing the tongue cleanly in two. David's face contorted in rage, the mouth in his gut letting out a strangled yelp.

Then—in a blink—the infinite corridor was gone. They stood in an ordinary hallway once more. David stood in front, small and barefoot, the thing in his stomach tucked neatly out of sight, like the monster had simply gone back into hiding.

"I just wanted more friends to play with," David whimpered.

The walls shook. One by one, every door opened, revealing hordes of ragged, undead humans stepping forward, weapons at the ready.

"Calm yourself, child." A tall man, poised and powerful, emerged from the crowd of undead and rested a firm hand on David's shoulder. Immediately, the boy relaxed, and the hallway folded back into the small, ruined room where they had first found him.

"But I'm hungry," David whined, grabbing at his rumbling stomach. The mouth that had split his torso shrank to a small, puckered hole. He tugged his shirt down to hide it—the wicked thing that had nearly devoured them whole.

"When Father speaks, what do you do?" the man asked calmly, his voice traveling with smooth, unshaken authority.

"I listen," David answered obediently, retreating into the crowd without another word.

The man turned toward Tavian and Aria. With each step forward, an invisible pressure bore down upon them. His mere presence radiated raw, terrifying power. An aura so dense and potent it seemed to shrink the room smaller. Tavian's heart hammered, each beat knocking at his eardrums, drowning out even his own terrified thoughts.

Tavian recognized him immediately, the same man that caused the car accident soon after leaving Valspire's walls.

It was Maeve.

"You two have disturbed the poor child," Maeve remarked. A cruel smile played at the corners of his mouth, never quite reaching his measuring eyes. "He's quite sensitive, you see. It's difficult to find friends who understand him. Not even I can quell his hunger."

Tavian's blood ran cold, an icy dread seizing his limbs and holding him hostage. Orin's warning replayed in his mind.

"I... I didn't mean to disturb him," Tavian stammered. He forced a breath, steadying himself before meeting Maeve's gaze head-on despite the crippling intimidation he felt. "But I was looking for people like you," he continued. "I need you to teach me how to bring back the dead, to better understand necromancy."

Maeve tilted his head like a curious hound, analyzing Tavian, dissecting every hidden secret and silent fear buried within. Then the recognition hit, he'd met these same two before. He seemed to savor Tavian's visible distress, allowing a pause to stretch painfully between them, amplifying the tension he so cherished.

"You want to learn necromancy?" Maeve mused, his deep voice rich with curiosity. "An unusual request coming from a Spirian. Most see that gift as abhorrent." Maeve's eyes turned to slits. "But you stand firm, demanding knowledge most fear to even utter aloud. Fascinating."

"Please," Tavian begged, tears welling in his eyes, proof of the pain he'd carried for so long. "There's someone I have to see. Someone who should never have died."

"And why should I help you? What's in it for me?" Maeve smiled. "Orin wouldn't agree to this, would he?"

Tavian began to feel exposed beneath Maeve's penetrating scrutiny. He took a shaky breath, hunting for strength he wasn't sure he possessed. "Orin has no say in this. I'll do anything. I'll pay any price."

The room fell silent at Tavian's declaration. Maeve took another step forward. Tavian resisted the urge to retreat, standing his ground despite the numb feeling in his knees.

Maeve's gaze softened, a peculiar brevity of warmth emerging through his usual coldness.

"You remind me of someone. Lyra, I think her name was. There's something about you, and I can't help but like it."

❀ ❀ ❀

Arnette twirled in delight, her excitement practically tangible. "Be sure to make it down in time for dinner. We're having roast duck tonight!" With a final flourish, she closed the door behind her, leaving Rowan, Cloud, Anastasia, and Lyra alone in their quarters.

The room was expansive, grander than most houses in Tenebral. A lavish living area stretched before them, its floors covered with intricately embroidered rugs and furniture draped in rich silks and velvet. Enormous windows framed an endless view of the sea, where gentle waves caressed the shore and birds soared gracefully across the cerulean sky. Three bedrooms surrounded the central space, each complete with its own sitting room and luxurious bath.

Rowan sprinted around excitedly, marveling at every detail. "Do you see this?" he exclaimed, holding up a golden fork and twisting it in the sunlight streaming through the windows. "Everything here is gold! What a waste." He slipped the fork and several other gilded trinkets into his bag, grinning mischievously.

Lyra sighed, shaking her head. "Rowan..."

He ignored her, rushing into another room. Loud clattering and excited gasps echoed back as he explored every drawer and cabinet for more valuables.

Lyra moved to the wide window, letting her eyes drift to the calm expanse of the sea, breathing in the tranquility. For the first time in what felt like ages, she felt an unusual sense of calm. A small tug pulled her from the moment. Anastasia was clutching her leg. Lyra smiled and ran a hand through Anastasia's hair, savoring the simple comfort of it. Something she'd nearly forgotten how to feel.

Some hours later, the group sat around an extensive dining table lavishly set for seven guests. Every inch gleamed with silver, gold, and crystal, the air rich in aromas of meat, vegetables, and sweets. Even Cloud had his own bowl, overflowing with food he eagerly devoured at Rowan's side. Across from them sat Seraphina, and beside her, a small, quiet boy.

Seraphina spoke first. "It's nice to see you all again. Rowan, you look well."

Rowan had indeed made an effort—his hair neatly styled, his finest clothes pressed, posture perfectly straight. Lyra couldn't help but wonder why he'd gone to such trouble for a simple dinner. She discreetly kicked him under the table. He yelped, rubbing his shin where her foot had struck.

"Thank you... Seraphina," he managed to get out.

"This is Baron," Seraphina continued, gesturing to the small boy beside her, who quietly played with smooth stones, seemingly lost in his own world. "My younger brother."

Everyone offered polite waves, but Baron didn't acknowledge them, fully absorbed in his task.

"Baron, put the rocks down and say hello to our guests." She nudged him with her elbow.

Baron looked up for a split second and smiled before turning his focus back to the rocks. "I need more practice before Vid comes back. I wanna show him my new trick."

Seraphina's smile thinned at the mention of the name; the corner of one eye watered, but her tight smile never ceased.

A refined, elegantly dressed man entered and took a seat at the head of the table. "Welcome, everyone. I heard we had guests. I'm Agusto Trubbman, Seraphina's father."

Lyra introduced herself and Anastasia, who waved absently in the direction of her sister's voice. Agusto's eyes widened upon noticing Anastasia seated at the table, but he quickly masked his reaction.

"And you, young man?" Agusto asked, pouring a glass of red wine and sliding it toward him.

"Rowan Lysander," he replied with a courteous nod. "A pleasure, and thank you again for your hospitality." Rowan graciously accepted the wine.

Agusto smiled warmly. "We've missed having guests. Things have been... quiet."

"I hope I didn't keep you all waiting too long!" Arnette bustled in, setting down an enormous silver platter of roast duck, the final centerpiece to a lavish spread of fruits, cheeses, breads, pastries, and decanters of wine. "Enjoy!" she said, taking her seat with effortless grace.

Rowan began piling his plate high, while Lyra sat still, untouched utensils sitting orderly and in place. Seraphina noticed, one eyebrow arching. "Not hungry, Lyra? On a diet, perhaps?"

"Just not hungry," Lyra replied curtly, then whispered to her sister, "Don't eat any of this." Anastasia nodded, lowering her hand down to her rumbling stomach.

Rowan paused his food-stacking, noticing Lyra's unease. "What's wrong?" he whispered.

Lyra leaned in, her voice barely audible. "What if it's poisoned?"

Rowan stopped chewing, eyeing his food for a moment before tossing a half-eaten sausage to Cloud. The dog sniffed it once, then devoured it in a single chomp. Rowan shrugged and resumed eating. "Looks good to me. Dogs can sense these things, it's fine."

Lyra gave Rowan a nasty side-eye and muttered, "Perfect. Poison the dog first, then we'll all die after."

Agusto refilled Rowan's glass of wine, maintaining a steady stream of conversation. "So, you all are old friends of Seraphina's, I assume?"

Lyra caught Seraphina's gaze—a silent cue to play along. Since they'd been formally "invited" to stay as *guests*, they had to keep up the pretense of civility, walking the tightrope between politeness and survival.

Lyra forced a grin and went with it. "Yes, we've known each other for a little while now. We were passing through Aipiron and thought we'd stop by."

Seraphina decided to add more to the story. "Lyra and I go way back. And Rowan," she flashed a coy smile. "He belongs to Lyra."

Rowan smirked rolled with it, realizing they were making things up on the fly. He didn't mind.

Baron glanced up briefly. "Ew, you're dating?"

Lyra cut in quickly, "We're not together anymore."

Anastasia looked puzzled, wondering if she'd somehow missed an important detail. She reached for a piece of bread amid Lyra's clumsy storytelling, but her sister's hand shot out, gripping her wrist just before she reached the crust.

Rowan took a sip from the rim of his wine glass. "Won't you tell them why we aren't together anymore? The heartbreak I endured so long ago—how you found someone else, a new lover, how you cheat—"

Lyra's jaw dropped. She kicked him much harder this time, passion laced into every inch of it. "I did not! Take it back!"

Seraphina burst into laughter.

"I told you, I forgive you!" Rowan cried out, gripping his bruised shin.

Agusto awkwardly chuckled, refilling Rowan's wine glass once more. "Apologies, perhaps I shouldn't have brought that up." He shifted back to Anastasia with polite curiosity. "Though I don't mean to pry, but may I ask about your sister's eyes?"

Lyra snapped out of her playful storytelling, protectively leaning closer to her sister. "She's blind—born that way. Our mother gave her this blindfold to cover it."

Agusto studied the worn cloth, noting its frayed edges and dark stains. With a small gesture, he motioned to Arnette, who quickly left her seat then returned soon after, holding a beautiful velvet blindfold. "Here, Anastasia," she said, placing it in the girl's hands. "This is far more fitting for our guest."

Anastasia's fingers explored it, tears staining her old blindfold. "Thank you," she whispered.

"Of course! We can't have our guests reduced to wearing such tattered rags. There are perks to this life, on occasion." Agusto took another sip of wine, then poured himself a fresh glass and drained half of it in a single swallow. He refilled Rowan's as well; the younger man's cheeks were already flushed bright red.

Arnette glared at Agusto with each sip he took, watching his slow descent into drunkenness.

"Baron, dear," she said, "are you finished eating? Would you like to go back to your room and play for a while?"

Baron nodded, slid back his chair, and darted from the table back toward his room.

When it became clear no one intended to eat anymore, a silent agreement among guests that the meal was over, Arnette rose and helped a drunken Agusto from his chair, bidding the group a cheerful goodnight. She looped an arm around him and guided him toward the kitchen, balancing his weight against her shoulder.

Before disappearing through the doorway, she glanced over one final time with a weary smile. "Sorry to leave so soon. I hope you all enjoy the night. I look forward to seeing you in the morning."

Moments later, she vanished into the kitchen with her husband. The sound of muffled voices followed, an argument breaking through the clatter of washed dishes. Only fragments reached the dining room table: "*Anastasia*" and "*dangerous*", slurred between Agusto's drunken words.

"I apologize for my father," Seraphina said, idly pushing the last scraps of food around her plate with a crystalline fork. "He has little sense of decency."

Rowan waved it off, accidentally toppling two empty wine bottles in the process. "It's all gooood," he hiccuped. "All the money and time to drunk, what else can you do?"

Seraphina's well-maintained smile began to sour. Lyra looked over to him and immediately sensed something was off. He reeked of red wine.

Lyra tapped his leg and whispered, "Are you all right? You look awful."

"I'm hot," he wiped sweat from his brow with a silk napkin. "And don't you always think I look awful anyway?" He downed another glass, reached for the bottle, tipped it—and nothing came out.

"That's a shame," he muttered, aggressively sliding the empty bottle aside. He slumped down in his chair to Cloud, still hiccuping every few seconds, and reached to scratch behind the dog's ears.

"Sorry, I don't know what's gotten into him," Lyra said.

"I'm used to it," Seraphina replied with an exhausted shake of her head. "The price you pay with men. What's that saying? *Can't live with them...*" She paused, feigning thought. "*Can't live with them.* I think that's it."

She started to laugh at herself, and to her surprise, so did Lyra.

"As much as I'd like to continue our conversation from earlier, it's getting late. Keep thinking about our agreement, Lyra. It's in everyone's best interest." Seraphina slowly finished the last of her meal, though oddly, one remaining scrap on her plate seemed to pulse with a faint white glow. Lyra blinked, uncertain if she'd imagined it.

She tried to recall what conversation Seraphina was referring to, but the thought slipped away like water through her fingers. Still, she went along with it. "I'll think about it."

"Good." Seraphina lingered briefly, watching as Lyra and Anastasia helped an intoxicated Rowan stumble back to their quarters, Cloud padding faithfully behind them.

She sat at the table, chewing on something she couldn't seem to swallow. When she opened her mouth, a white, wispy fragment rested at the base of her tongue. She bit down hard. It cracked open, and something poured down her throat.

Lyra reached the room with Rowan drooping over her shoulder. She dropped him onto the suite's couch and walked with Anastasia to the bathroom. "Don't go wandering off," she warned as he sat up wobbly.

"Yes ma'am," Rowan hoisted a sarcastic salute. "But where's more wine?"

In the bathroom, Anastasia removed her old blindfold and let it fall to the floor. Lyra unfolded the new velvet one and carefully tied it around her sister's sockets. Anastasia's fingers traced it in small circles, exploring the delicate inlays.

She couldn't help but smile. "It's perfect."

Lyra wrapped her arms around her sister from behind. "You look beautiful. I'm glad you came with me... and that you're safe."

Anastasia smiled wider. "Me too."

They walked out of the bathroom together, finding Rowan slouched on the couch with Cloud curled beside him. He lifted his head slightly with one eye closed and the other half-open. "That looks great, Anastasia," he said with a lazy grin. "Suits you well."

Anastasia blushed. "Thank you."

"Goodnight." Rowan's eyes suddenly rolled to the back of his head and he slumped into Cloud's thick, white fur, already asleep.

Late into night, as darkness draped itself over the palace, Anastasia and Rowan drifted into the comforting embrace of sleep. But Lyra lay awake, staring at the ceiling, chasing a thought that refused to be caught. She drifted off only when exhaustion pulled her under.

Unnoticed by the trio, an ethereal floating eye materialized into existence in one of the corners of the suite. Its iris glowed faintly blue as it hovered, observing each of them in turn, staying longer on Anastasia. When it had satisfied its silent inquiry, the glow dimmed, then dissolved with a soft ripple into the waiting dark.

"They're asleep," Arnette said, seated comfortably in a plush chair beside Seraphina's throne. She lifted a hand to her empty socket, pressing her palm against it. When she lowered it, the floating eye that had watched from Lyra's suite now rested whole in its place. Her face showed neither discomfort nor hesitation, only calm resolve. "Can we trust them?"

After several heavy moments, Seraphina finally spoke. "For now. But I need more time for her transformation."

Rising from her throne, she began her descent down the grand staircase toward the lower cells where Lyra had once been held. Arnette followed behind, her footsteps quieter, almost ghostlike in comparison. With every level they passed, the air grew colder, the light from the throne room losing its glow. The warmth and elegance above gave way to the stone walls and silence, the atmosphere hardening into something unforgiving.

At the bottom of the staircase, a narrow corridor sat ahead, lit only by sparse lamps that cast restless shadows upon the dampened stone walls. Rows of hefty wooden doors lined the passage, each reinforced with iron bars.

Seraphina stopped at the final cell at the end of the hall, peering through the rusted grate at a trembling figure huddled in the corner. Her expression shifted subtly, softening before she composed herself back into the poise of an aristocrat.

Arnette stopped beside her, her tone soft yet clinical. "His transformation is nearly complete. Why don't you ask him again? Let's see how deep the memories go."

"Lucan," Seraphina hailed.

The elderly man jerked his head toward her, eyes wide with sudden, overwhelming terror. His voice shook as he pleaded.

"Please... I'll do anything. Let me go... I-I have a family."

Seraphina stepped closer to the bars. "Family? Then tell me your wife's name."

He stared blankly, lips moving soundlessly, searching for the right answer. A thin whimper escaped him. "Sara... I think."

Seraphina tilted her head, a cold curiosity lighting her eyes. "If I released you now, could you find this... *Sara*?"

Lucan's frail body shuddered, his breathing turned shallow and rapid. His eyes darted frantically around the cell, searching the corners, each crack in the wall; anywhere an answer might hide.

"I... I don't know. I can't remember. Please, let me—"

Seraphina stared at him, her penetrating gaze unblinking, pressing firm into his mind. A thin wisp of white mist drifted from his forehead. She inhaled it.

Gradually, his trembling ceased. The panic drained from his face, leaving only a vacant calm. He neither moved nor spoke, he simply stopped.

After giving another second to readjust, Seraphina spoke to him again. "Lucan? How are you feeling?"

Slowly, as if roused from a long and distant sleep, the elderly man lifted his head. His eyes were glazed and unfocused—confused, devoid of recognition. He looked around the cell, lost in the unfamiliar surroundings, until finally making eye contact with the strange, freighting girl standing before him.

"Who?" He blinked. "Are you speaking to me?"

Arnette observed with detached interest. "Excellent. Your reach is expanding. I believe this one may be the last test."

Seraphina didn't look away.

"No, Lyra will be the last."

CHAPTER SIXTEEN
A SHIFT IN PERSPECTIVE

> "I couldn't tell you. I wanted to, but I was too scared to make you mad. Please don't be upset at me, Lyra. I only kill when I have no choice. I promise... please don't hate me.
>
> ~Anastasia Ashryn

"Please, come home. Love, Grandma."

Tavian's voice grew distant as he finished reading the note aloud. He stared at the brittle paper, his thumb brushing over the family's seal. It crinkled beneath his touch. With a bitter sigh, he crumpled it and let it fall, watching it land among the dirt and debris of the cold hospital floor. The letter soon vanished into a small streak of light, a thin beam shooting up into the sky.

"Doesn't she understand what I'm doing?" Tavian's words were layered with irritation and grief. "Does she not understand what I left for? They'll manage fine until I'm back... until *we're* back with Mom."

Aria moved over to him, her footsteps barely audible. She rested a tentative hand on him, feeling his tense muscles beneath her touch.

"Tavian," she said, "you should at least write back. Let her know we're safe."

His hand moved over hers, a gesture meant to reassure—but the moment their skin met, a troubling chill climbed up her arm. She suppressed a shiver, realizing how unnatural his touch now felt. Tavian had always provided a warmth she cherished, but ever since he began his training with Maeve, a coldness had settled in.

"Don't worry. We'll be finished here soon, and Grandma will see everything we did was for Valspire."

Aria slipped her hand out from beneath his and placed it into the warmth of her pocket, flexing her fingers to bring the feeling back from the bitter numbness.

A harsh laugh sliced through the thickening tension. From around the corner, Maeve emerged, the click of his bloodied boot heels reverberating off the walls. Even from a distance, his smile could be seen carrying malice.

"Don't be so certain," he said, hands folded loosely behind his back. "I'm beginning to wonder if you've forgotten the deal we made."

Tavian looked down to examine his palms. The deep, ink-dark scars from Maeve's quill still ached whenever he moved his fingers. Painful reminders of the promise he'd made.

Maeve continued. "You're not here simply to take what you want and vanish, boy. This is a mutual agreement, signed and sealed in your own blood. And soon enough, you'll deliver on your end." He leaned in, eyes shining. "Besides, should you decide to break your promise, I still have your collateral... I was surprised you were willing to offer something so precious."

Aria's stomach twisted at the mention of *collateral*. She glared at Tavian, demanding answers. "Collateral? What's he talking about? What did you offer him?"

Tavian turned away, unable or unwilling to meet her sight. His voice came out strained, clipped. "Don't worry about it. It doesn't concern you."

"Doesn't concern me?" Aria snapped, frustration tightening her throat. "How can you say that? How could it not—"

Maeve interrupted, too delighted not to speak out. "On the contrary, dear girl, it affects you more than anyone." He paused, letting the tension ripen. "But far be it from me to spoil the surprise."

As Maeve sauntered away, his dark laughter trailing down the hallway, Aria swiftly smacked Tavian on the back of the head. "Are you insane?" she hissed. "Why would you offer him anything? What happens if you fail?"

Tavian's eyes remained fixated on the shadows Maeve had vanished into. He spoke quietly, more to himself than to Aria.

"If I fail, the collateral will be the least of our concerns."

When Tavian and Aria arrived at the ground floor of the dilapidated hospital, they found Orin, Vid, and Cassius waiting there in silence. Their shoulders sagged, faces drawn with the weight of days spent in uncertainty and discomfort.

Orin's voice sounded considerate. "Sit down, Tavian. We need to talk."

Reluctantly, Tavian lowered himself into a chair, crossing his arms, eyes fixed anywhere but on the others. He knew exactly what was coming, though part of him wished he could delay it indefinitely.

"We've been here too long," Orin began, leaning forward. "You seem to think you know what you're doin', but it's high time we moved on. What's keepin' us here?"

Tavian shifted awkwardly, searching for words that wouldn't betray his own uncertainty. "I'm not finished yet. There's still more I need to learn."

Cassius broke the silence that followed. "We understand your need for answers, but the longer we stay, the more dangerous this becomes. These people aren't on our side."

A dark pulse rippled outward from Tavian. Aria felt it vividly, a sinister current she was sure no one else noticed. She glanced around, but the others didn't react. Perhaps they didn't feel it, or perhaps they didn't understand what it meant.

Vid edged closer. "Something's not right about this place or these people. Yesterday, I swear one of those things was watching me sleep. I get you want to bring Leora back, but—"

"Then leave," Tavian interjected. "You all agreed to come here. And now that I'm finally making progress, you decide to abandon me? Why even come at all?"

Orin lowered his gaze to the floor, Vid's shoulders sank deeper, and Cassius closed his notebook with a tired sigh. The quiet stretched painfully long, enough for it to feel like an ending.

"I still want to get to Aipiron," Vid said at last. "I don't want to go without you, but it feels like something I have to do."

Orin nodded solemnly. "We care about you, kid. We really do. But I've got my own unfinished business, and it's about time I see to it."

Everyone turned to Aria, waiting for her decision. Her chest constricted as she met Tavian's eyes. After a moment of hesitation, she spoke.

"I won't leave you. I chose to follow you here, and I intend to see it through to the end."

For a fleeting moment, relief lit up Tavian's cold eyes. A faint smile formed, one that sent warmth through Aria's cheeks despite her best efforts to suppress it.

Cassius gave a thoughtful nod. "I suppose I can stay a bit longer too. There's knowledge here about the afterlife that I won't find anywhere else. It may not be everything I need, but it's bringing me closer to the truth."

Orin rose, speaking directly to Aria. "You're stronger than you realize, Aria. I'd never leave if I had a choice, but some things can't wait. Not even for family."

He motioned for Vid to stand with him. "You need to reach Aipiron, and where I'm headin' isn't too far from it. We can travel together."

Vid now stood with him, Orin giving one final warning.

"This is a mistake, Tavian. I hope you can find what yer lookin' for, but I don't want you to end up like Leora. She never deserved this, and neither do you."

Tears spilled down Aria's cheeks as she rushed forward, throwing her arms around Orin. Her sobs came out in broken gasps as she clung to him, barely able to wrap her arms around his broad frame.

"Please... don't go," she choked out. "You're the only family I have left. I haven't even found Mom or Dad yet..."

He gently pushed her back, just enough to cup her face in his large, calloused hands. "I'm sorry, but this is somethin' I have to do. It's for Valspire—*actually* for Valspire. I've put it off for too long."

He leaned close and whispered in her ear. "But please be careful. Tavian isn't the same boy we knew. Promise me you'll keep your guard up."

Aria nodded profusely through her tears, refusing to let go. Orin held her for a long moment before finally easing her arms away. "No one's stronger than you. No man or woman I've ever met. I raised you right, and you've made me proud." His voice trembled just slightly. "I love you, sweetheart. Meet me back at Valspire... when you've realized the truth."

Vid embraced Aria next, his voice reassuring but fraying at the edges. "I'll be in Aipiron. Meet me there when you're finished here. Be safe until then."

Both he and Orin waved toward Tavian and Cassius, who returned the gesture with distant motions. Aria followed them outside, up until they reached the vehicle waiting beside the hospital.

As Orin and Vid climbed in, waving their final goodbyes, Aria stood static, heart aching.

Tavian stepped up behind her, his hand gripping her shoulder. She could feel the ring she got him buried into her skin—it was ice cold. "We're getting Mom back, don't worry," he said, a dark conviction burning beneath his words.

Aria turned, looking up into his eyes. A chill cut through her, sharper and more severe than ever.

They used to be inviting. They used to be brown.

When had they turned so dark?

The next morning brought with it a perturbed stillness, one that pressed on Aria more than the rest. Without Vid's easy jokes or Orin's comforting words to reassure her, she felt a strange hollowness that neither Tavian nor Cassius could fill. Their voices were an anchor she hadn't realized she needed.

Cassius woke with a disturbed kickstart, startling Tavian and Aria from their own restless half-sleep. Sweat poured down from his clammy face. His eyes were wide with terror, the whites stark against the dark shadows that lay within them.

"No!" he screamed hoarsely, lost between dream and reality. "Run! Get out!"

"Cassius! You're fine. It's just us!"

He blinked away the haze, his eyes refocusing slowly, the wild panic ebbing into embarrassment. "Sorry... another nightmare," he said, wiping the sweat from his brow with shaky fingers.

On the adjacent bed, Tavian sat up, rubbing away a thick crust of mucus sealing his eyelids shut. Before he could speak, a timid knock tapped on their door, followed by the slow creak of hinges as it opened on its own. Framed in the tall doorway, small and hunched in contrast to its height, stood David. He didn't move, his thin arms were wrapped around his gurgling stomach.

"I'm hungry," he announced. His penetrating green eyes locked onto Cassius, staring straight through Aria as though she were invisible.

Cassius chuckled, finally shaking off the last of his lingering tremors from the nightmare. He rose from bed and approached David with gentle amusement, ruffling the boy's unruly black hair. "Remember what I told you, Davie—have patience. I'm glad you enjoy my cooking, but a good meal takes time."

David's dissatisfaction was evident through his angered grumbles. He grabbed Cassius's hand and tugged impatiently. "We need it now."

"What have I said about manners?" Cassius asked patiently, folding his arms. "I'm waiting..."

David rolled his eyes and sighed with exaggerated frustration, before finally relenting. "We need it... *please*."

"Much better. Let me get sorted, and I'll whip up your favorite."

David's dwarfish body bounced with barely contained excitement. He turned and dashed away, the slap of his bare feet growing louder with each step. His stomach swelled, doubling, then tripling in size. Paintings rattled and fell off the walls, crashing noisily as he and the creature within him lumbered toward the kitchen.

"Quiet down, or you'll wake the whole building!" Cassius yelled out to him, shaking his head but flashing a smile. A smile for a monster, nonetheless.

Aria watched the exchange with mild curiosity, stretching her arms above her head to ease the tension from a sleepless night. "He's really taken a liking to you," she said through a yawn. "I'm shocked he's so comfortable. He doesn't strike me as the trusting type."

Cassius grew thoughtful, his fingers absently tracing the edges of his worn notebook in one pocket and the spice pouch in the other. "It's remarkable, really. There's something about that boy that's oddly familiar, like I've met him somewhere before. I suppose familiarity breeds comfort."

He flipped open the notebook, scribbling down his thoughts in tight, hurried handwriting before snapping the book shut again and stuffing it back into his pocket.

Now dressed for the day, Cassius made way toward the makeshift kitchen, only to find a line had formed in anticipation of his next meal. The line was filled with gaunt, undead creatures; their eyes both vacant and burning with hunger, all staring at Cassius with ferocious appetite.

One of them shuffled forward, its gray face creased with anxious hope. "You're cooking again today, aren't you? Tell us it's true."

"That may be true, but as always, there's only so much to go around. First come, first served!"

Bodies began to jostle and press forward, each one eager to reach the front first. The hunger etched into their faces was unsettling, but for now at least, it was for his food and not him.

From within the pressing mass, a shrill voice broke through. A skeletal, clearly agitated woman stepped boldly out of line. Messy clothes hung loosely from her bony frame, her body showing the unmistakable signs of prolonged malnourishment; days, perhaps weeks on end.

"Why does Davie always get special treatment?" she said, pointing to him standing merrily in front of the line. "He should be waiting like everyone else!"

The line had already been silent, but this silence was denser, so complete that any sound daring to escape would be swallowed in its entirety. Cassius pitied her, knowing what was to come, yet he had no power to change it.

David hobbled over to her, clutching his distended stomach, confusion evident on his juvenile face. His voice shivered. "Do you not like me? Did... I do something wrong?"

Several people frantically shook their heads, silently urging him not to get upset. Another reached out, yanking the infuriated woman back into line. She pushed them aside, standing her ground.

"Do you not want to be friends?" David asked.

"I don't give a damn about being your friend!" she barked. "Get to the back, brat! Just because you're a kid doesn't mean you get special—"

A gritty crunch followed. David's innocent facade evaporated as his stomach opened into a monstrous maw, rows of teeth jutting from its bottomless pit. In one fleeting, brutal motion, half of the woman's body disappeared within the gaping hole. Her legs dangled and twitched uselessly, nerves firing in vain as the creature inside David's body masticated and ground away at her torso. With one final gulp, the woman vanished entirely into the abyss, leaving behind nothing but a wet burp.

No one dared move, eyes cast firmly downward. David's voice, gentle yet chilling, broke the dreadful voicelessness. "I'm still hungry," he whispered, turning his innocent gaze toward Cassius, the blood around his lips a sharp contrast to his childlike expression.

Reality crashed harshly back upon Cassius. His hands fumbled for his notebook, struggling to hold the pen steady as he jotted down hurried notes.

"Of course, Davie," Cassius managed, forcing composure into his wavering voice. "Give me a moment. Your meal will be ready soon."

With an urgency he hadn't felt since his days as a chef, Cassius rushed into the kitchen, pots and pans rattling as he threw himself into preparing breakfast. David waited patiently back at the front of the line, humming a soft melody, oblivious to the terror of those around him. He'd earned his place at the front that day, and no one else objected.

There were no lights along the shore, yet the beach still glowed, bathed in the silver wash from the moon and starlight. The half-moon hung like an elegant jewel in the sky, surrounded by countless stars scattered in patterns as mysterious as the ocean's depths.

Lyra, Anastasia, Rowan, and Cloud strolled leisurely along the beach, their bare feet sinking into cool, damp sand outside their temporary home in Aipiron. It had been over a month now, and still, there was no clear sign of departure.

Anastasia pulled at the flowing threads of Lyra's dress, its delicate pink embroidery mirroring the bright outlines of shells scattered across the sand.

"When everything's done, we should get a dog too," she suggested, hopeful that her sister shared the same sentiment. She tilted upward, her empty sockets landing just shy of Lyra's face, a joyful grin illuminating her entire being.

Lyra returned a smile, though it felt strained. "We haven't even gotten close to Valspire yet..."

She watched Anastasia's excitement fade. "But I'll consider it," she added, "once it's all over."

Anastasia's felicity returned, more intense than before. She threw her arms around Lyra's hips, pressing her face against the embroidery. "And we can name it Cloud, just like Rowan's!"

Rowan, walking a few paces ahead, chuckled. With an easy flick of the wrist, he sent a stick sailing down the beach, Cloud bounding after it with joyful abandon. "That sounds like a great idea. Then Cloud could have someone to play with."

Anastasia hurried after Cloud, bending down to sift her hands through the sand until she found something to throw. Cloud bounded to her side with tail furiously wagging, both girl and dog drifting ahead of Lyra and Rowan, her laughter carried by the sea breeze.

Lyra stared after them, suddenly troubled by her sister's wording. "When everything's done? What did she mean by that?"

Rowan glanced sideways at her. "I suppose she means after you finally reach Valspire, after all the fighting's over."

Lyra froze, an invisible weight anchoring her in place. The question struck her harder than she expected. Had she ever really thought about what came after? Was there an end to any of this?

Rowan's voice broke through her troubled thoughts. "Haven't you ever thought about it before? What will you and your sister do when it's all over?"

"No. All I've ever thought about is reclaiming Valspire; restoring control to the Necromites. That's all that's ever mattered."

With a sigh, Rowan shaped his hand into a pistol—two fingers for the barrel, thumb for the hammer—and aimed playfully at her temple. He mimed a shot with a whispered *bang*.

Lyra flinched. The image flashed in her mind; her mother at the Rift, the finger gun beheading the attendant. She grabbed Rowan's hand and shoved it aside, bewildered and visibly shaken.

"What are you doing?"

He smiled sheepishly, holding up the finger gun again as if inspecting it. “It’s something I taught Cloud. When I pretend to shoot, he plays dead. Just a silly trick.”

Lyra raised an eyebrow. “Then why point it at me?”

His warmth blended with seriousness. “Because every time you talk about Valspire and your mission, you remind me of Cloud obeying a command. You move blindly, almost automatic, without thought.”

He raised the finger gun again and whispered *bang*. “But you’re not a dog, Lyra. You have a choice. And sometimes...” he hesitated, now softening. “Sometimes I just wish someone could shoot those heavy thoughts right out of your head and let you rest, even if just for a brief moment.”

Only the lapping of waves brushing against the shore followed the silence between them. Rowan watched her closely, uncertain of her reaction, but sensing he may have touched something buried deep.

He decided to press on in absence of her response. “Have you ever asked yourself what *you* want? Not what’s been drilled into you, not the mission, but what Lyra wants. For herself and for her sister.”

She continued to stand motionless.

Memories gushed forward like a raging tide with no walls left to hold it at bay: Ravenna’s wretched stare and the click of her spiked heels, Corvin’s hidden sadness behind the curtain of his cruel experiments, the frequent beatings, Slug’s lifeless eyes staring down at her with hands buried deep within, the first time she’d seen Anastasia’s empty sockets behind a bloodstained blindfold, the countless faces and screams of those she had tortured with her own powers...

And then—the first moment Rowan appeared, offering something she’d long forgotten existed.

She dug her nails into her palms as she did each time these feelings tried to resurface, but it did nothing to dam the storm. Her knees buckled, her breath coming in short, painful gasps. The screams of her past victims rang inside her ears, drowning out all else, turning the serene beach into a scene of personal torment.

Her legs gave out. Rowan caught her before she fell, arms encircling her as he lowered her to the sand. “Lyra!” he called urgently. “Breathe, it’ll pass. I’m sorry, I shouldn't have said anything.”

Anastasia sensed the shift instantly. She turned and ran toward them, Cloud close at her heels.

Several agonizing minutes crawled by at a slug's pace, each second an eternity before the relentless storm within her finally subsided. Lyra trembled in Rowan's steadying grasp. Her once-elegant dress was now marred by wet sand, and the salty breeze tangled loose strands of her hair.

"Are you okay?" he asked, rubbing her back in small circles, fingers grazing over the flowers laced through her hair.

She drew in a shaky breath, struggling to steady herself. "I—I think so," she whispered, attempting to rise only to fall back down. "Give me a second."

Rowan nodded, signaling for Anastasia to take Cloud back to their quarters. She hesitated but trusted him enough to obey, glancing back over her shoulder with every few steps as she led the dog away.

"I'm sorry," Rowan began. "I didn't mean to—"

"It's fine," she cut in quickly, not wanting to bring it up again.

Now alone, Rowan and Lyra sat in the sand, facing the sea as it shimmered under the moonlight, the waves whispering to them. Rowan stole a glance at her, the pale glow tracing the lines of her face. Before he could lose himself to thought, he reached into his pocket and produced a small rectangular object.

"I meant to show you both earlier," he said, trying his best to lighten the mood. "Look... I picked it up at the Eclipsed Bazaar."

Lyra turned the small device over in her hands, puzzled. "What is it?"

"It's a recorder," he explained. "You press this button, and it captures moments you can replay again and again. Like those videos you're always watching."

He pointed it playfully toward her, smiling warmly. "Do something interesting, I'm recording."

Lyra lifted her own finger gun to her temple, ready to half-jokingly fire the painful thoughts away. But Rowan moved quickly, lowering her hand into her lap and shaking his head.

"Don't do that," he said, filled with genuine care. "That's my job."

Lyra smirked, the corners of her mouth lifting as her mood began to lighten. She snatched the recorder, aiming it playfully back at Rowan, who struck a dramatic pose. She raised her hand again, formed the imaginary gun, and fired at his head instead, whispering *bang*.

In exaggerated fashion, Rowan collapsed backward onto the sand, eyes shut tight with a goofy smile. A sudden pang of panic flashed across Lyra. She lunged toward him, the device capturing every second of her genuine worry.

Oh gods. Did I just kill him?

Leaning over him, she saw his amusement and huffed in relief, until slight irritation took its place. She punched his shoulder lightly—her version of lightly, at least—and laughed, the sound freer than it had been in some time.

For a little while, she stopped thinking about the harsh reality of their situation and everything that was to come.

For a little while, she thought only of Rowan.

CHAPTER SEVENTEEN
FORTUNATE SON

Don't wait too long, now. Time doesn't stop for anyone!
~Thalia Moonbrook

UNRHYTHMIC, MUFFLED THUMPS.

Coming from the far end of the hall, that's all he could hear.

Corvin stood at one end, his fingers curling around the familiar handrail along the right wall. The sound came from the room just up ahead—accompanied by Ravenna's voice, labored and breathy, leaking through the cracks just beneath the door.

A warm orange hue spilled from those cracks, reminiscent of candlelight. He encroached, socks dragging across the worn wood. When he reached the door, he pressed his ear to the splintered surface. A few errant shards of wood bit into his ear, but he didn't flinch. Instead, he listened to the creak of the bed's headboard, the rhythm repeating: soft, then sharp, then still. The shared breaths of two people tangled in something far beyond sleep, their moans filling the brief empty spaces between movements.

A twitch pulled at his smile. He wasn't here for simple pleasure. He was auditing loyalties, ensuring the fly was trapped in the spider's web.

Beyond the door, Derewin sat on the edge of the bed, shirt half-undone, his back slouched. Ravenna stood across from him, slowly pulling up her stockings. Neither spoke; some things were best left unsaid.

Other things are best left said, Derewin thought.

"Why do we still do this?" he muttered. "Doesn't it feel... awkward?"

Ravenna simply smoothed her skirt with both hands and walked to the door. Before opening it, she glanced back. "You knew what this was," she said flatly. "And you know who's always listening."

He grimaced. The thought of Corvin listening through the door churned his stomach, threatening to empty its contents. Yet Ravenna's pull remained irresistible. He'd been caught in her web from the start, now too stuck to ever wriggle free. She had lured him in long ago; made promises she never intended to keep. Desire kept him close; leverage kept him obedient.

She pulled the door open. Corvin stood waiting, arms crossed, his face a mask of practiced joy.

"All done?" he asked with a sneer.

Derewin met his gaze for a half-second, then turned away. The shame had long since soured into something else, resentment maybe... or even grief.

On the wall beside the bed hung a crooked framed photograph; it was of Ravenna, Corvin, Lyra, and Anastasia. Derewin remembered that day vividly; he'd taken the photo himself. He recalled how Corvin had puppeteered the girls into position, how Ravenna had barked for their smiles before brandishing her discipline device as *encouragement.* Anastasia had grinned too wide, disturbingly so. Lyra hadn't smiled at all, even under Corvin's control and the sting of her mother's pole arm striking at her sides.

Derewin's own reflection, barely visible in the photo's glass, looked more like a ghost than a man. His skin had grown pale, his hair fallen out in clumps, and the heavy droop beneath his eyes sagged under the weight of painful years dragging on.

As Ravenna made a final pass by him, she dragged her knuckles along the wall, clipping the crooked frame. It rocked, slipped, and crashed to the floor. Shards of glass poked at his feet.

He stared down at the shattered image. He had traded everything for this illusion. He'd betrayed his own family in Valspire: Leora, Elyra, Tavian, and even himself.

He wondered:

If Lyra ever reached his old palace; if she'd seen Elyra and the others he once knew so well.

If she'd listened to his warnings, if she'd uncovered the truth behind her mother's lies.

If Anastasia was still alive.

If Valspire would ever take him back.

If Tavian would remember him.

If forgiveness was ever possible.

And he thought of Leora... why she had to die.

And why he had to be the one to kill her.

She stood in her garden of cotton roses, their white blossoms swaying in the breeze that swept in from the cliffs. Leora moved purposefully between them, watering each by hand, her touch tender and reverent. And yet, as always, the dark figure that trailed her followed just close enough to undo everything. Whenever its hand fell, the petals wilted and blackened, her careful work dissolved into futility.

"Please stop touching them," she said. Her voice was calm yet tired, pleading for an end to this tireless cycle.

The shadow didn't respond. It never did. Every time she restored a flower, it withered again beneath its reach, crumbling to ash. This cycle had repeated for so long that she lost count. Days blurred into years, perhaps decades. Time had no meaning here, only the constant pattern of bloom and decay.

Luna visited occasionally. Always smiling, always cryptic, never answering Leora's questions. Conversations drifted toward meaningless distractions: the weather, flower types, memories from long ago, but never toward what mattered.

"When do I leave this place? What comes next?" Leora would ask.

Luna would smile as if she hadn't heard. "These blooms are coming in nicely, don't you think?"

Leora would say nothing. She had grown weary of directionless small talk.

This place, what Luna had called the *Waiting Room,* was strange. Each day, a new image materialized before Leora like a floating portrait:

frozen scenes, some vaguely familiar, others utterly foreign. They were glimpses of places across the world; moments from the past, the present, and perhaps even the future.

Yesterday, it depicted an abandoned hospital in Ashford, where she could've sworn she saw Tavian and Aria wandering through its halls. A week ago, it depicted the gates of Valspire, where two girls and a fluffy white dog stood, peering through the cracks in the wall. Today, it revealed a small roadside town—an Erreeckan ruin. Corpses littered the sidewalks, and the buildings leaned at broken angles. There were no signs of life, only the occasional flower with burned petals and severed stems.

As always, when she moved closer to the image, it drifted back just out of reach. She longed to touch it, to press her fingers against the surface and feel what secrets it might hold.

But this time was different.

For the first time, the shadowed silhouette behind her moved toward the image. It stepped forward, and to Leora's astonishment, its hand actually touched the painted surface. The scene rippled, like a finger dipping into still water. Leora gasped as the ripples widened, tearing the painting open like paper splitting along a seam. The shadow slipped through, and the surface puckered behind it, no longer a portrait but a doorway.

By the time she reached the torn edge, the figure was already inside, walking the ruined streets below. From her vantage point, it looked as though she were watching from above, like a god looking down upon a forgotten world.

She tried to touch it, her hand finally passing through. Heat blasted up her arm, like pressing into the mouth of a furnace. Her heart pounded, but she didn't hesitate. She pushed forward—one foot, then the other—until the world consumed her whole.

She found herself standing in the street, surrounded by the wreckage. She hacked up a cough, a spray of thick green mucus splattered across the stiffened arm of a corpse at her feet. The air was dense and syrupy, each breath sticking to the lining of her lungs. Above, the sky burned a luminous crimson, as if it bled, much like the bodies below her. She clutched her chest, breathing grew harder with every gasp.

Ahead, the shadow walked slowly through the devastation.

Each step Leora took crushed brittle limbs underfoot. Bones snapped like twigs. She tried not to look down, but whenever she lifted her head, she lost her footing. The many faces of Erreeckans stared up at her in judgement, condemning her for sins she'd yet to atone for.

To her left: the remains of a playground. A swing set bent at an unusual angle, one chain snapped, the other still swaying. To her right: a shattered liquor store. Inside, two men laughed like lunatics, slamming bottles against shelves and at each other.

"Excuse me!" Leora called out. "Can you help me?"

No response.

"Please, I'm trying to—"

Their laughter didn't stop. One of the men lifted a severed Erreeckan head and flipped it over, pouring liquor into the hollow where the neck had once connected.

"To Leora, queen of all queens!" they cheered in unison, mock-saluting before sharing drinks from the skull. "Though she's gone, we still prevail. Onto the next!"

She spent not a second longer with them, quickening her pace, moving farther up the street toward the shadow.

She reached the entrance of an inn marked by the word *Gheget* etched across the front, its structure appearing to be carved from petrified chitin. The building reminded her of an old accordion, bent sideways and gathering dust. She stepped on another body just outside the door and stopped.

"*Favite yoyoti ema!*" the Erreeckan groaned, Leora's shoe printed across his face.

She jolted back in fear. "Why would I help you?" she muttered, trying to ignore the guilt knotting in her gut. She wiped the creature's blood from the bottoms of her shoes, smearing it across the pavement.

The man struggled to sit up, he wore a bright silver chain with a sizable opal set at its center, engraved with the letters "RC".

"*Rothanna rea iuo beneve? Iour benieres awesterry lvoioa nebes lla!*" he pointed at her with disgust. "Leora... Mariella's Executioner."

She stopped cleaning her shoes. Her foot froze mid-wipe, leaving a thin trail of blood from the toe.

She hadn't heard that name in years, *Mariella's Executioner*. A name used by her victims. A name ingrained into the minds of the Erreeckans.

Her collected facade began to crack, a small twitch forming at the corner of her left eye. "*Meh grandineh garet enna ghiva, tuve no quitalen iou lla*."

The man longingly looked down at the corpses beside him—his wife and his daughter, both mangled heaps of limbs and lost memories. Though gone, their eyes remained open, still staring at the bleeding sky.

He kissed his daughter's forehead. "It's about time, Rena. I'll be with you soon, along with the rest of the Carscells family... as I promised."

Leora was taken aback. "How can you speak my language?"

He shifted around, quietly unsheathing a dagger from his wife's side, moving with enough subtlety that Leora wouldn't notice.

"Never once did you try to understand us," he said. "Your wickedness cost us everything. You're just another tyrant, making us your scapegoat. Led by your villainous goddess. If I can't stop you here, someone will. The least I could do is try. *Burnea enna Hellios*."

He turned and hurled the dagger.

She had no time to react. It flew like lightning, slamming straight into her eye, yet passing clean through.

There was no pain, no impact, no sudden dark. She reached up, expecting blood pooling at her cheek, but found nothing. No wound.

The man folded into his wife's corpse, sobbing at his failed attempt. He dreamed of this moment, of standing before Leora and ending his people's plight. But instead, he was soon to become another casualty, another forgotten name buried beneath the growing, nameless body count. Another statistic on the evening broadcast, just a number, no longer a man.

The figure Leora had followed into the painting lingered in the background throughout this scene, now walking over and kneeling beside the defeated Erreeckan.

For the first time, it spoke.

"What is your name?"

The Erreeckan looked into its eyes. He noticed someone familiar in its shadowed reflection, someone he'd met once before, back at the inn, while working the front desk. He tried to smile through the tears.

"It's Radvisha," he said. "Please... don't let the memory of us die with her."

The shadow touched Radvisha's forehead and nodded.

Pieces of Radvisha's body began to dissolve into light. He reached out to grab the shadow's hand. "Funny you'd be the one to finish this. Though now that I see you clearly... it's strange I didn't realize it before, you look an awful lot like Leora—"

When the last fragment of Radvisha rose skyward and dissipated into the clouds, the shadow turned to face Leora. Fury was written all over its form, its fists were clenched, stance rigid, anger burning beneath the melancholy of the farewell.

Leora backed away and closed her eyes. "Please," she begged, covering her face with both hands. "I don't understand. Tell me what this is. Tell me what you want."

But the shadow didn't strike, nor did it speak.

Instead, the air shifted from oppressive humidity to a cool, cleansing breeze. The sky began to crack like broken glass, revealing slivers of gray seeping through. Then came the whispers, spoken like soft rumors, speaking of the truth yet to come.

She understood it then—for a split second, that this wasn't a dream nor some kind of hallucination. It was a realm built to mirror her choices, to ensnare her in moments long forgotten or not yet lived. A place Luna had called the *Waiting Room*, where souls weren't merely kept, but judged. Here, the dead could be touched but never torn; remembered pain could no longer wound flesh that no longer was.

Through the narrow slits between her fingers, she looked toward the shadow. Parts of its darkness were peeling away, flaking like dead skin.

What remained was Tavian, almost Tavian, hidden beneath leftover pieces of obscured shadow. This was not the boy that existed now, but a version of the boy who had once stayed at Radvisha's inn; the boy who had watched and listened to their plight, who had once frowned at the same man now faded into light. A version of Tavian who had, somehow, learned to help others move on... and in doing so, learned to let go.

"Is this what you wanted me to see?" she cried. "The ones I killed? The ones I forgot? Tavian... what is going on?"

The Erreeckan ruin collapsed inward, buildings folding in on themselves like paper origami. She squeezed her eyes shut, cowering away from Tavian and the destructive force of change itself. She screamed as shards of debris brushed her skin, and she prayed her second death would come quickly.

But when she opened her eyes again, she was back in the garden.

The cliffside. The cotton roses. The silence.

The painted image of the ruined city floated before her again, whole and untouched. She put a hand toward it, but as before, it slid just out of reach.

She sank down into the field of her precious flowers, looking up at the bleak, grey sky.

She had always longed for peace, but now that it had come, why did it feel so hollow?

Aria looked out the window at Tavian, who trained diligently with Maeve in the courtyard below. Though his movements still carried signs of strain, each day brought more progress; his strikes sharper, his control more focused. She felt a small sense of pride while watching him train, the kind that almost felt maternal, with quiet reassurance that staying had been the right choice.

But then she remembered his eyes.

There was little light to be found in them, no trace of the boy she'd once known. Something colder had settled in, taking root and threading into his being.

Aria had to turn away; she couldn't bear to watch her past love become something he wasn't. Leaving the hallway window behind, she wandered through the many floors of the hospital. She needed space to think, something to quiet the noise, to still the intrusive thoughts that refused to budge.

Near the front reception stood a rusty door marked *Hospital Staff*

Only. She pressed the release button... nothing. After a brief delay, the mechanism whined like a dying beast. With a grunt, she threw her shoulder into it, and the door crashed open, hinges splintering as dust billowed around her.

Inside, the hallway glowed bright as if staff still resided in this section. Faded plaques labeled various rooms, their lettering half-erased by time, but one door caught her attention.

Medical Records.

Driven by morbid curiosity, she entered. The room was in disarray, with tall filing cabinets looming over half-raided papers strewn like dead leaves across the floor. By the look of it, someone had torn through in a hurry to clear everything out. Overhead, a flickering light pulsed with strobes of artificial white light, dizzying and nauseating when trying to focus on one spot for too long. She flipped the switch, letting the calmer light from the hallway spill in.

She skimmed through the remaining files, rifling over brittle folders that crumbled to the touch. Most of the records were illegible, whether bloodstained, torn, or rotted by time. Still, a few entries stood out.

One detailed a man suffering from Fatal Familial Insomnia, slipping into deep psychosis before violently attacking the attending physicians, convinced they were plotting to kill him.

Another told of a seventeen-year-old girl who'd been bitten by a marrow rat. Her bones had begun to deteriorate within hours, leaving her unable to move.

Patient no longer able to feed herself. IV and feeding tube administered, the report read. The final line was barely legible: *Deceased on—*

Then, at the very bottom of the drawer jammed off its rails, a folder lay sealed in plastic. It had been archived, bagged, and tagged for litigation. Someone had written *DO NOT DESTROY* across the folder's tab.

Aria read the name, and for a moment, forgot how to breathe.

Patient Name: *Violet Valcrest*

Age: *30*

Weight: *120 lb*

BP: *90/60*

HR: *43*

Initial Observations: *Pale skin, bradycardia, difficulty breathing, bruising and bleeding along the fingers and other extremities.*

Background: *Arrived at approximately 3:00 a.m. with critically low blood pressure and heart rate. Chief complaint— chest pain and shortness of breath. Collapsed during transport.*

Husband: *Finnian Valcrest.*

Child: *Aria Valcrest. Traces of necromantic energy detected in blood samples. Exposure from the North suspected—patients believed to have originated from Tenebral.*

The room spun. Her stomach turned upside down, her heartbeat slammed against her ribs.

The Mycordians, she recalled the name they'd given her, Valcrest—the last human they'd seen pass through—Violet Valcrest.

The papers slipped from her loosened grasp as she stumbled backwards out of the room and raced to the nearest bathroom. She gripped the sink for balance, flipping her shaky hands over and back. She checked her eyes, her skin, her teeth. Everything looked normal, yet something felt wrong, like the truth she'd read had stirred something awake within her.

She splashed cold water on her face. Her reflection warped in the running stream.

Violet? That can't be her. I'm not from Tenebral. I'm not a Necromite.

She barely made it to the toilet before vomiting, bile painting the cracked tiles where her knees dug in. Sweat drenched through her shirt. Her arms throbbed; her knees burned from their friction with the floor.

Finnian? My father? No... it's a mistake. It has to be. Valcrest is a common name. Aria isn't unusual either. It's someone else.

But the panic kept climbing upward, even against all rationalization, rising like a scream she couldn't contain.

Then something inside her snapped for good; a kinked hose finally bursting.

A bright green mist snuck out of her eyes, her ears, the creases of her palms, the backs of her legs. Her veins distended, ballooning beneath her skin. Blood rushed in a tidal force through every limb, her muscles locking into steel-hard contractions.

Then came a knock at the stall door. She held her breath, forcing herself into silence, the only composure she could manage.

Another knock, louder. She tried to hold out, but her stomach betrayed her. Another fresh heave wracked her.

"Aria! Open up!" The voice sounded distant, even though it was near, but she couldn't hear over her heaving bouts.

Her strength gave way. She slumped sideways, her body striking the tile with a sudden smack. She could only see the bottoms of Tavian's shoes beneath the stall door before the world dimmed, everything cutting to black.

She woke to the cool press of a damp cloth resting against her forehead. Tavian leaned over her, his face taut between panic and concentration as he dabbed away the sweat beading at her skin.

"Hold on," he said, guiding her head back down to the pillow when she tried to lift it. "Just take a minute. You're okay."

Aria blinked, her limbs leaden, her head swimming with disorientation. She tried to sit up again, but her muscles protested in dull aches.

"Gods, I'm burning," she whispered with a raw voice. "I feel like I'm on fire."

He scanned the room for anything that might help. "There's no fan in here. Let me get these covers off."

He peeled back the sheets, revealing the sheen of sweat coating her skin. Her shirt clung to her body. She tugged at it weakly, frustration breaking through the haze.

"Help me get this off. I can't take it anymore."

Tavian froze. "I—uh—only if you're sure. I don't want to—"

"Don't be awkward," she gasped, fighting for a fresh breath. "Just help."

Trying to avert his gaze, he carefully lifted the drenched fabric over her head and tossed it aside. Flustered, he turned his back to her and squeezed his eyes shut.

"Okay. You're good. Anything else?"

"You're still being weird."

"I'm trying my best!"

"Look," she said, her voice suddenly hardening. "I need you to check if there's something wrong. My chest feels like it's about to burst."

Tavian peeked over his shoulder with the coolest composure he could muster. But what he saw made him flinch.

Thick, black veins had risen across Aria's chest, pulsing with an abnormal force. They curled across her skin like roots alive with power; he could feel them radiating even from where he stood. Her heart thudded visibly beneath the web of vessels, expanding and contracting every three beats.

"Oh gods..." he murmured, reaching for one of the veins.

Before his fingers could graze her skin, Aria's hand snapped up on reflex, slashing across his palm. Her nails were like sharpened steel, tearing into skin so fast it barely registered.

Tavian yelped and stumbled back, clutching his bleeding hand.

"I'm sorry!" Aria cried. "I didn't mean to... I just... My body moved on its own!"

"It's fine," Tavian said, wincing. He hovered his uninjured hand over the new wound, healing energy spilling from his palm in a warm glow. The wound sealed over within seconds, leaving only a thin trace of scar behind. "What happened to you? Are you sick? We need to get you help."

She let her head fall back onto the pillow. Her voice came out hoarse. "I'm not sick. It was from the vomiting earlier, now I'm probably just dehydrated. That's all."

Tavian didn't look convinced. Hard to, when distended black veins had just stared him down and split open his hand.

He sat beside her, his fingers brushing over hers, cautious now; ready if she lashed out again. "You scared me. When I found you on that floor, I thought—" He paused. "Does this have something to do with those patient records you were looking through?"

How did he know?

Aria opened her mouth. She wanted to tell him about Violet Valcrest, the possibility—no, the *truth*—of where she came from.

But when she looked at Tavian, his eyes had softened, carrying that same warmth she'd grown to love back in Valspire.

She couldn't do it. Not now. Not when her body felt foreign and the possibility of necromancy was now becoming a reality.

Did *she* still want Leora back? Was that even the right choice anymore? Or was she staying with Tavian out of comfort, clinging to the one steady thing left, even if his dream was impossible... a mercy she couldn't provide him?

"No," she lied. "It's just the stress. Everything's been too much. I was just trying to clear my head... needed something new to read."

"All right," he said, his voice heavily uncertain. "Then if it was just stress... it won't happen again, right?"

She nodded, hating how easy the lie slipped from her tongue. Tavian held her gaze for a second too long, as if waiting for the truth to surface on its own. It never did.

"... Then please, take it easy and rest. I'll handle things for a while, and I'll find someone who can take a look at you."

"Tavian..." she whispered, squeezing his hand. "Be careful. I don't trust these people, especially Maeve."

"Yeah," he said with a tired smirk. "Neither do I. But I'm getting closer. Soon, we won't have to hope for Mom back, she'll be right here with us."

She released his hand reluctantly, her fingers twitching with residual tension. "I'll catch up with you later."

Tavian stood, giving her one last worried glance before slipping out and closing the door behind him.

Aria stared up at the ceiling, the wobbling fan above pushing out troubled bursts of warm air across her sweaty brow. Her body was already beginning to pulse again with that same restless sensation from the bathroom, her veins trying to bloat and rise in pressure.

Aria exhaled a single heavy breath, one hard push through her nose, loosening the taut grip she kept on the volatile power simmering inside. She had been suppressing it, hiding it from Tavian. But now it erupted, spilling outward in waves—green energy blooming beneath her flesh, pooling across the floor like grassy ink. Her body convulsed, overtaken by the strength she could barely contain.

She clamped her jaw shut, fingers digging into the mattress, willing herself to resist the full flood.

Then came the sounds of scurrying footsteps beyond the door. It creaked open, but this time it wasn't Tavian.

Leather boots struck the floor with purposeful weight, kicking up flecks of dust. Maeve entered, his shadow blanketing her in absence of the ones Tavian had removed.

Maeve studied the network of veins mapping Aria's form. The closer he stepped, the more turbulent they palpitated, beating to a rhythm neither of them could hear; yet both could feel.

Aria's chest lifted, drawn by something in his presence. It tugged at her like being caught in a heavy current; a tether linking the two in subtle communion.

He crouched beside her, hovering a hand above her stomach. A faint orange mist escaped from his fingertips and flowed into her. It traveled through her bloodstream, flashes of smoldering heat mixed with stinging cold.

His power fanned the flames already burning, tuning it with a cruel hand of a master at work. The change was immediate. The veins expanded even more-so, straining until it felt like her skin was ready to tear apart. Then, like obeying a command, they relaxed. Her fever broke. The nausea fell away. Her muscles loosened; her mind, once clouded by panic and denial, went crystal-clear.

She had never felt stronger.

Maeve leaned in, satisfied beyond what he'd hoped for. "I knew you two were worth the trouble," he whispered. "Welcome to your new life, Aria. I'm glad I could be the one to introduce you."

He stood up, laughing to himself, giddy with some private joke only he understood. "I won't tell Tavian... I do love the suspense of it all."

He waved another man into the room who lingered in the doorway like a ghost. "Get her up and ready. We'll need to set a meeting to discuss next steps for her." Maeve looked back for only a moment before turning on his heel and leaving.

The man who entered was short and rail-thin, his face obscured behind a matted mask with rough holes cut for where the eyes and lips belonged. "Get up," he grunted, unsheathing a stubby sword with edges dulled by frequent use. "You heard Maeve."

Aria tried to rise, but her balance faltered. Her legs floundered, and she hit the floor. The man didn't move to help, he only tilted his head, studying her like a broken toy.

"I've seen corpses with more grace," he said, stepping closer. He crouched low, his eyes investigating her protruding veins.

"Maeve should've left you where he found you," he said. "What's so special about you, anyway?"

His hand moved fast toward her shoulders with bruising force, gripping them tight. He leaned in closer until she could smell the sour tang from his breath.

"You hear me, girl?"

She didn't answer. The veins had decided to resurface.

The man yanked her up, but her body refused to move, anchored to the floor like a statue clamped in iron.

"Move it! Don't make me—"

And then it happened. Slick viscera hit the floor with a plop.

He looked down to see the broad blade—deep maroon, not metal but hardened blood—jutting from Aria's abdomen, skewering him clean through like a kabob.

His mouth fell open. A thin stream of red trickled out, followed by a wet cough that splattered specks of blood across Aria's face. Then his body sagged forward, impaled on the weapon still connected to her.

As he went limp, the blade from her abdomen dissolved, melting back into her as if it never had existed. The corpse dropped onto her, weighing her down. She shoved him off with the last of her strength and remained lying on the floor.

Her eyes stayed open. Tears pooled.

Above her, the slick ceiling tiles reflected her image. She could see her bare skin, streaked with blood and ugly power. Her fingers brushed along the ridged veins on her torso, moving like a maze across her clavicle to sternum, down to her naval.

And she understood with a clarity that emptied her, that nothing would ever be the same again.

She was no longer just a girl from Valspire; she had been awakened —and the truth of it repulsed her.

Something in Orin's side flared... a sharp, burning twist that forced his hands to his ribs. He pressed his palm against the ache. A warning maybe. An omen.

Aria was getting close to the truth, he was sure of it.

He'd always known she would uncover it eventually, but he'd hoped to be there when it happened. That he'd have the chance to explain, to soften the blow before it shattered her.

He'd told himself the tracks were covered. There were no names, no records, nothing traceable that could lead her on. Only that single note the Mycordians had slipped her, the one he'd prayed she'd forget. But prayers didn't carry much weight anymore.

He reclined the driver's seat of the parked car, idling outside the gates of the royal palace in Aipiron. While Vid tried to talk his way past the guards, Orin let his eyes drift shut. Sleep found him quickly. So did the memories.

Orin was back in Valspire. Younger, lighter by a far margin. The sun held high in an unbroken blue sky. He stood in the East Garden with Gareth, nearest the cotton roses Leora had once tended to so diligently.

Gareth stood tall—regal, almost—his posture effortless even in casual conversation. His features were sharp, idealized; like a statue chiseled from marble by Mariella herself. He was everything Orin wasn't: eloquent, graceful, unflinchingly heroic. The kind of man others followed without question.

And Orin had always followed.

"Why the long face?" Gareth asked, clapping a strong hand on Orin. "Something troubling you on this fine day?"

"It's nothin' for you to fret about," Orin muttered, eyes cast toward Leora.

She was humming a tune, watering each flower with precise care, dressed in a gown that shimmered in shades of red, pink, and white. She matched the roses, as she always did.

"You've been distant lately," Gareth said. "If we're friends, treat me like one."

Orin swallowed, not taking much convincing before the words tumbled out. "What's wrong with me? I'm thirty-one, and I've got nothin' to show for it. You've got a wife, a newborn, a whole kingdom lookin' to you for direction. I'm just… orbiting your world."

Gareth's demeanor shifted. The warmth disappearing as fast as Orin's confession ended.

"Is that what you want? *My* life?"

"Well… yes. Why wouldn't I?"

Gareth turned to the garden. Leora glanced up at him and smiled. He smiled back with a carefully constructed expression, then kissed his palm and mimed tossing it to her. She pretended to catch it, pressing the invisible kiss to her lips.

Quietly, he said, "Do you know how many had to die to give me all this? How many more were exiled to be killed?"

Orin stood still. "What?"

Gareth's gaze never left the garden, paying especially close attention to the mounds of earth beneath the roses.

"Leora's flowers grow on graves," he murmured. "Our peace was purchased with exile, execution, and forced subservience. How many more must vanish so our children can run barefoot on clean grass, stomping upon the buried bodies that fodder our garden?"

"You're startin' to sound like one of them," Orin said carefully. "The ones we let go. You know there was a reason for that… a purpose for all of this."

Gareth turned to him. The light had left his face, replaced by something truer. His mask had slipped, and what stood before Orin was no longer a hero of Valspire, but a man who pitied their enemies.

"If peace demands blood," he asked, "is it peace at all?"

He stepped closer—close enough that, if he wanted, could seize Orin and add him to the garden's collection. "Have you ever watched someone die? Not in battle. I mean *really* die. A mother clinging to her daughter's corpse, begging the heavens while someone in Mariella's robes deems it righteous?"

Orin backed away, his hand finding the hilt of his axe.

Gareth followed, voice low. "Have you ever told a family their child's death was necessary, and watched their faith die before your very eyes?"

He grabbed Orin's face and forced him to look toward Leora.

"Look closely, Orin. *That's* the face of a killer. A quiet one. A devout one. The kind her own people don't fear because they believe she's saving them. But who's there to save the Necromites? Who saves the Erreeckans?"

Orin's voice cracked. "I... I don't know."

"There's no one left to speak for them. Only us, the privileged few, standing behind the barrel of the gun, pretending our finger isn't on the trigger. While the ones we claim need salvation wait on the other side, bracing for the bullet."

The sky above them cracked with a sound like breaking bones as Gareth continued.

"We are the fortunate ones, aren't we, Orin? The fortunate son's of Mariella, ordered to purge all those who stand in our way?"

The sky cracked once more, another fracture in the heavens, and a strange knocking sound resonated through the courtyard. It was loud, demanding to be heard.

"Orin!" a voice bellowed, booming across the clouds.

Birds scattered from the tree tops as rain began to fall.

"Orin!" it came again, pulling his focus upward, until the dream started to splinter apart.

He jerked awake in the driver's seat. Vid was outside, pounding on the passenger window. Orin fumbled with the lock until he could grasp it firm. Vid climbed in, rain dripping from his hair.

"Gods, you were out like a corpse," Vid said. "You all right?"

Orin wiped the warm sweat from his face. "Yeah. Just some rough dreams."

"Any luck?" Orin asked quickly, eager to change the subject.

"No. Guards wouldn't let me near her, but there's an inn close by. I'll try again tomorrow. You can head off if you need to, I won't make you wait around."

Orin looked toward the west, where distant, snow-capped mountains pierced into the horizon.

Tenebral.

His final destination.

The place where the truth waited, and where the friend he once knew had finally pulled the trigger.

CHAPTER EIGHTEEN
WHAT HIDES BENEATH THE EYES

> "Better not die on me, Lyra. We still have a deal to take down Tenebral. I'll handle the Riftbound Order in the meantime.
>
> ~Seraphina Trubbman

"You're doing well, Tavian."

The voice was guiding him. "We must preserve what remains of necromancy. Meet me in Traegos. We must continue forward at once."

The phrase played in Tavian's mind, searing itself into memory like a brand. As he stirred awake, a sharp throb in his lower back reminded him of the scar—deeper now, more pronounced than ever before. Yet it no longer troubled him the way it once had. Not since he'd spent more time around Maeve.

Traegos.

Was it another dream or a directive? Who was this voice that kept invading his sleep, dropping riddles like seeds in his thoughts? Tavian couldn't decide if it was a string of lucid dreams, madness, or something more. But it felt urgent. A summons.

As he got up and returned to his usual training spot, he pulled Maeve aside.

"Maeve," he began, voice hushed, "what do you know about a place called Traegos?"

Maeve paused, brow furrowing. "Who told *you* of that place?"

Tavian sighed. "You'll think I've lost it, but I've been hearing things... ever since I left Valspire. Dreams... voices maybe? A man keeps calling to me, and now wants me there. He says it's about necromancy. And there's this scar..."

He turned and lifted his shirt, exposing the zigzagged line that ran the length of his spine. It was thick and gnarled, a fleshy channel that seemed to throb like something alive moved just beneath the skin, bending through each vein in his body.

Maeve's eyes doubled in size. His usual grin began to expand, uncontainable.

"Why are you smiling like that?"

Maeve reached out toward the scar. The moment his skin made contact, the world warped. Maeve's body bucked as if yanked through a vacuum. Space folded, tearing him apart like meat through a grinder, then stitched back together in the center of a circular chamber, suspended in a half-lit smog. Beneath his feet, the floor squelched with a strange, meaty texture that stuck to his boots.

Before him stood a man, if he could still be called that. Body decrepit, half-rotten, suspended somewhere between life and death, limbs wrapped in threads that barely hid the hideousness. A clock's tick kept beating with the pace of his heart.

"I need the boy, now." The man rasped. "Your time is through."

Maeve dropped to one knee. "Of course. I would never defy the will of the Riftbound Order. Still, he and I struck a deal. I must see it through."

The withered man advanced, each step sounding mushy and gooey, dead skin sticking to the surface and peeling off his sole. He reached out and touched Maeve's forehead. A fresh scar sizzled into place, smoking like the tip of a used barrel.

"He will fulfill both purposes," the man said. "But send him quickly. Lyra and Anastasia can no longer be trusted. They must be disposed of."

Maeve bowed deeper, lowering himself to the floor. "As you wish, Eldric."

With a flick of the Eldric's decaying finger, the scar on Maeve's forehead ignited. In an instant, he was sucked backward, torn through space once more and spat back out into reality, fingers still pressed against Tavian's scar. The scar slid away from his fingers like a closing door, denying reentry.

Tavian pulled away. "Maeve? What happened?"

Maeve straightened up. "Traegos," he said, voice steady now. "That's where you must go."

"So it is real?"

"Yes, very much so." Maeve turned to look across his assembled horde, taking inventory of his troops, the restless undead scattered across the courtyard. Men and women lounged in the ruins, gnawing bones, cracking joints between their teeth. He pointed to one and let out a sharp whistle.

A meek woman shuffled over, her face hidden beneath a hood. She refused to meet anyone's eyes, her fingers fidgeting against the hem of her coat.

Maeve scratched his chin. "This is... tell me your name again?"

The woman kept her gaze to the dirt. "Aidra," she murmured.

"Right. Aidra will take you to Traegos. She used to be an adventurer of sorts, so she will guide you. And I trust she'll come back to me afterward... isn't that right?"

She hastily nodded.

Tavian stepped forward, offering his hand. "It's nice to meet you, Aidra. I'm Tavian. I'll introduce you to Aria and Cassius too."

She glanced up at him. His face, bright with sincerity, caught her off guard. In this grim place, he looked entirely out of place: too kind, too warm. And somehow... familiar.

Images flashed in her mind: a boy from long ago, laughing as he ran with a basket full of mushrooms, now reduced to ash in memory. And an older gentleman, his arm around her waist, looking at her with lips that called her name. He fidgeted with a necklace, one that held an old photo of her.

She couldn't remember their names, but something about Tavian felt like remembering home.

With the focus of someone desperate to master an art too soon, Lyra dabbed the brush against her skin. The foundation smeared unevenly—patchy, streaked, far from blended. With a frustrated huff, she hurled the brush at the floor. It snapped in two on impact, joining a small graveyard of frayed bristles and broken handles in the bathroom corner.

She grabbed the bottle of makeup remover and scrubbed at her face with excessive force, so hard that fresh rashes flared up across her already irritated skin. Her reflection looked blotchy, red, and exhausted. Still, she reached for another brush and tried again.

The bathroom door opened. Anastasia stepped inside.

"You've been in here forever," she said. "Are you okay?"

Lyra didn't answer. She was laser-focused on the screen propped up against the mirror, where a makeup tutorial played on loop, *How to Apply Foundation: The Basics*. The peppy voice of the instructor repeated the same two-minute segment again and again, each attempt ending just like the last.

Anastasia approached and touched Lyra's leg.

Lyra flinched. The brush flew from her hand and clattered into the sink.

"You've got to stop coming in unannounced," she snapped, pausing the video. "What's wrong?"

"I was asking you that. What are you doing? Is there another fancy dinner?"

Lyra turned back toward the mirror. The red splotches were impossible to ignore. She touched her cheek then winced at the sting.

"No," she said. "I just wanted to try something new. Doesn't matter. I give up anyway."

Anastasia's lips curved. "Rowan asked me what kinds of things you like for your birthday."

Lyra's head whipped around. A flicker of surprise crossed her face, followed by a shy smile. "What? Why would he ask that? What did you tell him?"

"I'm not telling!" Anastasia giggled, dashing for the door.

"Hey, wait!" Lyra chased in pursuit. "Get back here!"

Every time she caught Anastasia's arm, the girl slipped free again. Cloud, ecstatic from the havoc, joined the chase, barking, skidding, and knocking trinkets from the shelves as the living room devolved into playful disorder.

Rowan emerged from his room, rubbing sleep from his eyes. "What in the hells is going on? Can't I sleep past nine?"

No one heard him. The noise had claimed the room. With a resigned sigh, he grabbed his recorder and started filming. The sisters darting from couch to couch, Cloud weaving between them, furniture teetering precariously with each collision.

Lyra caught sight of him, her laughter faltering. She turned to face away, cheeks flushed. Possibly from the remnants of failed makeup removal.

"Put that away! Don't record me like this. My face looks awful—"

Cloud barreled into her legs, knocking her flat to the floor with a yelp. Rowan doubled over in laughter, nearly dropping the recorder. Anastasia kept running laps, oblivious to what went on behind her.

"This is perfect," he managed between laughs. "Keep it going!"

The floor trembled for just a moment, subtle at first, but enough to send paintings crashing from walls, their frames shattering against the hardwood with a cascade of glass and splinters. A few ornate vases toppled, one missing Anastasia by inches as she ran her loops. Cloud barked wildly now, not from excitement but fear, ears prickled stiff.

"What was that?" Anastasia asked.

"It should be fine," Rowan answered. "I think."

BOOM.

A second crash, louder this time.

Their entire suite tilted, gravity skewing sideways. They stumbled left, thrown off balance by the shifting floor.

"We need to leave." Rowan tossed the recorder onto the couch. It kept recording.

CRACK.

The walls split at the seams, drifting apart and hanging impossibly in the air. Rowan grabbed Anastasia by the arm and pulled her in close as debris crashed around them. Lyra followed their escape, shielding her face as they sprinted down the spiral staircase into the main chamber of the palace.

What awaited them was ruin.

The grand hall was collapsing. Its once-elegant architecture was reduced to cracked marble and statues turned to rubble. Debris rained from above. The roof had torn open, exposing an early morning sky. Sunlight poured in through the breach, catching on the smears of blood that streaked the once-immaculate carpet. Shattered stained glass crunched under their feet as they pressed forward, dust swirling in the air, constricting their throats, obscuring full view of the scene.

At the center of the destruction, near her fractured throne, knelt Seraphina. Her blonde hair, now streaked darker with signs of age, whipped round her face in the rising wind. Her silver eyes blazed brighter than the light pouring in from above. The calm, porcelain mask she once wore went missing. In its place was someone alive with passionate, unabated fury.

Beside her lay a boy, no older than twenty-three, slumped and bleeding profusely onto the ornate rug they'd only just cleaned. The blood spread fast, far too rapid to patch.

Opposite Seraphina stood a ring of hooded figures, watching carefully, weapons at the ready—except for the one at the front, who held nothing in his hands.

Rowan darted to the bleeding boy and rolled him onto his back. A sword protruded from the youth's abdomen; blood soaked through his clothes. Rowan's palms went slick as he tried to lift him.

"Put him down." Seraphina ordered.

"I'm trying to help—"

"Now." Her tone brooked no argument; he obeyed, lowering the boy back to the floor. He stepped away and melted into the edge of the group.

The hooded figures advanced with measured caution. Their leader pointed toward Lyra and Anastasia.

"The Riftbound Order has declared you traitors," he said. "Come with us for a fair trial, or suffer that boy's same fate."

Lyra grabbed her scythe, red spirals swirling and brewing like a storm. Her necromantic aura came through in steady waves. Anastasia didn't move, but the pressure around her became suffocating.

The hooded figures hesitated. A few stepped back. Rowan's hand went for his holster, one finger on the grip, another on the hammer.

Seraphina knelt beside the dying boy and whispered something to him. He blinked once, exhaled, then folded, eyes glazed in the quiet finality of end.

She remained kneeling, now looking up and locking eyes with Lyra. Tears fell freely down her face, darkening the pearl-white fabric of her dress.

"Help me," she whispered. "Lyra... he came back for me, and now he's already gone. I don't know if I can control myself."

Earlier that morning, before the blood and the screams, before Seraphina's loss of control—Vid had woken early.

Today was the day he'd been waiting for; another chance to see Seraphina. To tell her how he felt. To finally ask about the things he couldn't remember, the memories she might have taken from him.

He dressed with obsessive precision, checking his reflection repeatedly in the cracked mirror of the inn. Every stray hair was slicked down with spit; every invisible wrinkle smoothed flat with an iron; his body doused in cheap cologne he'd scavenged from a forgotten nightstand drawer. His fingers fumbled over the belt buckle, tightening it with a snap before he headed toward the palace.

As before, the guards stopped him before he could reach the palace steps. Not even his trademark juggling routine could win them over. One caught him by his collar, prematurely cutting the act short and hurling him back onto the dusty curb.

He adjusted his shirt and brushed off his sleeves as the morning sun climbed higher. That's when a blacked-out car rolled to a stop at the gates. The window buzzed down, revealing a familiar face. Agusto lounged in the back seat while small, shiny rocks orbited above his head.

"To what do we owe the pleasure of your return?" Agusto said, sliding over to make room.

Vid popped up and gave a dramatic bow.

The back door swung open. Vid hopped in, and it sealed behind him with a soft hiss.

Across from Agusto sat Baron, utterly absorbed in juggling the same set of polished stones Vid had once given him. The boy's concentration was fierce, fingers swift, moving in precise arcs. He'd improved a lot, surprisingly so, since their last encounter.

"Still at it, huh?" Vid grinned. "Careful. At this rate, you'll be stealing my job."

Baron looked up at the sound of the familiar voice. The stones slipped from his hands and clattered into his lap. In the next instant, he lunged, throwing his arms around Vid in a crushing hug.

Agusto chuckled. "He hasn't put those things down since you left. A real talent, that one."

"I can't believe it's you!" Baron beamed. "You really came back for us?"

Vid laughed, ruffling the boy's hair. "Of course I did. Had to make sure my protégé didn't forget who taught him everything. Thought I'd drop in for a few more lessons... if you're still up for it."

Baron scrambled back to his seat, gathering the stones like sacred relics, nodding so hard the car began to sway.

The car glided through the palace gates, a marvel to be seen in its own right. A long, polished stretch of obsidian and gold that circled around the entire structure. Guards parted without question, their puzzled glances following Vid as the vehicle passed... he gave them a small wave. The car came to a stop beside a massive crystal fountain, water arced high into the air before cascading around a statue of Mariella at the center.

"We'd love for you to stay awhile," Agusto said as he stepped out. "There are other guests here too, who are also friends of Seraphina's. I imagine she'll be thrilled to have you stay."

Vid flushed a shade too bright. "Friends," he muttered.

The palace doors swung open, blinding light spilling across his clothes. He raised a hand to his eyes as the interior revealed itself: gold-paneled walls, glittering chandeliers, towers of stained glass, marble columns nearly reaching the sky. The grandeur dwarfed even Valspire's royal halls. This was more than a palace, it was extravagance made divine.

Baron sprinted past. "I'll be upstairs! Come find me later!"

Agusto followed him leisurely, pausing to look back at Vid.

"Seraphina's likely in the main chamber, down that hall. Hard to miss it, just walk straight."

Vid nodded, though words failed him. His legs carried him forward through marbled corridors, past towering portraits and gilded archways that seemed to watch him as he passed. His palms were sweating. His heartbeat stumbled out of its usual rhythm, enough to make him wonder if he should see someone about that.

All right. Be cool.

He began to rehearse.

"Hi, it's good to see you again!"

Ugh, no.

"Hey, long time no see. You're still as beautiful as—"

Too much.

"Roses are red—"

Absolutely not.

He smacked his cheek. The sting kickstarted his thoughts, cutting through his nerves like a splash of ice water. His thoughts aligned, and in that moment he was reminded of the *other* reason he'd come. Not just to confess his feelings, but to uncover who Seraphina truly was.

He formed a bitter smile. "Maybe I should focus on her *eating my memories,*" he muttered. A pause. "And... also tell her I love her."

Better. Still needed finesse, though.

He'd reached the main chamber at last, walking for what felt like an hour down the same stretch of hallway. Large pillars extended so high he couldn't see where they ended. At the far end of the hall, a lone girl sat curled in a throne, meticulously filing her nails.

Vid stepped closer. But before he could say a word, a voice echoed from across the hall where she sat. "Dad, did you get the right crackers this time?"

Vid halted. "Uh—yes. I put them in the kitchen," he replied, imitating a deep voice.

Mr. Trubbman, perhaps. Not bad.

Seraphina moved on to another nail without looking up. "Odd. Last I checked, the kitchen door was behind me. How'd you manage that?"

Before Vid could scramble for a response, she lifted a manicured hand. An invisible force yanked him forward like a rag doll, hurling him down the chamber. His body jerked to a sudden halt a few feet from her throne, suspended midair by her grip.

"Tell me who you are before I kill you," she said evenly.

"Maybe look up from your nails first," he gasped through the binding force. "*Before* you kill me."

She sighed and rested one hand on the armrest, finally meeting his eyes.

She couldn't get the words out clearly. She paused while Vid continued to gasp for air.

"Vod?"

The invisible grip vanished and he dropped to the floor with a heavy thud.

"Vod!" she cried, rushing down the steps. "I'm so sorry! What the hells are you doing here?"

"It's Vid," he wheezed, rubbing his ribs. "I came to see you."

But she wasn't listening. "I told my family you'd come back! No one believed me, but I knew!" She crushed him in an embrace, squeezing so tight he thought his lungs might collapse for good.

"Okay, too much joy," he managed.

She stepped back just enough to grab his face between her palms. Her lips hovered close, but he flinched away, taking a step back.

Her smile faltered. "What's wrong?"

Vid straightened his posture. The tension returned to his shoulders.

"When were you going to tell me?"

She seemed confused. "Tell you what?"

His gaze didn't waver. He could see the guilt brewing, the small tremor in her hand as she nervously picked at a nail. He refused to say more, waiting for the truth to find its way out. If it ever would.

"The memories..." she said under her breath.

That was it. The confirmation he didn't want to hear.

"Why didn't you tell me? What did you take? Why me... and how?"

She looked down at her high-heeled shoes, too ashamed to meet his eyes. "I didn't *want* to take them, Vod. I had to. Consuming memories... it keeps me alive. Keeps me looking like this."

"But why me?" His voice cracked, leaking through the anger. "We were... *something*, weren't we?"

She shut her eyes. With delicate care, she pressed a fingernail into her temple. Her skin parted like soft wax, and from the gap she drew a white fragment constructed from mist. Her skin grew slightly paler, small wrinkles gathering at the corners of her mouth, and her hair dulled a shade. She held the fragment in her palm.

"It won't kill me to give this one back," she said. "I tried to only take the bad ones, or the ones I thought you wouldn't miss."

She aimed her hand at his head, formed into the shape of a finger gun, and the fragment fired like a bullet. It struck him square between the eyes and dissolved on impact. The memories hit him all at once.

Tavian, arguing with him over the last piece of cake at a birthday party. Orin, whispering stories about the undead, reveling through his many tales. His mother's funeral, watching her body—wrapped in layers of blankets—lowered into the earth. Seraphina at the Bazaar, her hand sliding behind his head, nails grazing his scalp as she drew a faint white fragment from his hair.

All of it.

He staggered back. "Even the bad ones matter, Seraphina."

Vid shook his head, trying to clear the torrent of images flooding his mind. "These memories are mine; they shape who I am. Don't ever take them from me again."

She nodded profusely, eyes watering. "I'm sorry, Vod—I mean, Vid. It's Vid, right? I didn't realize how much they meant to you. Please, forgive me. I never meant to hurt you."

He wanted to stay angry; wanted to hate her for stealing something so personal, but something about her disarmed him. Still, the questions clawed at him. How could he trust her, knowing she could take from him again and he'd never even know? But then again, was it really so terrible to lose what you can't remember, if it meant keeping her alive?

His contemplations tangled, but his body didn't wait for answers. His mouth spoke, his hands moved, as if they belonged to someone else. He was a young man after all, and it had been a long time, *admittedly*, since he'd found a woman who could tolerate him.

"You got it. It's Vid."

He smiled and reached for her hand. She met him halfway and extended hers. He turned it over and pressed a kiss to her hand, but before he could draw back, she caught his face between her hands and pulled him in.

Their lips met in static silence. The world seemed to still. They kissed for the first time, and the last time, savoring the moment he'd spent so long waiting for. Eyes closed, they stood in front of the throne, as the memory imprinted itself within them both; a new white fragment born and buried in the same breath.

"No need for the polite gesture," she said. "You're my equal here. No formalities, right?"

They kissed again.

For a moment, the palace was quiet. Just the two of them suspended in the illusion of peace.

Or so they thought.

Outside, not long after Vid's arrival, a group of cloaked men and women assembled before the front gates. Their leader, small in stature but clearly possessing great power, lifted one hand. The gate buckled and split down the center, metal shrieking as it folded inward.

The group marched forward in perfect synchrony. Several guards at the palace doors raised their weapons, shouting warnings, but the intruders didn't break stride.

The guards scrambled into position, forming a defensive ring with spears leveled. They advanced in, tightening the circle, their blades beginning to press into cloaks, but the fabric gave no resistance. No blood. No cries.

One guard pushed further, his spear plunging halfway into a hooded woman. Still nothing.

The impaled woman snapped her head toward the guard, a full rotation in a single instant. Her hood flew back, exposing her unsightly appearance: skin peeled back at the edges, remaining flesh sagging in ribbons, bone jutted like bark beneath a rotted tree, maggots writhing in the gaps left by time.

She gripped the spear still buried in her gut and wrenched it free, sending the guard hurtling backward with terrifying strength. Then she raised a hand, bones cracked and shifted from within her frame, snapping loose and floating outward until they knit themselves into a crude, serrated blade—an entire sword sculpted from her own skeleton. She flung it forward.

A second guard managed to deflect the blow, only for another hooded figure to appear behind him, driving a dagger clean through his spine. The man fell over, now lifeless in the dirt.

A third figure moved with fluid grace, seizing the fallen guard's spear as if it were its own. In one motion, before it could register with the others, it sliced through air and cleanly removed the head of another guard. The defensive ring wavered. Shields swayed. Spear tips quivered.

One panicked guard broke rank and bolted toward the palace side entrance, desperate to sound the alarm.

He turned a corner and vanished.

Another followed close behind, but when he rounded the same corner, all that remained was a single leg flopping on the ground, nerves still firing.

The guards, panicked by the sight of their fallen comrades, launched a final counterattack. Spears clashed, steel shrieked against steel, but the intruders put in little effort. With a mere snap from another half-dead woman, the ground ruptured with red-hot pillars, impaling the front line and hoisting them into the air like tasteless trophies. Screams rang out as the others could only watch.

Another snap.

More mountains of spikes burst upwards in waves, tearing through armor and bodies alike, lifting guards in twisted silhouettes against the morning sun.

The few who survived the carnage dropped their weapons and fled for the palace doors... but the arrows came faster. Their tips only grazed the skin, but it was enough. Stomachs churned and rippled through armor. One man fell to his knees, clutching his abdomen.

"My stomach... it's—"

Green-black slime burst from his mouth, followed by a multitude of small hands. Fingers clawed outward, tearing through his cheeks, hooking into eyes, splitting the face from within. Tiny malformed creatures forced their way free from their human hosts. They dragged bands of flesh along with them like afterbirth, leaving nothing whole but the scattered remains of innards.

The final guard stood paralyzed from horror, dropping to his knees. The hooded leader approached, his bony arm plunging into the man's throat. When he drew it back, his hand gripped a new weapon—an abomination of hardened blood and shredded tissue, forged into the shape of a sword. Bits of flesh clung to it like leeches feeding off its bloodied edges.

With the flick of his fingers, the palace doors detonated inward. They continued their march.

Seraphina had no idea what loomed. The main chamber was too far from the front door, and she remained locked in excited conversation with Vid, her voice soft but riddled with enthusiasm.

"I have so much to show you! I can take you through town, we can eat at my favorite place, walk the boardwalk along the water... you can stay with us for as long as you want! What do you like to do? I can't wait to—"

Her passion was palpable, excited questions flinging at him with no end, but the subtle rumble from the entryway caught Vid's ear.

He turned, just in time to spot the shadowed figures gliding through the threshold of the throne room.

His body moved before his mind could catch up.

A blade of viscera launched toward Seraphina. Though her back was turned, she sensed it at once and raised a hand, twisting the air to deflect, but Vid had already stepped in front of her. She was unable to control the sword with him in the way.

"Vid! Get out of the—"

The impact cut her short. Blood sprayed across her face. She glanced down to her bloodstained dress, expecting pain or injury, but neither was there. Then she saw it: the blade lodged clean through Vid's abdomen. It had stopped inches from her stomach, he had taken the full force of it.

He staggered, turning his head back toward her. He still wore that crooked, boyish smile.

"I shouldn't have done that, should I?"

He collapsed, but Seraphina caught him before he hit the floor, cradling him against her chest, his body already going cold.

"Vid... wait here," she whimpered, the tears already forming. "Hold on. I'll get help. You'll be okay."

Vid nodded but his shallow breathing seemed to disagree. He checked his hands, no longer able to recognize them, soaked in red and shivering beyond his control.

Seraphina rose, and something in her broke. The walls of the palace began to vibrate. The floor cracked beneath her feet. Her hair whipped upward as if caught in a storm, and the silver in her eyes blazed white-hot. With a violent twist of her arm, she unleashed a shockwave that hurled several attackers across the chamber. They hit the far wall with bone-shattering impact; one was vaporized instantly, reduced to little more than a puddle of bloody soup beneath the weight of her rage.

Gravity bore down with tenfold force. Bones snapped like twigs. Skulls cracked under the unseen pressure.

From both sides, archers emerged—dark arrows notched, firing in unison. Seraphina spread her arms wide. The arrows curved midair, ripped off their course, boomeranging back toward their masters. Each arrow that grazed fleshed birthed new life; the same small, green-black creatures clawing free from their hosts, unraveling them from within.

Seraphina turned to Vid, whose groans were fading to whispers.

"Leave," he breathed. "You won't get me out in time. It's my fault." He coughed. "I'm glad I could see you again. One memory you didn't take from me, was how beautiful you were."

Seraphina knelt by his side, refusing to accept the truth in front of her. She tried to lift him again.

"Please, don't say that. We have healers, people who can fix this. I just need to finish these people off... they just won't stop coming."

A steel dagger sliced past her head, embedding itself in the wall behind her.

"Leave," he gasped, "you're in danger."

By now, Lyra, Anastasia, and Rowan had reached the base of the staircase, weapons at the ready. They arrived just in time to witness the final breath of a boy who had never stopped smiling.

"I forgive you," Vid said. "For the memories. Thank you for giving them back. I'll hold onto the old ones—and these new ones—until the end."

His hand squeezed hers.

"Vid, no—please, stay awake a little longer! Give me more time."

Her tears now fell like rain, striking his face.

Then his hands went slack. His eyes dulled to grey. His chest rose and fell once, and didn't again.

Vid was gone.

Seraphina didn't register the hiss of blades cutting through the noise. Her gravitational field held firm, repelling them in blows of invisible force. She stayed hunched over Vid's body, tears dripping onto his bloodied chest, her hands pressed against his wounds in a vain, despondent attempt to hold him here—to keep him tethered to life.

Finally, she looked up at Lyra.

"Help me," she whispered. "Lyra... he came back for me, and now he's already gone. I don't know if I can control myself."

"We'd prefer to end this peacefully," the leader said, stepping forward and lowering his hood to reveal a skeletal face stretched thin with sinew. "The Riftbound Order has declared you traitors. Come with us for a fair trial, or suffer that boy's same fate."

He held up a wanted poster, one they'd already seen upon arriving in Aipiron.

Lyra stepped forward, placing herself between Seraphina and the Order, her stance unyielding. "We want no part of your Order. Leave. Now."

Anastasia remained far behind, her blindfold with a slight glow, allowing her sight to link with Lyra's. Rowan leaned into her ear.

"I need to grab something. Don't do anything stupid."

Anastasia gave the faintest of nods.

He sprinted up the stairs, heart pounding, navigating through the crumbling building. He tore through the room, finally spotting the recorder that was still on the couch, still running. He grabbed it then snatched Cloud's leash, the dog yapping anxiously at the chaos below.

When he returned to the main chamber, war had erupted.

The chamber was shattered beyond recognition: walls lay in heaps of rubble, the roof torn from its frame and suspended high above, the floor fissured like an earthquake had cracked it open. Lyra was at the center of the battle, her scythe carving wide angles that painted red circles of necromantic flame end-over-end. Each swing scorched flesh and bone the same, but even a weapon like hers could only do so much against them.

Above them floated Seraphina, eyes ablaze, hands aimed to the battlefield. The pressure from her palms intensified until several of the attackers simply ceased to exist—smothered into nothing under her raw gravity-born wrath.

Anastasia sat where Rowan had left her, her face blank, her sight bound through Lyra's perspective. Perfectly still, perfectly calm. Yet tiny fractures crept across the marble under her, webbing outward in fine white lines. The air around her had an eerie calm, its own fragile world sealed off from the battle.

Cloud strained against his leash, froth gathering at his jowls. Rowan tied him to a nearby pillar and set the recorder in Anastasia's lap.

"Hold this. Don't lose it. Watch Cloud."

Anastasia ran her fingers over the recorder, reading its shape. She nodded once.

Rowan turned back to the fray, pistol raised, firing in controlled shots.

Not yet, Anastasia thought. *I can't let them see.*

"Stop this madness!" their leader roared, his sword of flesh and bone clashing against Lyra's scythe. "We didn't come to kill! Our goals can align, but you *must* answer for what you've done!"

Lyra's scythe exhaled red smoke into his face, the air burning dry, draining the oxygen from his lungs. He moved back, slamming his weapon into the ground. Pillars of blood-red stone erupted from under her, lancing toward her neck and chest. She leapt aside, dodging their fatal edges, then brought her scythe clean down that shattered the next wave of pillars into dust.

Across the room, Seraphina stood atop a ruined dais, encircled by the mutilated remains of those that chose to engage. Entrails sprawled across the rug like repulsive confetti celebrating her rage.

A legless survivor crawled toward her. She seized him by the face and lifted him into the air. With a flick of the wrist, she sent him rocketing downward into the fractured marble, burying his body beneath the tile.

Another man groaned nearby, dragging himself through the gore, his escape futile. “Please, I’ll leave! I swear it. Fennwick, please!” He looked over to their leader, Fennwick, still locked in battle.

Seraphina brought her palms together, fingers folding and twisting until they pointed back towards her wrists. Her voice was ice. “I can’t make it *that* easy. I’m just starting to have fun.”

The moment her hands had fully twisted, the man’s body folded in on itself like a crumpled wad of paper, the vibrations rattling his insides. He burst apart, gore splattering her torn dress in steaming clumps.

By now, only Fennwick remained. Lyra and Seraphina flanked him, closing in from opposite sides. Rowan kept his distance, pistol trained but hand shaking.

“I wanted this done peacefully,” Fennwick rasped. “But I can’t return to the Riftbound Order empty-handed. Dead or alive... you’re all coming with me.”

He lifted his hands. Symbols etched into his palms began to glow. Color drained from the world.

Everything froze, leaving glass shards hung suspended in the air, dust arrested in the breeze. Even time itself had stopped to listen. Cloud remained locked mid-bark, fur turned shades of grey. Rowan, Lyra, Seraphina; each one of them trapped in a colorless plane. No breath. No motion. Not even thought could escape his snare.

Only Fennwick moved. His steps echoed as he advanced toward Lyra, dragging his fleshy sword behind him, leaving a trail of blood in its wake.

He reached toward her face, fingers hovering inches from her bleeding eyes. Then—his hand stopped. It wouldn’t move any closer.

“What...?” he pulled back before reaching forward again, only to be repelled away by some barrier he couldn’t spot. He tried once more, but in that instant, Lyra vanished.

In her place stood Anastasia.

She alone remained in color, the only hue left in this world stripped bare; untouched by the black-and-white entrapment that engulfed the others.

“How... did you move?” he stammered, flashing his etched palms at her, trying to pull her into his temporal trap. But nothing happened, she didn’t even flinch. Instead, she turned away.

With deliberate calm, Anastasia gripped at empty air with both hands and *pulled apart.* Reality tore open between her fingers. A diamond-shaped rift split the world before her, crackling with static and patterns of splendid color. The tear stretched nearly fifteen feet high, but lesser feet wide. Just enough space for what, or who, she intended to summon.

She turned back to Fennwick. Lowering her blindfold, she revealed the black sockets where her eyes should have been. Lights flickered within those voids, mass amounts of power surmounting from inside.

He stepped back. "No... what is this? What did they send me into?"

He spun to flee—his vision muddying, lungs scraping for air as he made his way for the palace entrance—but when he blinked, he found himself right back where he'd started, face-to-face with her once more.

"Please," he whispered. "Let me go. I'll tell the Riftbound Order it's finished. You'll never hear from me again."

He dropped to his knees, scooting forward, bowing low at her feet.

Anastasia reached down, resting a hand on his shoulder to help him rise.

"You're right," she said.

"Thank you," he sobbed, clasping her hand. "You're too merciful. You're—"

"No." Her voice was soft, almost kind. "You don't understand."

A pause.

"You're right," she repeated. "You're right that we'll never hear from you again."

Colors of all different hues bled from her sockets, painting the frozen world in a cascade of brilliance, a stark contrast from the black-and-white picture. She reached one arm behind into the rift and guided out a monstrous creature.

An amorphous blob with greasy, gray skin pulsating to a beat of its own. Three large eyes stared from its face, with a misshapen mouth and a sideways grin. From its body extended countless appendages, arms, and hands. It dwarfed her, towering behind like a living nightmare. Yet flowers crowned its head, growing out in all different directions, blooming in every color.

"Slug… I—I was told you were dead. How are you here? How are you *alive*?" Fennwick shuddered, losing all feeling in his legs.

"It's nice to be back," Slug said, voice dripping with malice. "Is this one for me, Anastasia?"

She nodded.

Fennwick whirled around to escape, but before he could take a single step, he was caught within a hundred greasy limbs. Slug's arms coiled and pressed into every inch of his being, dragging him backward, forcing their way in.

A blinding beam of multicolored light shot from Anastasia's sockets like a cannon blast. Fennwick screamed, but the sound was swallowed instantly. His body disintegrated, drawn into the radiant beam, consumed into the abyss of Anastasia's sockets until not a trace remained.

When the light faded, she slid her blindfold back into place. Slight stains of blue and pink clung to the velvet.

Behind her came the sounds of sobbing.

"Please," Slug wept. "Let me go. End my suffering. I gave you your gift… have I not earned mercy?"

Anastasia turned to him. "You cursed me and my sister. What mercy do you deserve?"

She placed both hands to his massive form and shoved him back toward the rift.

"You'll regret this!" Slug shrieked. "No mortal can survive such power! You'll go mad!"

"You made me this way," she pushed harder. "You gave me too much. Go and tell the rest."

Once he was inside, she pulled the rift shut.

Silence returned.

She opened a much smaller rift and reached inside, pulling out Lyra by the wrist, placing her back exactly as she had been before.

CHAPTER NINETEEN

WHERE DEATH ENDS, LIFE STARTS

> You want flowers? So be it. The flowers will grow on graves.
>
> ~Slug

LYRA AWOKE TO WARMTH BLANKETING HER BODY.

Above her, the gray sky shifted, wisp-like clouds drifting aimlessly. There were silhouettes of others far away, but too distant to make out. Around her, familiar structures began to take shape: her childhood home in Tenebral, the room she'd shared with Anastasia in Aipiron, Derewin's modest house.

She felt like she'd been in this place before, but her memories refused to cooperate. Everything was hazy, like a dream remembered seconds too late. She couldn't recall how she'd arrived... or what had come before.

She wandered through the conjoined residences. In one room, a bed was neatly made—corners tucked tightly, a lamp on the side with the switch still flicked on, pillows propped upright and angled against the wall. Hall lights were left on, casting a bright glow, but no one else was there. Still, the place didn't feel abandoned. It felt watched over.

Somewhere, she thought she had heard voices just beyond the door. But when she stepped outside, there was no one.

Eventually, she made her way through every overlapping doorway, until the stitched-together homes dissolved to sand. She now found herself on the beach outside the Aipiron palace—the same place where Rowan had first shown her the recorder. There, standing alone near the crashing waves, was a small, shadowed figure.

"Hello? Can you hear me?" Lyra called, but her voice was devoured by the thunderous surf. She tried again, louder. "Can you hear me?"

The figure didn't react. It seemed preoccupied, anxious even, shifting in place, eyes filled with some inner panic. Lyra stepped closer, only for it to bolt away.

She ran after it, but the faster she moved, the further it slipped ahead. When she finally closed the distance, now out of breath and frustrated, she stopped dead in her tracks.

Someone stood beside it. Rowan.

"Rowan? What are you doing here?"

He simply lifted a hand and waved.

Lyra pushed forward, but the sand fought her with every step. It felt like running on a treadmill that moved in reverse, each step pushing her back. Still, she fought against it, struggling forward until she could get just a little closer. He did in fact look like Rowan... yet something was off.

His face was the same, his smile and wave familiar, but the light in his eyes had gone vacant. A presence behind them had gone missing, leaving behind only the shell of the person she remembered.

"Is it really you?" she brought a hand closer to him. "Where are we? What's happening?"

Above them, seabirds cried and circled the pale moon, their feathers drifting slowly down like falling snow. Strangely, they didn't react to her aura as they usually did, no bodies thumped to the sand. They simply flew.

"Hi, Lyra," Rowan said at last. "How're you?"

She blinked, thrown off. "What? That's not... What are you talking about?"

He only shrugged and smiled wanly. His expression felt artificial, man-made by some foreign entity trying to prove its humanity.

She frowned, formed her fingers into the shape of a gun, and pressed it against his forehead.

"Bang," she whispered.

Nothing about him changed. He tilted his head. "What was that for?"

"Forget it," she sighed, lowering her hand back to her side. Her attention shifted back to the small shadow she'd been chasing. It hadn't moved all this time. Still small, still quiet, still watching.

"Who's this?" Lyra asked. "Who are you?"

She heard nothing but the cadence of the ocean and the cawing of gulls. The tide had crept higher, soaking through the bottom of one of her shoes.

She stepped closer, one final time. This time, the figure didn't move. It stood still as Lyra's hand reached forward, closer than ever before. Her fingers nearly brushed the top of its head when her hand locked in place.

The figure turned. A blindfold was wrapped around its eyes.

Then, the world drained of color. Everything turned black and white.

A tear in space spilt open in front of her. From it, a small girl's arm emerged, reaching through the rift. The hand grasped Lyra's wrist and yanked her in.

When awareness returned, she was back in the grand chamber of Aipiron. The hooded attackers were gone. The battle was over.

Lyra took a shaky step forward. Her shoe squelched as if she'd stepped into a pool of water. She looked down; one shoe was soaked, but no puddle was in sight, yet the brine reeked unmistakably of the sea.

Seraphina stirred beside her, groaning as she clutched her temple. Rowan shook his head, clearing the fog from his mind. Cloud let out a soft whine, tailed tucked beneath itself.

Lyra summoned her scythe and braced for battle. "Where'd he go? ... Is it over?"

"I don't know," Seraphina said. "One second he lifted his hands, and the next I blacked out."

"He's gone now," came Anastasia's voice. She crossed the room and handed Rowan the recorder.

The others turned to her. Her clothes were torn, her blindfold stained with faint splotches of color, but she didn't look shaken. Not like the rest of them.

Lyra crouched beside her sister, inspecting her end-over-end. "Were you here the whole time? Who touched you? Are you hurt?"

"I'm fine," Anastasia replied, putting her hands behind her back. "He ran away. Got scared, I guess."

Lyra grabbed one of Anastasia's hands and flipped it over before she could fully hide it. Sigils were faintly carved into her skin. Something about them tickled a memory Lyra couldn't place.

Weren't these on Fennwick's hands? She wasn't sure.

"What are these?" she pressed.

Anastasia pulled her hand back, tucking it behind her once more. "Cuts."

Before Lyra could press further, Seraphina stepped beside her and tilted her head. "Forgot to mention, Lyra, but your foundation looks awful. I could always help—"

Lyra moved faster than thought. The air bent around the arc of her hand, slapping Seraphina hard across the cheek.

Seraphina reeled back, padding her injured cheek. "Ow! Damn. Offer revoked. Keep looking like that, then."

Rowan inspected the recorder, thumbing the playback button in an attempt to replay what had just happened, but the screen flickered and went dark.

"Battery's dead," he muttered. "Damn it. We need to get more."

Lyra rolled her eyes. "You and that dumb toy."

She turned back toward Seraphina, who stood silently over Vid's body. When Seraphina looked up, her expression had turned detached and resolute. "We need to leave. Now."

Lyra raised a brow. "Why? Can't we—"

"SERAPHINA TRUBBMAN! COME HERE THIS INSTANT!"

The shrill voice shattered what remained of the glass windows. From the far end of the collapsed hall stormed Arnette, brandishing a massive metal spoon like a war hammer.

"*This* is why..." Seraphina groaned and rubbed her temple. "Mom, I'm sorry, okay? We'll find someone to clean—"

Arnette moved with the speed only a mother in full fury could muster. The spoon came down with a resounding *smack*, leaving a perfect imprint across Seraphina's cheek, right next to the one Lyra gifted her.

"Don't give me that! What the hells were you thinking? Half the house is in shambles!"

From a staircase above, Agusto and Baron leaned over the railing to watch.

"Wow," Agusto muttered, taking a long swig from a flask he'd fished out of his coat. "I assumed there was a party. Who caused all this?"

Baron, unfazed, continued practicing his juggling—until Seraphina moved to the side. That's when he saw Vid.

"Oh my... what happened to the poor boy? Vid, wasn't it?" Agusto stammered, downing another swig. "What did he do to earn your wrath, my dear?"

Baron's rocks clattered to the floor and rolled away, forgotten.

He sprinted down the stairs, small legs splashing through pools of blood and viscera left by the fallen Order. He threw himself to the ground beside Vid, tears already welling in his eyes.

"Vid? You never saw what I practiced! Please, Vid!"

He rocked Vid's shoulders hard. The body didn't move. His neck hung stiff, head slumped to one side, eyes an empty stare.

"Baron, let him go," Seraphina said, kneeling beside him and gently prying his hands away. But the boy only clutched tighter, sobbing into Vid's bloodied shirt.

Seraphina wrapped her arms around him and buried her face into her brother's shoulder. Her tears mingled with his. Arnette and Agusto moved in closer, their earlier anger dissolving into stunned silence. Arnette slipped her hand into Agusto's and leaned against him.

Rowan came forward and joined alongside Seraphina and Baron. He spoke to her brother. "I'm sorry for your loss. He meant a lot to you, I'm sure."

Baron looked up, eyes red and swollen, nose leaking with streaks of snot.

"We should do something for him," Rowan continued. "Put him to rest properly."

Baron's face crumpled. "No... he can't be dead. Vid, come back!" He shook his head, trying to deny what his eyes already knew.

Behind them, Lyra and Anastasia stood waiting. They had seen death too many times to flinch at it now. In their world, death was only a turn in the cycle, another step forward. It would always come full-circle.

"We can bring him back, if he means that much to you." Lyra said.

Their cries stopped, the only sound left was the thud of birds falling through the open ceiling, their bodies joining in on the devastation.

Baron turned toward Lyra, and through his tears he could now see the intense necromantic energy drifting from her figure like smoke, almost beckoning to him, calling for his attention.

"You can do that? Yes, do it!" He leapt to his feet, hope finding its way through the misery. "Bring him back!"

Agusto and Arnette exchanged a look, equal parts alarm and worry.

Seraphina stared down at Vid, hands weak against the sides of her dress.

"No," Rowan said firmly, stepping in front of Lyra. "It's not right. You both know what happens when someone's brought back. It won't be *him*. It'll only look like him."

Baron screamed, grabbing Lyra and tugging frantically, his hands leaving crimson prints over her coat. "No! He'll still be here! I don't care if he's different! He'll still be alive, please!"

Lyra looked at Rowan again, his expression was grave; he gave a silent signal with a head shake. Then, she turned to Seraphina.

"What do you want, Seraphina?"

Seraphina didn't answer at first, still turned away from them, staring into what remained of Vid.

"What I want," she whispered at last, "is for Vid to still be alive. For him to laugh again. For him to show Baron new tricks. But what I *don't* want is some... thing, some reanimated shell pretending to be him. What I want—what I truly want—is for necromancy to be erased from this world entirely."

She looked up at Lyra, silver eyes burning with conviction. "Don't bring him back. Don't touch him. Don't even *look* at him."

A long silence followed.

"We bury him this afternoon." Seraphina concluded.

Then she rose against the full weight of her decision, her voice turning to cold marble.

"And I'm coming with you to Valspire."

Arnette's mouth fell open. "What? Seraphina, you can't leave! This is your city... we're your family!"

Seraphina began walking up the stairs. "I want to be there when Lyra goes for Tenebral—when she burns it to the ground. I want to be there when she sets fire to all those narcissists in Valspire. Then, and only then, will we go for the Riftbound Order. I want to watch them all die."

Her footsteps faded. A door slammed.

Lyra's head struck with pain. Her memories fragmented. She thought of Tenebral, but something new was eating at her mind, replacing those old memories with new ones. She had never once thought to destroy Tenebral, yet Seraphina's words lingered in her skull like commandments. They *felt* true, words bound like law.

Her will began to splinter. For the first time, she imagined it: flames rising through familiar streets, the town center in ruin, her mother's body riddled with wounds. She almost *wanted* it. Even as she tried to tell herself against it, these poisoned and soured memories were seeded in... those buds now beginning to bloom.

Arnette broke down crying into her husband's collar, and this time, he didn't reach for his flask.

Baron's tears didn't stop. Not that night, not the next morning, not even at the funeral.

He wept until his shirt clung to his skin, soaked through as if he'd walked out of a pool fully dressed. His throat burned raw from the sound of Vid's name on repeat.

On the grave, Baron placed the juggling stones Vid had given him. They were worn smooth, the colors faded, but still his. Seraphina added her own offerings: a handful of small trinkets, things that reminded her of him, small pieces of memory laid out in the dirt.

The funeral was brief. Only the Trubbmans and Lyra's group stood beneath the broken sky. A soft melody played. Vid was buried in the courtyard beside the palace.

Seraphina recalled his words: *I shouldn't have done that, should I?*

The line repeated over and over again in her mind like a cruel lullaby. She thought about it when she slept, when she woke, when she showered, when she ate.

I shouldn't have done that, should I?

"Why did you have to try and be a hero? I could have stopped that sword. Your death was pointless."

No one moved even after the last shovel of dirt fell. The courtyard felt incomplete. Leaving so soon felt wrong, but staying offered no comfort either.

And so, eventually, they decided to move on, and to leave Aipiron for good.

At the entrance where the palace gates once stood, Arnette, Agusto, and Baron waited for Serpahina's departure. She turned back to them one last time, crouching beside her brother and planting a kiss on his forehead.

"I'll be back before you know it. Keep Mom and Dad safe, all right?"

Baron nodded, wiping away the last of his tears.

She stood, then embraced her father. He held on a little too long.

"This is foolish," he said. "You're safe here."

Seraphina pulled away, meeting his gaze. "Was any of what happened safe? Nowhere is safe with the Riftbound Order still out there. Not with Tenebral standing. This may be my only chance to see this through, now that I have Lyra."

Agusto reached for his flask, but Arnette caught his hand before he could. "Let it be this once. At least for her goodbye."

He exhaled and lowered his arm.

Arnette hugged her daughter and slipped something into her bag without a word. "Be careful out there, sweetheart. Send us word whenever you can. We'll be waiting."

Seraphina wept into her mother's arms. "Yes… I will."

She turned to the road. Lyra and the others were already waiting. Together, they passed through town, their silhouettes fading into the horizon.

In Seraphina's bag, the object Arnette had hidden glowed a misty white. An unspoken memory waiting to be remembered.

Tavian explained his plan to meet with Eldric and the Riftbound Order. At first, Aria and Cassius were wary, but after enough persuasion, they finally conceded to go with him.

"Who's going to make me food?" David whined, chasing after Cassius, who was already walking beside Tavian toward Traegos.

Cassius stopped, crouched, and placed a hand on the boy's head. "I left some recipes on the counter for you. I'm sure someone will take over."

David looked down, defeated. He pressed his hands to his stomach, where a small mouth parted showing several rows of its eager teeth.

Maeve stepped in, nudging David aside. "Don't bother our guests, Davie. Their time here is over. They've served their purpose."

Then he turned his attention to Tavian. "Don't forget our deal," he said. "It's of the utmost importance. We wouldn't want to have to involve Aria, would we?"

Tavian avoided eye contact, fiddling with his fingers. "Yes. I understand."

"I don't want to lose my friends," David muttered, tugging at Maeve's sleeve. "Father, when will I get more?"

Maeve patted his head. "Friends come and go. I'll be sure to add more to your collection. Maybe one of them can help with that hunger of yours."

David beamed, clapping his hands together. He wandered off, humming a half-remembered tune that Cassius had once taught him.

As Tavian, Aidra, Aria, and Cassius pulled away, Maeve's hand slid out and caught Aria by the arm. The others continued along.

"And you..." he said with a lowered voice, fingers gliding down her forearm until they paused over the faint, dark veins that rose under her skin. "You're something special. A shame we didn't have more time to talk. I would've loved to—"

Aria wrenched free and spat at his boot. The blood-tinged mucus rolled off the toe and gathered at the base.

"I don't care what you think," she snapped. "Stay away from me and Tavian. Whatever deal you've made—if you so much as lift a finger toward him, I'll make sure you suffer. Slowly."

Her eyes darkened. The veins along her neck distended into thick, black cords.

Maeve stepped back, hands raised. "Don't shoot the messenger. You can't deny what you are; it'll only make things worse. You'll need people like me sooner than you think. Don't come crawling back without an apology."

His grin crawled under her skin, boiling her blood beyond the point of evaporation. She wanted to tear him apart, but there would be another time for that.

She turned and rejoined Tavian and the others. Maeve waved from a distance, and several of the undead gathered around him, snickering like children.

One of Maeve's companions jabbed him with an elbow. "Why didn't you tell him? I wanted to see the look on his face. Did he really think you could teach him necromancy? Only pure-blood Necromites can do that."

Maeve's smile sharpened, his fists flexed.

"Those damn Spirians," he spat. "They waltz in, cozy up to us, try to take back the power we were exiled for, and think they can just leave with it. Entitled bastards."

He drew a scimitar, its rusted edge basking in the sun, and turned on the man that elbowed him. The man flinched too late. The blade sang; a head hit the ground with a thud.

"They don't know what we went through," Maeve said as he continuously drove the weapon into the man's beheaded body. "What we endured to get here. Tavian's on a date with death. And what waits for him will make our suffering look trivial."

Tavian led the way, head held high, quiet confidence building in him. He hadn't mastered everything yet, but the power inside him buzzed, ready to be unleashed.

For weeks they traveled: through rivers and over lakes, across deserts and mountains, until finally they reached the edge of an impassable wall of green. A vast forest stood in their way, the canopy rising like a cathedral roof. Towering trunks, as wide as city towers, with acorns littering the forest floor like marbles spilled from a child's game.

Aidra stepped in front of Tavian. "We should go around," she warned. "These woods don't take kindly to my kind. It's safer to take the long way."

Tavian shook his head, already moving ahead. "We've wasted enough time. We can't afford more detours."

He didn't wait for her response. The moment his foot hit the forest floor, the world fell silent. No wind. No birds. No rustling leaves. Only the soft crunch of an acorn beneath his heel.

When the others followed in, the sounds slowly returned, but warped in a way they hadn't sounded before.

Each step disoriented them more. The forest seemed to bend in on itself. Trees repeated, paths twisted, time stretched and snapped like thread under tension. They were in a loop that they couldn't manage themselves out of.

"I swear we passed that tree an hour ago," Cassius muttered, pointing to a crooked trunk bent at a perfect ninety-degree angle.

"Just keep moving," Tavian said.

With each passing minute, his aura was darkening like a storm cloud gathering heavy, unspent rain. Aria stayed close but quiet, keeping her own energy veiled, wary of letting it become detected.

As if tired of the charade after hours upon hours, the trees began to part, opening a path to a clearing ringed by even more of the imposing trees. The canopy above thinned just enough to let sunlight trickle through.

The trees surrounding the glade were watching.

Faces bulged from the bark, wooden masks carved with countless expressions, some weeping, another grinning, several glaring with hatred. There was one wincing in anticipation of what was to come.

Their branches bent into arms. Their roots uncoiled into legs. Together they sat silently in a ring, their masks fixed on the center.

From the soil at the center, a hut rose, woven from bark and root, spiraled with living vines that crawled along the sides of its surface. It was small, no larger than a single room, yet its presence was immense and radiating strength familiar to that of Maeve's. It was different though, not cruel, rather cautious.

"This is it," Aidra whispered, stepping back onto another acorn. "I can't go near it." She leaned in close to Aria's ear. "You shouldn't either. *She* doesn't tolerate the undead, or Necromites."

Tavian marched forward, unfazed and pride inflating with the power he'd come to wield. Cassius begrudgingly followed, leaving Aidra and Aria behind. As Tavian drew closer, the faces on the trees shifted. Their masks flipped like shuffled cards—sadness, confusion, anger, remorse, pain. By the time he reached the hut's door, every mask had settled on the same expression: pure anger.

"Tavian, don't go closer!" Aria shouted. "Let's just leave. Look at the trees, they don't want us here."

Cassius glanced around unnerved. "I think she's right, Tavian. These trees are sending a pretty clear message." He gave one a sheepish wave. Its wooden arms crossed in disdain, its face switching from sorrow to seething rage.

Cassius swallowed. "Okay, no waving..."

Tavian ignored them both and reached for the doorknob.

"I'm sure we can handle a few angry trees," he muttered. "Let's find out who's in charge and get this over with."

The moment his hand met the handle, six-inch thorns erupted, driving into his palm and wrist, impaling him cleanly through. The barbs twisted and burrowed his grip deeper into place. The more he struggled to pull free, the deeper they pushed through, far enough until their tips emerged from the back of his hand. He dropped to his knees, jaw clenched so hard he could feel a tooth chip.

Maeve's training, for all its cruelty and hidden ruse, had left Tavian with a few tricks. Dark energy flared from his palms, curling and hissing in smoke as it ate through the thorns. The wood shriveled into ash before it fell away in wisps.

The hut shuddered in reaction to the sinister nature of his newfound power. The door blew open with a gust of wind, the blast hurling Tavian backward into the others, leaving the remaining thorns lodged into his hand.

The inside only showed black, all light vanished save for a single candle on a small table, the flame a lone witness.

From the doorway, a sandaled foot stepped into view. Its nails were painted a sky blue. A leg followed. Then, slowly, out came the woman—middle-aged, long brown hair falling down her back. Her clothes were plain, humble, yet the forest bowed to her, the tree's branches leaning in deference.

"Leave," the woman said, her voice smooth but laced with authority. "You don't belong here."

"We're trying to," Tavian called back, hauling himself to his feet, blood still dripping from his hand. "We got lost. We just need directions out of here."

She noticed the white glow from his hand, healing his fresh wounds. Her eyes narrowed. Around them, the tree's masks shifted once more, cycling to surprise, suspicion, and resentment.

An acorn shot from the canopy, embedding itself in Aidra's shoulder. It split open, vines and roots burst from it, wrapping around her body, binding her arms to her sides. The tendrils climbed her neck, digging into her skin and wrapping around her throat.

"Stop!" the woman commanded the trees. "Not yet. Let me speak to them."

Aria stared into the trees, realizing now they were not alone. Hundreds of tiny creatures lurked among the canopy, nearly invisible until they reloaded their slingshots with more deadly seeds. They had acorns for heads with twig limbs, almost microscopic from a distance.

"How do you wield that power?" the woman asked, stepping near Tavian. "You heal with one hand and destroy with the other. You burned my thorns with judgment, yet healed through Mariella's grace."

"I've been practicing," he said. "Regardless—we're trying to get my mother back. I just need to reach Traegos and meet with some important people. We need to get through here, fast."

The woman stopped short of him, inspecting from head to toe.

"You shouldn't go there," she said. "Traegos will devour you. You seem to still have some good in you. Run while you still can. Forget what you've learned."

The woman's head tilted, her nose pointed upward, sniffing the air, picking up on another scent. She had felt it, another darkness close by. Her head turned to Aria.

Green light glowed in the woman's palms. She laid both hands on Aria's neck.

At once, Aria's veins bulged beneath her skin. Her eyes twitched, jaw locking until the grind of her teeth became audible. The forest reacted, the masks shifting again. Moving through anger, mourning, disgust.

The woman whispered close to her ear. "You're hiding something heavy, awfully dark, yet you're fighting it." She looked at Aria with a touch of pity. "Like that boy… you should turn back. Save yourself."

Aria shoved her hands away, the veins retreating through a controlled breath. She couldn't let Tavian see, but Cassius caught a glimpse. His eyes flicked to Aria's arms, narrowing on the remnants of a single black vein.

"How do you know all this?" Aria asked in a low voice. The woman smelled of earth and rain, of roots freshly torn from the soil.

The woman pointed to the ground behind Aria where she'd walked, each footprint marked by blackened, dead grass. Even the body of a young squirrel lay nearby, its half-dead state twitching and staring with clouded eyes at Aria.

"The trees don't hate *you*," the woman said, "but they fear what's *inside* you. I've never met anyone who could hold so much darkness at bay. That's a good sign. Don't waste it."

She finally turned her attention to Aidra. "But you have no reason to be here. If not for the others, I'd have buried you already. You should know better, trespass from the undead means death."

The vines constricting Aidra loosened and crumbled away to dirt. She staggered back, bowing in relief.

"I've already given you all more time than I intended," the woman continued. "Heed my warning. Do not go near Traegos. Take yourselves elsewhere."

She returned to the hut. The tree's masks shifted a final time, some calm, some curious, none angry.

Her last words came from inside the doorway. "The forest let you live because I commanded it. Next time, it may not listen. Even I may not."

Through the hut's small window, her hand made a single, dismissive motion. The forest screamed in reply. A gale tore through the glade, uprooting grass, branches, and small trees, hurling the group off their feet. The world flipped upside down, flinging them beyond the tree line and sending them crashing into a grassy plain. They stood up coughing, covered in dirt and petals.

Tavian sat up first, brushing debris from his shirt. "That went great."

"We were lucky," Aidra said, already starting her forward march. "Next time, listen to me. I have experience with these things."

Cassius wiped bark and soil from his neck, studying Aria closely now, unsettled by what he'd seen. She noticed his lingered stare and shifted her body away from his, speeding up to get ahead of the group until the weight of his gaze had lifted.

Aidra led them onward, her stride deliberate and purposeful. Every so often she paused to kneel in the dirt, examining massive impressions in the earth, turning up to scan the horizon like she was a hunter following a trail.

"It moves," she had said earlier. "Always has."

The others looked to one another puzzled but never questioned her. Whatever she meant, they would find out soon enough.

Their travel continued. Through heat that blistered their backs and cold that bit at their ears. Across plain grasslands and brittle rock, through dust storms and dry winds. They camped beneath the watchful guidance of the stars and rose with the weary dawn. Each step carried heavier than the last, each moment passed longer, heavy with anticipation.

Cassius broke their labored tension. "I never asked, Aidra—but what brought you to Maeve? How did you end up with the likes of him?"

Aidra shook her head, the discomfort palpable. "He's a Necromite; his followers are all those he's killed and brought back." She nervously tapped her fingers against her leg. "I was one of the many unfortunate ones who crossed his path."

Cassius reached for his notebook, the pages rustling as he flipped through them. He started scribbling down notes. "When you were brought back, what changed? Did you notice anything unusual about yourself? Do things look different now? How did—"

"Cassius!" Aria interrupted, elbowing him in the side. "Don't be rude."

"No, it's all right," Aidra patted Cassius on the shoulder. "It's natural to want to know more."

She drew a deep breath. "But yes, everything changes. You feel... awful. Every part of your aches. Your memories blur, emotions dull, and something ugly gnaws at you. It makes you angry, violent, unable to control a building hunger. And whoever brings you back," her eyes dimmed, "you're tied to them. Like a string pulling you wherever they will it. You can fight it, but not for long."

Aria frowned. "How did he find you?"

The look of remorse that followed spoke louder than words.

"I'm not sure," she admitted. "Those details are... foggy. I remember having a family; a husband, a little boy, and I remember leaving them. My husband cried, my son begged me to stay," her voice frayed. "I remember the guilt, the shame of walking away. But there was a reason I had to go. I just... can't remember what it was."

She turned to Tavian with softened eyes. "Oddly enough, you—you remind me of someone. My son, I swear he was just like you."

A distant crash split the air like the crack of thunder. They stopped abruptly, looking to where the sound had come from.

Another crash followed. Then another—each one louder, closer than the last. The ground heaved, rattling loose stones and startling birds, taking off to the sky. The rumbling grew so fierce it nearly lifted them off their feet.

Aidra pointed toward the mountains. "We're here."

They looked in her direction, but saw only the tops of mountains and piles of brown snow.

"We're where?" Aria asked. "There's nothing but rocks."

"Just wait."

The crashes multiplied. The sky itself seemed to shake the birds free, the ones trying to fly to safety thrown to the dirt. Then, beyond the mountain ridge, a massive silhouette came into view. A hunched shape, larger than the mountains that had obscured it, steadily carried something atop its back.

It took a single step. In that one stride it covered half a mile.

At last, the figure emerged into full view: a colossal being made of stone and metal, its limbs like pillars and a body crusted in moss and ancient, rusted armor. Its joints groaned like the hull of a ship trapped in a storm, each tread accompanied by the sound of deep scrapes and age-worn gears.

And anchored across its back, held fast by chains thicker than the masked trees of the woods, was a city. A sprawling metropolis of towers and clockwork, of chimneys and curling steam. Gears the size of buildings rotated in opposing directions, the sounds hidden beneath the boom of the colossus's steps.

Life thrived upon the giant's spine. Trains screeched along tracks set uneven by the curvature of its back, cars rattled over bridges of steel, streetlights flickered on at the signs of dusk. The air was alive with noise; honks, shouts, cries, laughter, the city was in full view, full of life, in full swing. Atop a giant, the city of Traegos lived.

Tavian stammered, eyes darting from tower to tower, not able to settle on any one sight. "That... can't be it. That's Traegos?"

His heartbeat spiked, pounding in his chest like a beating war drum. He clutched his shirt, unsure whether it was fear or awe that was killing him faster.

Aidra nodded. "Yes. The city is named after the colossus. Now step back. I'll get its attention."

From her coat she drew a pistol. It was sleek from recent cleaning but chipped and scared from frequent use.

"A pistol?" Tavian asked. "What's that going to do?"

Aidra raised the weapon without answering. She aimed for the creature's ankles and fired.

The shots shattered the air with a deafening noise, louder than any footfall of the colossus, echoing for miles. Twin streaks of fire struck the plated joints of the giant's legs. Metal rang like struck bells, sparks flew off the surface. The bullets hadn't pierced far, just enough for the colossus to take notice.

The earth stilled, the creature stopped.

Its head moved mechanically until a single domed eye locked onto them. The eye resembled an ancient diver's helmet, the surface glowing with blinding intensity.

"Go," Aidra whispered. "Now."

Tavian stumbled forward, legs shaking. He didn't know what to say, or if it could hear him, but he had to try something. He cupped his hands around his mouth and shouted, "It's Tavian Fenwyn! I'm here for the Riftbound Order!"

The light within the colossus's eye flared ever so brighter, now removing the horizon from view. It burned through their vision. They raised their arms to shield their faces as waves of molten air blanketed them. The sky turned white, sweat poured from their bodies.

Tavian dared to look again, just a sliver through the cracks of his fingers. He saw the light grow in intensity, converging to a singular point.

Then the beam struck.

The world disappeared in white light, sound vanished; there was no time to scream, no time to understand. Their bodies unspooled, fragmenting into something far beyond flesh, purifying into liquid matter.

Their human lives had ended in that instant.

ACT III
BEFORE YOU CAN BE FOUND

CHAPTER TWENTY
THE FEW CONTROL THE MANY

I'm so sorry, Tavian. Go find your mother.
~Aria Valcrest

Cassius awoke to warmth blanketing his body.

It quickly turned to raging heat, intensifying and suffocating with every small breath. The smell of burning wood filled his nostrils as he sat up just in time to see flames devouring the walls of his bedroom.

He turned. His wife lay beside him, unmoving. He grabbed her shoulder and flipped her over. Her face was charred like an over-roasted marshmallow, skin flaking into soot. Beneath it, the whites of scorched bone bled through the blackened skin. Cassius opened his mouth to scream, but only a hoarse whine escaped.

Then the screams of children, just beyond the bedroom walls. They pounded their small fists against the plaster, crying for him.

He ran over and pressed into the wall, shouting for them to crawl low and find the door, but their voices had already muted.

Flames climbed higher, eating through the drapes and licking across the ceiling. The bedroom door was gone, reduced to molten metal and burned frame. He turned to the window, but it refused to open, jammed tight. Smoke poured and began to cloud his vision through its black density. He waved his arms trying to clear the smoke, but the motions only fed the fire. His sleeves caught; his hands and legs ignited.

He screamed, tumbled to the window, and slammed it with all his weight. The latch finally snapped. He dove through the opening and crashed onto the grass below, rolling again and again until the fire died away, leaving raw pain and the smell of burnt flesh as a reminder.

As he stood, the pain vanished. His body was whole again: no scars, no burns, no smoke trapped in the lungs. Only a cool breeze brushing beneath the gray sky.

When he looked back toward the house, it was untouched. The walls were clean, the curtains still drawn. The world, somehow, had rewound.

The front door opened. His wife stepped out onto the porch, smiling sweetly. She wore a patterned apron, faded and dusted with splotches of flour. Her high cheekbones framed a long face, her nose still bent from that age-old break. A single braid trailed over her shoulder to her chest.

"What are you doing out here?" she asked. "It's too early to be wandering around the yard. Come back inside, Cassius."

He stared at his hands, his unscarred legs, then back to her, then back to the house.

What's happening?

He tread closer, hesitant at first, as if a wrong move may rewind time again. But he couldn't stop himself, he moved closer without regard for any more delay. Her face was untouched. Her skin was warm and soft beneath his fingers, exactly as he remembered.

"What happened? The fire... where did it go?"

She chuckled and cupped his face between her palms. "Fire? The one from years ago? We've long forgotten that, love. You're here now. That's what matters."

"We?" he asked.

Children's laughter came from behind her. The voices he knew. The joy he remembered, but buried long ago.

"Come inside," she said, turning to gesture at the door. "They've been waiting for you."

He tried to follow, but his feet wouldn't move past the porch. He looked down, but his legs were stuck, rooted into the earth.

Her smile faded into heartbreak. She wiped a tear from the base of one eye, stepping close and pressing a kiss to his temple.

"Maybe it's not time yet," she whispered. "We'll be waiting. We've waited this long... we can manage a little longer."

She turned and walked back toward the door. Cassius tried to follow, tried to call out for her, but his body refused to listen.

"Wait! What do you mean? Where am I? Don't go!"

She didn't answer, didn't even look back. Her face remained hidden as she stepped through; bearing her grief alone. She wouldn't tell him, couldn't tell him. He would understand in due time.

The door creaked shut behind her, and with it, the children's laughter vanished.

"No! Please, wait! I'm still here!"

"Cassius!" a voice boomed from the sky.

He looked up, but saw only the churning of gray clouds.

"Cassius!" it called again.

Flames burst beneath his feet once more. He screamed, but the pain stole his breath. The fire devoured him whole, and this time he couldn't run.

Rain fell. Darkness folded in.

"Cassius!"

The burning consumed him, then shattered into a blinding light that he could no longer see through. When his vision returned, he was choking on water, hauled back into a new reality.

No house. No gray sky. Just Tavian, Aria, and Aidra crouched over him with a group of robed strangers.

"Cassius! You're all right!" Tavian exclaimed.

A hand grabbed him and hoisted him up to wobbly feet. His head spun. Something was missing, some vital part of himself. His soul felt fractured between the place he'd just left and the one he'd returned to.

There was weak light coming from each corner of whatever room he was held in. In those corners stood odd creatures: thin, human-shaped, short, with jerky, almost zombified movements as they paced in circles. Instead of heads, thick candles burned where their necks ended, wax dripping down their shoulders, melting their flesh. They weren't guards nor servants, they were the light source.

"Where am I?" he wheezed.

They guided him to a chair.

"We made it!" Tavian beamed. "We're in Traegos. We can finally get Mom back!"

Cassius blinked hard in an effort to steady the flashing lights burned into his iris. "No... I remember the light from that monster. Immense pain. Then, my family. She said... it wasn't my time."

"I saw things too," Aria said, crouching at his side with curious intent. "Did they tell you anything else?"

Cassius searched his memory, but everything came back blurred. He shook his head.

A robed figure helped steady him. "Don't dwell on it," the stranger said. "Transporting souls to Traegos is never clean. Many don't survive the transition."

"What, like they can't be brought back from death?" Aria asked.

The lead stranger stepped an inch closer. "Usually, yes. But—"

"Eldric brought us back, Cassius!" Tavian interrupted, face manic with excitement. "We died! But now we'll live forever!"

Eldric's hand lashed out and struck Tavian. He collapsed, groaning. "I told you not to speak. What's wrong with you?"

"I'm... excited," Tavian muttered through the sting. "He needed to know."

Eldric adjusted his robe and regained composure. A faint ticking sound, akin to a clock, picked up tempo then died back down. "What I *meant* to say," he continued cooly, "is that yes, you died. All of you. The colossus must kill before it allows passage into Traegos. But you were the chosen few we deemed worth reconstructing, to be brought back better than before."

Aria already knew, but hearing it aloud struck a chord she avoided playing.

"I was killed..." Cassius's fists clenched. "You brought me back?"

"Yes," Eldric said. "But now you'll never age, never fade. Time no longer holds you. You've been given power beyond death itself."

Cassius looked down. "Then... how do I get back to my family?"

Eldric knelt, lowering himself until their eyes met. "You don't need them anymore. You have eternity."

Cassius's voice hardened. "No." He looked up, eyes blazing. "Take me back to my family."

He lurched to his feet and made for the nearest door, whipping it open and storming out. One of the candle-headed creatures shuffled over and closed the door behind him. The flame atop its candle rippled from the gust of air, then steadied back to a point.

Tavian watched him leave, part of him wanting to follow. But Eldric's hand pressed against him, guiding him back.

"Not everyone sees this as a gift, but I'm glad you do. You understand the vision."

Tavian nodded apprehensively. He looked over to Aria and noticed her discomfort, her silence, her distant stare, the way her hands wouldn't stop twitching. She didn't appear to share his same enthusiasm for their new lives.

"I'm glad my messages reached you. I feared you'd never make it. We have important business to attend to." He motioned for them to follow.

Metal hummed through the floor as the colossus shifted its titanic weight. Every half-mile step resonated up their legs and into their bones, knocking them slightly off balance. None of them had found their land-legs yet.

Eldric led them through a labyrinth of steel corridors until they reached a vast, circular chamber. At its center was a grand throne flanked by eleven seats aligned in a half-moon arc. Eldric flipped a switch. Lights flooded the chamber in a blinding surge. When the glare subsided, Tavian squinted and saw that every chair was now occupied. Eleven robed figures sat before them, unmistakably powerful.

"This," Eldric declared, ascending to the central throne, "is the Rift-bound Order. We built this council to maintain the balance of Rifts across our fractured world. Each member before you is the most gifted soul in their respective area, personally chosen by their region's Watcher."

Tavian and Aria scanned the room. Though the robes concealed their faces, their presence was undeniable.

"We're under threat," Eldric continued. "A few have decided to upend the balance we've sacrificed everything to preserve."

"Forgive me," Tavian said, "but if you're all so powerful... why bring me here?"

Eldric leaned back. "Your mother was once an informal member of this council. Before her passing, she told us you were the future of our cause. Consider this your trial, a chance to prove yourself worthy of a seat she once sought."

Tavian smirked. "What would you have me do?"

Eldric nodded toward one of the council members. A parchment slid forward, then into Tavian's hands. A wanted poster. His eyes locked onto the two faces staring back at him: Lyra and Anastasia.

He recognized them instantly, the two girls from the bazaar. Even then, their aura had lingered, their power unmistakable. One of them, the small one with the blindfold, had left a distinct impression unlike anything he'd encountered before. She'd made Maeve feel insignificant, even.

"They threaten everything," Eldric said. "If left unchecked, they could destroy all that we've built. And there are rumors they've set their sights on Tenebral as well... where necromancy lives. I imagine that's not an outcome you're willing to accept; the end of rebirth."

Tavian's blood boiled. *No necromancy meant no mother.* That was not an option. His hands tightened around the poster, crumpling it with his fists.

"No, it's not."

"Good. Then—"

The doors burst open, slamming against the stone walls. A woman tumbled in, breathless and wild-eyed.

"What is the meaning of this interruption?"

"Apologies, Eldric," she panted. "A report just came in. Seraphina has joined with Lyra and Anastasia. They're coming for us."

Eldric laughed. "Seraphina, that self-righteous idealist? She thinks she can speak to us now?"

"They're not coming to talk. Fennwick's retrieval team killed someone close to her. She's coming for blood."

"They don't even know where we are—"

"They do," she cut in. "The young girl, Anastasia, she accessed everything Fennwick knew. She knows *everything* about us."

Eldric paused. A sharp pain lanced through the hollows of his chest, all his composure cracking for the briefest moment. "That *damned* Slug! To give that kind of power to a *child*, to a Necromite? What of the balance? Fool!"

He rose from his throne and stormed toward Tavian, stopping inches from his face. His breath stank of years-old fish and preserved cabbage, an odor that clung to every syllable. "Now you understand. This is no longer a task that can wait. Intercept them before they reach us. That is your test."

"But... if they're coming here anyway, wouldn't it be better to—"

"*Enough*!" Eldric growled. "This is your chance to prove yourself. You want your mother back, don't you? Then stop asking questions and *listen*."

Tavian nodded, stepping back to put space between them. "I understand. Where are they?"

Eldric retrieved a strange helmet from beside the throne and fitted it over Tavian's head. A high-pitched whirring filled his ears as the device powered on. Through the lens, a bird's-eye view flicked into focus—the forest they had passed through on their way to Traegos.

"They're there."

Eldric tore the helmet off and hurled it out of view.

"Go before it's too late. And take this."

He handed Tavian a dagger marked with alien symbols. "The undead are no easy task. You'll need specialized tools for the job."

Tavian grabbed the weapon and looked closer at the markings. "Undead? Who's un—"

"*Go*!" Eldric snapped.

Tavian turned to Aria and Aidra. Aria wouldn't meet his eyes. She clasped her hands, and the tip of her shoe traced small circles across the floor, an anxious tic he knew too well.

"Let's go," he said. "We have to find them."

Aria agreed and fell into step beside him, as she always did. Aidra too agreed, and joined alongside.

Tavian took a step toward the door, but his foot wouldn't budge. He looked down, watching his leg tremble. A deep-seated chill ran through him.

Can I do this? he thought. *What if I fail?*

He looked sideways and caught the image of Aria's shadow at his side. Aidra too, waiting on him.

Am I ready?

❀ ❀ ❀

"It's been nearly ten years, Finnian. We need to go back. I doubt anyone's still looking for us."

The axe struck the stump again, splitting through the dried wood. The repetitive *thud* sounded between them.

"Finnian," Violet tried again, softer this time.

He didn't look back at her. He raised the axe, brought it down, wiped the sweat, repeated.

"Finnian!"

"What?" he snapped, voice sharp as the blade in his hands. "Can't you see I'm busy?"

Violet rose from the back porch, the sting of his tone visible in her eyes, but she held her ground.

"I miss our daughter, Finnian. Don't you? We need to go back and find Orin. It's time to be a family again."

"We can't. It's not safe. You want our first reunion to be as corpses lying out in front of her?"

She stepped behind him, her hand pressing against his back. He stiffened, but didn't move away.

"It's been hard on both of us, I know. But we can't hide out here forever. If nothing else... we bring her back here, where it's safe. She's older now, she'll be ready this time."

He finally turned to face her, pain carved deep into his aging features, the first wrinkles settling under his tired eyes. "What makes you think she's still at Valspire? It's been years, Violet. She could be anywhere."

"We won't know until we try. And what if she's already discovered who she is?" Her voice broke. "We need to be there when she figures it out, before she becomes like those who lost themselves in Tenebral."

This was the moment he'd dreaded, yet always knew would come. The day safety finally yielded to love. The day they risked everything again.

"Finnian," she said softly, stepping even closer until her head rested against his chest. "The time's come. We can't keep hiding. Don't you want to see her again? To hold her in your arms? Raise her the way we always dreamed we would?"

He didn't answer. The memories came unbidden—his newborn daughter asleep in Orin's arms, the bustle of the port as they handed her over, the last look Aria gave him before they crossed the ocean.

His grip on the axe loosened. It slipped from his hand and struck the dirt, the blade burying itself halfway into the soil, where a few flowers were just starting to bud. Then he leaned into Violet, his forehead pressed to her shoulder as the first sob escaped.

She wrapped her arms around him, holding him steady as his knees began to wobble.

It was time to stop running, now was the time to find Aria. Not just to be a family again, but to keep her from being swallowed by the same darkness that had nearly consumed them both.

A row of trees barred the path ahead, their gnarled bark contorted like furrowed brows. Within the dense canopy, dozens—no, hundreds—of eyes waited. They weren't merely watching; they were judging, studying each step forward, probing intentions before the group had even crossed the threshold.

"Are we heading through?" Rowan asked, turning back to the rest. Seraphina and Cloud were a few paces ahead, while Lyra and Anastasia trailed behind, both staring at the forest's edge as if expecting the trees themselves to speak.

"I don't wanna go in there," Anastasia whined, as she reached out and clutched the seam of Lyra's shirt. Her hand squeezed, crumpling the fabric in her fist.

Lyra glanced down at her, then back to the forest. "We have to, though I feel it too, but there's no other way." Gently, she pried Anastasia's hand loose and interlaced their fingers. Together, they took the first step forward.

The forest closed around them like a living maze. Vines clung to their boots, damp moss proved slippery, and the light grew soft with a green tint. Time seemed to blur as they wandered; minutes, maybe hours, until they came upon a flattened outcrop. And one by one, the trunks began to turn to face them.

They wore masks that shifted across bark and branch; faces carved from living wood. Some bore wide, blank eyes, others twisted into abstract shapes without discernible emotion. None conveyed rage or sorrow or joy, only a wary curiosity. It was far different than what Tavian had encountered here, watchful rather than hostile.

From somewhere deep within the glade, a violin's melody drifted, thin and elegant, weaving between the trees. It came from a hut nestled at the clearing's heart, bathed in the same green light. The tune carried the wistful ache of something half-remembered.

"I used to love that song," Seraphina said. Her voice was soft, touched by memory, as she began to hum along.

Rowan looked up, noticing the tiny figures sitting there quietly along the upper branches. Acorn people, partially hidden among the leaves, clutching miniature slingshots carved from twigs. Rowan lifted a hand in greeting. A few of them waved back, their little arms moving to the beat of the song.

"Shall we?" he asked. "I'll go first."

Lyra gave a nod, stepping back and holding Anastasia's hand tighter. There was something coming from the hut; an odd, greenish energy that shimmered faintly around its edges. It beckoned, but there was hostility in it too. Something that couldn't be placed, ambiguous in nature.

Rowan approached the front door. "Hello? Is someone there? We're lost and looking for a way out."

The violin hit a sharp note and screeched into silence. What followed was not just quiet but expectance, waiting for more. A low rumble stirred the ground. The trees groaned in response as their roots twisted, their limbs folding into cross-legged shapes, sitting like ancient monks settling for meditation. The acorn people lowered their weapons and stilled.

Still, no reply came.

He knocked this time. "Hello? We just need some directions out of here—"

The door burst open with a violent creak. Rowan flinched back, just avoiding being struck. The hinges wailed, and the door swung wide, revealing a figure silhouetted in the frame.

A short, middle-aged woman stepped out. Her nails were long and lacquered a deep green caught in the dappled light. Silky hair spilled down her back, stirring in the wind as the forest's scattered light played across her flowing sundress.

"Why are you here?" she asked, her voice resonant with the weight of centuries behind it. "Must people always disturb my peace?"

Her eyes swept over Rowan, then to Seraphina, and finally fell on Lyra and Anastasia. Something shifted.

The trees began to stir. Their masks spun wildly through emotion—confusion, awe, sorrow, hope—faces revolving like a wheel that could not stop turning.

The woman's gaze softened, then hardened again, caught somewhere between reverence and alarm. "Why do I sense danger, yet feel no threat?"

Lyra tensed, pointing to herself. "Me?" Then to her sister. "Or her?"

The woman's voice went soft again. "What are your names?"

"Lyra," she answered. "And this is my sister, Anastasia."

The woman nodded and turned toward the door, motioning them inside. "I'm Thalia. Come in. Quickly."

They traded uncertain looks. Rowan and Seraphina offered half-hearted shrugs before stepping forward. Lyra crouched down to Anastasia and whispered in her ear. "Stay close. If I tap your shoulder, we run."

Anastasia nodded and gripped her sister's hand again. Together, they crossed into the hut. The door closed behind them and locked with a *clink*, sealing them inside. The hum of the forest resumed outside.

Inside, the hut was even smaller than it had appeared from the outside. A cluttered table to the left overflowed with bundles of dried herbs; beside it sat a crooked fireplace, a tiny stove, and three wooden chairs that looked handmade and uneven. A violin leaned against one of them, resting next to a stack of worn sheet music.

"That song," Seraphina said. "I recognized it. Where did you hear it?"

Thalia moved to the violin, tracing its neck as if greeting an old lover. "My husband used to bring me music. He traveled often, always chasing something new. Trinkets, songs, stories from faraway places. This one came from Aipiron," her eyes drifted to the window. "We used to play it together."

Seraphina's eyes wandered the walls, where hundreds of portraits lined the hut. Most were of the same man; always smiling, laughing, and standing beside Thalia in different locations.

"Is this him?" Seraphina asked, pointing to one of the photos, a scene outside the palace of Aipiron, the same place she called home.

Thalia's lips curved into a nostalgic smile. "Yes. He was everything to me. We loved it there."

Thalia walked over to the only window and waved to a tree outside. It responded with a small rustle, a leafy wave of its own.

Lyra looked to her suspiciously. "The trees... have they always been like that? Why do they act so human?"

"It's one of my *blessings*. A curse too, depending how you see it." Thalia grinned with a tinge of sorrow. "This entire forest was born from souls seeking peace. I stay behind to protect them."

Lyra stared out the window at the trees. Some looked serene, others restless. The one Thalia had greeted seemed almost anguished, like it still held onto regret from its past life.

"What happened to him?" Rowan asked. "Your husband... if you don't mind me asking."

"He too entered a Rift, after seeing what I had been given. But it hollowed him out. He was never the same after that day. There was malice behind his eyes that hadn't been there before. He lost passion for the things he once loved, and started saying things that didn't sound like him."

She looked away, blinking rapidly. For a long moment, the only sounds were of rustling trees outside the window. When she finally spoke again, her voice was scarcely above a whisper.

"Whenever I looked at him, it felt like I was staring at a stranger, a placeholder wearing the shape of my husband."

A single tear hit the floor, darkening the wood where it landed. "He took his life shortly after, I suppose searching for freedom beyond the madness."

A sharp pain flared in Lyra's temple. Her thoughts spiraled to the gray beach, the metallic scent of blood, the weight of her own killings. The woman at the port, the boy named Vid. The screams. The corpses. All of it surfacing unbidden.

"You wouldn't believe the torment these powers bring..." Thalia shifted her attention to Lyra. "Or maybe *you* would. The insanity, the loss of self. I know because I live it. I regret every moment I ever stepped into that Rift."

She rolled up her sleeves, revealing arms as a gallery of scars—some self-inflicted, others carved deliberately in bizarre, ritualistic patterns. "These marks are all that remain of that day. When they took me by the arm and etched their *gifts* into my bones."

"Is it all that bad though... the abilities you were given?" Seraphina asked, wrestling with her own uncertainty. "It's awful what happened to your husband, but... not all powers have to demand that kind of sacrifice, right?"

"Intent doesn't matter when the power itself is poison," Thalia replied. "If I could choose, the Rifts would vanish from this world entirely. But some cling to them and can't let go. The Riftbound Order ensures they never do. They keep them alive."

Lyra straightened. "The Riftbound Order?"

"They keep the cycle spinning. Immortal tyrants, obsessed with control. They offered me a seat among them once. I refused. After what happened to my husband, I fled here, hoping to shelter other lost souls and provide them a chance at a new beginning."

She took a step closer to Lyra, who instinctively mirrored a movement and took a step back, one hand rising in caution.

"I mean no harm," Thalia said. A green mist curled from her fingertips as she reached out and touched Lyra's collarbone, then Anastasia's. Her eyes widened.

"You're both powerful. Necromites, without question. But you don't *feel* like it."

The green light passed harmlessly through their skin. Their bodies didn't resist. They absorbed it, welcomed it.

"There was another boy here not long ago, not a Necromite, but corrupted with something festering. His darkness poisoned the air of this forest. He was hungry for Traegos." Thalia withdrew her hand. "You aren't like him. You'll find no enemy in me."

A stomach growled, breaking the tension.

"Sorry," Rowan said sheepishly. "Getting a little hungry."

Thalia chuckled. "The cupboard's all yours. Help yourself."

Rowan hesitated. "I shouldn't... well, maybe just a quick look." He scurried off, rummaging through the shelves. Seraphina joined him, happily pulling out whatever looked edible and assembling a small, chaotic feast from the forest's offerings.

Thalia turned back to Lyra, whose look still spoke of confusion and hesitation.

"You wonder why I brought you in," Thalia said.

"Yes. What's your plan here? Why bring us inside just to tell us about you and your husband?"

"Because I sense the same thing in you that I saw in him. That same war in your mind. You've been having nightmares, haven't you? Hallucinations?"

Lyra's guard shot back up. "How did you know that?"

Thalia's smile was small, knowing. "That more than answers my question." She got closer, her voice low and hushed. "You still have time. You can still change. There's hope for you. These are the things I wish I could've told him."

Lyra edged back, pulling Anastasia closer to her hip.

"You came from a wicked place," Thalia went on, "and were given power no one should have to bear alone. But remember this: people aren't born evil. They're shaped into it, taught it, and can be changed for the better. The Rift doesn't have to be a permanent scar, a constant reminder of your plight."

Thalia looked toward Rowan and Seraphina, but still speaking quietly enough for only Lyra to hear. "You need someone who reminds you what it's like to care. Someone to pull you out of the storm when you've forgotten yourself."

Lyra joined her gaze, looking right at Rowan. He was laughing now, a real, unguarded sound. His smile was easy, so bright it almost felt foreign. When he noticed her watching, he lit up.

"There's plenty left, Lyra! Come eat!"

A reluctant smirk tugged at her lips.

For a second he made her feel… light. Safe. Normal.

Thalia leaned in. “You look at him the way I looked at my husband. Don’t let time slip away. Regret comes too easily… before you know it, the moment’s gone, and it never comes back.”

Anastasia still clung to Lyra’s side, hearing every word. Tears welled in her eyes; not because of Thalia’s wisdom, but because every word had echoed the guilt she’d tried to bury. Thalia’s message dragged her secrets to the surface and pried open what she sealed away.

She’d lied to Lyra. She’d hurt her.

And now, standing in this quiet hut, Anastasia couldn’t tell if she’d made the right choice back in Tenebral.

Maybe Lyra didn’t need to die.

Maybe Anastasia never should have done it.

CHAPTER TWENTY-ONE
'TIL DEATH DO US PART

Tenebral doesn't welcome outsiders, Tavian. You won't find mercy there.
~Lyra Ashryn

ANASTASIA CURLED UP IN A LARGE, WORN CHAIR.

It was tucked in the corner of Thalia's hut. The cushion swallowed her, and before she realized it, her eyelids grew heavy, gravity pulling them shut as exhaustion claimed her.

The others' voices faded into a distant hum, muffled beneath the haze of sleep. Images from the day flickered behind her eyes, gradually twisting into something darker from her past; back at the Rift where she had been given her powers.

Slug hovered above her, a disgusting figure whose mere presence repulsed her. Behind him, Ravenna and Corvin waited, seated and eerily composed, their mouths twitching with anticipation like starving animals forced to sit still before their meal.

"This one is special, Ravenna," Slug rasped, his voice slithering across the stone walls. "You've a knack for producing valuable offspring."

Ravenna clasped Corvin's hands so tightly that their veins bulged along their wrists. "Yes, I know," she purred. "But don't leave us begging. What will she be getting?"

Slug's slimy limbs continued to probe Anastasia, each touch invasive and unnervingly precise. Abruptly, they shot back into his gelatinous mass.

"I want to test the true limits of the human form," he declared.

"With this one, I'll experiment. If she survives, the future is limitless." His grin widened grotesquely, revealing too many teeth. "She'll become a new commander of the Rifts."

Inside, his thoughts swirled. *They mock me. Call me a failed Watcher. Let them laugh. I'll show them all—the Riftbound Order, the Watchers, every last arrogant husk. I can command the Rifts as well as they can. And this girl will be my proof.*

He bent down, his face inches from hers. "I have one question, dear girl."

Anastasia stared up at him, her violet eyes shining even in the nightmare.

"What do you want from me?" There was a disturbing false kindness in his tone. "I know what your parents want, but what about you? I owe you that much, at least. A small reciprocity for offering your body."

Anastasia tilted her head, thinking hard. Placing a finger to her chin, she answered with childlike sincerity. "I like flowers, but Mom says they can't grow in the snow. I want to grow my own and give my sister some."

Slug's head snapped back as a thunderous laugh shook the chamber. The ceiling tilted as Ravenna and Corvin steadied themselves against the floor.

"Children," Slug hissed through peals of laughter, "always full of surprises."

His arms lunged again, plunging into Anastasia's body. This time, they dove deeper; past flesh, into muscle, organs, and bone. She dropped to her knees, gasping, her fingers clawing at the cold stone floor. Pain rippled through her, searing every nerve.

The hands retracted.

"You want flowers?" Slug bellowed. "So be it. The flowers will grow on graves."

Anastasia staggered to her feet, swaying but refusing to fall. Her gaze met his again, filled now with defiance.

"On graves? What does that—"

But the question couldn't escape her lips before one of his fingers shot forward, driving straight for her eyes. A flash of agony, blinding pain, exploded through her.

Anastasia jolted awake with a gasp, heart pounding at a sporadic pace. The nightmare—no, the memory—dissolved in the warmth of Thalia's hut. Her hands were clenched into fists and sweaty, she could still feel the phantom pain in her sockets.

Laughter floated through the air.

Still half-sunken in the chair, she turned her head. Around the wooden table sat Lyra, Thalia, Seraphina, Cloud, and Rowan, bathed in the cozy flicker of lantern light. Their faces were calm, gentle, and safe, with the warm smell of fire burning and herbs roasting.

"My mom and I used to go into the fields behind our house and collect wild mushrooms for dinner," Rowan said, reminiscing at the memory. "A small thing, but it stuck with me all these years."

He turned to Lyra. "What about you? Did your family have any traditions?"

Lyra glanced down, fingers fidgeting in her lap. "No, not really."

The table fell quiet. Rowan placed a hand over hers. "That's okay," he said with that same unshakable optimism. "You've still got plenty of life left to live."

Lyra looked up, expecting mockery. But his wide, genuine grin disarmed her. She wasn't used to kindness so effortless, so unearned. It was light meeting shadow, sweetness to balance her bitter edges.

She smiled despite herself.

"I never noticed the flowers in your hair before, Lyra," Seraphina commented. "Rowan get those for you?"

Lyra's cheeks flushed. She gently nudged Rowan's hand from hers, not to reject him, but to hide the building warmth.

"No. Actually, Anastasia gave them to me a while ago, the night before I left Tenebral, while I slept. I'd almost forgotten I still had them."

She turned toward her sister, who was now sitting upright, fully awake.

"Isn't that right, Anastasia?"

She yawned, still recovering from the dream's grip, and nodded.

"Yes," she replied. "Slug gave me that gift. The eternal flowers. Flowers that grow on—"

She stopped herself and immediately began to cry.

Lyra was at her side in an instant, pulling her into a hug. "Hey, I love them. No need to cry."

"I know," Anastasia said through her tears, hugging her sister tighter. "I just—"

One day I'll tell her. Just not yet.

A day later, Lyra's thoughts forcefully flashed back to Rowan. Not the hut, not the violence, but the small moments between, before everything fell apart. Those memories rolled through her like a persistent tide, refusing to recede.

In this memory, she sat beside him in the dirt, looking through the film of the recorder during their travels together. The moon above poured silver light across the clearing, full and bright enough to feel like day. A gentle wind rustled the grass, and Lyra shivered from the cold.

Behind them, Seraphina, Anastasia, and Cloud were clustered around a modest makeshift fire, preparing food beside the tent they'd thrown together, sagging to one side. This was not long after leaving Aipiron, one step closer toward Valspire, but the road still felt endless.

"You know what's funny?" Rowan said, clicking through the various videos that had been captured. "I didn't realize how often you smile until I looked back at these. You seem a lot... lighter now. Maybe Seraphina's makeup lessons are cheering you up?"

Lyra laughed and punched his arm, not too hard. "Not at all. I just think it's nice being away from home... nice to feel like we're getting closer to something."

She turned toward the horizon. Valspire wasn't visible yet, but she could feel it.

Rowan followed her gaze. "It's getting closer, yeah, but I'm glad we found each other first."

When she turned back, his face was closer than before, too close. Neither of them moved. Their eyes met, hands hovering inches apart, an invisible thread drawing them in.

A voice called from behind her, shattering the spell. Lyra turned toward it, and the memory dissolved. The moonlight vanished, replaced by the rhythm of waves, the scent of salt, and the creak of a boat hull. In this new memory, she found herself standing on a boat. The same one they'd taken when fleeing Ashford, their wild escape from Maeve.

"Lyra! Rowan said I can play with Cloud! Wanna come?" Anastasia tugged at her pants, grinning wide and innocent.

Lyra crouched beside her, brushing a stray lock from her sister's face. "Not right now. But you go have fun, okay?"

Anastasia scampered off, nearly hitting her head on the doorway.

At the helm, Rowan was hammering at the ship's console, frantically trying to adjust unmarked knobs. "Please help, I have absolutely no idea what I'm doing."

Lyra stepped close and nudged him gently out of the way, their bodies brushing. A warm flutter stirred in her chest.

"I'll figure it out," she insisted, trying to sound composed even as her cheeks burned.

Rowan watched in awe as she twisted dials and tapped at glowing panels. When the ship righted itself, he placed a hand to his chest and gave a dramatic bow. "Brilliant work, milady."

Lyra rolled her eyes and started to walk away, but when her back was turned, she formed a quiet smile.

She braced her arms on the railing, letting the ocean spray cool her face, watching Anastasia chase Cloud across the deck. Then Rowan's voice called again.

"Lyra."

She sighed, still smiling. "What do you want now?"

She turned, but the memory fractured again.

The deck, the sea, the sunlight all bled away, replaced by walls she half-remembered. The next memory placed her inside a building, a suite of some kind. Rowan sat on a couch beside Anastasia, while Lyra stood behind a corner, hidden, eavesdropping on their conversation. She remembered this day, but only in fragments.

"You and your sister are pretty close, huh?" Rowan asked.

Anastasia nodded.

"When's her birthday?"

She tilted her head. "We never really did anything for that. I don't even remember mine."

"What?" Rowan gasped, clutching his chest in mock offense. "You expect me to believe you don't celebrate the day you were *born*? That's criminal!"

Anastasia giggled. "It's true! I always wanted to, but Mom and Dad would make us work or do chores instead."

Rowan shot to his feet, indignant. "Unacceptable. Tell me what she likes. We must celebrate immediately! We've got *years* of birthdays to make up for."

Anastasia clapped. "Yay! And cake too, right?"

"Obviously. A cake the size of this palace. Maybe bigger."

She danced in place, the joy bubbling out of her.

"I'm gonna tell Lyra!" she sang, skipping toward the door.

"Wait! It's supposed to be a surprise!" Rowan chased after her.

Lyra stepped back from the corner, heart fluttering, careful not to be seen. But as she turned another hallway, this memory dissolved to a new one, the final one.

She now stood in the Aipiron ballroom, caught in one of the palace's formal gatherings. The hall gleamed with gold chandeliers, diamond-crusted tableware, and lavish dishes from across the lands. The air was fragrant with perfume and sweetened with the tang of wine. A string quartet performed while nobles, dressed in their finest attire, twirled in slow circles in the background.

Rowan stood before her in a perfect-fitted suit, every trace of his usual clumsiness replaced by nervous grace. He extended his hand to her.

"Do you need something?" Lyra asked.

He cleared his throat, swiping sweat onto his jacket. "No... well, yes. I was wondering if you wanted to dance. Everyone's doing it."

"I can't dance," she said quickly. "No one wants to see that."

"I do," Anastasia said. She reached into Rowan's eyes, borrowing his sight, and saw her sister the way he did.

Through him, Lyra was stunning—no frown lines, no bruises, no weariness lining the ridges of each cheek. Only beauty. Her dress hung awkwardly in places, but the imperfection only made her look all the more real, all the more breathtaking. Her slight dimples that formed when she spoke, the fall of her hair brushing down to her ribs, her lightly applied makeup that was done with more care than she put on, the faint freckles dotting the bridge of her nose... Rowan had memorized them all.

Anastasia blinked, overwhelmed by the depth of what she saw. To see her sister through his eyes was to rediscover her, to remember beauty beyond the scars and sorrow.

She missed seeing Lyra that way. Missed seeing *anything* that way.

Lyra crossed her arms. "Can you even dance? We're going to look like fools."

"That may be true, but I'm willing to take that risk."

Before she could protest, he took her hand and led her away from the edge of the dance floor. The crowd parted as he guided her to the center, repositioning her hands over his shoulders.

"Here," he said. "Follow my lead."

And somehow, they were dancing. Not gracefully like Seraphina and her father, who soon joined them on the floor, but with something better: with heart. Their steps were uneven, improvised, clumsy yet alive.

Anastasia sat in a tall chair in the corner, seeing through Rowan's eyes as she swung her legs and pet Cloud beside her.

The audience gathered. Applause rose as Rowan dipped Lyra with exaggerated flair, spinning her until her hair brushed the floor. Seraphina winked at her from across the room.

Lyra leaned in closer, flustered. "They're all watching."

"Then don't mess up," Rowan laughed, leading her into another spin.

They moved together in sync, their rhythm guided by instinct more than skill. The clapping grew louder, but to her, it faded in the distance. Lyra locked eyes with him and, for a fleeting moment, the world no longer seemed to matter. There were no nobles, no music, no eyes upon them. Only him.

But screams managed to break through her trance. Muffled at first, but then that same metallic scent crept into her nose: iron, salty, and thick.

Lyra stayed in his arms, clinging to the warmth of the moment, trying to keep the memory alive.

But then came another scream. Cloud's barking. Anastasia's voice shouting something incoherent.

"Anastasia?" Lyra turned to look back, but the crowd was too dense to see through.

She turned to Rowan again, only to find his face drenched in blood.

Crimson spilled from deep gashes in his forehead, streaking down his cheeks like tears. His body was riddled with holes, leaking life faster than an over-flowing bucket.

Lyra jolted back into reality, no longer caught in the long-forgotten memories replaying in her head. The ballroom, the music, the chandeliers: all gone. Instead, she was surrounded by trees in an open expanse, the outside air brisk and rainy.

She was kneeling over a body.

Blood pooled beneath her, absorbing into her clothes, hot and endless. Her hands were pressed into open wounds, trying to stop the flow, but it was already too late.

Her vision was blurry, trying to readjust to the outside world. Her breathing became uneven. The scene felt detached, like she hadn't fully left the dreams and snapped back to actuality.

"Lyra!"

Anastasia's voice. Lyra looked up.

Her sister stood above her, hands painted red. Her face was contorted in horror, tears pouring like the rain.

"I couldn't tell you. I wanted to, but I was too scared to make you mad. Please don't be upset at me, Lyra. I only kill when I have no choice. I promise... please don't hate me."

Kill?

Lyra's pulse spiked.

She looked down, and the daze finally shattered.

The body beneath her, the eyes staring lifeless into the sky.

It was Rowan.

Her mouth opened, but no sound came. Her mind was unable to

process the weight of what had happened. The memory of their dance still beat in her chest, but now it felt like a cruel, mocking illusion.

Rowan's body lay broken, a partner she could never dance with again.

He was dead.

Had Anastasia killed him?

CHAPTER TWENTY-TWO

BEFORE DEATH: CAUGHT IN THE CROSSFIRE

> All things must die eventually. This is no way to live.
> ~Lyra Ashryn

EARLIER THAT DAY, BEFORE HIS END, ROWAN STOOD.

He was found beneath the trees, unaware of what was to come.

The sky had grown to a deep grey. The trees sounded whispers as the breeze shuffled through their branches, and a cold unease threaded itself through Rowan's chest like a constricting knot.

He placed a hand over his stomach, nausea rising in swirls. A feeling of impending doom took root, like his body knew something his mind did not.

"Are you all right? You sure you don't need to rest any longer?" Thalia asked, her brows raised as she caught the pallor in Rowan's face.

"No, I'm fine." He forced a weak smile and quickly let his hand fall to his side. "Probably just ate too much."

Thalia studied him for a moment longer, reading something deeper into his posture, but said nothing. She walked forward and extended a hand to the forest. "Let me show you the way toward Valspire."

With a soft creak and shuffle, the trees parted as if they too understood the importance of this moment. Their limbs groaned like old bones, creating a passageway forward.

"Follow that path. It's still some distance, but you'll reach it in due time."

One by one, the group gathered to say their goodbyes. Thalia offered hugs, well-wishes, and lingering glances to each of them. But before Lyra could step away, her hand reaching for Rowan's, Thalia caught her elbow and pulled her aside.

"When do you plan on telling him?" Thalia asked, a sly smirk formed.

"Tell him what?" Lyra asked, voice low and quite defensive.

Thalia tilted her head knowingly. Lyra looked away, cheeks reddened.

"I'll get to it when the time is right," she muttered, then jogged ahead to catch up with the others.

Behind her, Thalia's voice echoed. "Don't wait too long, now. Time doesn't stop for anyone!"

They left Thalia's woods behind. The trees thinned until the air grew bare and open, the smell of moss replaced by mountainous wind. Beyond the forest, the terrain had changed, and the sun, once golden and warm, now cast an amber glow across steep cliffs in the far distance. They came upon a rocky clearing, where the forest broke into mountains.

It was there, in that emptiness, where movement caught Lyra's eye. Three silhouettes approached from the far ridge.

She stopped in her tracks, squinting hard to make them out. "Let's go around," she said. "We don't need to run into anyone out here."

Rowan tried to keep the mood light. "It'll be fine. Maybe they know the way to Valspire. Couldn't hurt to socialize a little, right?"

Lyra sighed, wiping her tired eyes. "We don't need socialization right now, Rowan. We—"

A gunshot tore through their conversion. Lyra moved her hand away from her face.

Rowan's body jerked as if struck by lightning. Blood burst from his chest, scattering red across the mud. His expression froze in shock before his body slumped over like a ragdoll.

"Rowan!" Lyra screamed, his name traveling through the wind as she sprinted toward him.

Across the way, the silhouetted woman lowered her pistol, its barrel still trailing a thin wisp of smoke. Two others stood beside her; a girl wielding an impossibly large sword, and a boy with one hand holding an engraved dagger with strange markings. All three were still, stunned by what had happened.

The woman who shot, Aidra, blinked in disbelief as she caught the name Lyra had screamed.

"Rowan?"

Her eyes moved to the dropped weapon laying beside the fallen boy. She knew it immediately, the engravings were unmistakable, the same as on her own, tally marks indicating the undead body count. As Rowan hit the ground, a photograph slipped from his pocket, into the dirt, and unfolded in the wind.

Aidra's stomach turned to stone. Her fingers went slack, the pistol slipped from her grip, landing on the ground with a muted thud.

The photo stared back at her: Rowan's smile, her arm around his shoulder, the both of them younger, carefree.

She had shot her own son.

"No," she whispered, inching forward in disbelief, the reality refusing to settle.

Before Lyra could reach his body, Aria threw her sword from across the way like a javelin, driving clean through Lyra's torso, into the ribs and muscle, out the other side. Her blood joined his. She staggered, gritting her teeth from the initial jolt of agony, but kept running.

Aria recoiled. "How the hells...?"

Lyra looked down at the hole in her side, her clothes now drenched red. Her fingers pressed against the wound, and she felt her flesh slowly knitting together, organs mending like time had run in reverse.

"What's happening to me?" Lyra cried as she dropped to her knees beside Rowan. "How am I still alive?"

Ignoring her own suffering, her shaking hands pressed against his chest, trying to halt the flow, but it only poured faster.

Flashes of memories crashed onto her: birthday whispers, laughter on the boat, their first dance in Aipiron. She couldn't lose him. Not after all that.

Anastasia's voice cut through the blur. "I couldn't tell you. I wanted to, but I was too scared to make you mad. Please don't be upset at me, Lyra. I only kill when I have no choice. I promise... please don't hate me."

Lyra's mind turned to confused panic. "What are you talking about? You didn't kill Rowan. Who did you kill—"

Anastasia raised a shaky finger and pointed toward Lyra. "I had to. Mom made me. The flowers, Lyra... they grow on graves. Mom said we could be a family forever. Please, don't be mad."

The wind picked up, curling through Lyra's hair. The flowers woven into her locks swayed with the breeze. A few petals dropped off and fell beside her, landing beside Rowan's hollowed chest. Not a second later, new petals sprouted in her hair, vivid and alive again.

"Flowers..." Lyra's fingers reached up and plucked one from her braid. It wilted, crumbling to dust in her palm. Another bloomed in its place, already tangled in her hair, seamlessly replacing the old one.

Anastasia threw herself against her sister, wrapping her arms around her waist. "I was going to tell you, but Mom made me promise! She said if I killed you, I could bring you back so you'd never leave me again and we'd be together forever!"

Lyra could only stare at Rowan. Too many things were happening at once for her mind to focus on any one of them. His breaths were ragged, sounding more like a struggle with each passing exhale. He was trying to speak.

"Recorder... remember..."

She leaned closer. "What, Rowan? I'm here. Stay awake. I'll get you out—"

He touched a finger to her lips, weak and reeling.

"Remember. The recorder." He reached into his pocket, fingers slick with blood, and pulled out a small device. He placed it against her chest. "Watch it... all of it."

"No, Rowan, don't go. You'll be okay. You have to hold on. We can fix this, somehow."

Her mind screamed for time to stop, for just one more moment with him, but the words couldn't reach her throat.

He smiled faintly as if the recorder was enough, as a way to keep him alive in her memory once he was gone. Then his eyes began to cloud. "The Watcher. My deal. They took it away from me."

She moved in closer. "Took what away? What was the deal you made for that gun?"

He coughed up small gouts of blood, staining his lips. "For the gun, I can't be saved. It's over, Lyra. It's what I chose."

She turned, frantically grabbing her sister's hands.

"Do what you did to me, Anastasia. Bring him back, keep him with us. Please."

"You want him to be like you?" Anastasia whispered. "Forever?"

Lyra desperately pleaded. "Please. I can't be the one to do it, please do it for me."

A scarlet glow enveloped Anastasia's hands, her entire body rocked as power moved through her. Her blindfold slipped loose. The sockets bled in multicolored hues, her hair began to lift upwards, her skin lined with distended veins pumping blood at an erratic pace. She reached her hands over his corpse, summoning the deep-seated powers within to keep him alive, the same force that made flowers grow on graves.

"Wait! Stop!"

It was Aidra.

Lyra raised her scythe.

"I'm his mother!" She shouted, falling to her knees alongside them. "Stop what you're doing!"

Anastasia stopped. Her hands dimmed, her sockets losing some color.

Aidra cradled Rowan's face, brushing back his hair with twitching fingers. Her tears streamed freely, splashing onto his cheeks.

"Rowan... I can't believe you found me. I'm so sorry." Her voice cracked under the weight of forgotten years. "I should've never left you and your father. There's so much I never said."

Rowan's glassy eyes found hers. A few tears rolled from their corners, his last living reflex.

"I missed you," he whispered. "I'm glad you remember me."

He reached for the photo lying in the dirt and held it beside her face, comparing her to the smiling woman he had once known. Then he placed it in her hands and turned toward Lyra, gathering one final breath.

"Keep Mom safe for me... and Cloud too. I'll miss you, Lyra. I wish I could've... told... you—"

His light flickered out. His chest stopped rising, relaxing back to its breathless state.

Time had moved on without her. Lyra was too late, even too weak, to save him. His mother cried, folding over his broken form, while Anastasia lay near him, hands with a partial glow, still unwilling to let go of all chances to bring him back. Lyra only stared, lost, her attention fixed on a speck of dirt clinging to his eyebrow. Her vision pulsed in and out. She had never lost someone she couldn't bring back.

"Take him home," Aidra coughed. "Back to Westwick. His father, Rodrick, deserves to see his son one last time. To give him a proper goodbye."

Her resolve lasted only seconds before it crumbled. She fell forward again, weeping over her son's emptied chest.

Lyra said nothing.

Cloud emerged from the tree line, tail low, ears folded back. The dog padded over the bloodied ground and licked Rowan's face before curling beside him, whimpering.

They had failed. They were too late. And something dark began to stir.

"What are you doing, Aidra? We need to get them, not cry with them!" Tavian shouted.

The ground underfoot Lyra began to quake with a force akin to the colossal steps of Traegos. Cracks split the earth, red haze coiled upward like smoke from hell itself. The putrid stench of decay followed. Lyra's tears, once clear, now fell as blood—thick spheres sliding down her face and splashing across Rowan's arms. Her veins bulged beneath her skin, dark and throbbing.

The trees around her withered in seconds, leaves curling to ash. Birds circling overhead dropped like stones, their bodies limp with beady eyes staring at Tavian.

Aidra scrambled to her feet, slipping on the bloody grass, bolting for the tree line. She didn't look back; she didn't need to. There was a storm building at the center of Lyra's grief, the pressure unstable and asphyxiating. Anastasia joined Aidra, she too was frightened at what may become of her sister.

Thunder cracked overhead. The air vibrated with continuous tremors, the earth groaning from deep underground. Rain now fell in heavy sheets, washing away the last traces of Rowan's blood as it vanished into the blackened grass.

Lyra's cries transformed to laughter; high-pitched, raw, and unhinged. She looked down at her hands, now glowing with unstable necromantic energy. Rowan's image appeared again and again around her, surrounding her in a cruel form of taunting. Her head throbbed violently, her thoughts glitching and incoherent.

Without hesitation, she lifted her scythe with one hand. She swung, the blade cleaved clean through her wrist.

Her severed hand dropped to the mud, twitching once before going still. Impossibly, a new one began to regenerate in its place. Skin formed over bone, veins snaked through flesh, muscles reforming within seconds.

She dragged the blade's sharp tip along her torso, methodically, parting flesh from belly to collarbone. Blood gushed from the wound, pooling in a semicircle around her, steaming against the cold rain. Yet she did not die. The gash stitched itself closed, her body whole again.

"I've been killed," she cried, caught somewhere between wonder and madness. "But I can't die." A broken chuckle escaped her. "Rowan's dead, and they won't let me bring him back. He's gone forever."

She reached for him, her palms producing necromantic energy, eager to spill life into what remained of him. But as her fingers brushed his thigh, a hand caught her wrist.

Rowan stood before her, or rather the image of him. He was translucent and solemn, his look filled with disgust, as though Lyra was committing a horrific act that displeased him.

She recoiled, stumbling backward on herself. They stared at one another, and she raised her fingers, mimicking a pistol. With a flick and a silent *bang*, she shot at the image of him.

He didn't flinch, didn't fall over, didn't laugh. Instead, he disintegrated into wind.

"Please," Tavian shouted. "Come with us. We don't want to hurt you. No one else has to die."

He edged closer to the manic girl, Eldric's dagger concealed behind his back, only the blade's edge glinting as it peeked past his hip.

Lyra's head snapped toward him. Her eyes were bleeding heavier now, the streams running down her face faster than the remaining blood that still trickled from Rowan's body.

Tavian flinched and averted his stare. He was reminded of Eldric's warning: *Never look into her eyes when they bleed.*

"You don't know what it's like to lose someone you love," he said with fixed attention to the ground. "Just come with me. They need you so I can bring Mom back."

Few words could've struck Lyra deeper. The irony was venomous.

The earth had now fully split open beneath Lyra like a beast clawing its way free from the underworld. The red smoke condensed into honed blades, shooting up from the ground at Tavian with terrifying speed. He dove aside, the barrage slicing through parts of his coat, leaving shallow cuts across his arm.

With a grunt, he took the dagger and hurled it toward her. But the instant the blade neared her, it ricocheted off an invisible barrier, burying itself deep into a nearby tree trunk.

Seraphina stepped in, raising both hands, maintaining the small shield she willed for Lyra. She glared at Tavian, the image of Vid's death now bright and hot within her mind.

From behind her, Aria burst into motion, sprinting at inhuman speed toward Seraphina with her massive sword arcing high. Seraphina saw through her tactic and thrust both palms forward. A gravitational wave slammed into Aria's chest, launching her backward into the dirt with a bone-crunching thud.

Lyra rose to her feet, scythe clenched tight, the storm now raging at its peak.

I don't know what it's like to lose someone I love?

She shot forward like a missile. Her foot cracked the ground beneath the heel at the force of her launch, closing the distance in a breath. He barely had time to raise his arms before her shadow overtook him.

As her scythe came down, a metallic clash rang out. Aria, already recovered from Seraphina's blow, intercepted the strike with her sword held high.

Lyra's hair whipped wildly, her scythe held firm in both hands, her dark jacket fluttering like torn wings. Her stance was sharp and guarded, but her glare flickered with something more. Something about Aria felt familiar, but most of all, something about her was frightening.

Aria stood opposite her, feet braced in the mud. The earth clung to her boots and forearms; lines of blackened blood and distended veins popped from the sides of her neck. Her hair hung in knotted strands, with eyes brimming an unrestrained rage. Her necromantic energy pulsed visibly, dark veins trailing from her collarbone down her arms and legs.

For a suspended moment, neither moved, steel grinding against steel.

Then Aria shoved her back with a labored push, breaking the lock.

"Who are you?" Lyra hissed, catching her balance. "You're a Necromite, I can feel it, but I've never seen you in Tenebral."

Tavian crouched behind her with hands covering his face in defense, peeking through the cracks in his fingers.

"Necromite? What is she talking about?"

Seraphina didn't give him a chance to think it over. She surged her power downward, slamming Tavian's body into the dirt. He gritted his teeth, planting both hands on the ground and pushing against the weight, only enough to hold himself from being crushed entirely.

"Don't touch Tavian."

Aria swung at Lyra, her massive blade falling in a wide arc that nearly took off Lyra's head. The sword cleaved the ground, creating a geyser of soil and stone exploding into the air.

Lyra retaliated, flinging her scythe forward in a whirling blur. It spun end-over-end, a streak of red light through the dark storm. Aria kept clear, only for Lyra to vanish and reappear where the weapon landed, vaulting off its snath and kicking Aria square in the chest.

The impact sent Aria skidding through the mud. She rolled and came up on one knee, slamming the tip of her sword into the soil. Obelisks of hardened blood erupted upwards, their bloodied spikes lancing toward Lyra from every angle.

She spun with her scythe, carving through them in a crimson

cyclone. Each shattered spike liquified, raining down as warm, viscous blood that splattered across her face and arms.

Then, returned the visions.

Rowan; his face, his voice, his death.

They engulfed her senses, bending around her like vines of grief wrapped around her throat. Her swings grew erratic. Corpses rose in her periphery, whether they were hallucinations, reality, or memory, she could no longer tell.

Red lightning cracked from the sky in sync with her screams, spearing the ground near Aria. Each strike came faster and closer, far too fast to dodge. One bolt found its mark.

Aria's body lit up and crashed to the floor. Before she could breathe again, Lyra was already over her, the rain dripping off her bloodstained face onto Aria's torn shirt.

A blade of hardened blood shot from Aria's abdomen; Lyra swatted it aside, then drove her boot into Aria's stomach.

Raising her scythe high, Lyra sliced downward in a clean, merciless sweep through Aria's throat. Blood sprayed across the grass, Aria spasmed, clutching at the gash in her neck, her eyes closed and wet with pain. She choked and flailed, the wound gurgling liquid as she fought for air.

And then her body healed. Flesh sealed. Breath returned. Aria gasped back in the fresh air, her throat glistening with a new layer of skin.

"We're awfully alike," Lyra said sardonically. "Not just a Necromite, but another undead victim."

She grabbed Aria by the collar and hauled her upright. "You and that boy need to leave. Now. Or I'll kill you both." Lyra's hands flashed Rowan's pistol from under her coat. The metal presented a cold promise.

Aria leaned in, throat still ragged from the knitted wound. "W-we can't leave. You might be able to convince me, but Tavian can't walk away. The Order won't let him. He's bound to them."

Lyra pivoted toward Tavian, still pinned under Seraphina's crushing gravity, his limbs scrabbling for purchase on the torn earth.

"You, Tavian," she said coldly. "Let us handle the Riftbound Order. It's your time for you to go."

"No." He spat the single word. "I won't let you destroy them. I won't let necromancy die with you. I need it."

Lyra moved toward him. Each footfall was heavy and thunderous. She leaned over, the blood still wet around her eyes and her gloss smearing. Tavian flinched and turned his head, careful not to meet those bleeding eyes.

"They're using you," she hissed, yanking his jaw so he had to look. "Open your eyes, stop obsessing over meaningless things, and leave before my patience runs out."

Lyra motioned for Seraphina to loosen her grasp. Seraphina reluctantly released her hold like a sigh. The pressure lifted from Tavian's spine, and he lurched up, body still tense with arms raised halfway in defense.

"What are you talking about?" he panted. "Why would they do that to me?"

"I don't know," she replied. "And I don't care. If you want necromancy, the answers are found in Tenebral. That's where it lives, no one here can teach you what you need."

Tavian paused, brushing blood off his forehead, the wound slowly knitting closed. But something in his eyes had shifted, an inner conflict rising to the surface.

"You don't understand," he said. "I made a deal with Eldric and Maeve. For everything they've done for me, I owe them my body and soul."

Lyra's expression darkened at the name Maeve. Her patience was razor-thin. "You're testing me, Tavian. I don't give a damn about your deals. Do you want to die here and be rid of your contracts?"

She stepped close, one hand gripping her scythe, the other sliding the pistol up to his head.

"I won't leave," he said simply. "You can't kill me with empty threats. I'm undead. I—"

A crack rolled through the mountains.

Lyra lowered the pistol and shot him in the thigh.

Tavian howled in agony, collapsing onto his side. He clutched the torn muscle, but this time the wound didn't heal. The regenerative powers in his blood proved useless to the bullet. He looked down at the mangled flesh, at the crater where flesh should've been.

"You're not immortal," Lyra said, standing over him. "Not to this. I can kill you. Both of you. Want another demonstration?"

Aria rushed to his side, lifting him upright. He leaned against her heavy, breath shallow. "We'll go. Don't mind him—please."

Aria took a quick glance at Rowan's body on the ground. The recognition hit her like a swift gut punch. The boy from the Bazaar, the one that bought her the ring. Tavian's ring.

What was he doing with people like this?

She didn't have time to linger. She hoisted Tavian's arm up around her and began guiding him away. Lyra's voice followed with one final warning. "Tenebral doesn't welcome outsiders, Tavian. You won't find mercy there. You've chosen the wrong field to lay in. You should've stayed home—you should've let your mother go."

Tavian gave a blood-slicked middle finger without looking back. With Aria's arm around him, he limped into the horizon, vanishing past the stone ridge toward the land of the dead.

"You're letting them go?" Seraphina asked, incredulous. "We could've ended it. Both of them."

Lyra remained silent, still looking to where they'd gone.

"They didn't kill Rowan," she said softly. "And he never liked it when I killed without reason."

She balled her fist, restraining her tears. She turned, walking toward her sister and Aidra, both huddled near the trees.

Aidra had her arms wrapped around Anastasia's shoulders, her head buried in the girl's shirt as she wept. She looked up as Lyra approached and flinched, expecting judgment.

But Lyra only knelt beside her. The fury was gone from her face. What remained only was sorrow, exhaustion, and the weight of death clinging to her bones like never before.

"Get up," Lyra said.

Aidra struggled to rise, barely able to steady herself. She clutched the photo of her and Rowan, though the rain had blurred the ink so that only parts of their faces remained.

Lyra seized her collar and yanked her close. "What kind of mother abandons her child? He spent years searching for you, believing you were out there. And when he finally reached you, it was your gun he met first."

Aidra's composure decomposed back to wracking sobs. "I didn't know. I would never hurt Rowan!"

Her body shook. She caught a glimpse of her son's gun tucked inside Lyra's coat and pulled it free. The metal seared her palm but she didn't let it go. She placed it in Lyra's hands.

"Let me see him again," Aidra whispered.

The gun Rowan had carried, the one he had used to kill the undead. A cursed weapon with a holy purpose. One that could kill the unkillable. Aidra forced Lyra's hand around the grip and guided her finger to the trigger. She then placed the barrel against her own forehead. At last her hands stilled.

"Please," she whispered again, "bring his body back to Westwick. His father's name is Rodrick. Tell him... tell him I was wrong. I should've never left. I was selfish—a terrible mother, a terrible wife." Her voice faltered then steadied—calmer than it had been. "But tell him I'm all right now. I'll be with Rowan. We'll be waiting for him."

Lyra stared, unable to picture lifting the gun against Rowan's own mother. "I can't—"

"Do it!" Aidra screamed. "Has a damned Necromite ever waited this long? I can't live with what I did... knowing what I've done to my son. Don't send me back to Maeve. End it. Let me see him again."

Lyra's throat tightened, her eyes welled again. Aidra's face was a mirror of Rowan's; the same bone structure, the same voice, the same eye shape. For a moment Lyra couldn't move a muscle.

"Just because you killed him," Lyra's voice broke into pieces, "doesn't mean— it was your fault—"

Aidra cut her off, taking Lyra's finger and clicking the pistol's hammer into the locked position, ready to fire.

"Enough talk. If you care about him the way you pretend, then do what he would have wanted. *Let me see him.*"

Lyra gave a slow nod.

She's right. Why am I hesitating? I'm a killer, this is what I was made for.

She removed Aidra's hand from the grip and lifted the gun on her own. For the first time before a kill, she averted her eyes. Anastasia covered her ears.

A long, steady breath. A pull of the trigger.

A mother reunited with son.

CHAPTER TWENTY-THREE
MOTHERS AND SONS

> All things must die eventually, Eldric. This is no way to live.
>
> ~Anastasia Ashryn

LYRA PULLED AN 184-POUND CART BEHIND HER.

The wheels squealed and struggled against gravel as they approached the nearest train station. Their clothes, unchanged for days, were still soaked with a mixture of blood, tears, and rain, stiffening the fabric.

At the counter, Lyra spoke first. "Three tickets to Westwick, please."

The clerk didn't look up right away, but then came the smell: the putrid and unmistakable scent of death. Her nose wrinkled as she finally lifted her head.

"Excuse me, ma'am, but I can't allow you on a public train in your *condition*. And..." she glanced past Lyra to the cart. "May I ask what's in the cart?"

Lyra looked over at it. A sagged sheet covered the load, mottled with dark splotches. Bloodstains had seeped through the fabric, and a foul odor radiated from within.

Her hand found the scythe, she could end this exchange in seconds, just one clean swipe would do the trick. But then she saw Rowan's face flash in her mind, the quiet disappointment that always followed her needless killings.

A hand caught her wrist.

"Let me handle this," Seraphina said, tugging Lyra behind her.

She smiled with effortless charm, stepping up front. "I'm sorry for my friend. I'm Seraphina Trubbman, *the* Seraphina of Aipiron. I'm sure you understand that this is a matter of urgency." She tossed her hair over one shoulder and adjusted her dress. Despite the chaos that ensued over the last few days, not a thread was out of place. Her perfume clung to her like armor, elegant and untouchable.

Recognition dawned on the clerk. "M-Ms. Trubbman? I... of course. My apologies." She gave a nervous bow. "But... I'm still required to ask... what's in the cart?"

Seraphina leaned across the counter, blocking Lyra's view. Her eyes met the clerk's. Wisps of white light began to slip from the clerk's forehead into Seraphina's parted lips. More memories for consumption, drifting over like moths to a flame.

Then Seraphina straightened, smoothing her collar as if nothing happened. Her hair returned back to its blonde sheen, her hunger subsided for a moment. "Thank you for your help. We'll be taking those three tickets to Westwick now."

The woman blinked. She touched her forehead, disoriented, like she'd forgotten what she was doing all together.

"Of course," she slid the three tickets below the glass. "Next, please!"

Seraphina handed the tickets to the group and walked ahead with practiced poise. Lyra watched her stride forward toward the train, her movements effortlessly confident. Not a trace of blood or dirt marred her appearance, as if the past days had politely avoided her. Lyra wanted to ask how she managed it, but the exhaustion pinned her tongue.

The train ride felt shorter than it was. Hours slipped by like minutes. The landscapes flew past like streaks of blurred color. Other passengers shifted seats or quietly left for different cars, the smell warding them off like evil spirits.

Anastasia leaned onto Lyra's arm. Lyra looked down at her, a heaviness settling in her chest that refused to lift.

She killed me, was all Lyra could think about. *Ravenna ordered it, and now I'm undead.*

Lyra looked down at her hands that lay over her lap. They were still pale, still warm, still hers nonetheless. Was being undead really that different from living? She hadn't felt the change... would she have ever known if Anastasia hadn't confessed?

Had Rowan known?

She wanted to be angry and needed someone to blame. Anastasia? Ravenna? Herself?

Her thoughts mulled over that night, about her death, about everything she hadn't been able to stop. Then her mind crawled back into the space she always tried to push down, that she always hid from the public eye. Her mother.

Her mother's voice made the anxiety spike again. Lyra put a hand to her cheek and the sharp sting of the slap still felt fresh on her skin. The discipline device still left an ugly map of scars that could never be replaced.

She thought of Aidra looking down at her son's body, and wondered if Ravenna would feel the same of her own death. A tear for a fallen soldier, perhaps, but would there be grief for *her*? Or only inconvenience for another lost tool?

Anger coiled under the questions. She pictured Ravenna and the want to kill her flared hot.... for what she forced them into. For stealing Anastasia's childhood, for setting this ruin into motion, for being the reason Rowan lay still in a cart covered with tattered cloth.

Anastasia slept on her arm, breath soft and steady. Lyra let herself smile, though small and frayed, and hugged her sister tight.

Seraphina peeked her head over the seat. "When this is over, we're heading to Traegos, right?" Her voice was calm, too calm. There was something behind the question that didn't sit right with Lyra.

"*After* Valspire. But you didn't have to come. Westwick is something only I have to do."

Seraphina rolled her eyes. "Of course I have to. You did the same for Vid. It's time to return the favor." She toyed with a fingernail idly. "Besides, Rowan was a cutie. His death stung me too, you know."

Lyra bit down on her tongue, enough for it to bleed. A beat of dark energy emerged around her.

"I'm joking! Too soon?" Seraphina raised her hands innocently.

Lyra threw a punch, but Seraphina caught her wrist, her power pressing Lyra's hand gently but firmly back down.

"Please, Lyra. Enough with the impulse. It's not very lady-like."

Lyra clenched her jaw, then slowly let her hand drop.

The train came to a sudden halt, tossing Seraphina back into her seat. Through the window, Lyra saw a small town nestled between rolling, barren hills. Dust caked the land; what little vegetation remained was brittle and sparse under the unforgiving sun.

Cloud leapt off the train the moment the doors opened, nose pressed low to the dirt as he caught a scent. The group followed him, trusting his instinct to lead them to Rodrick.

He moved with purpose, tail low, paws padding along the hot pebbles until they reached the town's center. Women sitting on porches looked up from their knitting, whispering to each other as the group passed by. One stood abruptly and rushed inside, slamming the door behind her.

They passed modest homes, crooked shop signs, and shuttered supply stores. There was little commotion, almost as though the town had known they were coming. At the far corner, Cloud stopped, sniffed once, then bolted down a narrow side road.

The group chased after him, and the deeper they went, the more faces that gathered. People peeking from windows, porches, over fences, gathering along the street edges, watching from their front yards. Lyra pulled Anastasia closer, gripping her hand tight and keeping her head on a swivel.

Seraphina waved cheerfully at the onlookers, basking in the familiar attention she missed from Aipiron, though many gave her confused looks in return rather than admiration. Whispers followed them, many of the townsfolk pointing to the cart Lyra towed behind her.

Cloud turned another blind corner and vanished from sight. They heard a man's voice coming from where the dog had turned. Seraphina rounded the bend first, leaving Lyra a few paces behind with her sister.

She quickened once she heard laughter coming from around the bend. Turning the corner, she saw an average-sized man with a neatly trimmed beard, crouched beside Cloud, scratching the dog's fur with tenderness. But when Lyra and Anastasia came into view, the man's expression flipped.

The smell of death hit him with force. An unnatural sensation prickled across his skin. His hand moved to the butt of his gun, the click of the hammer snapping loud in the dry air.

"Where's Rowan?" Rodrick's voice dropped from laughter to a deep boom. "Why do you have Cloud?"

"Are you Rodrick?" Lyra asked, approaching with the cart in tow.

"Who's asking?"

A gust swept through the alley, flinging her hair across her face, leaving a moment where she couldn't see him. In that second, Rodrick had raised his gun and aimed squarely at her chest.

"I'll ask once more. Who are you, and where is my son?"

Anastasia reached into empty air, tugging at it, the shimmer of a miniature rift appearing before her—just small enough for her to notice.

Seraphina shifted, hands poised to crush him into the dirt.

But Lyra stepped forward, placing one hand on Anastasia's head and the other in front of Seraphina's raised arms.

"I'm Lyra. This is Seraphina. And this is my sister, Anastasia. Aidra asked us to come. She wanted us to find you."

Rodrick's hand trembled. The gun shook in cadence with the tremor. His mouth went dry as sweat beaded along his hairline.

"Where is she?" he gulped. "And where's Rowan?"

Lyra pushed the cart forward until it nudged against his shin. The stench from it was unbearable.

Rodrick's gun fell from his grip, his hands rose instead to cover his mouth.

"What is this?" he whispered through his hands. "What did you do?"

Lyra's words came out heavy. "We were too late." She hesitated, but added. "I'm sorry. He meant a lot to us too."

Rodrick's fists clenched. He swung at Lyra. She ducked, but his other hand caught her shoulder and shoved her hard into the ground. With quivering hands, he reached for the sheet and carefully pulled it back. Parts of the fabric clung to scabs, peeling away old flesh in strings. A few strands of hair hung to the cloth, and more was matted to a skull that had caved in on one side.

Then he pulled it back further and saw the face. Sunken eyes, grayed skin, maggots wriggling within hollowed holes, but unmistakably Rowan.

Rodrick reeled backward and threw the sheet back over the body.

His stomach heaved, and he turned to vomit against the alley wall. His body felt the immense weight of grief subdue him, dropping to his knees, gripping both sides of his head.

"My boy," he cried, rocking back and forth. "My boy... what happened to him?" His fingers dug into his scalp until clumps of hair came loose. "Who did this to him?"

The noise drew others. Townsfolk gathered at both ends of the alley, their faces pale in the narrow stripe of sunlight that reached the cart through the gap in the rooftops.

Anastasia turned away, covering her ears, tears soaking through her eye covering. Seraphina stared at her shoes, awkwardly kicking around a pebble. Lyra knelt beside Rodrick and placed a hesitant hand on him, trying to mirror what Rowan used to do to steady her. Comfort never came naturally to her; she fumbled for words that would make the smallest dent in his grief.

"We don't know," she lied, for Aidra's sake. "But... he found his mother before the end," she said gently. "She... she wanted me to tell you something."

Rodrick's red-rimmed eyes lifted with a flicker of hope. "His mother? What did she say? How is she?"

Lyra swallowed. "She said she misses you. That she never should have left. And that she and Rowan will be waiting for you."

His face crumpled back to anguish. He leaned against her shoulder and wept profusely.

"Why couldn't you save them?" he whispered hoarsely. "Why are you still alive?"

"I don't know..." Lyra's voice cracked, no longer able to hold back her own ache. "I tried. I'm so sorry."

Their agony intertwined, joined by the same loss. Around them, the watching crowd bowed their heads and clasped their hands. The hero of Westwick, the boy who had once slain a Watcher and given his people hope, lay dead in a stranger's cart.

And the world had to learn to move on without him.

By dusk, neighbors were already at Rodrick's door bringing water, food, clean sheets, and anything else they could spare to help him endure the night. Lyra and the others stayed to assist, helping prepare for the funeral to be held the following evening.

When the next sunset came, the town assembled in a wide field near Rodrick's home. The golden light of dusk stretched along those same rolling hills, gliding across the grass. Unpicked wild mushrooms grew in small clusters between the graves and along the bark of trees, the same kind Rowan and Aidra had collected when he was a boy.

Everyone in town attended, no one stayed behind. They brought offerings: simple things chosen with care, like toys, tools, trinkets, tokens of friendship, and laid them atop Rowan's grave. Each mourner also carried a bouquet of flowers to cast into the bonfire at the ceremony's end.

Beside Rowan's tombstone, a second grave had been dug, its marker already carved:

In Loving Memory: Aidra Lysander.

Speakers approached one by one, sharing stories that turned grief to reminiscence. Laughter broke through tears. Memories became testimonies. The legacy of mother and son lived in every voice.

When Rodrick's name was called, he stepped to the podium, realizing with a sigh that he had left his speech at the house. He gripped the wooden podium anyway. For a moment he looked over at the sea of faces and exhaled.

"I didn't write anything down. Rowan always told me I talked too much anyway."

A soft ripple of laughter passed through.

"What my son did was leave a lasting mark on Westwick. He showed the world that the tyranny of the Rifts could be broken. That gods, monsters, and even shadows can bleed. And they can be stopped."

Rodrick paused, scanning the faces.

"But what made Rowan special wasn't just his strength. It was how he never gave up on people, even when they gave up on themselves. He saw light where others saw dark. And somehow, he carried that light with him through every fight and through every loss. I saw it the day his mother left, and again when he came home with the gun and a purpose."

His voice trembled, the cracks breaking through his composure.

"He taught me how to be better. To listen more. To fight for something that mattered. And Aidra... she gave him that heart. She gave him the gentleness I never could. Together, they made something beautiful."

Rodrick gripped the podium tighter. "He wasn't only a hero. He was my son. That was his most important title, my son. Everything else came second."

A few heads in the crowd nodded.

"And Aidra was the best wife anyone could ask for. I still regret those last days—arguing about things that seem so small now. But time doesn't stop. You can't turn it back."

He wiped his eyes with the back of one hand.

"I think that's what they would want, for us to keep moving. To protect each other. To carry what they gave us, and pass it on."

He turned, facing the two gravestones.

"Today, Westwick lost two incredible souls... the love of my life and my son. When we light the bonfire, let it mark not an ending, but a new beginning. A reunion. A mother and son, walking together once more." He drew in a deep breath. "As our doctrine states: 'One does not simply cease to exist, but live out a second life anew with those who are waiting for you.'"

His voice rose slightly. "So let us ignite the fire and cast in our flowers, sending its embers high into the sky and to light the path for their journey ahead. A journey full of love, free of pain. A journey they'll walk together."

One of the townsfolk bent to strike a match. The dry branches caught, flaring bright. One by one, the townspeople stepped forward, tossing their flowers into the blaze. Petals curled and vanished to orange flame, the ashes carried upward by the wind. The night glowed in a sea of drifting specks lifting slowly upward, painting the sky in warm hues like a second sunset.

Lyra, Anastasia, and Seraphina stood together, hands linked. As they threw in their flowers to the fire, Lyra whispered her own farewell.

That night, something inside her snapped loose and reshaped.

She forgave Anastasia for what she'd done.

She forgave Seraphina for the careless comments about Rowan.

And, at last, she forgave herself for being blind from the truth for so long.

The truth that Ravenna had never cared for her best interests, that her mother had raised her wrong. The truth that people she'd met since, the ones she had chosen rather than been born into, had shaped her better than blood ever could.

Tenebral was not home.

Valspire still had to pay, but so did her own city for what it had done to her and her sister. For the blood on her hands, for the people like Rowan who would never go home again.

Valspire was no longer her only target. Tenebral was next.

And beyond those names and places, there was something deeper. Something the Riftbound Order had seen long before she had. They knew someday she would turn on necromancy itself. Its unnatural grasp chained souls in torment. She could no longer bear the thought of another Aidra wandering this world in pain, trapped between life and death, forever cut off from those they loved.

Rowan's death had broken the last chain that linked her to that cursed town. She was free now; from her mother, her past, her fears.

She looked up at the sky, her eyes following the drifting embers.

Thank you, Rowan.

In the flickering light she saw him, his outline appearing in the rising sparks.

Wait for me, will you?

She reached toward the stars, and in that fleeting moment it felt as though someone reached back.

I won't be too long. I promise.

Cassius hadn't spoken to anyone since storming out of Eldric's chamber, since learning what his immortality truly meant. He wandered the halls of Traegos like a prisoner awaiting their final sentencing. His hopes of studying the afterlife, to finally learn how to reunite with his family once more, were gone. Though his body remained, he no longer recognized the man he'd become.

They called it a *gift*, but to him, it was prison without bars.

His family hadn't been saved. All of them burned, buried, and rotting in their graves. And now, he could never join them. Death was the only mercy he'd wanted now, and even that choice was stolen from him.

He didn't know if it would work. Maybe Eldric had truly severed his ties to mortality and death could no longer hold him. But he had to try. He *had* to believe that somehow, if he did it himself... he could slip past whatever power bound him to this never-ending life.

Nothing dulled the ache, not prayer, not silence, not fury. Nothing changed the fact that he still existed when they did not.

He stood in the center of a small, dark room and dragged a desk behind him.

"Looks about good," he muttered, climbing on top. Its loose construction wobbled beneath his feet, nearly throwing him off balance.

From the ceiling hung a rope, its loop swayed lazily above the desk. He reached for it, slipped it over his neck, and cinched the knot tight. His feet shifted, unsure, slipping more with every breath.

Now, time to kick this out—

The desk slipped out from under him. His body dropped, legs dangling inches off the ground. The rope snapped taut around his throat. Whatever air had been stored in his lungs had dissipated. His face began to turn different shades of blue as his hands clawed for the rope, legs kicking uselessly in the air, searching for something—anything—to relieve the pressure.

The door creaked open. Eldric stood there, arms crossed, expression cold.

"It's not that easy," he said with a chuckle. "You don't think you were the first to try that, do you?"

Cassius thrashed harder, no closer to death. His limbs flailed, toes scraping for purchase that wasn't there. His lungs burned as he tried for a broken rasp. "Help... me."

Eldric stepped closer, head tilted in mild amusement. "What was that?" he asked, not lifting a finger.

Cassius couldn't respond. All of his remaining air was used for that plea. All he could do was reach out, just short of contact.

"You don't appreciate our gift, do you?" He gave Cassius a light push, swinging his body back and forth like a morbid pendulum. "Why don't you stay here a while? Think about what you've done."

He grinned, watching Cassius's puffed, purple face struggle for air, then turned to leave. "Oh, and your friends? They're gone. I sent them off... probably dead by now. Thought you'd want to know."

Eldric stepped through the doorway and gave a cruel parting wave, slamming the door shut.

Darkness reclaimed the room. The only sounds were the creaking ceiling tiles, the stretching rope, and the wet choking noises of a man no one was coming to save.

Aria laid Tavian down on a bench, miles away from their encounter with Lyra. He brought his hand close to the gaping wound in his thigh, where shredded flesh still refused to heal. His palms glowed with a fading white light, illuminating the injury in a dim halo.

"It's not working," he said, trying everything in his power to heal himself. "I've never tried to heal something this bad before."

Aria pulled gauze from her bag and pressed it over the hole, doing her best to stop the bleeding. "I'm sorry I couldn't stop them. I tried, but—"

"It's not your job to be my guardian." He forced a meek laugh. "Guess I'm not as strong as I thought. Those girls were terrifying. And clearly, Maeve taught me nothing worth knowing. That bastard."

"I don't think we should go to Tenebral." Aria passed by his attempt at humor and drove straight to the point. "You saw what those people are like. The moment we show up, we're dead. They won't let us walk in and bring your mother back."

"No." The word carried that familiar edge, the one that always surfaced when questioned about his mother. "We have to try. We need to bring her back... to save Valspire."

Aria gave him a long, searching look. "Are you really here to save Valspire, Tavian? Or are you here to save your mother?" Her voice lowered, tight with suspicion. "It's been too long, and things are probably worse in Valspire than we know. But here we are, chasing ghosts. And you know how much I hate those."

Tavian stayed still, eyes fixed on the blood draining from his leg.

"I've been with you through everything," she continued, "even when no one else would. But this time you need to think. Have you considered that bringing her back might not be what you want?" She looked down at his infected leg. "You've seen what happens to the ones who return. You've *felt* it yourself. It isn't living."

She exhaled, more tired than angry now, but she persisted nonetheless. "When is it enough? Vid's gone to Aipiron. Cassius stayed behind in Traegos. Orin left us. And I—" she hesitated. "I chose *you* over the man who raised me."

For a long time, he said nothing. When he finally looked up to her, there was no warmth left in her gaze. He had lost some of that too.

"Since we're being honest," he said, "what was Lyra talking about earlier? About you being a Necromite. Is that true?" He narrowed his eyes. "Have you been lying to me this whole time?"

Aria pulled her hands away from his leg and turned her back. "It's not that simple."

Tavian stood shakily, his wounded leg limp. Blood trickled down his shin and splattered against the dirt.

"Not that simple?" he snapped. "Are you a Necromite or not? Have you *been* to Tenebral? What else are you hiding from me?"

A soft breeze traveled through the clearing. Pink petals drifted past his face, their unique but familiar color catching his attention like a memory.

He turned his head toward the breeze.

Beside the bench, a field of cotton roses swayed, their blossoms shedding petals by the hundreds. Countless cotton roses grew wild across the slope, their hues shifting in the dimming evening light. Each flower seemed to capture a different moment in time—some pale pink, some streaked in red, and others already fully dark maroon.

"They're beautiful," Aria said, stooping to lift a fallen petal. She rubbed it between her fingers and smiled. The petal began to wilt, its edges curling, decay only just setting in.

"Don't change the subject, Aria. Are you—"

"You and your mother loved these," she interrupted, still waiting for the petal's fully decay in her grasp.

Tavian nodded. "She used to say they reminded her that people change—some slowly, some all at once." His mind set off on a tangent. "The cotton rose blooms white in the morning, turns pink by midday, then red by night." He paused after reciting his mother's lines, his voice thinning. "Sometimes… it felt like she loved those flowers more than me."

He paused. "But to get back to the point—"

Aria shook her head. "Nonsense. She cared about you deeply." She reached out, offering the petal. "Here. Take it."

She placed the petal in his open hand. The moment it touched his skin, it shriveled and died. The pink hue drained into black, crumbling into ash that scattered from his palm.

Tavian stared at it, his hands cold and barren of the lines that used to streak across his palms, then limped toward the field of roses. He reached out to touch them. As his fingers brushed each top, the flowers wilted in his wake, folding in on themselves, dying with every pass of his hand.

He stood silently, surrounded by a field of decay. Aria approached and rested a hand on his back. He didn't move.

"Tavian… *this* is why I'm saying these things. Look at what we've become… what people like Maeve have turned us into. Please, come back. Sit down. We can talk about what comes next."

"She always loved the cotton roses," he said, still facing away from her. "And all I do is kill them."

When he turned to her, his eyes were reddened and glassy.

"When will it be over? When can I stop searching? When will Mom come back to save us? I hope she's not disappointed when she sees me. This was all for her."

His hands clutched what remained of a few errant stems. His leg bled freely, the dark crimson pooling among the fallen petals, mixing into a muddy swirl of pink and brown.

"Would you still buy me flowers?" Aria tested. "Like you did before... at the Bazaar?"

"Flowers? When did I do that?"

The memory was slipping, consumed by his undead nature, just as Aidra had promised it would. The tiny joy she felt in that moment back at the market, when he handed the dahlias over to her in a large bouquet, was gone.

She already knew what she needed to do.

She tenderly pried the wilted stems from his hands and pulled him into an embrace. His blood soaked through her pants, warm and spreading fast, but she didn't mind. She wrapped her arms around him and held still.

Then she pulled back just enough to meet his eyes. For a moment, they only stared at one another in silence. She leaned in and kissed him.

He flinched, yet didn't resist. The tension drained from him as he melted into her, their lips meeting with subtle desperation that said everything neither could. When she pulled back, her body shivered like it was cold. She pressed her head against his shoulder, arms tightening as though she feared that loosening her hold would cause him to fall apart completely.

Her smile faded.

"I'm so sorry, Tavian."

He tilted his head in confusion. He could feel a drop of water strike his back. He looked up, but there was no rain. "You're sorry... for what? I've always wanted to do that—"

A bird cawed somewhere in the distance. The field went windless. A single cotton rose petal drifted from a flower near his feet, spinning slowly until it came to rest in the dirt. It was red.

Then came the click of a hammer. The cold press of metal against his ribs.

"Go find your mother."

His world went mute. The gun fired.

Pain tore through his ribcage all at once; a dull, final ripping sensation that stole his breath. His knees caved in and his strength fled. Blood rushed up his throat and spilled from his lips across Aria's back.

A pistol—the one Aidra had left in the dirt—was pressed firm against him. Aria held it, but her hands began to quake, jerking the smoking barrel.

His body went limp, dead weighting in her embrace. Aria lowered him to the ground, cradling his head in her lap. He stared up at her, eyes wide in terror.

"Why?" he choked, sucking in air that wouldn't come. His heart stuttered. "Am I... going to die?"

She pressed one hand to his forehead, the other clasping his trembling fingers.

"It's been too much, Tavian. You wouldn't listen. I had to do what was best for you, for Valspire, for everyone. We can't keep running around like this. You know that."

He looked down at the wound, willing it to close. But like the one to his thigh, it didn't listen.

She lifted his head, cradling it against her chest. "And yes, I'm a Necromite. I found out at the hospital. I knew I couldn't tell you."

"You could've brought Mom back..." He tried to raise his hands, the white glow of Mariella's gift returning weakly to his palms, but he couldn't reach the wound. His arms fell limp.

She caught his hands and placed them at his sides.

"Close your eyes. It'll be over soon." Her tears splashed against his brow.

"Please... help me," he begged. "It hurts so bad."

His fingers twitched toward her face. She gently pushed them away.

"Now you can be with Leora again." She wiped away a stray tear, her words coming out like a prayer. "Now your suffering can end." Her voice broke. "I couldn't leave you here alone... but I couldn't bear to see how you've changed. Don't you remember what I told you before we left Valspire?"

"No..." he said, coughing up more blood onto her chest. "I haven't changed."

He tried raising a hand again. The ring Aria bought him caught in the dying light of the sun, a tiny glint casting a fragile shadow over his right cheek. She guided his back back into her lap. Aria's face began to blur before him, shifting and changing in and out of shape.

He squinted. Her hair had changed, her features transformed before his eyes. It wasn't Aria's anymore. Someone else, someone faint, someone familiar replaced her.

"Mom?"

The sky above drained to grey. There were faint images appearing in the corners of his eyes.

Aria's breath hitched, clutching his hand. She reached out and closed his eyes.

"Goodbye, Tavian... I hope you find what you're looking for." His body slackened. "I just wish I could've been enough."

Aria squeezed his corpse, while his final breath escaped in a soft, almost relieved exhale. His arm slipped from her grasp and thudded against the ground.

He went still, surrounded by a dark pool of blood and wind-scattered petals.

Within a moment's time, his eyes flew open.

His head still rested in someone's lap, but the world had changed. He looked up at the charcoal sky; petals now lifting instead of falling.

And the face looking down at him was no longer Aria's.

It was Leora.

"Welcome home," she whispered, cradling her arms around his head.

"I've been waiting for you."

CHAPTER TWENTY-FOUR
VALSPIRE

I side with the victors, Eldric. Your time has come. Soon, flowers will grow on your grave—just as they did upon mine.

~Mariella, Mother of the First Rift

COLORFUL, VIBRANT TOY FLOWERS LAY IN BLOOD.

They were a little girl's favorite. Her golden curls, once bright as sunlight, were now soaked through and stained red. She crawled forward on scarred elbows, screaming for her mother, unable to look back, unwilling to see what chased her.

Her mother lay only a few feet away, though the body was far from living. A hideous undead creature, with jaw unhinged like a broken mask, gnawed savagely at her mother's arms. The girl dragged herself closer, sharp pebbles tearing deeper into the wounds on her knees with each inch she gained.

Screams cascaded from every direction. From the corners of her vision she saw neighbors fleeing toward the heart of Valspire, some towing children, others dragging loved ones unable to run fast enough. A column of fire erupted from behind her, unleashing a blistering heat that rolled over her body like a suffocating blanket.

Bodies fell around her, one falling right atop her, crushing her into the cobblestone. She squirmed free, but then came a sharp sting at her ankle.

She gasped and twisted around. Lyra stood over her, a sharp-heeled boot buried deep into the girl's flesh.

The child kicked and thrashed, but Lyra pressed harder. Above them, the great walls of Valspire began to crumble. Waves of undead, reinforcements sent by Ravenna, scaled the ruins like a swarm of insects, pouring into the city's center.

Church bells rang. It was noon on a Saturday, the prayer hour.

The girl turned her head as the church doors burst open. Inside, limp bodies dangled over the pews. The pastor stumbled into view from beyond the wreckage, before another creature scooped him up and ripped him clean in half.

"Please," the girl pleaded to Lyra. "Please stop. My mom—please help her!"

Lyra's iris bled red, the sharp intensity piercing into the girl's mind. She grabbed the child around the torso and lifted her effortlessly, their faces inches apart.

Tears tracked down Lyra's cheeks, mixing with burned embers and dirt.

"Why?" Lyra whispered. "Why did you make me do this? Why did you all send us all away?"

The girl gasped, struggling to breathe under Lyra's intense grip.

"I... I don't know you. I didn't do anything..."

"You sent us away," Lyra insisted. "All of you. I have to do this, don't you understand? Don't you see I never wanted any of it?"

The girl's lips trembled. "Please... don't hurt me... Please... help my—"

Her fragile plea struck something in Lyra, a splinter of clarity of her own self as a child. Her grip loosened slightly.

But—

A sharp hiss through the air.

A barbed arrow tore in from a distant rooftop. It struck the girl, silencing her. Her tiny body went limp in Lyra's hands.

Lyra froze, her fingers slacking, the girl thudding onto the ground. Nausea surged; acid rose in her throat.

Around her, Valspire burned. They had arrived less than an hour ago, and already the city's center was a wasteland. Undead swarmed the streets, smoke stung her eyes but she didn't wipe it away.

She looked up.

High above, perched on the crest of a hill, the palace's spire pierced the clouds. Pristine, untouched, the place that cast her people out and left them to die.

This wasn't for Ravenna.

Nor Corvin.

Nor Derewin.

This was for Tenebral. For every family Valspire had damned to starvation and disease. For every child and mother who faded into the ground without a name or grave. Tenebral would have its vengeance.

A small tug pulled her from her spiraling thoughts. Anastasia stood beside her, her bloodied hand reaching up for her sister's. Lyra took it and squeezed.

"Are we going up there?" Anastasia asked, pointing toward the palace.

"Yes. That's where they are. The people that built this place. We'll make it quick."

Behind them, the bodies of thousands of Spirians were heaped like discarded refuse. On some, flowers had begun to bloom. On others, rot had already taken hold.

Anastasia stooped down beside the golden-haired girl. She picked up the toy flowers that floated in the puddle of blood and turned them over in her hands, studying them with mournful curiosity. She then leaned forward and tucked them into the girl's lifeless fingers, arranging them as though the child may wake and hold them again.

"She liked flowers too," Anastasia said. "Maybe we would've been friends."

Lyra stared at the girl's body. She reminded her of her sister in little ways.

But she wasn't.

No Spirian could be.

They were vile, raised to turn their backs on the suffering of thousands. To cast people out like Anastasia, innocents with no hand in whatever crime Valspire believed justified their exile. No amount of children's innocence could rewrite history.

And nothing in this place was worth saving.

So Lyra thought.

Seraphina watched the smoke rise from Valspire in the distance. She sat alone on a train toward Traegos, chin resting against her knuckles, eyes on the window's reflection. Though she and Lyra had agreed to split paths for now, she knew their roads would cross again. She would make sure of it.

Better not die on me, Lyra. We still have a deal to take down Tenebral. I'll handle the Riftbound Order in the meantime.

She dug into her bag for lipstick, but something small and white slipped out and clinked to the floor. It was a misty-white fragment. The same one Arnette had slipped into her bag before she left Aipiron.

She stared at it. "When did that get in there?"

She picked it up and swallowed it. The memory overtook her mind, transporting her back in time.

She stood again in the bazaar, but not as herself. She was inside someone else's perspective. From behind unfamiliar eyes, she saw herself —and she looked... stunning. More beautiful than she ever believed she was. Admired, idolized, revered even.

In this memory, they were standing outside the Hidden Moon Circus. She watched her hand come forward for a polite shake, and instead felt the body she inhabited kneel and press their lips to the back of her hand.

Vid. This was his memory.

The vision shifted to the performance they'd watched together. Vid hardly looked at the stage, his gaze kept returning to her. Every thought, every nervous fidget, centered around her and nothing else.

Does my hair look right?

He adjusted it anxiously, trying to be subtle.

Does this shirt make me look fat?

He puffed out the front awkwardly.

Am I supposed to hold her hand?

She shimmered like rays of light caught under water. Vid reached slowly across the space between them, leaving his hand halfway.

Seraphina, in this memory, smiled with easy confidence and placed her hand in his.

Holy shit, he thought. *Please don't notice the sweat.*

They held hands the entire performance.

Do I love her? His heart pounded. *That's crazy, right? It's the first day. Gods... maybe it's been awhile...*

Before the thought could finish, Seraphina had already leaned in and kissed his cheek.

Vid smiled like a fool and leaned in closer.

Maybe it's not too crazy.

The memory dissolved, gone as suddenly as it arrived.

Seraphina sat motionless on the train, the reflection of her own face ghosting in the window. She let the rhythm of the tracks fade, replaying that moment again and again like an old, grainy, forgotten film tucked away in her mind. The warmth of his hand, the timid way he'd admired her, the way he'd looked at her like she was the only person in the world worth seeing.

This is why she was going back. Why she had promised to burn through the Riftbound Order. Why she refused to die before meeting with Lyra once more.

She couldn't forget—and she wouldn't.

But there were things she had tried to bury; Lucan most of all. The man she'd broken in the cell, drained to strengthen her power, then erased from her thoughts as if the deletion could absolve her. Whenever his disheveled face resurfaced in her mind, she'd forced it away. Yet she could never outrun what she'd learned after devouring his memories.

Unlike him, she knew his wife's name. It was Seraphina, the same as hers. Twisted, delicious irony.

Maybe that was the Order's cruelty, maybe the Rift's, or maybe both... teaching her how easy it was to forget mercy, to sever away empathy like a rotten limb. Whatever the reason, she knew now that the answers lay in their blood. Once every one of them was gone, perhaps she would return to that cell for Lucan and grant him the release she once denied.

But not yet. Not until she was finished.

Lyra kicked down the palace doors. The golden slabs crashed onto the marble, crushing the last few guards beneath its weight.

She stood in awe for a moment, taking in the obscene wealth of the grand foyer. Polished floors, pillars wrapped in sheets of gold, gemstones inlaying railings and walkways that were brighter than street lamps. The wealth here could've fed all of Tenebral for months.

"Disgusting," she muttered. "Arrogant pigs."

She stormed down the halls, boots slapping with blood she dragged in with her, following a path toward Elyra's quarters. Halfway up the main staircase, a framed portrait caught her attention. It was of Tavian, younger but unmistakably him. He stood smiling with his mother, grandmother, and Aria.

Lyra's gut twisted, her memories collided. The boy from the bazaar... the same one that was tied to Rowan's death.

Her rage surged.

He was a Spirian? And I let him go?

With a punch she broke through the portrait glass. With another, her knuckles drove deeper into the wall behind it.

I'll remember that.

Her dripping shoes left rust-colored prints across the pristine carpeting as she reached the landing. At the top stood a large wooden door carved with symbols of Mariella. She shoved it open.

Inside, an elderly woman stood at the window, hands clasped around a miniature idol of Mariella. A soft, blurred light surrounded her body.

"I'm too old to fight now, you know," Elyra said calmly, still facing the window. "My powers have faded. I'm no match for someone like you."

Lyra shut the door behind her. "Are you the one who rules Valspire? The replacement for Leora?"

"I suppose you could say I inherited her sins, yes."

The soft glow around Elyra thickened into the shape of a woman. Arms formed, draping protectively around Elyra's shoulders like a guardian spirit. Legs formed next, then a face so bright Lyra had to shield her eyes against it.

They called that radiant woman Mariella.

"Mariella still protects us," Elyra said, leaning into the divine warmth. "But without Leora, we have little hope. I was never able to decipher the texts. Tavian never came back for us. I'm sorry, Mariella."

Mariella whispered something only Elyra could hear.

Lyra took a step back. The sight curdled her insides; the divine comfort wrapped over a woman who had benefited from years of cruelty. A woman who ruled the same land that cast her people out. It made her sick.

Why would a goddess choose them? Lyra thought. *Why comfort the ones who cast us aside, while my people still pray to you in the dark?*

The injustice crawled under her skin, but the sheer power exuding from Mariella kept her from lashing out. Worse still, the goddess didn't even spare Lyra a glance.

Her hands balled at her sides. "Your people must atone for what you did. I don't care if it was by your hand or someone else's, the debt still remains."

"You're bold, reckless even." Elyra replied, faintly amused. "You remind me of Tavian. He was so desperate to bring his mother back... he forgot what really mattered."

She turned toward Anastasia, Mariella still holding onto her from behind. "That child with you—she's blind?" Elyra pointed to the blindfold that covered her eyes.

Lyra nodded once.

"And yet, despite your sight, *you're* the one wandering in the dark. Just like my grandson. I suppose it's fitting, watching the blind lead the blind."

In a flash, Lyra was inches from Elyra, scythe half-drawn.

"You have Spirian blood, you know," Elyra said, Lyra's sudden appearance having no impact on her poise. "Many in Tenebral do. Strange, isn't it? We exiled you to keep you far from us, out of sight, out of mind, only to discover we're now woven from the same cloth."

Lyra bared her teeth. "Don't you *dare* compare us to your kind." She unsheathed the scythe fully.

Elyra shook her head. "Tell me, do you know the name Derewin—if that's what he still calls himself these days...?"

Lyra paused. "How do you know that name?"

"He was one of ours. Gareth is his true name. He fled after making a grave mistake. He's now fathered many of your kind."

Lyra's mind snapped to Derewin's parting words the day she left his home in Tenebral, when Anastasia had just returned from the Rift:

Not everyone from Valspire is as bad as you think.

Her stomach sank. Another lie. Another betrayal.

"You can kill me if you wish," Elyra said, her voice soft, "but it won't change the truth. You're as much a part of us as you are them, whether you accept it or not. Ending my life would be no different than killing one of your own."

Mariella placed a reassuring hand on Elyra. Her hair floated as if underwater, the silk of her robes like mist. For the first time, her gaze moved toward Lyra, but not with judgment nor anger, rather with something far worse: a deep, aching pity.

She leaned in and whispered something else in Elyra's ear. Lyra caught only a fragment:

"...fear... the one with the blindfold."

Then Mariella began to fade. Her form unraveled into strands of golden light, leaving behind only a slight shimmer that eventually vanished.

"She never stays long," Elyra said. "But she's wiser than the rest of us. I can't fault her for that."

Without the goddess beside her, Elyra looked unbearably small as she stared out the window at the burning city.

"I wish I could've told Tavian about his father, but he was too young... too angry. I couldn't have planted such hatred for your kind in him, even if I wanted to."

Lyra said nothing.

Elyra continued, clenching her fists, bracing for one of these words to be her last. "Honestly, I hope he never found out how to bring his mother back. I couldn't bear to see my daughter in that state."

With not a word from Lyra spoken, Elyra turned, expecting a scythe to be rocketing toward her.

But instead, the room was empty. Elyra was standing alone, the walls still chipping away, the sounds of Sprians deaths still squealing.

Standing atop a crumbling wall, Lyra and Anastasia looked out over the devastated city. Bodies carpeted the streets. Congealed blood clogged the storm drains in thick, unmoving pools. Flames danced across rooftops. The screams faded as the corpses finally settled into their resting places.

Cloud could be spotted in the distance, a beacon of white light among the darkened gore, pattering around the wreckage.

Lyra spotted the body of the girl with golden curls, her hand outstretched toward her mother's, the two separated by inches. Her other hand was stiffly grasping the toy flowers that Anastasia had so gently placed there.

Lyra wept and tried to hide it, but the tears came anyway. She turned to the hills beyond the walls, green and alive. The trees swayed steadily, the lakes sparkled bright blue.

She thought Rowan had changed her.

But she had killed again, needlessly, it seemed. Entire families erased. Mothers, daughters, sons, fathers, brothers; gone, never to return, never to be whole again.

I thought I was someone else, she realized. *But I'm the same as I've always been. Who can I believe anymore?*

She was still Lyra the killer. Taking lives without reason, without meaning, and never once saving them. She couldn't save the ones she loved most; she couldn't even save herself.

The outline of Rowan's face appeared before her, a phantom of grief. His eyes were wary; and again, carrying that same disappointed look he'd always give when she killed without reason.

I had a reason this time, didn't I, Rowan? Or was this Ravenna's doing?

"I thought I changed, Anastasia. But I'm still the same as before." She held her sister's hand. "Please... don't become like me. Learn from my mistakes."

Anastasia rested her head against Lyra's side.

"You only did what Mom told you to do. It's not your fault," she nestled closer. "But... we can fix it."

Lyra followed her sister's gesture toward the distant mountains.

"If we ruin Tenebral like we did Valspire," Anastasia said, "maybe it'll be better. No one else can hurt us. No one else can lie to us."

Lyra stroked her sister's hair. Hearing such cold, violent certainty from a child made her nauseous. But this was a wound she herself had carved, Anastasia was only following the script Lyra had written for them both.

"Maybe," Lyra said. "Or maybe not. Maybe we'll kill them all... and nothing will change."

She sat down beside her sister, pulling her close.

"But if I'm to be a killer, then there's truth in what you say. There's still one more person who needs to pay. After that... we're done. Then we'll make our home. We'll get the dog you've always wanted, a friend for Cloud."

Anastasia squeezed with all the strength she had. "You promise?"

Lyra nodded. "I promise. And I don't break promises."

She looked up at the sky.

Don't forget my promise to you, Rowan, she thought. *I'll be with you soon.*

Derewin's fingers tapped against the wooden table, the only sound coming from the empty house. Empty, besides the man who sat across the table, burly with a hardened expression. They stared at each other, neither willing to blink first.

"So?" Derewin finally straightened his slouch. "Got something to say?"

Orin slammed his fist onto the table.

"How could you be so damned ignorant? How many years have passed, how many people have suffered, and you've got *nothin'* to say?"

He stood and shoved the table forward, jamming it into Derewin's chest. "And Leora? What about her? Did you forget yer wife? Yer *child*?"

Derewin covered his face with both hands. A single tear slid between his fingers. "I think about them every day. Don't pretend I don't."

Orin slammed the table again, harder this time, enough to rattle the floorboards.

"Great. You *think* about them. After killin' yer wife, abandonin' yer son, and leavin' yer city to rot, 'thinkin' is all you've got?"

"You wouldn't understand. My choices are not your problem. Don't tell me Leora meant that much to you."

Orin's face went blank. He lunged over the table and swung. Derewin dropped to the floor just in time, the punch sailing over his head.

"I told you, Orin! Leora wasn't who you thought she was. What happened *had* to happen!"

Orin moved to the floor where Derewin lay and landed a brutal punch to the bridge of his nose. He led with another. Punch after punch landed, blood scattering across the wooden floor as Derewin's face turned into a ruinous smear.

Only when his old friend's arms twitched did Orin stop, panting, his knuckles dripping red. He recoiled in horror, lunging back, as Derewin's body began to melt. It liquefied into the slits of the floorboards like water from a sink flowing down into the drain.

Behind him, Derewin's liquid form resurfaced and reshaped back into its whole, unbroken figure.

A tinge of pain hit Orin's shoulder. Derewin's blade rested there, like a ceremonial knighting, a thin trail of blood already leaking from the cut of the sword's tip.

"Can you justify what she did?" Derewin asked. "Or were you blinded by emotion? By love? You do remember she was *my* wife, correct?"

Orin turned, grabbing the blade with his bare hand. Metal split the skin, but he held firm, refusing to let go.

"I don't give a damn what she did. She did it for Valspire. She was yer wife. The mother of yer son. You don't get to poison her and walk away like none of it mattered."

With a sudden yank, Orin ripped the weapon from Derewin's hand and tossed it to the floor between them.

"So what now?" Derewin hissed. "You came here to guilt-trip me? What's your purpose?"

Orin planted a foot and stood tall. "I've raised a girl like a daughter of my own. A Necromite, born into a world that calls her evil, when she's the purest soul I've ever met."

Derewin scoffed. "Good for you. And?"

"And people can change, Gareth. You did. And yer son did too... only he's changed into a version of you I prayed we'd never see again. I came to drag you out of this hole and make you face the mess you started. To help fix it."

Derewin slumped back into his chair. Orin remained standing.

"It's too late," Derewin said, defeated. "By now Valspire's already gone. Ravenna has already sent in the troops. Lyra and Anastasia are too strong. Even if I wanted to fix anything, even if I regret all of it, the deal's done."

He buried his face in his hands, weeping.

"It's not too late," Orin said. "Not yet. We've still got Mariella, Tavian, Aria, Elyra... you and me. There's still a chance." He offered his hand.

Derewin stared at it, then slowly reached for it.

"I know you regret it," Orin said. "It's written all over you. The time to change is now. Come home."

Derewin took in a shaky breath. "Ravenna will kill me."

"I'll be sure she doesn't, but I need to know you're all in."

Derewin nodded, and his hand hovered inches from Orin's.

Before they could touch, the front door detonated inward. The explosion sent planks of wood hurling from its hinges, flinging debris through the room. A woman stepped through the dust and splinters.

Her energy exuded dark, raw power—a sensation that coiled around her like a serpent. Black ink dripped from the bulging veins at her throat. Her presence smothered the air.

She blurred out of vision, reappearing in a blink in front of Derewin, clamping his throat, slamming him onto the table. From her back she drew a sword nearly as tall as she was, its blade cloaked in swirling necromantic haze, blazing like a wildfire.

It was Aria.

She never returned to Valspire. She stopped in Tenebral instead, to return to the place that birthed her. Tavian's death still screamed in her skull, and after hearing the rumors of someone named Derewin; a Spirian tied to the royal bloodline, now living in Tenebral from his alienated family, her grief sharpened into purpose.

She had to see him… she knew it had to be Gareth. She had to make him pay.

Orin tried to stop her, but the force surrounding her created an impenetrable wall that pushed him back.

Aria's blade rose. It cracked along the ceiling as she brought it down. The strike obliterated the table and tore a gaping hole into the floorboards. Derewin was just able to roll clear, the attack cleaving the house neatly in two.

"Aria, wait!" Orin shouted over the toppling home. "Don't kill him! Listen to me!"

She didn't hear… she didn't care to hear.

She turned to Derewin; no, toward *Gareth*, eyes burning with the passion of a girl who'd just discovered her purpose.

"Tavian told me about you… the father who walked away. And now I find you here, alive and in hiding, while he bled for you and his mother." Aria squeezed the hilt of her sword.

"This is for Tavian."

She raised the sword again, the black fog twisting around the blade.

"Go find your son."

CHAPTER TWENTY-FIVE

TENEBRAL

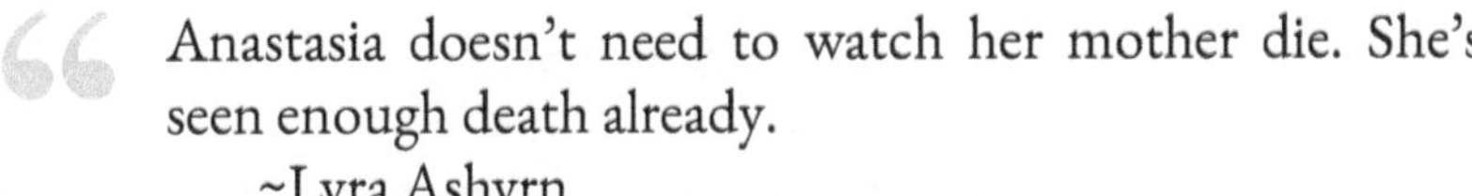

> Anastasia doesn't need to watch her mother die. She's seen enough death already.
>
> ~Lyra Ashyrn

SHE SAT ON THE BLOOD-SOAKED BENCH.

It lay near a field of cotton roses. Close by, under a dying tree, lay a makeshift grave with no marker but a small bundle of cotton roses at its base. The name *Tavian* had been scraped weakly into the dirt, already half-erased by wind and time. The tree above the grave shed its leaves in a black rain. Every tree surrounding the grave withered in the same way.

Lyra stared at the name. She hadn't realized that the boy she and Anastasia had once spared, the boy who'd limped away bleeding and stubborn, had come here to die before ever reaching Tenebral.

An undead boy dead again, buried in soil where life refused to grow. It felt almost symbolic, inevitable, and tragic.

She stood over the grave much longer than she meant to. Something about it rooted her there. Something about the person buried beneath the earth resonated with her.

Having a half-brother can do that to you. She just didn't know it yet.

When she pulled away from the grave no one would remember, she returned to the bench where Anastasia sat in peaceful silence, legs swinging, blindfold pointed in the direction of the rotted tree.

Lyra went into her coat and pulled out the recorder, but hesitated in clicking it on. She wanted to watch it. Rowan had asked her to, but something inside warned her she was about to uncover something that could upend herself. Maybe even ruin her.

Still, she pressed play. The recorder clicked alive, clips rolling in sequence.

The first clip showed Anastasia handing Rowan a bouquet of flowers.

"We got it from the bazaar. Lyra said you'd like them."

"Anastasia! I told you not to say that!" Lyra's voice scolded from behind the camera. Rowan turned to the lens and smiled.

"Thank you for these. They're beautiful... *Anastasia*." He shot a smirk where Lyra stood offscreen, before the video abruptly cut out.

The next clip opened on the beach at night in Aipiron, the night they'd patented their infamous finger-gun routine.

Lyra pointed her finger at her own head, pretending to shoot herself. Rowan had stopped her hand, saying, *"That's my job."* She had grabbed the recorder from him, and the next shot was of her hand firing at him. He dropped dramatically into the sand, with fake death cut by laughter.

A good memory. One of the few. She remembered the shape of his smile more vividly than she wished she did.

The next clip followed. It was short, chaotic, and filled with momentary joy. Lyra chasing Anastasia around the living room with Cloud barking and trailing behind. This was back in Aipiron, when her sister interrupted her makeup tutorial. Then the camera fell sideways at the rumble of the earth. The screen only showed an empty living room while the audio caught the distant thud of fighting below. A moment later Rowan appeared in frame, grabbing the recorder and taking it downstairs.

Another jump cut, now only Anastasia sat on screen.

At the sound of her own voice coming from the device, Anastasia shuffled off the bench and lunged to snatch the recorder away, but Lyra held it out of reach.

Rowan narrated from behind the camera, with a voice bright and theatrical. "Now introducing the greatest singer Aipiron has ever known, the artist people travel the world to hear, the one and only Anastasia Ashryn!"

Anastasia gave a shy bow on-screen. Then quietly, soft enough to not wake the others, she began to sing. Even hushed, her voice carried: it was steady, warm, and heartachingly pure. The recording played for a few minutes, as Anastasia continued reaching for it out of Lyra's grasp, ending with Rowan's whispered applause and Anastasia's flustered scolding for him making her do it.

"I never knew you could sing," Lyra said, turning to her sister.

Anastasia buried her face into her hands with bright red cheeks. "I can't, it was only once. Rowan made me do it for the camera."

"I think it's great," Lyra said, pulling her into a hug.

The next clip played. Seraphina's voice rang out from behind the camera this time, early in the morning after what must've been a long night.

"And here's Lyra! How was your night? Did the vomiting eventually subside?" Lyra groaned and shoved the camera away, her hair a mess, her patience thinned.

Seraphina panned to Rowan next, half-asleep and clearly hungover. "And here's the self-proclaimed king of drinking. Your majesty, a question if I may—how many shots does it take to get you passed out beside a riverbank?"

Rowan moaned, rolling over just enough to aim a sluggish middle finger at the camera. His back was still caked in mud and river water.

Then Seraphina swung the lens to Anastasia.

"And we've saved the best for last, sweet lil' Anastasia!" Seraphina pinched her cheeks.

Anastasia giggled, swatting her hands away.

Seraphina leaned in. "Go tell Lyra that boys aren't allowed next time! I do hope she brushed her teeth before sneaking over to Rowan's tent and—"

Lyra appeared in front of the camera out of nowhere, a toothbrush hanging from her mouth, hands covering the lens. The video cut before she could say, or smack, anything.

Lyra flicked through the next few clips quickly... nothing of importance that Anastasia needed to see or hear.

Over an hour of muddled memories later, the final clip began.

Rowan was sitting on the floor with Cloud against his thigh. They were in a small, familiar room, though Lyra couldn't place it. He cleared his throat, his nerves ever so present.

"Maybe it's my awkwardness, but I had to get it out somehow," he said, stroking Cloud's fur. "I wanted to keep a record for you, Lyra, in case I never get the courage to say it aloud. I'm not as straightforward as I pretend to be."

Her heart skipped.

"Once we find my mother, and you... do what you need to do at Valspire, maybe we could all go somewhere new. Across the sea maybe, somewhere no one knows us. No history, no horrid powers, no Rifts. We could live free, the life we've always talked about, no prior baggage weighing us down."

His fingers fidgeted around Cloud's ears.

"I've seen how you've changed. And I know I've changed too, because of you. Whether you've noticed or not, I think we work pretty well together."

He glanced behind him, lowering his voice to not wake the others.

"I love your hidden smile, I love your impatience at my terrible jokes, I love how fiercely you protect your sister. And I... love you, Lyra." He swallowed. "I don't know if you want to hear that, but I had to say it at some point. We'll call this is practice for the real thing. Once I man up and do it in person."

There was a knock at the door behind him.

"You may not feel the same—I'll admit you're not the easiest to read—but you've changed me in ways I didn't expect from the first time we met. When you nearly killed me. And thank you, Anastasia, for changing her mind. I owe you one."

Another knock on the door, someone whispered through the cracks.

"I just wish more people were like you, Lyra. Necromites get a bad rep—and yeah, even I held my biases. But you're just like anyone else. Better, even. You opened my eyes. And your eyes... are special. Not because of the Rift, but because they're yours. That alone has more power than any Rift-born abilities."

A louder knock startled him.

"You're not a killer, Lyra. You're a savior. You saved Anastasia from Ravenna, you saved me more times than I'll admit, and you saved yourself from that hell you were raised in. That counts for something."

"Rowan! Are you in there? Is everything okay?" Thalia's voice could be heard through the door.

"I hope one day we can watch this back together, and you can punch me for not telling you sooner. I love you, Lyra, and I hope whatever comes from Valspire makes everything you've endured worth it."

He reached a finger toward the lens as the recorder shut off.

The final frame froze on his face, just as the mention of Valspire had darkened his expression.

Then the recorder's lights blinked out.

Lyra frantically pressed rewind. "Why isn't this working?" She slammed the play button again. "C'mon! Replay!" But the device only clicked weakly. The battery was dead.

She gripped the recorder tight in one hand, Anastasia's hand even tighter in the other.

Watching those memories, those fleeting, imperfect, precious moments, pulled something out of her she didn't know still lived.

After several trying breaths, she gave up and leaned back against the bench, watching cotton rose petals drift on in the breeze. She hadn't realized how much she loved the look of those flowers, turning to stare at their white blossoms.

"It's funny," Lyra said aloud, not to Anastasia but to the empty field, to the mountains, to the trees, maybe to the world. "You spend so long chasing something that you forget life is still happening around you. And sometimes, while chasing that one thing... you miss everything that actually made life worth living."

She put the recorder back in her pocket and stood.

You should've told me, Rowan.

You're right—I would've punched you.

She looked toward Tenebral.

And I would've loved to see that stupid look on your face when I told you I loved you too.

They had finally arrived in Tenebral. Snow fell in thick, steady sheets, blanketing the rooftops and cobblestone roads. The town looked smaller than they had remembered. Much smaller, and much bleaker.

"This is it," Lyra said, glancing at her sister. "You ready?"

"Yes."

Anastasia turned, tearing open the empty air behind her. A human-sized Rift split wide, presenting an endless void within. Lyra was too stunned to speak. She had never seen her sister do anything remotely like this. Her body wouldn't move.

"Anastasia... what did you just do? What is that?"

She didn't answer, instead she reached into the void, her hand disappearing into the dark. For a moment something hesitated, the swirling lights of the Rift seemed to stutter as a boy's body was pulled out, tumbling into the snow.

"Rowan?"

No, it couldn't have been him, not exactly. His body was hunched, cold and unmoving with small flowers sprouting front the crown of his head, from the jaw, from his wrists.

"Anastasia... did you—how—how did you kill him? When did this happen?"

Her knees buckled, the snow cushioning the fall, but the shock of seeing him once more stung far greater than the cold ever could. She had forced herself to move on, they had buried him, she was just starting to let go... and now he was here.

Anastasia lowered her head.

"I finished him, before the bullet could kill him. I—I wanted him to be with us forever." Anastasia's voice trembled with guilt. "I know I should've listened to Aidra, but I couldn't let him go like you could. I had to take him with us. I had to."

"Then whose body was in that cart? When I took him to Westwick... when I buried him?"

Anastasia paced nervously in the deep snow.

"That was Rowan. But *this* Rowan is... different. He isn't all the same, he's what the Rift gave back when I pulled him out, but it's close enough. Like you."

Lyra looked back at him and reached out to touch his face. But something was horribly wrong.

His skin was tinged blue like he was seconds away from death, his eyes were glazed and cloudy, exactly as they had been once he died. His breath barely left a fog in the cold air. He didn't react to her.

Mechanically, he rested a hand on his gun, readying himself to enter Tenebral. Following some unheard instruction instead of paying mind to the woman he supposedly loved.

"No," Lyra said. "No, no... this isn't right."

Lyra raised her hand, mimicking a finger gun, and pointed it at him. And as their old joke went, she fired, whispering *bang* as she shot.

No response. No teasing, no laughing, no pretending to fall over.

She let her hand drop and shook her head. "I figured."

But she couldn't stop looking at him. She traced the outline of his cheek with her gaze, searching for something... anything that could show it was *him*.

"Rowan?" her voice cracked around the name. "Are you... in there?"

He looked at her with a dull stare. "Yes."

Lyra blinked to push out the tears that were beginning to sting. "Right."

The three of them stood before Tenebral's gates. A once-familiar sight, now turned to an unwelcoming reunion. The gate guards spotted Lyra and Anastasia and exchanged confused looks, whispering commands to one another, then opening the gates without question. No one dared to bar their path. One sprinted off, clearly to warn the others.

Anastasia squeezed Rowan's cold hand, then reached for Lyra's with the other.

Together, they walked forward, a family forged through trauma and death, walking toward the end of their long, blood-paved road.

The town was eerily quiet, which wasn't unusual for Tenebral, but something felt different. Residents peered from behind windows or scurried past, barely acknowledging their return.

When they reached the main square, someone waited for them. Ravenna.

She stood exactly where Lyra had once dropped her father's pail of water as a child. The slap that followed, humiliating and sharp, rang in Lyra's ears. This time would be different, though. She wouldn't make another mistake, she would listen to her mother's lessons, and not fail like her useless father.

Snow concealed Ravenna's outline, but even so, they could feel her wicked intentions hidden beneath a facade of motherly intent.

"Lyra! Anastasia!" Ravenna called to them. "You're back." Her grin was far too large, far too rehearsed. "I heard about Valspire. Wonderful work, you two. Come give your mother a hug."

She spread her arms wide, but no one moved.

"What's wrong?" she asked, her smile still rigid. "Aren't you happy to see your mother? Lyra, darling, you did exactly what I asked. I'm so proud of you."

Behind Ravenna, the town echoed with the collapse of a building, toward where Derewin lived. Metal clanged as smoke spiraled into the sky.

Lyra's senses sharpened.

Ravenna took a step forward. "If you won't come to me... then I'll come to you," she took another step. "And who's this boy? Someone I should know about?"

Anastasia raised her hand, stopping Ravenna's forward progress.

"Don't come closer," she warned.

Ravenna's smile twisted to a scowl. "What kind of reunion is this? After all we've been through, after everything I've done for you—"

"We're not here to celebrate. We—" Anastasia faltered.

Lyra tore Rowan's gun from his holster and pressed the barrel to his head. Her palms sizzled and stuck to the grip as it burned straight through her skin.

He barely had time to turn toward her.

"Lyra, what—"

The shot exploded.

"I'm sorry, Rowan."

His body vanished the second the bullet hit him. Rowan was gone, finally gone. Erased from Anastasia's grasp, deleted from the world he was trapped in.

Lyra's hands quaked as she lowered the gun. A high-pitched ringing screamed in her ears. She thought back to Westwick, the grave she dug for him, the weight of the soil as she buried the body. She thought of the promise she made as the bonfire sent the embers skyward.

Anastasia recoiled at the shockwave, disoriented for a second.

"What was that? Lyra, what happened, are you okay?" She reached blindly for Lyra, attempting to link their vision, but Lyra moved first.

I'm sorry, Anastasia. Please forgive me. I can't let you be here for this.

Her kick trailed through the snow and slammed into Anastasia's temple. The girl collapsed instantly, her small body folding into the snow drifts, swallowing her into a pillow. Lyra stood over her unconscious sister, foot throbbing, breath out of sorts. She had already lost Rowan twice; but she would not let Anastasia see what came next. She could not ruin her.

"How vicious!" Ravenna laughed with a delighted smirk. "You're starting to act a lot like me. You'd make a *wonderful* mother. Never thought I could be so proud of—"

Lyra stood between Ravenna and Anastasia's limp body, her stance protective.

"I'm nothing like you," Lyra hissed, in a tone quite like her mother's. "And you're no mother. You're a breeder—just a vessel pushing out slaves to do the work you're too weak, too pathetic, to do yourself."

She grabbed her scythe, red energy warping from her arms down to the blade. The snow hissed at her feet as it vaporized to steam.

"I did this for my sister. Anastasia doesn't need to watch her mother die. She's seen enough death already."

Ravenna scoffed, incredulous. "Die? You want to kill me? After everything I've done, and with Valspire gone, this is how you repay me? This is how you—"

Lyra didn't let Ravenna's guilt-soaked rambling last another second. She was already inches from her mother's face when the scythe came down.

Ravenna ducked with the grace of a dancer, narrowly avoiding the blade that sung past her cheek, but she never saw the follow-up. Lyra's boot snapped upward, connecting hard under Ravenna's jaw and launching her skyward.

In a blink, Lyra disappeared and reappeared beside her, driving her fist into Ravenna's gut. She plummeted down like stone, ice shattering beneath her fall. She rolled, gasping for breath, summoning her pole arm into existence.

"You psychopath! What's gotten into you? You don't think you can kill—"

Lyra swung, the scythe's arc screaming past Ravenna's face, shearing off a strand of her hair. The residual shockwave rippled through an entire line of buildings behind her, separating them to imperfect halves.

Ravenna raised her pole arm. Lyra flinched at the sight—her body didn't mean to, but the beatings still imprinted in her mind. Her mother noticed the hesitation and smirked, slashing down into her daughter's neck. It just grazed her throat, but Lyra moved faster than Ravenna could focus, every counterstrike uncontrolled, only carving shallow wounds across Lyra's fast-regenerating skin.

She's stronger than I remember. Ravenna thought.

Panic set in, Ravenna bolted toward the denser alleyways, where more distant crashes echoed behind her. Lyra chased.

Through narrow corridors and icy walkways, Lyra smashed through the walls of houses, fracturing stone and splintering wood, tearing after her mother like a natural disaster given human shape.

Ravenna risked a glance back. Lyra's eyes glowed like twin furnaces from the depths of the shadows. Ravenna turned sharply, racing toward Derewin's home, guiding her to the one place she thought she could find refuge.

But Lyra landed in front of her, slamming the scythe's blade into the snow-packed earth. Red spires erupted beneath Ravenna's feet, spearing toward her legs. She leapt aside last-minute, swinging her pole arm in a jab, but Lyra met it with the blade of her own.

From the impact point, energy detonated like a bomb, the blast overwhelming Ravenna and hurling her backward. She smashed through the wall of a house, wood and stone spraying outward, then blasted through the other side, rolling to a stop at a pair of boots. Familiar boots... Derewin's.

He was battered and bloodied, hardly in better shape than Ravenna.

"Couldn't you hear me?" Ravenna gasped, staggering upright. "That daughter of yours has gone psycho!"

"Lyra? She's here?" Derewin twisted toward the direction Ravenna pointed, but he didn't notice Aria disappear from his periphery.

Aria reappeared with sword raised high, necromantic life flowing through her distended and molten-hot veins. The blade came crashing down with a heave. Ravenna and Derewin just avoided her range, the ground exploding beneath the blade, earth flung skyward in a violent plume.

Lyra approached carefully, watching from a distance with her weapon burning with potential but held behind her. Her gaze passed from Ravenna to Aria, then to Derewin. Her fury ignited after seeing him. The Spirian—the traitor hiding under a stolen name.

Daughter? So Corvin was nothing more than...

She then slid back to Aria. The same girl who'd fought her the day Rowan died, now fully drowned in the power of necromancy. But clarity struck: they shared an enemy. Aria wasn't striking Ravenna, she was after Derewin.

"You were a Spirian all along?" Lyra called out, eyes fixed on Derewin. "And worse yet, my father?"

Aria's swinging halted, Ravenna went stiff, Orin braced himself, Derewin's face contorted. She swept her scythe outward. A red crescent ejected from the blade, sharp as a razor's edge, wide as a collapsed building, humming with hatred.

They all scattered. But Derewin wasn't fast enough, the edge of the crescent wave gouging through one leg, severing a massive portion of it, painting the snow red. He crashed sideways, gripping his mangled stump.

But Lyra didn't stop. She swung again and again, each arc leveling the surrounding buildings, streets upending, her powers now at an all time high. She had never reached such heights before, her abilities had never been so lethal.

Through the agony, Derewin forced his body to liquefy, melting into the earth much like he had done with Orin. His liquid form slid beneath the frost and reshaped behind Lyra. He reformed whole, everything but his dismembered leg.

"It's not what you think, Lyra," he said. "I did this for Tenebral. Everything I've done was to make us stronger."

She turned. Their eyes met too quickly for him to turn away. Her blood-red pupils dilated, locking him in to her trap. The world fell away before him, an eternity of suffering opened in its place.

He collapsed to the ground, images flooded to his mind, Lyra's powers stripping him open. The first memory was of Valspire, the night he had been given the poison from Corvin.

"Feed this to her. In due time, she'll pass from what looks like sickness," Corvin pressed the vial into Derewin's hand. "Only a little. No need to go overboard."

The scene skipped, now Derewin, or Gareth, sat beside Leora with a tenderness he didn't feel. The sparkling grape juice swirled innocently between them.

"Cheers!" he said brightly, tapping his glass to hers. "To a wonderful new beginning for Valspire... and our future prince, Tavian." He patted her distended stomach lightly. She drank, he watched, encouraging her to finish every last drop.

Then his nightmarish world shifted yet again. Now he stood on the bodies of thousands of Erreeckans, women, men, and children, screaming beneath his feet. Their hands crawled up his legs, trying to drag him back under. Hands of babies, of infants, of mothers reaching for their children that they would never hold again.

He tried to look away, but Lyra's power wouldn't let him. Burning buildings rose like towers of hellfire, people hurling themselves from high rise windows, cracking onto the pavement below. Spirian soldiers tore families from homes, dragging limp bodies onto the streets to be tossed into overflowing carts like trash.

A small boy stood beside him on top of the thousand-body heap. The child turned to look at Derewin, tugging at his side. "Why did you leave?" the boy asked.

Gareth caught himself. The child's face resembled him. It was Tavian. "You wouldn't understand. I don't expect anyone to."

Tavian's bones stretched, face elongating into adolescence. Two more people materialized beside him—another adolescent boy and a girl. Vid and Aria.

"Why did you kill Leora?" they asked in unison.

Gareth grabbed his head. "I had to! You don't know what Valspire was. It was camouflaged evil, just like everywhere else. All of these wretched cities, hiding under a cover of lies and false peace!"

The three adolescents aged again into young adulthood. Tavian now looked so painfully familiar to his mother.

"Did Mom have to die? Why did I have to die? Was it worth it? Has peace finally been made?"

"Tavian... when did you get so tall?" Gareth reached out in disbelief.

But as his hand neared, Tavian's face collapsed into ash, leaving nothing behind but a void.

"Please, Tavian, forgive me! If only you knew! I regret it, but what was I supposed to do? Your mother wouldn't stop. Mariella wouldn't *let* her stop. Ravenna offered me solace..."

Tavian stood over him, body still intact but face now an ashen hole. He hefted a scythe overhead and sent it spiraling toward Gareth. A flash of searing pain radiated through his arm.

Then, Derewin snapped back from Lyra's control, her power receding like the tide pulling back from shore. He had no idea how long he'd been trapped... an hour, a day, a lifetime. But in reality, only seconds had passed.

"You disgust me." Lyra stood over him where Tavian had left him, her scythe planted in his arm. "But I'm not here to kill you—I need something instead."

She yanked him up and ripped the blade free. His liquid body seemed to reform around his wounds, but his leg was still absent, unable to fully mend.

"Take my sister and leave. Your guilt won't allow you to abandon another." She grabbed his collar with a strength he couldn't contest. "Take her to the port. There's a shack you can hide in. Then take her across the sea, out of this place for good. She can start anew there. Do something worthwhile for once in your life, keep Anastasia alive for me."

Derewin profusely nodded, his body still shuddering, his mind still reeling from the scraps of the nightmare. "I'm so sorry. Not just to Tavian, but to you and your sister both. My gods how you've grown... I'm glad there won't be another Ravenna the world has to face."

She jerked her chin toward Anastasia's distant, unconscious body.

Then she kicked him hard, sending his body flying across the ice, off in her sister's direction.

"Go. Before I change my mind."

"No! Don't let him go!" Aria shouted, bolting after him—Derewin dragging himself as fast as his ruined body would allow.

Lyra stepped into Aria's path, blocking her advance with the scythe raised.

"Your vengeance is not my priority," Lyra said. "If you're searching for death, keep chasing him."

Aria kept her stare low, away from Lyra's. Her anger burned, veins and arteries nearly on the edge of bursting.

"Move," Aria commanded, brandishing her sword again. The black ink seeping from her veins spilled onto the ground, crawling toward Lyra's feet.

Lyra unholstered Rowan's gun, pointing it at Aria's head. She could hear the click of the hammer, her anger draining, replaced by fear.

"I'm tired of these games," Lyra said. "I'm only here for one body. Leave, or I'll make it two."

Aria's hand slipped behind her, reaching for Aidra's pistol. Before she could clasp the grip, Orin barreled in, wrapping his arms around her and pulling her back.

"We're sorry. She's... she's not herself right now. Please forgive us, ma'am." Orin bowed low, wrestling Aria away. "We'll be leaving now."

With the distractions from Gareth, Orin, and Aria, Lyra failed to notice the opening she'd left. But Ravenna didn't.

The pole arm punched through Lyra's back, bursting out the other side of her abdomen. It sent air flying out from her lungs, taking her to both knees. She didn't scream, instead clamped both hands around it, locking it inside her own body.

Ravenna tried to wrench it free, cursing under her breath, but Lyra held on tight. Taking her scythe, she swung it backward, striking Ravenna in the neck.

Both women stayed in a locked, bloody clinch, each refusing to let go of the other's weapon buried into them.

"I only... wanted to keep my family whole. Is that too much to ask?" Ravenna gagged up blood, spitting it onto the back of her daughter's hair. “To keep us from drifting apart, to bind us together. United forever as undead, tied together without end.”

Lyra violently tore her scythe free from Ravenna’s neck and released her grasp on the pole arm. Ravenna tore it through her daughter’s stomach. Both of their wounds healed shut in an instant.

“You’re... undead too?” Lyra watched as all of her mother’s wounds closed up.

“Of course I am! How else could I spend eternity with you? With all of you? Everything I do has been for us... for our family, for our home.”

“You don’t care about us. You never have. We were weapons... tools. Extensions of your will.” She gripped onto her weapon. “You’ve never once told me you loved me.”

Ravenna rolled her eyes. “Gods, are you four? Do you need your mommy to reassure you?” She shrugged dismissevely. “Fine. I love you.” Her tone dripped with mockery. “Feel better? Ready to stop this childish tantrum?”

The ground rocked, a crack tore open the center of Tenebral and separated it into two distinct halves. Bodies of the deceased buried deep underground began to claw their way up from the crack. The snow stopped falling. The icy wind paused. The remaining buildings continued to crumble and buckle as the power around Lyra intensified.

She held her scythe out to her side, a second blade grew from the other end, creating a double-edged weapon. A barrier of blood-red energy gathered around her, pushing Ravenna back.

“Rowan tried to warn me for so long, but I was blinded by your hatred, by your lies.” Her tears vaporized in the heat that coated her. “How did I not see through you sooner? How was it that the first time I heard *I love you*, was from a dead boy I barely had the chance to get to know?”

Her right foot dug into the ground; the cobblestones began to float upward.

“I saw Aidra sob over her son’s dead body, I finally saw how a real mother acts. You are no mother. You’re nothing... and when I’m done, you’ll be a forgotten stain on a ruined city. A memory only to those you tormented.”

All of her energy concentrated into her leg as she launched forward like a cannon. A sonic boom followed her take off, buildings vaporizing behind her in the backwash. Before Ravenna could blink, Lyra's scythe carved into her stomach, folding her in half and launching her through street after street. Homes exploded, glass shattered, Necromites peeked from broken windows—not fearful, not mourning, some even smiling.

Lyra was already there when Ravenna crash-landed, standing over her mother and slashing through bone. Ravenna screamed and lashed out, her heel snapping into Lyra's hip, sending her skidding across the street through an adjacent wall.

Lyra rose from the rubble just in time to see Ravenna soaring at her. The punch drove Lyra through one side of a home and out the other.

They collided again, locked in a never ending battle. Out of the corner of her eye, Ravenna spotted movement. Corvin was standing alone on the sidewalk, sending invisible strings in Lyra's direction, trying to grasp onto her.

Lyra swept Ravenna's legs and slammed her into the ground so hard it cratered.

Corvin flicked his strings to grab hold of Lyra, but she severed them before they could latch. He blinked, and now she stood in front of him. Rowan's pistol was already in her hand, and with a single shot, his head burst open, sending bone shards spraying. His body crumpled, a few shards landing at Ravenna's feet.

Ravenna wailed like an animal. "What have you done? Your own father—" she hesitated, "well, not your father. But regardless... you're still a vile, ungrateful little girl!"

She grabbed a few sharpened chunks of Corvin's skull and hurled them like throwing knives. Lyra ducked under them, the pieces bursting from contact with the wall behind her.

"Why can't you SEE? We could lead our people to salvation, take back what the Spirians stole, but instead you defend *them*? The same ones that sent us here to die!"

Lightning struck the ground in front of Lyra. In its flash, Ravenna appeared, now wielding not just one, but two pole-arms, ready to skewer her. Her smile was twisted and triumphant, thinking she had gotten the best of Lyra.

But in her overconfidence, Ravenna made a fatal mistake. She had made eye contact for just a fraction of a moment, but it was enough.

She fell to her knees, where the memories began to flood. "No... no... stop—"

Lyra stepped forward and rammed her scythe through Ravenna's leg, pinning her to the ice.

"Lyra, please!" She battled through the memories that tried to eat at her, flailing at the scythe trying to rip it free. "Think of what we can accomplish. You, me, and your sister. No one could stop us!"

Her rambling broke as horrifying images flooded her vision. Her head throbbed in agony.

Lyra reached for the pistol. She leveled it to her mother's forehead.

"You nasty wretch!" Ravenna spat at Lyra's face. "I knew I should've never had a daughter—let alone two! This is why I wanted a boy!"

In desperation, still fighting the mental assault, she snatched a rock from her side and hurled it. Lyra stepped aside, it clattered harmlessly across the street.

"Even if you kill me, then what? What does this accomplish? What kind of sister are you? Anastasia will grow up with no mother. You're fine with destroying her family?"

Lyra reflected. "You're right. I am taking away her family."

A shrug.

"But we're used to it."

The gun clicked.

Ravenna's eyes widened. "Don't you da—"

She fired.

One shot.

Then another.

Then another.

Two more after—five in total.

Ravenna's body jerked with each, its final spasms traveling through her torso until it went still, slumped sideways in the snow, blood blooming out like an opened flower.

Lyra exhaled and held the burning gun firm within her shaking grip. Then she fell onto Ravenna's body and began to swing into the lifeless flesh. Again, again, and again she punched. For every punch, another year of lies, another year of childhood stolen, another year of wounds that wouldn't heal.

By the time her strength waned, Ravenna couldn't be recognized.

She stood back up and hovered over what remained of her mother, the last breath of hatred finally leaving her. But there was no relief. No satisfaction. No triumph. Only silence and the hollow throb of her pulse bouncing off the insides of her ears.

The wind returned, soft at first then bitter and sharp, carrying with it the weight of what had been done. Her coat flapped against her sides, stained in blood, snow, and ash. She took in what remained of the city that shaped her, tortured her, made her strong, then broke her down again.

She never realized how cold it was here.

Lyra wandered through the city aimlessly. Past the charred remains of the bakery where she would steal bread, past the cracked statue of Mariella in the town square now bisected down the center, past the bent lamppost she and Anastasia used to hide behind during Ravenna's bouts of rage. A memory flickered: Anastasia giggling, Lyra shushing her as they crouched behind the post, hands gripping each other in terrified excitement.

The past was a ghost, and she was its last haunt.

She stopped at the edge of a torn-down home and stared into the darkness within. In the shard of a shattered windowpane, her face stared back. It was pale, full of smeared soot, eyes glowing a vivid red. Alive indeed, but she felt nothing.

"Is it over?" she whispered to her reflection. "Is that it?"

She'd imagined this moment a thousand times over, but victory felt empty. Ravenna was gone, and nothing was left but the destruction Lyra had helped create.

The sky began to lighten, not from the rising sun but from the remaining ash thinning in the wind. The storm was clearing, revealing more devastation. She could hear the final breaths of the undead as they dissolved around her, one by one, their deaths silent and peaceful, yet impossibly loud. The last of Ravenna's mark on this world, her undead community that she chained into existence, now freed after their captor was gone.

A child's voice sounded from behind. "We just wanted to live a little longer," they said, a tear running down their cheek. "Without Ravenna, we're gonna die."

Lyra turned. Those words pierced her deeper than any blade had.

Tenebral wasn't just a city, but a mausoleum of memories, held together by grief and Ravenna's refusal to let go. The people here weren't *really* living; they were fragments of a past she couldn't release, brought back repeatedly by her necromancy. Her friends, her neighbors, old teachers, guards, family... had died long ago but were bound to this city. Tenebral had become their prison, and now with Ravenna gone, the links of their chains were dissolving.

The child reached for her, fingertips scattering to grey flecks. "I don't want to die. I'm not ready."

Lyra took their fading hand. A part of her wished she could vanish with them too. "It's your time... Ravenna bound you here. It's everyone's time. No one should have to live like this. All things must end."

"But we're a family, Lyra," the child couldn't stop the ever-moving disintegration. "You killed them."

The child vanished. Hundreds followed.

Lyra stared at Rowan's gun. She remembered the time before she knew she was undead. The memories that felt real. That made life worth living.

I should be dead. I'm no different than them.

She bent, grabbing a sharpened piece of stone fallen off a nearby building, etching three tally marks into the metallic barrel of the pistol —one for Aidra, one for the life she'd just ended, one for the life she was about to.

Anastasia stirred awake, slung over a shoulder, struggling in their grip.

"Let go of me!" she demanded, but her powers were weak, still spent.

Gareth tightened his hold. "Stop squirming so much. Lyra told me to do this. Please don't make this harder than it needs to be."

Anastasia froze at the name.

Lyra. Where is she?

Anastasia quickly overtook Lyra's vision, distance meaning nothing to her gift. Lyra tried to shut her out, but even when drained, Anastasia's power overtook her own defenses.

Anastasia could see Tenebral in ruin. She saw the stillness of the dead, their remainders floating up into the sky. She saw Rowan's gun glinting in Lyra's shaking hands.

"You weren't supposed to wake up yet, Anastasia. Please, let go." Lyra fought again to shove her off, but Anastasia latched on with every last bit she had.

"What's happening? Where's Mom... did you kill her? And where's Derewin taking me?"

Lyra's tears fogged their shared vision. Anastasia could hear her sister sniffling, wiping her nose with the sleeve of her jacket.

"Everything will be okay," Lyra whispered. "After I'm gone, you'll have nothing to worry about. You'll find your peace across the sea." She placed a single bullet into the chamber. "I'm sorry I couldn't get you a friend for Cloud. That's... one promise I won't be able to fulfill."

She placed Rowan's gun against the side of her head and cocked the hammer. She wanted to at least follow through on one promise—the one she'd made to Rowan at his funeral.

"I'm so tired, Anastasia," she said, smiling through the tears that flowed fast and unbroken. "All things must die eventually. This is no way to live."

"Lyra, no! Stop! STOP!" she screamed through their connection. "Please, don't leave me! Don't—"

"I love you, Anastasia," Lyra whispered. "Be good for me."

Her voice cracked. "We'll see each other again... just not for a little while."

Lyra closed her eyes, but before she pulled the trigger, something grazed her arm.

She opened her eyes to see Rowan; his hand placed on the grip of the gun.

"That's my job, remember?" he said.

Lyra's free hand flew to her mouth, the sobs no longer restrained. The sight of him, the real him and not some created copy from a Rift, stole the breath from her lungs.

"Are you ready?" he asked.

Lyra nodded weakly. "Yes... please."

She lifted her hand as if holding up an invisible recorder, framing the two of them in a final, make-believe shot.

"Do something interesting, I'm recording."

Rowan understood, smiling through his own tears, taking hold of the gun for her.

But before he pulled the trigger, he whispered *bang*.

Anastasia reached her arm out, her cries unable to be heard over the worsening snowstorm. "NO—!"

Through her sister's eyes, Anastasia saw a final bloom of white—an ending so bright it severed their connection forever.

There was constant ringing. A pounding, relentless pain that filled her skull and would not ease. A torrent of agony and sorrow felt like an unbearable weight that could not be shaken. She tried to look up to see what remained, but her mind buckled under the force and went blank.

Then, only darkness.

CHAPTER TWENTY-SIX
THE END OF THE BEGINNING

When will I see you again?
~Anastasia Ashryn

Anastasia opened her eyes.

But the underlying feeling of grief clung to her, unyielding. Her memories were shattered glass, reflecting fragments of a life she could no longer assemble. She didn't know how she had arrived here. She didn't know who had brought her.

But as she came to, someone's stare met hers, a wordless exchange of understanding passed between them, though she couldn't yet place why they'd felt familiar.

In the corners of the room, the shadows from the lantern danced along the cracked wooden walls. A single warped table, spotted with dark-red stains, sat unevenly at the center, supporting a flickering lantern in its last moments of life. A dog slept beneath it, white and fluffy.

The air was damp and carried a strong, briny stench, as if a school of fish had met their untimely end not too long ago. Tools lined the walls and others were spread across the table among unmarked buckets and boxes all pushed to one corner nearest the door.

A lone boarded window allowed only a thin sliver of light to squeeze through, offering a narrow glimpse of the outside world. A faint, repetitive ringing sounded somewhere beyond the door, though she couldn't tell if they were distant bells or something far more sinister waiting outside.

Anastasia braced her palms against the seat and tried to stand, but a sudden weight pushed her back down. The burden of something unusually heavy kept her planted, like an invisible hand pushing down and preventing her escape.

Memories crept into the edges of her mind, taunting her, but nothing resolved into something she could trust. Though one question refused to let go:

How much time had passed?

The man in the corner did not move; watching her closely, with an aura that was impossible to ignore.

"They're signaling for our departure," said the man.

The voice ricocheted around the room, a whisper wrapped inside a roar. Anastasia flinched. It took only a few seconds for recognition to settle in, though even recognizing him brought no comfort.

She steadied her breath, forcing her voice forward despite how uneven it felt. "Departure? Where are we going?"

He rose, unstable on his single remaining leg, not yet experienced with his newfound form. "We'll start anew across the sea. My orders were to take you there."

A spike of pressure stabbed at her blindfold, like invisible fingers burrowing toward her eyes. She remembered that feeling. She *hated* that feeling.

"While I'm around, nothing will happen to you," he continued. "And... I'm sorry about your sister. But we need to leave at once. The Riftbound Order will not take this lightly."

His urgency sharpened his words, but it didn't show in his expression. His callous demeanor was shielded by a new face, a face like that of a father, trying to assume his new role in their journey ahead.

Sister... Riftbound Order...

The pressure behind her eyes tightened, then snapped. Her memory returned.

Lyra. Tenebral. Rowan. Seraphina. The Riftbound Order. Derewin —Gareth—the traitor, now standing before her.

Her knuckles cracked under her firm grip. Sorrow transformed into rage. Their entire journey—following Ravenna's orders, chasing the illusion of purpose, death and blood spilling from loved ones and strangers alike—*all of it* had been for nothing.

Rowan was dead. Lyra was gone. Her family, shattered beyond

repair. And what did the world leave her in return? Ripped-out eyes, an empty childhood, and a life built from scraps of other people's lies.

But this was no ending. Not yet.

The Riftbound Order. The Rifts. The Watchers. Mariella. They are the ones that began this nightmare. I have to be the one to end it.

"For Lyra," she whispered. "And for everyone else who suffered like me."

"Anastasia?" Derewin asked. "Did you hear me? We need to go. I'll keep you safe—"

She stood. Even against the pressure that dug into her, she forced her spine upright.

Gone was the fragile, uncertain girl... that version of her had died in Tenebral. What stood now was someone new, someone baptized by suffering. A vengeful force of her own making, ready to turn the world inside out. She had followed others orders for too long. Now... they would follow her.

"Go tell that to Tavian," she said with a renewed sense of self.

He froze. "Tavian? How do you know his name? Anastasia, what are you—"

She inhaled, feeling the power residing within her crack open as though it had been sealed shut with an everlasting lock. Power surged up her spine and electrified her veins. It thrummed, begging to be used once more.

The walls folded inward. Windows exploded into glittering shrapnel. Out on the docks, the ocean heaved great waves that slammed onto the pier. Anastasia lifted her hand.

Derewin's body writhed to the floor. Organs shifted inside him, twisting, folding, and bending in ways no living thing should endure. Blood splattered from his lips as he searched for ways to end his suffering.

Then, his spleen found its way up and out of him.

"W-Why?" he managed to choke out between gurgles.

"Tavian is waiting for you." There was little hatred, no heat, but only truth in those words. "I never needed a father, but maybe he did."

He reached for her but she stepped over him, the gesture not even worth noticing.

"You left Lyra to die," her footsteps splashed through the blood left at his soon-to-be corpse. "She had no one... and now not even I can bring her back."

Those words traveled empty; he was long gone before the message was received. Only his husk listened to her pain.

She walked through what remained of the doorway, emerging into the cool air of the port. She was barefoot, drenched in viscera, a velvet blindfold hanging loosely over half her face. Workers nearby set still, fear holding them down. One of them stepped forward, unwillingly drawn as her power wrapped around his mind.

She spoke directly through him, his will diminished through her grasp.

"Take me to the nearest Rift," she commanded.

The man scurried off and prepared the ship for departure.

There's work to be done.

Some time after the downfall of Tenebral, Eldric and Maeve met in Traegos, the machinery humming in the background as they bickered.

"You sent him to die?" Mave spun away on the heel of his boots in an exaggerated twirl. "I had plans for the kid! He was supposed to die by *my* hands."

"His mother had been a liability, and he was set to become one too. Mariella's meddling with the Rifts contaminated them both. I refused to let it fester." Eldric said.

Meave whipped back around. "Don't pretend as if you didn't use him too."

"Of course I used him," Eldric said, unbothered and rather bored. "He was naive enough to obey and durable enough to survive... for a while. He led us to what we needed. Although he couldn't kill Lyra or Anastasia, he still served some purpose."

Maeve sighed dramatically, still pouting like a child, hands thrown into the air. "Next time, at least tell me *before* you go killing my people! It's incredibly rude."

Before Eldric's retort, a muffled voice from behind a closed door shouted something unintelligible but furious.

Maeve's eye twitched. "Can you tell that girl to shut it already? She's the most aggravating hostage I've ever had the displeasure of being around."

Eldric stomped over to the door and pounded his fist into it. "Seraphina, quiet down! I have company—"

"Eat me!" she screamed from the other side.

He threw the door open, revealing Seraphina bound to a surgical table, her wrists and ankles clamped in thick restraints, wires snaking across her skin.

"What did you say?" He stepped toward the control panel.

"I said—" Seraphina began, but her words snapped in half to the queue of the whirring machinery coming to life.

Electricity ripped through her; she arched violently against the restraints. Her scream was high and raw, enough to sound over the stomping of Traegos. Her restraints tightened, biting deep into her skin, leaving red lines where she fought with the remaining strength left within her.

"Gods, can you keep it down? You know my ears are sensitive!" Maeve called out from the next room, covering his ears.

Eldric switched the machine off. Seraphina slumped forward, twitching, her breathing ragged.

"Please," she rasped. "Please, just stop. Let me go. I'm done. I don't resent you. I don't... I don't care anymore."

"That's not for you to decide," Eldric replied, flipping the switch again. Her screams returned, louder and sharper this time around.

He shut the door behind him, but it remained slightly ajar. He walked back over to the main chamber where the Riftbound Order's inner circle sat in a half-ring beneath a wide, glass ceiling.

"We should've sent someone for Lyra sooner," he muttered as he sank into his throne. "Tenebral is gone. The Rifts are collapsing. Every passing day drains us further." A few of the Order members shifted. "But Anastasia is still alive. If we bring her to heel, if we can harness whatever abomination she's become, her power could restore what's lost. With her, we—"

A turbulent tremor struck. The entire room lurched out of alignment. They were weightless for a second, stuck in a suspended float, before gravity took hold and slammed them back to the ground. Groans of confusion and pain rippled.

"What the hells was that?" a council member gasped.

Eldric rushed to a window and looked out in terrified awe. They were no longer elevated miles high above the world. The city stood at ground level.

The colossus that carried their city had fallen. The mountains now towered above them like tombstones. Something had killed the behemoth.

Then, a knock at the front door. Not frantic, not timid either, just a steady rhythm.

Eldric held up a hand, silencing the others.

Another knock, harder this time.

"Eldric? Are you in there? Something's happening outside. I need you out here!" The voice was familiar.

Eldric approached the door carefully. The voice continued from the other side, pleading. "Please, Eldric. It's urgent. We need you."

He cracked the door open. Standing before him was the spy sent to Aipiron to capture Lyra and Anastasia; the one who'd never returned. The one Anastasia supposedly killed.

"Fennwick?" Eldric breath halted. "You're alive? I swore she killed you. What—"

Before Eldric could finish, one woman from the Order passed him by and threw herself around Fennwick.

"I can't believe you're alive! They said you died. I was so scared—" Realizing her transparency, she blushed and quickly backed away. "I mean, not that I cared personally... but the others did."

Fennwick didn't react. He simply stared ahead, mouth slightly opened, eyes like fogged glass.

Eldric placed a hand on Fennwick's cheek. "Fennwick, you seem... not yourself. Come inside. Sit."

But Fennwick remained glued to the entryway, muscles locked as though any sudden movement would cost his life.

That's when Eldric noticed the petals. Tiny blossoms sprouted from

Fennwick's scalp and the backs of his hands. The flowers that grow on graves, as Slug would've said.

"Run," Fennwick pleaded in a muted whisper. "She's here."

His body folded inward, spine curving until it snapped to three distinct segments. Tendons stretched, muscles tore; he was contorting like a performer who had never trained a day in their life, each motion jerky and unnatural.

The woman who'd hugged him ran back to his side. "Fennwick? Somebody help him!"

A shadow fell over her, so heavy she couldn't lift her head up to see who it belonged to. It pinned her neck down, a weight placed directly onto her back.

Fennwick unwound for a breath, provided enough time to speak his final words.

"I'm sorry," he choked out. "She's too strong. I couldn't stop her... I missed you."

He didn't twist again. This time, he simply melted, his body liquefying into black tar that seeped between the cracks in the floor, disappearing entirely.

The weight pressed on her neck lifted. She looked up.

Anastasia stood above her. Her head was half-cocked, her expression patient, almost polite, as she waited for the woman's reaction.

"What did you do to him? You... you killed him?"

Without giving Anastasia time to reply, the woman screamed and lunged forward with an engraved dagger in her hand.

Anastasia caught her by the forehead. The woman melted beneath her grasp, flesh sliding off bone, turning into a fresh puddle of human soup.

Anastasia's voice was soft, far too soft. "Now they can be together."

Eldric inched back.

"A-Anastasia? Is it really you?" he stammered. "That's... wonderful! I–I've been meaning to talk. P-Please... come in."

Behind her, Cassius stepped into view. Rope burns ringed his neck like a noose still clung to him, the flesh bruised and purple. Death had come for him once, and now he carried it along with him.

From the adjoining room came a familiar scream. "Once I'm out, I'll kill you!"

Eldric rushed to close the half-shut door. "Sorry, don't mind that one," he nervously laughed. "Now, please, join us—"

Anastasia shoved past him, throwing open the door.

Light spilled into the room, revealing Seraphina along the back wall. Bruised, bloodied, and broken. Her once-polished appearance was now reduced to a disheveled mess of tangled hair, smeared makeup, torn clothes, and a face swollen and slanted in pain. But even through it, her pride still showed.

Anastasia ran over to her, unfastening her restraints. The moment they loosened, she was sent to the floor. She lifted her head to look up. "Anastasia... you came. Thank you. Where's Lyra?"

A single tear slid beneath Anastasia's blindfold, splashing onto Seraphina's leg with a soft tap.

Seraphina's face crumpled. "I'm so sorry." She pulled her into an embrace that Anastasia didn't resist.

From the doorway, Eldric tried again. "Please, let's talk. You, Cassius, Seraphina, we can all work together and start over."

Anastasia raised a finger to her lips to signal silence. Eldric obeyed.

"I didn't come here to talk," she said. "I came to end the nightmare you created. One I can't wake from... not until every last one of you is gone."

The Riftbound Order rose as one, weapons unsheathed. Their power was already evident, exuding colored energy sent snaking up their arms, flowing with deadly intent.

Only Eldric remained calm, calculating his next move.

"Don't be ridiculous, Anastasia. You don't want that," he spread his arms out wide like addressing a room full of children. "Think of what we could accomplish together. The Riftbound Order, the strongest force left in this world. You, Seraphina... even Cassius, if he's done wasting my gifts."

He glanced at Cassius, who held a cold, unyielding stare. Eldric's smile twitched but he pressed on.

"Together, we can restore the Rifts. We can bring power back to mankind. Live forever. Hold the world in the palms of our hands. We could even bring your sister back…"

He extended his hand.

"Join us, Anastasia. You and your friends. With our strength combined, we could accomplish what even the gods never dared."

Anastasia's hand moved slowly toward his. For the briefest moment, she almost wanted to believe him. Seraphina and Cassius both tensed, watching her hand nearly meet his.

But before contact, Anastasia stopped. Her thumb flicked into a pretend hammer, her index and middle finger turning to a barrel. Her hand was now a finger gun, aimed at his forehead.

"Bang," she whispered.

"What… What was that? Is that supposed to be a joke?"

Anastasia's expression didn't change.

"All things must die eventually, Eldric. This is no way to live."

Eldric recoiled by the gesture, pulling back as if insulted. "This is your last chance," he snarled. "You really think you can take all of us? Slug told me everything. I know what you are."

She quickly turned.

"Please leave, both of you," she said to Seraphina and Cassius. "I don't want to kill you too."

Seraphina stepped close and placed a small kiss on her forehead.

"You'd be stupid to think I'd let you face them alone. And even more stupid if you thought I'd let you have all the fun." She winked, playfully ruffling Anastasia's hair.

Cassius approached next and took Anastasia's hand. "Funny you should mention that," he said, voice tense. "Please… help me. Like you said, this isn't really living. My family is gone, and I'm still stuck here."

Anastasia didn't need explanation, it was written in the lines carved in his face. She nodded and laid a hand on his forehead. "I understand."

"And take this." He pressed a battered leather journal into her arms. "I've spent far too long on this to let it die with me. Keep it safe."

The cover was warm, as if the pages still remembered his touch. There were scribbles all over, notes on the afterlife, on David, on Tavian, on Aria's worsening power. His entire life, bound to a single book.

She placed it in her coat.

Cassius exhaled, her touch breaking him down and flaking him apart, chips of him removed like crumbling bark. His hand rubbed along the crease of the spice pouch one last time.

"Thank you," he whispered, as he dissolved into dust.

Anastasia turned back to Eldric. By now, the Order had fully surrounded her. Eldric had shed his outer robes, revealing his skeletal, half-decayed form.

"That reminds me..." Anastasia took both hands and ripped a long, vertical slash through the air. A Rift split open, large enough for something monstrous to walk through. "I brought someone for you, Eldric."

From the Rift slithered out Slug, his oozing form dragging across the room.

"Eldric," Slug croaked, hollow and hungered. "Good to see you again. I hope you've prepared for her."

Eldric scowled. "You think this will help you? Slug couldn't even rise above the *lowest* ranks of the Watcher hierarchy. He's useless."

"I made a mistake," Slug said remorsefully. "She's stronger now... *much* stronger. I gave her too much. My experiment failed."

Eldric's brows snapped together. "Experiment?"

Slug winced. "Maybe I should've listened to the whole 'balance' thing. I just wanted to prove to myself—to show you all I was worth more." His expression turned sour. "But letting her absorb the powers of those she kills, and having her grow stronger with every death, seemed to backfire. And uh... letting her create Rifts... I'll take the blame on that one."

He looked at her with a mix of fear and pride. "I never knew I could create someone like her. I never knew she would live this long... or that she would kill this many. She was just a young girl, after all."

Eldric's eyes blazed. "You *what*?"

A ripple stirred within the Rift. Another figure stepped out, not quite man or woman, draped in cloth that flowed like water. It had three dangling arms that hung like loose threads, with a mask that covered up a face with too many eyes peeking out from the sides. Its form hunched like a puppet without its master, skin made of old, chipped bark. It was another Watcher that she had slain.

"Hello again, Eldric," the being murmured. "Care to join us?"

Eldric's posture strained.

Then, another Watcher emerged.

And another.

And another.

One by one, every Watcher she had killed stepped through the glowing tear, surrounding her in an ominous ring. All bore sorrowful glances and flowers, reminders of the ones she had already claimed.

Even the colossus that once carried the city on its back lumbered from the Rift. Its massive, helmeted head punched straight through the glass ceiling, the shards falling onto their heads. Through the new opening snow fell in small clumps. A full moon hung low, peeking from behind scattered clouds like the whites of an eye.

Eldric backed away. "All our work... undone by one girl. The Rifts are gone. We have nothing left." He looked down to his decrepit hands, his strength dwindling with each passing moment. "You think we'll give up because of this? We'll speak with Mariella—we'll rebuild—"

As if the very name conjured her, Mariella—the mother of the Rifts—gracefully stepped out from the Rift, adorned with flowers stemming from her fingertips. But one stood alone: a single cotton rose sprouting from her middle finger, its base pale white, its tip stained deep red. She lifted her hand skyward, aligning the blossom with the moon.

Her voice carried the calm of a prophecy already fulfilled. "I side with the victors, Eldric. Your time has come. Soon, flowers will grow on your grave—just as they did upon mine."

"No... not her too... how could you manage—"

Anastasia smiled for the first time in what felt like ages. Her cheeks lifted, nudging the blindfold upward until it slipped free and fluttered to the floor. Where once there had been hollow, mutilated sockets, something new now sat.

Nestled within flesh were two whole, sparkling, violet eyes.

"Your eyes!" Seraphina gasped. "Have you always had those?"

"They were a gift," Anastasia said. "Slug gave them back to me after some time... after some *convincing*."

Her smile widened. A scythe manifested in her hand, the same shape, the same weight, the same dual-bladed weapon that her sister once carried. With a single upward slash, she dragged the blade through the Rift, elongating it far beyond the building's frame. The Rift was now visible from miles away, stretching to the heavens.

It roared with its own gravitational pull, beginning to suck in whatever was near, the very fabric of reality fighting against its force.

Anastasia's newly violet eyes began to bleed like her sister's once had, and those foolish enough to look into them collapsed instantly—lifeless before their bodies struck the ground.

Maeve shrieked and bolted for an exit. "Lovely chat, Eldric! See you... well, probably never!"

Eldric and his remaining members shielded their faces as the Rift ruptured. A flood of the dead spilled forth, every one of her victims spread out in a sea of gored mass. They reached out toward the Rift-bound Order, beckoning them into their nightmare.

Eldric vanished, reappearing behind Anastasia with a blade almost pressed to her throat. But it never touched her; she bent backwards with a boneless, serpentine motion, spine dislocating with an audible *snap*. In a flash, she twisted upright again, grabbing the blade, shattering it with a slight squeeze.

Her bleeding violet stare locked onto him. Around them, Order members hacked and screamed as the undead poured in waves through the Rift.

One of the Order members spotted Eldric interlocked with Anastasia; and with a snap of his fingers, he hurled a compacted orb of white-hot, concentrated radiation—a miniature bomb—directly at her head.

But with only the swipe of a hand, she caught it, tossing it aside like a pebble. When it hit the ground under her, stone vaporized and dust flew outward in the explosion, yet her body remained whole and intact, not a hair out of place.

He lunged toward her in a final attempt, but never made it. The colossus brought its foot down in an earth-shattering crash, flattening the man into nothing but a stain beneath its heel.

The buildings of the city began to crumble under the Rift's pull, dragging them in like sinking ships pulled deep underwater. Out of the tear came waves of static, colored only in black and white, that flooded streets, swallowed railways, consumed clocktowers, evaporating everything and anything it touched. The cries of the townsfolk permeated the havoc as hundreds were consumed by the tsunami of distortion. The Rift widened steadily, each life taken increasing its size and dominance.

Seraphina struggled to stay upright, locked between two Order members. One launched into the air, diving at her like a metallic-winged hawk, but Seraphina rolled aside. The woman drilled headfirst into the floor. She rose with a snarl, but Seraphina was faster.

She used her gravity to grab the woman and force her further back into the ground, snapping bones like brittle branches. The makeshift metal wings folded inward and separated.

The second member swept their hand forward, controlling a halo of spinning ash. The dust swarmed the broken body of their comrade, piecing together the mangled wings and ruined flesh. Skin began to regenerate, her pulse returning in quiet thumps. But before the resurrection could complete, a shadow fell upon him.

A Watcher stood behind the healer, shoving their long, sharpened fingers through the back of the Order member's skull, emerging from the top like an antenna. The halo collapsed, as did the man.

Anastasia and Eldric remained locked together at the center of the storm. He was on his hands and knees now, the full bulk of Anastasia's violet eyes pressing on his mind. Memories assaulted him: of death, of family, of failures... flashing in nauseating strobes.

"Please... Anastasia," he pleaded. "Spare us. We'll serve you. We'll do anything. Just let us go."

She pulled him to his feet. His legs barely held. A cool wind brushed the back of her neck, carrying with it the smell of pine and dampened earth. The smell of the forest.

A sign that the one she sought out on her journey back to Traegos had finally arrived, just on time. Anastasia turned to a familiar face.

"I'm not the one meant to kill you," Anastasia whispered in Eldric's ear. "But she is."

Eldric lifted his head to where Anastasia stared.

Thalia had returned.

"Anastasia," Thalia said. "You've done what I never could. Thank you. My husband gives his regards as well."

Anastasia offered the scythe, but Thalia declined. She reached beneath her coat and pulled out a stiletto, its edge dulled by age.

"My husband saved it for a moment like this. Told me to keep it safe in case the day ever came."

She stepped forward, each footfall riddled with repressed, years-old resentment. She pressed the point to Eldric's throat.

He struggled against the sharp tip. "You resent us," he yelled. "Yet you wield the power we gave you! Hypocrite! None of you understand our purpose. Humanity always craves for more power. We served to provide balance, and now you leave it to *her*, to Anastasia, to rule without limits!"

Thalia slid the blade along his neck, not enough to kill, but to bleed.

"You are no martyr," she said, "You cared nothing for balance. Nothing for humanity. You cursed us, all of us." Her voice only wavered for a second. "I do this for my husband... for everyone you've damned."

She shoved the blade straight into his neck. Blood erupted in great sheets, splashing across the stone and pooling unnaturally fast. Before even half of it could drip to the floor, the blood thickened and congealed—transforming into odd shapes. The blood took the shape of thorns, bursting outward, impaling deep into Thalia and Anastasia. Either twitch of them forced the barbs deeper, keeping them anchored in place.

"How juvenile to think I'm that weak." Eldric's wounds healed, blood still oozing but in lesser streams. "Come, Anastasia. Let me fix you."

He pressed a hand to her forehead. His fingers sank to the deepest parts of her skull. Fingers emerged from her ears, her eyes, her nostrils—tangled inside, fumbling through her mind like someone searching through drawers.

Anastasia screeched. Her blood-curdling yells caught the attention of the Watchers.

The Rift widened even further in response to her pain. Static rushed out in force, engulfing the remaining buildings in seconds. Civilians, Order members, anyone not already dead—sucked into the flood, erased in a blink.

Thalia ripped an arm free from the thorny blood, shredding her own skin in the process, then cast a violent gale forward. The compressed wind struck Eldric, crashing him through two members of the Order that stood behind him. One took the spell head-on, stripped down to the bone, skin plastered to the wall beside them.

Eldric hit the ground hard and scrambled upright, but Anastasia was already there. Her scythe pierced straight through his back and out the chest.

He threw his hands back and laughed. "You think that's enough?"

He grabbed the blade, prying it loose, but the scythe reacted to his touch. Red filaments spread from the metal like a web, taking over his forearms and up his sides, down to his legs and across his torso. The web burned and constricted tighter.

Thalia approached Anastasia and rested a hand on her head. "Thank you again, dear. I think I've lost my touch over the years."

She bent down to meet Eldric's fading stare. "This ends now. You've lived long enough, it's time to let go."

"Wait—please," he begged again. "I can change. I'll do anything... I'm afraid to die. I still have so much to do."

Anastasia covered her ears. She couldn't bear another plea, another scream, another pitiful grasp for mercy. Not after so much death. She was tired of the killing.

But Thalia gently pulled Anastasia's hands off her ears.

"I'm sorry, honey, but I need your help again. I'm not what I used to be, I don't have what it takes to finish him. This will be the last time. I promise."

Anastasia nodded, weariness bending her posture. Her eyes began to leak a multicolored wave, the same that spilt over Fennwick in Aipiron, staining her clothes in glowing streaks. She stepped toward Eldric.

His head drooped, whispering to himself.

"Why has it come to this...?" he mumbled. "Why won't they just let me live...?"

Anastasia ignored his mutterings, now stretching her arm out in his direction. Eldric looked up at her, wet trails marked his cheeks yet an unsettling smile remained.

"If I must die here," he said, "then so shall you and everyone else. It's only fair. A girl like you cannot live unbounded."

Behind him, one of the last remaining Order members gasped as they watched Eldric rip through his own chest, pulling out his own heart. It was an amalgamation of flesh fused with intricate machinery and metalwork. Gears spun deep within the ventricles, thumping to a pattern maintained by an internal clock, with a tiny timer placed in the center. And beneath the glass window of the timer, red numbers began to count down.

Ten. Nine.

Eldric laughed, but not with joy, rather with the realization of what he'd just unleashed.

Eight. Seven.

"Oh gods—" The Order member turned to call out the remaining few. Eldric had warned them of this, the final measure. None of them had believed he'd ever use it.

Six. Five. Four.

Anastasia spun around to shield Thalia and Seraphina, but even with all her power, her hands couldn't move fast enough.

Three. Two.

"SERAPHINA—THALIA! *RUN*!"

One.

Zero.

Eldric looked directly into the heart. It lit up like a newborn star. A violent flash swallowed Traegos whole. Pure white heat annihilated anything it touched. The Rift melted in its wake, any last remaining building vaporized. Streets, towers, bridges, all gone before their very eyes. Wind shrieked across the ruined land.

In less than a heartbeat, the entire city had evaporated.

The sound rolled over the distant mountains, into the horizon. Far away, Aria and Orin stopped, turning their heads back toward the noise, where a white sun had bloomed then died.

Silence followed. No birds, no voices, no breath of wind, no powers, no undead, no Order, no Watchers.

Though among the quiet, there was a shifting of rock; a single hand emerging from the rubble. Seraphina dragged herself free, her pearly-white dress hung in ribbons, her face caked in soot, her nails chipped to stubs.

"Anastasia!" she wheezed, coughing up blood onto rock. She blasted away the debris that weighed her down, tossing bodies, stones, and broken glass along with it. "Anastasia!"

A groan, quiet but close, answered her.

She limped toward it, buckling from the first step, dragging herself forward on her brittle legs. Her palms burned though the hot ash as she continued to drag along. Her feet throbbed from numerous broken bones. Her hair was singed, her skin blistered, her eyesight blurred.

She managed to reach the pile of corpses where the groans came from, raising both hands and summoned, with whatever strength she had left, her gravitational energy to push away the top layer of bodies. They peeled back by the layer, until a body with some remaining life was discovered.

There, Thalia lay buried—though in her current state, Seraphina had to squint to make out who it was.

Seraphina hoisted her upright, brushing dirt away from Thalia's face and keeping her body steady.

"Sorry to... ask for something right now," Seraphina said with visible panic, "but I need your help. Anastasia's missing. Please, help me find her."

Thalia nodded, coughing up a ball of phlegm and soot.

Shoulder to shoulder they moved in tandem, overturning each piece of ruined city until they could locate the body. They called for her name on repeat, but got no answer. With each empty patch of stone, their hope dwindled. The moon dipped lower over the horizon, the air growing warmer, the world brightening from the early morning sun.

Their hope diminished with each passing hour, reality setting in. Maybe Anastasia had sacrificed herself. Maybe this was the cost of their survival. Maybe she was meant to die with the rest.

Then a cough—small, fragile, and young.

They stood still, listening for its origin. Then another one, off to their left. Their heads snapped toward the sound, now sprinting in that direction to the best of their ability.

A small body was caked in dust out front. Shrapnel had torn through her side; her arms and legs were raw and cleaved, but she was alive.

Anastasia was nestled in the dirt, crying not because the battle was over, but because she had killed again.

Again and again and again.

She was exhausted, she was jaded, she was empty. All she wanted now was peace.

Thalia and Seraphina dropped to their knees beside her and pulled her into their arms. She gripped them back as though if she'd loosened her grasp for even a second, they would dissolve to dust like everything else she touched.

"When will I see you again?" Anastasia whispered, not because Thalia was gone, but because she felt something stirring in the silence. A voice in her ear that wasn't Thalia's. She was looking through the empty air just beyond them, at something invisible but patiently awaiting her.

Thalia tilted her head. "See me again? But, Anastasia... I'm right here."

CHAPTER TWENTY-SEVEN

LOST N' FOUND

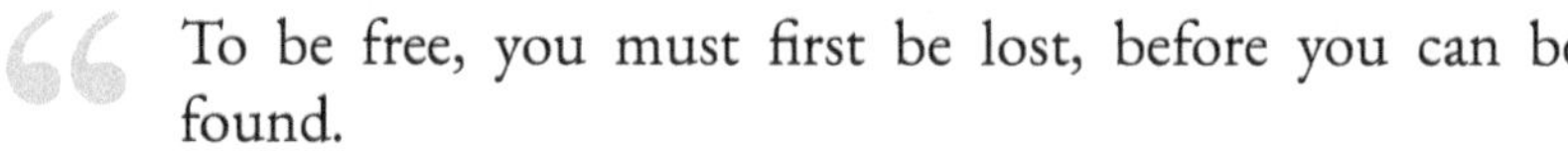

> To be free, you must first be lost, before you can be found.
>
> ~Luna Gray

The smell of fire lingered in his nose.

An ashen home, a stovetop left burning just long enough to turn a house into a funeral pyre.

Cassius stirred beneath a colorless sky, sprawled in a field of wind-tossed grass. The clouds above rolled in slow motion, heavy and gray, like the world had gone still, caught in between breaths awaiting him to understand where he was.

He sat up, disoriented from Anastasia's final touch. There was no cityscape, no mountains, no people. Only a lonely structure far off to his left.

His home.

The shabby, beloved thing was just as he remembered before the fire: an unfinished paint job, green wooden shutters faded by sunlight, a crooked porch with five different sized rocking chairs facing the same direction, the chipped front door he'd always meant to fix but never got around to.

Did... did she do it? Am I home... actually home?

Cassius staggered to his feet and rushed to the front door. He reached the porch and pounded his fists against the door.

"It's me! I'm home! Please, open up! Let me see you. Let this be real."

Nothing.

No footsteps. No laughter coming from his children. No warm voices to sooth his restless mind.

His fists dropped to his sides, his forehead pressed to the door. He turned and his back slid down the door until he sat on the porch boards with awkwardly folded legs. The tears came fast, but not even hands covering face could dam the years of guilt he'd built up inside of him. Their deaths all on him and his cooking, the one thing that unified them, killing them just as easy.

Maybe he'd waited too long. Maybe the last time he'd seen them was the last chance he'd ever have.

But the front door flew open without warning. The force of it sent him tumbling end-over-end. His head smacked against the porch with a dull thud, stars bursting in his vision. Pain shot through his skull as he groaned to try and sit back up.

Then three small faces leaned over him—beaming, bright-eyed, and so achingly familiar.

"Dad's home!" they squealed in unison, giggling as they dove onto him in a tangle of arms and joy.

Cassius gasped, clutching them with all his might, the once sorrowful tears now rolling freely down his face by the overwhelming miracle of it all.

"She did it," he whispered into their hair. "You're really here. I thought I'd lost you forever."

Their giggles vibrated against his chest. Tiny hands tugged at his sleeves, little fingers pressed into his cheeks and tangled in his hair.

Footsteps softened on the floor of the porch.

He looked up through tear-blurred vision.

And she was there.

Standing on the landing, wearing a lemon-yellow dress she saved for special occasions, her hair curled just the way he liked it, one hand resting delicately over her heart. Her eyes glistened with the kind of love only time could sharpen.

"I told you," she said, her smile full of light. "We just had to wait a little longer."

She descended slowly, letting the moment breathe. When she

reached him, she lowered herself to her knees beside the tangled family, her arms slipping around him and the children. She gathered them all close like she had done a hundred times before.

Her scent was the same. The smell of clove and allspice, the same that lived forever in the little spice pouch he carried in his pocket everywhere he went.

"Welcome home," she whispered against his ear.

Cassius closed his eyes and let the world fall away.

For the first time since their passing, he wasn't running, wasn't sacrificing, wasn't breaking himself to understand what lay beyond the opaque curtain of life and death.

He was simply where he belonged.

With them.

"We waited too long."

Orin and Aria stood in stunned silence before the gaping ruin where Valspire's entrance had once stood. Walls crumbled, falling into the blood-slicked streets below. Fires licked the sky. Bodies were strewn across the wreckage—some burned to charcoal, others split wide open—each one sprouting flowers from their hands, feet, and throats as if nature tried to apologize for the horror.

Their boots sank into the curdled puddles, viscous with bloodied viscera. The stench was almost unbearable. The rain worked hard to cleanse the devastation, but it wasn't enough. It couldn't hide the truth.

Aria dropped to her knees, her breathing troubled and chest stabbing her insides. A small bundle of toy flowers sat beside the lifeless forms of a mother and daughter, their hands outstretched but not quite touching. She grabbed the toy flowers and hugged them to her.

"I knew we were too late. I never should have listened to him... gods, why did I listen?"

Orin stepped behind her and rubbed her back.

"There's nothin' we could've done, even if we'd stayed. We would've ended up just like them. We need to search the palace, see if anyone is left."

She forced herself to look up. The school where she and Tavian had whispered secrets was pulverized. The chapel where they prayed on weekends was reduced to scattered stone. The little corner shop where they'd argued over sweets was split clean in half.

She reached up, letting Orin help her to her feet. One hand covered her mouth to stifle sobs, while fighting against the rising vomit.

As they stepped through the shattered palace entrance, Aria paused on the first stair. A lone photograph hung sideways on the wall, the glass frame broken, a hole punched through into the back wall.

Tavian's face was depicted along with his mother and Aria, the hole gaping in the center but still recognizable. She lifted the picture gingerly out of the frame and held onto it like something sacred. She then tucked it into her pocket.

They reached the upper floor and turned the corner, just in time for a dagger to whistle past Orin's head and embed itself in the wall.

Aria's hand snapped to her sword, but before the hilt could clear the sheath, a weathered hand caught hers.

"Easy, Aria."

The voice was calm but commanding. Aria spun around, and it was Elyra who stood there. She was bruised and off balance, but alive. Her look held the wisdom of someone who had just seen the worst and survived it.

Aria gasped and launched forward, hugging her tightly, nearly squeezing out what breath Elyra had left.

"I thought everyone was dead. I'm so sorry I left. I should've come back sooner."

Elyra rested a hand on her head. "Shh. You're here now. That's what matters."

She looked up at Orin, whose face still hovered inches from the dagger that was planted in the wall.

"You're lucky my aim's not what it used to be." Elyra gave an exacerbated wink. Orin managed a thin smile.

Aria exhaled a breath she hadn't realized she was holding in.

"Should I ask where Vid and Tavian are, or... do I already know?" Elyra's voice darkened.

"I... I don't know about Vid," Aria murmured. "But Tavian... he's gone. He changed. I couldn't bear to see him like that anymore." She resumed crying, doing her best to hide it with both hands.

Elyra closed her eyes. "He's with Leora now."

Aria grazed the photo through her pocket. "I couldn't save him. He went mad. There was no stopping him."

"He was never yours to save," Elyra said. "You did more for him than any of us ever did." She pulled Aria into another tight embrace before guiding her back. "But now we have something for you to save."

She pointed down the steps.

"The throne is empty. Valspire needs someone to take the seat. Someone to help rebuild."

Aria didn't hesitate. "It's the least I can do."

Elyra gave a quick smile, but was soon interrupted by a guttural grumbling from below the stairs.

"There are still a few lurking," Elyra warned. "Remnants from the invasion. I'd check myself, but... Mariella is no longer with me."

Elyra shuddered at the memory. The moment Anastasia appeared in Valspire, alone, like a terrifying omen with bleeding violet eyes. She had snuffed out Mariella's presence like a hound and ripped her away, severing Mariella's light from her own like it was nothing. There were no words exchanged; only Mariella's fading screams as she was pulled into the Rift.

Aria drew her sword. "I'll finish it."

Orin followed.

The noise grew louder as they neared the performance hall. The stage where Vid once performed was littered with a pit of bodies, some fresh and pungent, others old and rotted. Among the ruined grandeur, a single undead creature crouched, ripping flesh from a corpse with animalistic glee. It looked half human, half lizard, with sharp ridges along its spine and scaly skin to match.

Aria slowed as she approached. Her mind cascaded with memories: laughing with Tavian during Vid's concerts, elbowing through the crowd to find good seats, worrying over nothing more than how she could sit nearest Tavian and feel his side brush against hers.

That world was gone now, replaced by the husks of those same friends and families, watching the empty stage from their prone positions.

They crept closer to the creature.

As the outlines of the bodies came closer into view, Orin did a double-take at one corpse in particular. Her face was gashed, but her image still remained clear.

"My gods… is that Violet?"

He instantly regretted saying her name out loud, it came out without warning.

Aria looked at him, confused. "Violet?"

The name tumbled around like loose stones, stacking together one by one. She'd heard it somewhere before, read it even, but couldn't place it. Not until the memory swept through her like a tide.

It reached shore.

Violet. Her mother. From the records in Ashford.

There, on Vid's old stage, lay Violet and Finnian. Freshly dead, still warm to the touch. Violet's scent, jasmine mixed with something floral, was now tainted by iron.

The lizard-like undead creature hunched over her parents, using Violet's dismembered arm like a puppet. It waggled the severed hand in greeting.

The creature cackled. "Judging by your faces, I'm guessing these two are yours? Missed 'em by minutes. Wanna taste?" It patted its scaly back with her limp hand. "Hah—gods, I crack myself up."

Aria's vision tunneled. Before the creature could bark another laugh, black smoke piled into the room. Every corner was obscured by darkness, the stage, the seats, the walls, only allowing enough visibility to see a few feet ahead.

A small pocket cleared for the creature to see, and there stood Aria, a foot away. She was shaking uncontrollably, her veins were pulsing at full throttle with her sword raised to the heavens.

The creature screamed and stumbled back. "N-now hold on…"

He slipped on entrails and loose bones, hitting the ground. She threw her blade down into his chest. It pinned him like a dart on a board, with dark energy flowing from her hands, crackling through the weapon and into his ribcage.

He couldn't breathe; his stomach inflated like a balloon, and his lungs ruptured from his chest. Blood painted the ceiling.

She yanked the sword free and went feral. She tore the creature into scraps, hundreds of them, carving with the deranged precision of an unhinged surgeon. Only when the red haze of anger drained from her did she stop. Her arms sagged, her breath worked to keep up, tremors signaled her exhaustion.

She dropped the sword, then she turned to them, to her parents.

Kneeling between their mangled bodies, she placed a hand on each of their chests. A powerful glow spread from her palms, her necromantic energy surging at full force.

Orin hung back, turning away. He'd seen what comes from forcing life back to where it no longer belonged. Mycorida still existed because of him; an empire of bodies that refused to die, and even still regretted what he'd done. He prayed this wouldn't become another tragedy forged by necromancy.

"Be careful with what you bring back," he mumbled. "Some things don't return the way we hope."

Her parents' eyelids twitched, their mouths opened, gasping for air, and their limbs stirred awake as life flowed back into them.

"Aria... is it you?" Finnian's voice was strained but strengthened with each syllable. "We really found you..."

His hand found her palm on his chest. She grabbed it and squeezed hard enough to hurt.

"Dad? How did you know where to find me?"

Beside him, her mother's body sat up slightly, her head creaking up to meet her daughter's sight.

"It really is her. I can tell... you have your father's eyes." Her dried lips cracked into a smile.

"Mom..." Aria let go of her father's hand and wrapped around Violet. Her mother's remaining arm still found its way around her daughter's body; she was still a mother by nature, even in this broken state.

"How could we have possibly made such a beautiful girl, Finnian?"

"She takes after her mother, that's for sure." He shuffled close and joined in their embrace.

Violet soothed Aria's shaking body, petting her hair in long, patient downward strokes.

"I'm so glad you're okay. That's all I ever wanted... just to know my baby was safe. I told them all you were special—who could've guessed how right I'd be."

"Please don't leave me again. I have so much I want to ask—so much I don't know." Aria buried her face deeper into the shattered ridge of Violet's collarbone.

"Orin," Violet turned to him, gesturing him closer. "Orin... thank you. For keeping your word, for protecting our little girl. She's everything I ever imagined, everything I'd hoped she'd become. She's in good hands with you."

Orin turned to her, his tears joining the rest. "I always keep to my word."

Aria interjected into their reunion. "Why does it sound like you're trying to leave me again? I can't let you go. I finally found you."

Violet and Finnian gently released her, settling her back in front of them. They laced their fingers together, united even in undeath, both looking straight at her.

"You'll have to let us go at some point, Aria," Violet's demeanor was unshaken. "Just because you're a Necromite doesn't mean you have to continue on this vile tradition. The undead are far worse off than the dead—trust me." She reached over to Aria and wiped away a stray tear.

"Save your tears, sweetie. This won't be the last time we're together. When we see each other again, I'll answer all those questions you have for me."

"No..." Aria's necromantic pulse grew stronger. She was forcing the powers to their limit, trying her best to keep her family whole.

"You too, Orin. You'll always be family to us." Violet took Orin's hand and gave it a small shake. "Continue to keep your word and look after Aria. Though by now, I'm sure she's looking after you."

Orin laughed through his sorrow. "The girl's stronger than ten full-grown men. I'm more worried 'bout myself than Aria."

"Orin, stop! I'm not letting go. They're staying with us—forever." The words soured in her mouth. Aria couldn't even convince herself of the lie.

No. Why do I sound like him? She thought of Tavian and his obsession for bringing back Leora. *Was it really this hard for him? Did Tavian feel like this all the time?*

Her parents' shame was masked behind soft, loving smiles. "We can't control you, Aria. We're at your mercy. Do with us as you please."

Aria's hand rose to her chest, where her heart *should* be, and squeezed until she couldn't grasp any harder. Her whole life had led to this moment. Every step she'd taken, every fear she'd swallowed, every trail she chased... all of it was for them.

And now she was going to let them slip away again? Was their suffering worth their survival?

There was an answer behind the shroud of confusion. It was clear, simple, and plain as day, one she had always known. She had told it to Tavian countless times, guiding him toward the truth:

Some things are better left off dead. Some things don't need to stay around forever, no matter how much you want them to. You must learn to let go.

But now this was *her* family, now that it was *her* turn to choose...

"I was always afraid of ghosts," Aria said. "And now I think I finally understand why." She cupped her hands to their cheeks, one hand on each.

"It wasn't because they were scary or horrifying to look at. It's because they weren't people any longer, just empty containers... imitations of their old selves. Maybe I was scared because someday I'd become one too. Or worse... that someone I loved would become one and haunt me with that same fate."

The glow in Aria's hands began to settle.

"And I'm still afraid. Afraid of what happens after. Afraid of losing you both. Afraid of being alone again."

She leaned her forehead into theirs.

"But if I have to face those ghosts someday, go to wherever you end up after this life is over, it's comforting to know I'll have you both to keep me company."

They both smiled their last smile. Violet even let out a chuckle. "Kids are always scared of ghosts, it's in their nature. But once you grow up, you realize there's nothing to be afraid of. Funny, isn't it? You're father and I were the ghosts all along." She squeezed Aria's hand. "I guess they're really not that scary after all..."

The necromantic energy in Aria's palms finally ceased. She let go.

Their bodies slackened. The last spark dimmed as their souls slipped free. Aria let out a shuddering breath and stepped back.

"I found what I'd lost so long ago," she whispered. "But I don't want it anymore."

She turned to Orin and collapsed into his arms. Tears ran free, not able to shake the images of her dead parents from behind her eyelids. "Why is it so hard to let go?"

He held her close, cradling her shoulders and bracing the back of her head. "Because we always think there'll be one more day," he said. "But you were stronger than I. You did what's best. Hard doesn't mean wrong, Aria."

He leaned back and looked at her.

"And maybe there's somethin' more waitin' for us than pain."

He brushed her hair.

"We let go because we know they're waitin' for us: Tavian, Leora, Violet, Finnian. When the time's right, we'll see them again."

He turned toward the stage, watching the last of the black haze clear into the rafters.

"But for now, we endure. We live to carry on what they left behind. We'll make their sacrifices mean somethin'. Even if it's too late to erase the damage we've done."

As his voice faded into the halls of the palace, somewhere beyond, another soul stirred awake. A son reunited with his mother for the first time in years.

Tavian continued staring up at Leora, scratching at his eyes, trying to rub away the illusion. Any second now, he expected her to distort back into Aria.

But the more he blinked, the more Aria faded, and the more clearly Leora came into focus.

He panicked and straightened up, checking his body for wounds, but there were none. Not even pain remained in his untouched body.

He threw his arms around his mom, holding her with intense desperation. His voice struggled beneath the weight of all the words he'd carried alone.

"I'm sorry I couldn't bring you back. I tried, I tried so hard. I did everything I could."

Leora wrapped him close, cradling the back of his head. "It's okay, darling. I'm here now. We're back together. That's all that matters."

A few petals drifted into Tavian's hair, delicate cotton rose blossoms. He plucked one out, admiring its vivid color. When he followed the direction it floated from, he saw it. Her old garden; just as beautiful and pristine as he remembered, like no one had ever stopped tending to it since her death. Every flower was carefully arranged, each plant vibrant and thriving.

Leora stood up, still holding his hand, guiding him toward the rows of flowers.

"I've been waiting for you," Leora said, her gaze scanning the petals with fondness. "I tried to send you signals. I hoped you'd feel them."

Tavian turned to her. She hadn't aged a day. Not a single line. She was his mother exactly as she'd been before everything fell apart.

Then he remembered the rumors. His voice dropped. "Mom... the rumors. About the Erreeckans. Please tell me they aren't true."

Leora continued gazing at her garden, serene as ever, without a fracture to her smile. "Isn't it beautiful? When you were my little shadow, you used to try the silliest things—always ruining the edges when I tried to keep everything neat."

"Mom," Tavian cut in, his tone harder this time, "those rumors... they weren't true, right? You didn't actually kill all those people."

She froze.

Leora turned to face him. For a brief second, her eyes dulled a shade, like someone grabbed the warmth from them. Her smile stayed but sagged, remembering the expression but no longer feeling it.

"There's no need to dwell on the past, darling. Overthinking's not good for your health."

Tavian's stomach firmed. He forced himself to look back at the garden. The flowers were indeed beautiful, perfect even. The only inconsistency was the soil. It wasn't smooth, instead it rose in strange, uneven lumps. Misshapen mounds pocked the ground.

He stepped deeper into the rows, the soft petals brushing his legs paired with the cool mountain breeze. He knelt beside one of the mounds, pushing his fingers into the dirt. A strong, unpleasant odor rose from the disturbed earth. Frowning, he dug a little deeper.

Beneath the surface, something metallic sparkled.

A chain necklace.

He scooped away more soil, revealing a delicate silver chain. At its center was an opal engraved with the letters R and C.

Why's this buried here? Why do I know these letters...

The sweet perfume of the garden soured, and every bloom seemed to look darker than he'd remembered. As he worked his hand further into the soil, a hand rested on his back. He turned to it.

Leora stood over him, her smile now visibly stretched too thin.

"Darling," she said with forced cheer, "don't go digging around in places you don't belong."

She took his hand and lifted him to his feet with gentle insistence. "Come now. Let's get you cleaned up. I don't want you all muddy and messy."

She moved quickly, almost urgently, guiding Tavian through the twisting halls of the palace. He struggled to keep pace, nearly tripping over rugs that never used to be there, or dodging doorways that were misplaced.

"Mom, slow down!"

"Sorry hunny!" Leora chirped. "Lots to do today. Keep up!"

But the halls kept bending, turning to places that shouldn't have existed. Tavian knew his home like the lines on his palms, but here nothing was the same. It felt like someone was changing the layout as they moved, and it wasn't Leora's doing.

He rounded a corner and nearly collided into her. She'd stopped dead in her tracks. Her back was straight, and even from behind, he could sense her tension.

Someone else stood before her. A tall, lanky woman in flowing robes, floating a few feet above ground level. She oozed an aura of other-worldly power.

"You've waited long enough," Luna said calmly. "And as promised, the one you wanted is now here." She extended her hand toward Leora. "It's time to go."

Leora's face twitched. "Now? Can't we wait a little longer? I still have gardening to—"

"Enough," Luna said. Her voice held no cruelty, only finality. "This place was a gift, a kindness provided to you out of my own goodwill. You and I agreed: once Tavian arrived, you would be sent on."

Tavian stepped back. "Go where? I thought this was it. I thought this was home."

Leora turned to him, her face softening, a mother trying to save a moment that wouldn't last. "To where people like us go after lives like ours. This place isn't meant to last forever, Tavian. But at least... we'll head there together."

Leora reached for her son's hand, both hidden behind his back.

Tavian didn't extend one in return. "I just got here. Can't we just stay? Just for a while?"

Leora shook her head. "No, sweetheart. Come with me. I've always protected you, haven't I? We'll be fine. Just take my hand..."

He stared at her.

She looked exactly as she had when he was small. Safe, loving, the familiar kindness and caring he always imagined of her. The version of his mother he put on a pedestal. The one he remembered through a warped lens of childhood longing. But the truth he knew now warred with the comfort he recalled of those memories.

"Tavian," Luna said, "you may stay. Those close to you: Aria, Orin, Elyra, are still coming when their time calls. You can wait for them here. You are not the same as your mother. The choice is yours."

A crack in Leora's veneer. "Don't tell him that! He belongs with me!" She reached for him again like a lifeline. "Tavian, come. Please."

"Tell me the truth first," he said. "What did you do to those people?"

Leora's hand twitched. "Nothing happened, Tavian! I'm your mother! I love you!" Her pitch climbed the more she spoke. "You wanted me back so badly, and now you're here! You can't let me leave now!"

Luna tugged at Leora's arm. Where she touched, Leora's body began to fall away petal by petal, floating up into the air.

"Tavian!" she screamed. "Please, don't let me go! Grab my hand!"

She stretched toward him one last time.

He turned his head away, squeezing his eyes shut. He knew too much now.

In the moment before she finally unraveled, some truth had finally escaped. "...Tell Orin I made the wrong choice. Gareth never cared for me, he only chased lust. Tell Mom I should've listened to her sooner."

Tavian's head snapped back at her. The words struck deeper than any accusation or plea. They were the first real, human, honest words she had spoken since his arrival.

"Tav—"

But she couldn't finish. Her body was gone. Hundreds of cotton rose petals, fully white, drifted high into the sky, disappearing into the air.

Luna approached, her presence soft enough to dull the jaggedness of what had just happened. Tavian backed away.

"Don't worry," she said. "I'm not here to send you away."

He nodded, breathing hard. "What... what will happen to her?"

"My job is to guide souls to where they truly belong. Your mother walked a long, merciless road to get to where she stood. She had debts that had to be repaid."

Tavian anxiously rolled around with something in his fingers, still hidden behind his back. "How long will I wait here for the others?"

"As long as it takes," she said with a gentle smile. "You're safe. I'll be here to check on you from time to time."

A pause.

"Welcome to your new home... for now."

Luna faded, leaving him standing alone in the vast, empty palace that once held everything.

Only then did Tavian unclench his hand. Behind his back, his fingers clutched the pendant of the silver chain, dirtied with soil, with the letters R and C engraved in the center.

I'll be waiting for you, Aria. And this time... I won't forget to buy you flowers.

Her head beat like a drum—sharp and deep, like a bullet had passed clean through her skull.

Lyra moaned and clutched the sides of her head, forcing herself upright. Beneath her was powdery sand, warm from the remnants of the day's sun. Gentle waves lapped against the shore, their quiet rhythms soothing the pain by a fraction.

The sky above was bruised purple, twilight stretching wide as the stars began to pierce the darkening canvas. A cool sea breeze brushed through her hair, drying the sweat on her skin.

It all felt too peaceful. It was too normal, like she had never really left this place.

She pushed herself to her feet, nails digging into the sand for balance. Her body felt light, maybe even weightless, but something was missing. Something vital—or someone.

She instinctively reached for her scythe, but her hand closed on nothing but air. She tried to call on her powers but nothing could be channeled. There was no blood leaking from her sockets, and her eyes, once overwhelming with power, saw only what was directly before her.

Only him.

Along the shoreline, a tall, lone figure walked along the water's edge, his silhouette rimmed in silver by the rising moon. He was tossing a stick into the sea, where a dog went chasing after it.

She crept toward him, half-dreading who it may be, half-afraid she already knew. He didn't turn to face her, simply meandering along the line of the water's tide. His hair, his gait, his posture; it all struck a distant chord in her memory. But the moonlight hadn't yet broken through the clouds to illuminate him fully, and shadows played tricks on her.

Then the clouds shifted, just enough to allow a beam of moonlight to reach through. The moon spilled across the ocean, and the beach lit up in its glow.

Air snagged in her throat. The figure that wandered the shore was now in full view.

It was Rowan.

He turned, his face catching the stray moonlight. That same warm smile she had memorized had settled, the one she loved far before ever admitting it. She couldn't make herself move, her brain refusing to believe what her eyes insisted were true.

"Is it... really you?" her voice carried as an echo over the beach.

Rowan nodded, eyes brimming with quiet joy.

The tears came quicker than breath. She stepped closer to him until only a few paces separated them. She lifted her shaky hand and made her fingers into the shape of a gun, aimed playfully at him, and whispered *bang*.

But Rowan didn't move.

She waited for his laughter, but it never came. She waited for him to fall over like a well-trained dog, but nothing happened. No reaction.

She immediately turned away, laughing in a miserable exhale as the realization hit her like a slap to the cheek; it was another impostor.

Of course, of course it wasn't him.

Why did I think that would work?

But from behind, she heard a gritty thump, the sound of a body falling into dampened sand.

That's when her heart fluttered. A bout of dizziness took over.

No... don't do this. Don't torment me with hope. Don't make me believe this time is different.

She took a deep breath, closing her eyes. She spun around and then opened them.

Rowan was lying flat on his back in the sand, grinning up at the sky like a fool, the sounds of his laughter carried by the wind. It sounded nostalgic, like something she never wanted to forget, replayed through her mind endlessly in his absence.

Lyra choked back another wave of tears and collapsed into his outstretched arms. She wrapped her body around his, laughing and crying at once. With unsteady hands, she mimed holding an invisible recording device up between them.

"Do something interesting, I'm recording," she whispered.

He pretended to snatch the imaginary device, exaggeratedly wound up his arm, and tossed it into the ocean. "We don't need that anymore," he said.

Lyra snorted... an ugly sound, but not to him. He leaned in closer to her. She too moved in, their lips almost touching.

Then their lips met. They kissed with eyes shut tight, their lips lingering in a lock, mouths familiar enough to feel like coming home. He carefully placed a hand on the side of her face and kept them intertwined together, the sounds of the pattering waves disappearing behind the gravity of the moment.

She pulled back, just enough to see part of him, never enough to let go. "I'm so sorry I couldn't save you, Rowan. I tried everything. Why did it have to end like that?"

He kept her close, brushing a thumb across her cheek to wipe away the tears gathering along her waterline, smudging off whatever bit of makeup she had left.

"It didn't end," he said. "This is just the beginning."

She searched his face. "I watched your recording. I want to hear it from *you* this time. In person."

"Hear what?" He raised a brow, teasing with that familiar lopsided grin.

"You know what." She sniffed, giving him a soft punch on the shoulder.

Rowan took her hands in his.

"Now that there's nothing left to lose..." he said, leaning closer, "I love—"

A soft cry cut him off.

They both turned toward the sound, where the moonlight revealed another figure curled into the sand, its body heaving with uncontrolled bawls.

"Who's that?" Lyra tried to focus her vision on the small shadow in the distance.

"I'm not sure. I was heading over there when you arrived," Rowan said. "Let's go find out."

He stood, dusting off sand from his palms, then pulled Lyra to her feet and pressed another kiss to her lips.

"Sorry, I have to make up for lost time."

Lyra laughed, letting his warmth settle her nerves. They walked toward the weeping figure together with their fingers twined.

Farther behind them, off of the sandy beach, sitting quietly on a bench, Aidra watched them with fondness, content to let their reunion unfold before joining them.

Thank you for listening, Lyra. Aidra thought.

Kneeling over the childlike shadow was Luna, her white robes matching the pale complexion of her skin. She looked up as Rowan and Lyra approached.

"Welcome back, Lyra. And hello again, Rowan," she said, bowing her head. "I'll allow this moment of crossing, but be mindful, this one isn't ready to join you both. Not yet."

Lyra and Rowan lowered themselves beside the shadow. Lyra didn't need to wait for the darkness to subside to recognize the form—Anastasia was imprinted so deeply into her heart that she could recognize her sister with eyes closed.

Bits of shadow peeled away in thin sections, her younger sister's face coming into view like pieces of a puzzle slotting together one by one.

As they reached out to embrace her, their comforting beach transformed to the ruins of Traegos, placing them into her sister's world temporarily, where she lay with Thalia and Seraphina. The ocean's tide receded, pulling the beach away grain by grain, replaced by the rubble and devastation of a forgotten city.

Anastasia lifted her head, now seeing Lyra's face where Thalia's had been, and Rowan's face where Seraphina's was.

Lyra, Anastasia, and Rowan held one another in silence. Cloud approached, lying beside Anastasia's feet.

"Live the life I never had the chance to," Lyra said. "There's no rush to join us. Enjoy your freedom."

"When will I see you again?" Anastasia asked, looking up at Lyra, though Thalia believed she was speaking to her.

Lyra held her even tighter, her own heart swelling with painful emotion, but she maintained her composure. She rested her forehead against her sister's.

"When your story ends," she whispered, "ours begins anew."

She laced her fingers through Rowan's, smiling down at the child.

"We'll be waiting for you."

And beyond reality, where life and death intertwined, their stories did not end.
They simply bloomed again, like flowers that grow on graves.

ABOUT THE AUTHOR

K.F. Black is an IT technician by day and an author by night. Originally from Texas, he now lives in Maryland with his wife. Drawing on his background in teaching, he writes stories with a strong focus on people; their choices, their flaws, and the ways they try to understand one another. Outside of writing, he enjoys cooking new dishes, planning trips, and losing track of hours over a game of chess.

Flowers That Grow on Graves is his debut novel.

www.ingramcontent.com/pod-product-compliance
Lightning Source LLC
Chambersburg PA
CBHW020915310726
48980CB00011B/902/J

* 9 7 9 8 9 9 9 7 7 7 2 0 1 *